KILOTON
THREAT

LTG (RET)
WILLIAM G. BOYKIN
Former Commander of U.S. Army Special Forces and Founding Member of Delta Force

and TOM MORRISEY

KILOTON THREAT

B&H
PUBLISHING GROUP

Nashville, Tennessee

978-0-8054-4954-9

Published by B&H Publishing Group
Nashville, Tennessee

Dewey Decimal Classification: F
Subject Heading: IRAN—FICTION \ ARMS CONTROL—FICTION \
NUCLEAR WEAPONS—FICTION

Authors represented by the literary agency of Alive Communications, Inc.,
7680 Goddard Street, Suite 200, Colorado Springs, Colorado, 80920,
www.alivecommunications.com.

All Scripture is taken from the New International Version (NIV),
copyright © 1973, 1978, 1984 by International Bible Society.

1 2 3 4 5 6 7 8 9 10 • 15 14 13 12 11

Author's Note

Kiloton Threat is written in the language of the military and intelligence communities, and as such makes use of phrases and acronyms common to those communities. The authors realized that not all readers may be familiar with these terms and phrases, so a glossary is provided in this volume, after the epilogue of the novel.

*. . . Honor is
not a sufficient
reward of virtue:
yet nothing in human
and corporal things
can be greater
than honor . . .*

THOMAS AQUINAS
SUMMA THEOLOGICA

*We have grasped
the mystery
of the atom
and rejected
the Sermon
on the Mount.*

OMAR N. BRADLEY

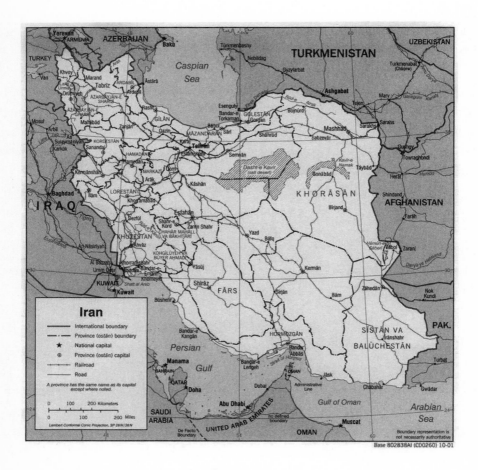

Iran

Chapter One

The presidential security detail checked each attendee with a thoroughness that was at first what one would expect, then became rude and, finally, was little short of humiliating.

As a retired Iranian air force colonel, Farrokh Nassiri would have objected to the groping—not once, but twice, rubber-gloved hands manipulating his armpits and his crotch—to the confiscation of his Cross pen, and to having to remove his stockings so some over-muscled thug could inspect the soles of his feet. But an admiral beside him, still on active duty, was subjected to the same indignities, so Nassiri held his tongue.

And then like an abusive father who first strikes his child and then placates him with sweets, the captain of the security detail saluted him and led him out of the anteroom and into the lobby of Shahidayn Seminary—"Martyrs Seminary," the name the Shiah Haghani Seminary was given after two of its founding ayatollahs were assassinated—where white-jacketed stewards were attending to an after-prayer breakfast of baked goods, figs, and cheeses.

There was an ornate silver coffee urn being warmed by a small blue-flamed burner, but no one went near it and the tray of cups at its side remained untouched. That morning, two of Tehran's leading mullahs had commented in the newspaper that coffee, although broadly thought of as *halal* by most clerics, should be considered *haram* because of the addictive nature of caffeine.

It reminded Nassiri of the year before, when the only decent Chinese restaurant in Tehran went out of business because some cleric discovered that soy sauce, a fermented product, contained trace amounts of alcohol. In modern-day Iran, a mullah could twist the Qur'an any way he liked, make a stern pronouncement, and the population would react like chastened puppies. It disgusted Nassiri, but like his peers, he avoided the coffee urn and accepted instead a steaming cup of freshly spiced chai tea and a thin china plate with a slice of *baqlava* and a couple of golden, egg-shaped *bamieh*, sticky with honey.

The fifty or so men in the room were a mix of senior military officers and dark-suited administrators like himself, and Nassiri had worked for the government long enough to recognize most as having strategic responsibilities in the rapidly developing nuclear program.

At the far end of the room, he caught the profile of Zudi Maberi, the young Quds Force major. Nassiri had little to do with the Quds Force; it was quasi-military, quasi-police, and fully under the control of Mahmoud Ahmadinejad, the Iranian president. And as for Maberi himself, the rumors were that he changed his name, his past was an enigma, while Iranian-born he spent most of his life elsewhere, and he was a favorite of Ahmadinejad himself. Avoiding the young major was not entirely possible; Nassiri and he had too many areas in which their responsibilities overlapped. But on this morning, Nassiri avoided eye contact. The last thing he wanted was to spend the next two hours sitting anywhere near an officer of the Quds Force.

The invitation—the emissary delivering it called it an "invitation," although Nassiri was under no illusions that it was anything but an order—loftily proclaimed, "the Supreme National Security Council of the Islamic Republic of Iran requests the pleasure of your company." Yet Nassiri had yet to spot a single member of the Council. Nor had he seen Ahmadinejad. No doubt the president and his council entered the seminary through another route . . . one that did not require them to have their most private areas pawed by silent, rubber-gloved minions.

It did not escape Nassiri that the president was becoming less and less a stranger to the trappings of power. When he'd first entered politics, Ahmadinejad went to great lengths to convince whoever he was speaking to that he was a common man. When campaigning in poor neighborhoods, he would talk about studying the Qur'an late at night with his father, a blacksmith. When his travels took him to middle-class neighborhoods, he would arrive in the 1977 Peugeot that he drove for years. And when speaking to academics, he would mention the fact he had a doctorate in engineering—in civil engineering, the type of engineering created to help the people.

The PhD in engineering was very much real; Nassiri's own degrees were in engineering and physics and he found Ahmadinejad to be the first politician who could keep up with him when he was speaking about his areas of specialty—not only keep up, but ask questions that showed he was every bit Nassiri's intellectual equal.

Still, Ahmadinejad's early actions in office—attempting to conduct his presidency from his Tehran home and sending all the rugs from the presidential palace to a carpet museum—seemed to Nassiri to be orchestrated messages to the proletariat. In a way, he was glad the president was finally traveling in convoys, living in the palace and taking advantage of his station. The man was finally showing his true colors.

A chime sounded, doors opened, and the small crowd of men—there was not one woman among them—filed toward a large hall with richly tiled walls, verses from the Qur'an written on the cornices, and an ornate rug that covered every centimeter of the floor. It looked, at first glance, like a prayer hall and some of the attendees hesitated before entering, going in only after the stewards assured them they need not remove their shoes.

The room was set with ten rectangular tables arranged classroom style, each table set with five chairs facing the front of the hall and its platform, which was also equipped with skirted tables and chairs, as well as a rich, mahogany lectern standing to the far left of the platform. A video camera and its operator were off to one side and on the table before each chair was a leather-bound tablet. Nassiri opened his and found that it contained a tablet of blank paper, but no agenda and no pen or pencil. Around him, men were patting their jacket pockets and coming to the same realization as he; that, as their pens had been removed from them in the security check, the tablets were there for the benefit of the camera only. No one would be taking notes this morning.

The doors at the far end of the room opened and the members of the Security Council filed in, taking their seats at the table on the dais. Then the red light on the video camera winked on, Ahmadinejad entered and everyone in the room, Nassiri included, rose and applauded.

The president smiled and waved to his guests. Nassiri wondered how many of his peers were applauding because they truly admired the man and how many were simply fawning for the benefit of the videotape.

Then something unexpected happened. The president turned to face the door he just entered through and in walked a bearded man wearing a shawl and a dark turban. And now the president was applauding as well.

There was a pause, an audible gasp, all around the room. Then the applause continued anew.

It was Ali Khameini, the ayatollah for whom Ruhollah Khomeini—the leader who acquainted most of the world with the title, "ayatollah"—changed both Islamic tradition and the Iranian constitution to allow Khameini to succeed Khomeini as Supreme Leader. And it was almost unheard-of for both the president and the ayatollah to be in the same room at the same time. It was an unmistakable signal to everyone in attendance; whatever the president was about to say had the full endorsement of every level of the Iranian government.

Khameini was seated and the president stepped to the lectern. The room fell immediately silent, the assembly retaking their seats.

Ahmadinejad looked down at his notes, then up at the ten tables of listeners.

"In the name of Allah, the compassionate, the merciful," he began in his native Farsi. "Oh, Allah, hasten the arrival of Imam al-Mahdi. Grant him good health and victory and make us his followers and those who attest to his rightfulness."

There was no murmur of response, but the man next to Nassiri squirmed slightly in his seat.

Nassiri fully shared his discomfort. It was not unusual for Ahmadinejad to open with a prayer, but it was notable for a leader of an Islamic republic to open with a prayer that made no mention whatsoever of the prophet Muhammad.

That was especially true when it came to Ahmadinejad. Early in his presidency, he referred to and quoted Muhammad often. In interviews with the western press, whenever he mentioned the prophets of Judaism or Christianity, he would unfailingly follow that up by describing Muhammad as he is described in the thirty-third surah of the Qur'an, "the Seal of the Prophets"— the final messenger of God.

But in recent years Ahmadinejad was more and more vocal concerning al-Mahdi, the "twelfth imam" of Shiite Islam. Believed to be a direct descendant of Muhammad himself, al-Mahdi—the title was Arabic for "the guided one"—was held by Islamic tradition to have gone into hiding in AD 931 and to have stayed in hiding throughout the centuries. Shi'a believed al-Mahdi would one day return during a time of great chaos and strife and would lead the world into a period of global Muslim peace and tranquility.

And there was this nuance; by not mentioning Muhammad, Ahmadinejad was seen by some as underplaying the prophet's importance and allowing the possibility—held by a small, but growing number of Muslim theologians in the Middle East—that Muhammad was simply the forerunner for another, greater prophet. In Nassiri's mind, it was not so great a leap to assume, if that was the case, the prophet the president was leaving room for was either the Ayatollah Khameini or Mahmoud Ahmadinejad himself.

Nor was the omission of Muhammad a mere oversight. Nassiri remembered the video of Ahmadinejad addressing the United Nations in May of 2010, which opened in precisely the same manner. To Farrokh Nassiri, it was an obvious shift in presidential messaging.

"My brothers," Ahmadinejad continued, "for years now, Israel has tried to pass itself off as a beleaguered nation of Jews. Nothing could be further from the truth. Judaism is a religion of prophetic tradition. They are people of The Book. They herald the truth of Allah, the one true God, and in fact they are only one step away from eternal consecration as believers. But the men who founded Israel and the men who rule Israel are not beleaguered and they are not Jews. They are criminals. They have hidden behind their Torah to justify murder and theft and the rape of land that is holy to believers and to Islam. So I ask you: what do you do when a criminal has taken over your house? Do you do nothing? Can you do nothing?"

The assembly rumbled in response.

"And that great Satan, America, protects these criminals by disarming those who would defend their homes. The American leaders say they are Christian, but again I tell you this is a lie, because Christianity too has the tradition of the prophets and The Book. Those who rule America are liars and thugs, the puppeteers of the West and the murderers of millions. They lie to the world about the Holocaust because they hope that in the supposed death of three million, they can lead us to somehow forget the deaths of sixty million. They put their boots upon our throats to suppress us. Would you have the boots of Satan on your throat . . . on your children's throats?"

"Three million" and "sixty million"—it was typical Ahmadinejad rhetoric: understate the deaths from the Holocaust by half, and then invest some outrageous number that supposedly represented the wrongs of the West. Nassiri was tempted to roll his eyes, but he did not; he knew the cameras were watching. And all around him, the rumble of assent grew louder.

"In all the history of mankind, only one nation has ever used nuclear force in anger and they used it, not against a massed army or a fleet of ships at sea, but against cities . . . against cities crowded with women and heavy with children."

Someone to Nassiri's right stood up and shouted his agreement. Ahmadinejad smiled and held up his hand, urging the listener to sit.

"Your family is like my family," he said. "Never for an instant would you stand by and do nothing while infidels defiled your sister or your daughter. There is a saying I heard growing up and it is coarse and indelicate but, my brothers, I repeat it because it is true: 'The honor of a Muslim man lies between the legs of his women.' My brother believers, I say to you, Israel has defiled the sacred ground of Islam. America has held their cloaks while they did it. And we as Muslim men can no longer sit by and do nothing. We must act."

"But," someone shouted from the back, "Israel has weapons! Nuclear weapons."

"My brother . . ." Ahmadinejad smiled. "Just because your enemy has a knife, is that any deterrent to keep you from using a knife of your own . . . a knife of your own in an urgent matter of honor?"

The room went absolutely silent. The president just said—or at very least implied—that Iran possessed nuclear weapons.

Nassiri shivered and hoped no one around him noticed.

"Do not be afraid," Ahmadinejad told his listeners. "We know from tradition that al-Mahdi stands at the threshold, ready to return. The signs indicate his return. He is eager to walk again among us. We have only to open the door, to complete the signs that herald his return. And in raining death and fire on Israel, we shall do just that. We shall complete those signs."

Now more men were standing and shouting agreement and Ahmadinejad allowed them to shout.

"Prophecy," the president said, "has led us to this place. History has led us to this place. The guiding hand of Allah has led us to this place. We have only to act. Brothers, shall we act?"

The entire room rose to its feet. Cognizant of the video camera, Nassiri joined them, his knees shaking. He put a hand on the table before him to steady himself. He could not believe what was going on around him.

He was witnessing the start of World War III.

SIXTEEN HUNDRED KILOMETERS TO the northwest, the waters of the Black Sea were clear and inviting, sapphire and emerald under a cloudless late-summer sky. Yet for a kilometer to either side, the beach north of Anapa, Russia was virtually empty. No families sunned themselves on holiday, no swimmers splashed in the gentle August waves. In the distance, only two people walked slowly on the sand and both of them were plain-clothes guards, Groza bullpup assault rifles slung discretely from their shoulders.

On the verge of the beach was a spacious cabana, pennants above it snapping softly in the gentle morning breeze. Inside the cabana, a silver pot in one hand and a strainer in the other, the president of the Russian Federation was pouring tea. He was serving it Russian-style, not in a cup but in a glass, and the glass was set in a *podstakannik*, an ornate tea-glass holder with a curved handle. Like the teapot, the podstakannik was made in Kolchugino, the town in Vladimir Oblast known throughout Russia for its metalsmiths. And like the teapot, the holder was embellished with the seal of the federation, a double-headed eagle wearing three crowns.

The president handed the tea glass to his guest, whose smile blossomed whitely in his dark gray beard. The old man bowed slightly in thanks, his *yarmulke* showing thinly, like the edge of a waning moon. While both spiced milk and cubed sugar were set out on the serving tray, the president offered neither to his guest, nor did the rabbi ask for them. It was obvious the two were old friends; each man knew how the other took his tea.

"And your family, Sergei Nikitavich," the rabbi asked the president, continuing a conversation interrupted by the arrival of the tea. His Russian held only a trace of the accent of the south. "Your wife—she is well?"

"She is very well, Rabbi." The president cocked his head at the older man. "You know, I have always wanted to ask you . . . you are a fine man.

Responsible, levelheaded. Any man would have been proud to give his daughter to you. Yet I have never heard you mention a wife; how is that?"

The rabbi smiled. "There was a girl . . . once. She lived on a farm next to the yeshivah, when I was taking my studies. But her father wanted her to marry a man of substance, a merchant or a farmer. To him, a man who leads a congregation in a temple is little more than . . . do you know the Yiddish expression, *luftmench*?"

The president had studied French, English, and German at university and he worked the word out in his head: "A man of the air?"

"Precisely," the rabbi told him. "A man with no visible means of support. This farmer had no son, this daughter was his eldest, and he was not about to let everything he worked for slip into the hands of anyone as impractical as a country rabbi."

The president cocked his head. "What did you do?"

"We took the path of Esau," the rabbi said, smiling again as he said it. "I spoke to Vasya—that was her name. Then, with her permission, I went to her father and told him that, if he would give me her hand in marriage, we would give up her right to the inheritance . . . allow it to pass to her younger sister."

"So you did marry?"

"We did." The sparkle left the rabbi's eyes. "And in the second year of marriage, when she was expecting our first child, she died of influenza."

"You were still a young man."

The rabbi nodded. "But my Vasya was . . . perfect. And if such a thing is possible, she became even more perfect in my memory as the months and years wore on. There was no other woman I could wed. It would not have been fair; any second wife would always be that to me: second."

"Rabbi . . ." The president shook his head. "You are a hopeless romantic."

"True." The rabbi smiled. "But at least on Tuesdays, when I lunch with the Orthodox bishop, he and I have something on which we can silently commiserate!"

He laughed as he said it, but the president shook his head.

"I cannot imagine a life such as that."

The rabbi shrugged again. "When I was young, it was difficult, at times. But now? I will be eighty-nine next winter, my friend. Eighty-nine! Celibacy is probably the only thing keeping me alive!"

Both men laughed at that.

The rabbi set his tea on the table at his side. "So, Sergei Nikitavich, why does the president of the Russian Federation want to have tea with a poor, *luftmench* rabbi on this beautiful morning Hashem has given us? Surely not to discuss my misfortune in matters matrimonial."

The president cleared his throat. "Last Wednesday, Rabbi . . . do you remember what happened five years ago, last Wednesday?"

The rabbi smiled and nodded.

"We were summering in Novorossiysk, up the coast," the president said, as if he did not see the nod. "I was prime minister then, and my son, my Mikhail, was out on a motorboat. He was driving, and you know how it is when you are a teenager; he thought he was invincible. As he crossed the wake of a freighter . . . the boat capsized, struck him on the head. He was rescued, praise the Almighty, but fell into a deep coma. Second day in the hospital, they put him on life support; his heart was failing. Then, three weeks later, the doctors said there was no hope. They told me I should give them the order—take him off the machines. You were there in the hospital, making rounds, and I asked what you thought, whether I should allow the doctors to take away . . . take away the things keeping my only son alive. Tell me, Rabbi. Do you remember what you said?"

The rabbi nodded. "I told you the story of Abraham and Isaac: how when Hashem told Abraham to sacrifice his only son, what he was really doing was asking Abraham if he trusted Hashem—trusted him with that which meant the world to him. You told me you were born to a Jewish mother, but you abandoned Hashem because of your years as a communist leader. That not even your mother's dying wish, that you would return to the faith that had sustained her, moved you away from that path. And I told you the law is clear; that if you are a child of a Jewish mother, then you, too, are a Jew . . . that, deny it as you may, you are one of the chosen people. I told you he who was the creator of the world is still loyal to the covenant he made with your fathers —that this is what Jews believe. And I told you that, if you trusted Hashem, truly trusted him, you should let the doctors do as they wished."

The president nodded, tears in his eyes. "I always knew there was a God. My mother was so passionate about her faith. Yet I had to deny him in order to progress in the party."

"And I said that perhaps Hashem was eager to show his love to you through this difficult situation."

The president patted the rabbi's hand. "You did more than that, old friend. You told me God loves me even more than I love my son. And when I asked if that meant God would save him, you said you could not guarantee that, but you could guarantee that, whatever the outcome was, if I did it in faith, it would be for the good."

The rabbi nodded again.

"A great peace came over me when you said that," the president told him. "I told the doctors to take him off the machines. And my son's heart continued to beat. On its own. The doctors . . . they were astounded. Then, three days later—five years ago today—he awoke from his coma. And next month, he graduates from Gargarin; he will pilot a fighter-bomber, the same as I did, when I was his age."

Neither man said a thing. The breeze had picked up, the pennants snapping more sharply in the breeze.

"My life changed that day, Rabbi," the president finally said. He wiped his eyes with the back of his hand. "And then, once I accepted the Almighty into my life, I wanted to learn Hebrew. I studied in secrecy. You gave me my bar mitzvah—just you and me."

The rabbi shrugged. "It was not as either of us truly wanted it, but it was as it had to be. To this day, my congregation asks me who the mysterious stranger is who so generously funds our temple. And I tell them simply that sometimes Hashem still sends angels in our midst. Sergei Nikitavich, why do you now recall in such detail that which we both remember so well?"

The president leaned forward, hands clasped. He had not touched his own tea.

"Rabbi, all my life, I have colluded against Israel. Do you know that?"

The old rabbi nodded.

"My teachers in school and even my professors at university were great supporters of Stalin," the president continued. "I grew up ashamed of my heritage. I hid it. I thought of Judaism as undesirable, a faction to be eliminated. When we were Soviet, I served in the KGB. And once I came to power, I conspired against Israel. I armed her enemies: armed her *greatest* enemy."

The rabbi nodded again slowly, his brow furrowed.

"You have told me this before. And I have told you before that Hashem spoke of this in his Psalms: As far as the east is from the west, that is how far he has distanced our rebellious acts from us."

The president finally picked up his tea and put his hand against the glass, frowning at its coolness.

"God has distanced us, Rabbi. But me? I have not distanced myself. So I have taken steps: steps to protect Israel even from that one country which has sought most zealously to destroy her. I wanted you to know that . . . in confidence of course."

"Of course." The rabbi reached for his own tea and then stopped. He cocked his head. "But how, Sergei Nikitavich? If their enemy is already armed; how can you possibly protect the Jews now?"

The president sighed.

"Forgive me, my old friend, but some things must remain unsaid for now." He smiled. "After all, you are my rabbi, not my confessor."

Chapter Two

HAHO—high altitude, high opening: the mission prep had not included a night HAHO jump. That left a major risk, a possible flaw in the plan and now the proof of that was frozen in the doorway of the altitude-modified de Havilland Twin Otter jump plane. Red strobe blinking on the back of his black plastic helmet, gloved hands clinching either side of the hatch-frame, a frigid hundred-mile-an-hour slipstream roaring past as he stared down into five miles of empty blackness, the Iranian was a human statue, unable to move.

The American loadmaster pounded on his shoulder, shouting instructions, but the man remained stiff, immobile.

Thighs aching from the effort of keeping his balance with all his equipment on, Blake Kershaw moved forward. His gear bag sagging beneath his butt like an over-full diaper and the civilian clothing bunched and folded tightly under his jumpsuit by the too-tight straps of the parachute harness. But he moved as swiftly as he safely could, ducking his helmeted head in the low overhead of the cramped cabin. A big white plastic auxiliary fuel tank, strapped down on the deck and full at the beginning of the flight, was now just an obstacle to squirm past, its clear wire-mesh, reinforced hose spotted with the last dregs of avgas, sucked up before the pilots switched over to the wing tanks.

Blake unsnapped his oxygen mask and let it hang from one strap. The airplane was flying at an altitude greater than that of the summit of Mount Everest. He knew he had to work quickly before he became hypoxic in the high, thin air.

"*Massoud*," he shouted, leaning in to be heard over the rushing wind.

The man in the doorway turned. Even through the clear bubble jump-goggles and even in the dim red interior lighting of the airplane, Blake could see his eyes, wide enough there was white showing all the way around. The man's black beard, flecked with gray, was damp with sweat where it stuck out from under his oxygen mask, despite the sub-freezing wind rushing in through the open door. They were close enough now that, even over the wind, Blake could hear the regular, high-pitched whine of the man's helmet-strobe as it cycled.

Blake patted his shoulder. "Put your hands on top of your head."

Shirazi had to know what was coming next. They'd done this once before, on the older man's second training jump. Yet he nodded gravely and did as he was told.

Blake kneed the back of the Iranian's leg, causing him to buckle slightly. Then, when Shirazi was off-balance, Blake put both hands on the bottom of the man's parachute pack, took a breath, and shoved.

Shirazi pitched forward and fell out into the blackness, his helmet strobe a momentary red tear in the night. Then the man was gone.

Stepping forward into the open doorway, Blake re-snapped his mask over a month-and-a-half's worth of beard and gripped the hatch on either side. He knew the Gulf was down there, somewhere, nearly six miles below, but saw nothing but blackness. Leaning back, he took a full breath of pure oxygen.

Then he followed his partner and hurled himself out into the dark.

Chapter Three

Blake tumbled at first, maybe a second or two: the red and white beacons of the jump-plane careening past, leaving luminous trails in his dark-adapted eyes. He arched backward, hands and feet out, and stabilized his fall. The air at altitude was well below freezing and the skin above his cheek-bones—the only exposed portion of his face—went numb immediately.

He scanned the void beneath him, looking for Shirazi's helmet beacon, found it, and groaned into his oxygen mask.

The tiny red light would describe a half circle, wink out, miss a cycle, and then describe a half-circle again.

Meaning the other jumper was still tumbling. *And* spinning.

Blake brought his hands together, spreading his legs to stay stable as he fell. There was an altimeter mounted on the back of his left glove and he thumbed the display. The backlight came on, a dim red, black numerals showing him that he was at twenty-five thousand feet and change, losing better than one-hundred-sixty feet a second in the thin, cold air.

That gave him about half a minute before he reached 20,000 feet, their opening altitude. The oversized high-altitude/high-opening canopies would glide better than 6 feet for every 1 foot of drop, meaning that, from 20,000 feet, they could glide approximately twenty-three miles to a landing at sea level.

Only they weren't landing at sea level. They were supposed to navigate to a drop zone well up in the hill country and the landing zone was nearly ten miles inland.

One thing that helped greatly was the wind aloft; the wind at altitude was a virtual gale and a parachutist could, for all intents and purposes, surf the rapidly moving air to cover more distance. But surfing the winds aloft meant they had to open while they were still high up in that layer of moving air. Beneath it, they lost that assistance.

That left very little margin for error . . . no margin for error. The only way to be sure to make it to the drop zone would be to follow the mission plan. And to to do that, he would have to let Shirazi go and hope the Iranian would somehow be able to sort it out on his own.

That's what Blake thought.

But what he did was bring his arms in next to his body and close his feet. The wind roar around him increased as he picked up speed and became a human missile, aiming himself at the distant spinning, flashing red light.

Fifteen seconds later, he flared, arms and legs out, when Shirazi was still fifty feet below him. And moments after that, they were level with one another. From a dozen feet away, even in the dim starlight, Blake could see the other man flailing, trying to right himself.

Blake knew the chances were he'd get a kick in the head for his trouble—a kick that could knock him cold. He knew, if he did this wrong, he and his partner would both wind up dead in the Gulf.

Blake drifted nearer. He could see the cause of the tumble now; Shirazi's gear bag had come unclipped on one side. But there was no way to easily jettison it; the straps were still tight around the older man's legs.

Blake thumbed his altimeter again: they were at 19,200 feet and dropping. Arms outstretched, he grabbed for one of Shirazi's flailing boots, missed it, drifted in for another try, and got the kick in the head he'd been worried about.

It didn't knock him out, but it did stun him. It made him see stars and the hit was hard enough to start Blake tumbling as well. Blinking, shaking his head, he arched his back, flared, and stabilized.

There was nothing but empty, black sky before him. Blake opened his right hand, canted his left boot, and rotated slowly to the left. He did that for a full twenty seconds and saw nothing but blackness and then, briefly through a break in the thin clouds far below, the lights of a freighter headed up the Gulf.

Blake looked up. Sure enough, there was the spinning, tumbling strobe light and a dark spot that occluded two stars for a moment. Somehow, after the kick, Blake must have fallen head-first or feet-first for a few seconds, because he was now two hundred feet *below* Massoud.

That presented a problem.

In free-fall, it's relatively easy to catch up with a skydiver even a considerable distance below you. All you have to do is streamline yourself, arms in tight, legs locked together, and dive head-first so you create as little wind-resistance as possible. You'll fall faster, and quickly reach your partner.

But when the other skydiver is above you, it is *his* speed that closes the distance. And a tumbling man falls only slightly faster than one dropping in a controlled flare.

Blake spread his arms and legs wide, opened his gloved hands, canted his boots to either side, and then cupped his body, trying to present as much surface area as possible to the cold night air as he plummeted through it. He glanced up; the distant red strobe seemed to be just as far away as before.

Flaring wasn't working. Not quickly enough. . . .

Blake thought through the situation for just a second; just a second was more time than he really had. Then he reached for the ripcord D-handle on his right-hand side and pulled it.

A dark blossom rushed away from him into the night sky and then there was a huge jolt to his groin as his main parachute opened. Despite the oxygen mask over his beard, he smelled burning nylon—the HAHO canopy was so large that the friction of the deploying lines melted their sheaths slightly. Blake barely registered Shirazi's helmet-strobe plummeting past him. Then Blake brought his left hand in, found the quick-release pillow on his left chest strap, and pulled it, cutting away the canopy.

Standard HAHO protocol called for the use of a "Stevens rig," a system that would deploy the reserve canopy as soon as the main had been cut away. But Blake had rigged his parachutes the way a sport skydiver would—the two parachutes independent of one another. And now he was glad he'd done it. It had allowed him to use the main canopy as an air brake, and then get rid of it.

There was a brief moment of near-weightlessness and then Blake was at speed, in free-fall again. He could see his tumbling partner's helmet strobe about three hundred feet below and he kept it in sight as he streamlined himself and again oriented his dive head-first.

Another freighter appeared momentarily in a gap in the thin cloud-cover below. The strobe on the other man's helmet developed a halo and dimmed to a deep pink.

Clouds. Blake barely had time to think it before Shirazi's strobe disappeared. A second later, the air around him became even colder, his clear goggles streaking with moisture as he entered the clouds as well.

Blake flared to slow himself. He couldn't risk passing his partner in the cloud cover; his primary chute was gone. Only the reserve was left, so there was no repeating that trick.

Altimeter check: 12,300 feet. They had dropped beneath the fastest of the assisting winds aloft. In perfect conditions, they could glide nearly twelve to fourteen miles, were they to open now. But that would only get them past the beach and not to the drop zone. They would still be roughly fifteen miles short. And again, that was only if the wind agreed to fully cooperate. And Blake couldn't open now. Not if he wanted to save Shirazi.

"What am I doing here?" Blake surprised himself by saying it aloud, into his mask.

Lights appeared off to his right and his goggles cleared, as they dropped out of the cloud cover, still miles off the coast. The lights he was seeing were from a few buildings standing miles apart on the distant shore. The freighters in the Gulf resolved into individual lights running the lengths of the ships; they were less than two miles beneath him now.

And there was Shirazi's strobe; Blake had drifted far to the left of his partner, but the other man was just a few feet below him. Angling in, Blake stayed clear of the feet this time—even though they were no longer flailing—and grabbed the older man by the arm of his jumpsuit. The two of them began tumbling together and Blake flared until the tumble resolved into a spin. Then he stuck a leg out in the opposite direction of the spin and slowed them until they were dropping cleanly.

Shirazi was motionless, so Blake reached for the D-handle on the other man's harness and pulled. The Iranian seemed to levitate just a bit and then rocketed up into the black night.

Blake canted to his right and then, as he oriented himself feet-first, reached with his left hand and pulled the ripcord to his reserve chute, conscious of the fact that, if it didn't deploy properly, there was nothing between him and the sea below.

The reserve canopy was the same design as his primary, but packed so it would open more quickly. That meant the jolt to his groin this time felt more like a kick. That, plus the stench of melted nylon, was enough to make Blake sick to his stomach. He swallowed and forced himself to ignore it.

Blake reached up for his steering toggles and executed a slow left turn. Like the primary, the reserve parachute was black and difficult to see in the low light, but he could make it out clearly enough to verify he had a full canopy, the ballooned cells a defined and rectangular shape against the lighter black of the cloud bottoms.

Altimeter check: 5,786 feet. That they were far out of range of the landing zone was a foregone conclusion. His sole concern now was gliding far enough to reach the coast.

Blake unsnapped his oxygen mask and removed his helmet.

"Massoud?" He called the man's name and waited.

No reply.

The oxygen bottle was attached to his harness with Velcro straps; he ripped them away and dropped the bottle, the mask, and the helmet.

Pulling his knees up so he could reach the rucksack straps around his thighs, Blake began loosening the straps. When they were hanging loose, he reached behind him, found the carabiners clipping the rucksack bottom to his harness, and opened them.

The rucksack contained gear he needed, but none of it would be useful if he wound up swimming. He dropped the rucksack, confident it, like the oxygen bottle, was heavy enough to sink when it hit the sea a mile below: no risk of compromising the mission.

"Massoud . . ." Blake called again. The only comms they were carrying was a single Iridium satellite phone, secured in a Witz case in the bellows pocket of Blake's jumpsuit—no radios. The Iranians had listening stations all along the coast; they would quickly triangulate on the radio signal from a slow-moving parachutist.

"Massoud?"

Silence.

"Massoud!" He yelled it this time, not worried about the noise carrying. They were still better than five miles off the coast.

This time he got a response: a groan from far above him.

"Can you hear me, Massoud?"

Another groan. "I can hear you."

Blake canted to his right, making certain he was not beneath the other parachutist.

"Drop your gear. The oh-two bottle, the rucksack . . . drop it."

"The rucksack?" The other man's voice was faint. "We need it."

"Too heavy. Need to shallow the glide—get more travel. Drop the gear."

"I will try."

For a minute Blake swayed in silence under the canopy. Then Shirazi called down to him.

"I cannot loosen the straps." His voice was nearer now. "One side is under my harness, and when I try to lift my legs, I . . . I cannot loosen the straps. My gear. I cannot drop it."

Blake took a deep breath. "That's fine. Aim inland. Feels as if we have a tailwind. It'll push us. Go with it."

"Aim inland. Yes. I can see your parachute. You are just below me, to my right."

His voice sounded close. Blake thought about it; they were above the sea at night, with no thermals to keep them aloft.

"Please, Lord," he whispered, "give us glide."

He looked up.

"That's it," Blake called to his partner. "Just follow me."

Chapter Four

Alia Kassab peered over the edge of the casserole, oblivious to the smudge of flour on the side her nose, and verified that her creation was just beginning to bubble. Pushing her jet-black hair back, she consulted her slick, new cookbook, put on a pair of oven mitts, and opened the oven door, a sauna of heat spilling out and wafting over her. Tongue in the corner of her mouth, she transferred the simmering casserole from the stovetop to the oven, slid the rack in, and closed the door. She looked at the book again—it was first published in 1961, twenty-five years before she was born—and set the stovetop timer.

"Three hours," she muttered as she did it. "Julia Child, you had *way* too much time on your hands, girlfriend."

Then again, truth be told, she could use the three hours to finish picking up her apartment.

And, truth be told, there were any number of recipes in *Mastering the Art of French Cooking* that took much less time to prepare. But it made Alia feel good to make a dinner that took half a day to cook. Besides, she liked the name.

"*Boeuf bourguignon,*" she murmured as she peeked inside the oven and verified the casserole was still simmering. It would be a suitably elegant dinner, particularly for a Saturday evening.

Elegant dinner—Alia went to her bedroom closet, pushed aside the dresses on hangers, got up on her toes, and found the box she'd brought back from colonial Williamsburg two winters before. Inside were four beeswax candles, lightly scented with vanilla, each pair joined at the wick. She extracted the top two, noted with pleasure that they had not melted or drooped, and took them into her tiny dining room, where she snipped the wicks to separate them, softened the candle bases with a lighted match, and then set them into a pair of brass candlesticks.

She smiled. The view from her dining-room window wasn't the best in Washington—it looked down onto a street crowded with shops, three walk-up floors below—but a pair of burning candles could make all the difference. They would make the room romantic.

She turned the candlesticks, looking at them. Her smile melted from her face. Romance made her think of weddings, and a wedding . . . well, a wedding was out of the question.

Alia Kassab was in love with a spy. There was no plainer way to put it than that. She was in love with a man who had no legitimate identity; the one he was born with could be found on a headstone at Arlington National Cemetery, marking the grave of an individual burned beyond recognition in a helicopter crash staged the year before.

Alia knew the crash was staged because she'd been there for the briefing. She worked for the CIA; worked directly with the deputy director of operations, just as she had with his predecessor, a man who died in a car-bomb attack the autumn before. She knew her spy was a spy because she'd helped create him and coached him as he learned his "legend"—his agency cover story—for his very first mission. He was a Special Forces lieutenant then, and still was, if one knew which top-secret documents to consult. Alia's boss had personally trained him in spycraft, and Alia was now one of a highly select handful of people who knew the young officer was still alive. Even his own mother thought he was dead.

Alia was in love with a ghost, a person who no longer existed, not in the legal sense. She remembered a phrase from *Hamlet*—"hoist with his own petard"—it meant "to be destroyed by the very weapon you created." It seemed appropriate. She and her spy talked about a future together; they discussed family, a farmhouse in the Virginia countryside. But she knew it was not possible: not while his life remained covert.

Alia set the candlestick down and went back to the kitchen.

Time to make sure the boeuf bourguignon was still simmering.

THIRTY MILES AWAY, LYING prone on the rifle range at Fairfax Rod & Gun Club, Blake Kershaw made an adjustment to the Redfield riflescope, chambered a round, and fired.

"That's it." The man at the spotting scope was Amos Phillips, deputy director of operations for the Central Intelligence Agency. "You're zeroed. Let's see what you can do."

Blake reloaded and then worked the bolt, chambering another round. Under a thin cloud cover, the light was diffuse, the image in the scope clear and crisp. He put the reticle on the "X" at the center of the bull's-eye.

The rifle belonged to Phillips. It was a Remington Model 700 with a hard rubber recoil pad—essentially the standard-issue bolt-action sniper rifle of the early Vietnam era. Compared to what Blake carried with his Special Forces team in Afghanistan, the Remington, with its walnut stock, was a dinosaur. But it was an extremely familiar dinosaur; his father had taught him to hunt deer with a Model 700.

Blake took three full breaths, held the last one and then blew it out slowly, feeling his heart beat against the nylon pad on which he was lying. He relaxed, allowing his heartbeat to slow. Then, when it dropped beneath forty beats per minute, he tightened his squeeze on the trigger, allowing it to break when he was between heartbeats.

"Center of the X," Phillips told him.

Blake only half heard. He chambered the second 30.06 round and fired again.

"X, just below, touching your first."

In the twelve seconds following, Blake fired three more times, working the bolt each time without taking his eye off the target. When the fifth round was downrange, he left the action open, slid in a yellow plastic empty-chamber indicator, and said, "Clear."

He looked up at Phillips.

"One ragged hole," CIA's deputy director of operations told him. "You don't appear to have lost a thing, my friend."

"This is only a hundred yards," Blake told him. "And it's not moving. Or shooting back. You want another whack at it?"

"Nope." Phillips shook his head. "Let's pack it up."

Fifteen minutes later they were stowing the cased rifle, the mat, and the spotting scope in the back of Phillips's Suburban.

"Nice club," Blake said, looking around.

"My father was a charter member," Phillips told him. "You want to be an active member here, you have to acquire or inherit it—that, plus be vetted by two other actives."

"Pricey?"

"Not really. But they limit membership to five hundred actives and five hundred associates. Keeps things from getting too crowded. I can bring guests, though. Anytime you want range time, don't want to make the trip down to Bragg or Quantico, just let me know. We may not have targets at a thousand yards, but it's still a pretty nice place to shoot."

Phillips closed the back hatch and the two men got into the SUV.

"Got your membership from your father . . ." Blake said, looking out the window at the landscaping, the hedges. "He in the business?"

"This business?" Phillips asked. He started the Suburban. "Ours? No. Government, yes, but not intelligence. He was a physicist with the Bureau of Standards. Joined here because he knew I was interested. He was that kind of dad, you know? The thing that made me happiest about being selected for Annapolis was he wouldn't have to pay for it—he and my mom could finally go to Europe on something besides a business trip. Because otherwise, they would have eaten macaroni and cheese for four years to put me through school."

Blake turned away from the window. "I can relate. Had a father like that myself."

"He still around?"

"No." Blake swallowed, finding his words. "Died in Desert Storm. SCUD attack."

Phillips nodded, making the turn out of the club's gate. "My dad was on Air Florida Flight 90—the one that hit the 14th Street Bridge, back in '82. It was my last year at the Academy. We'd just finished Christmas break together; Dad splurged and took us—my mother and me—to Grand Cayman. He was going to try and sneak in a trip to Tampa at the end of that, but the professor he was supposed to meet at USF had to reschedule; snowstorm—couldn't get back from a ski trip. So I guess you could say the weather killed him twice: it was weather that put him on the flight, and weather that brought the flight down."

Blake thought about that. If his father hadn't volunteered to go to Desert Storm in 1990 to get the overseas pay . . . Blake thought about that too often. Time to change the subject.

"So why'd you leave the Navy?"

Phillips turned on the blinker, shrugged. "I elected Aviation out of the Academy, but the Navy berthed me in intelligence—temporary berth until there was room in aviation: not enough Tomcats and Hornets to go around. After a year there, turned out I had an aptitude for it. Made my way up, got promoted, and made it to commander by the time I got assigned to DIA. Colson Atwater was recruiting for the Agency and met me there, sweet-talked me into civilian work: CIA. Guess I never planned it that way, but I've been in intelligence all my life."

When Phillips mentioned Colson Atwater, Blake's mind drifted back to the day he met the legendary CIA operative. It was at Hampden Sydney College during his senior year. Like Phillips, Atwater recruited Blake into the spy business. And now Colson was gone; killed in a terrorist bombing in Islamabad just a year earlier. It was just one of the risks people take when they get into this game of espionage, but Blake missed his old friend. And after all, it was Colson who'd introduced him to Alia, the love of his life, beautiful and Egyptian-born. He was planning to see her for dinner that very night.

They passed Chantilly National Golf and Country Club and got onto the eastbound ramp for I-66.

"Ever a field agent?"

Phillips shook his head. "Took the training and I've been in the field—been in the field a lot. Always as a case officer, though; never a deep-cover NOC. I'm first to admit that what you do takes aptitude."

Blake looked at the car next to them. Ever since Afghanistan, he'd been edgy whenever a car kept pace with his own on the road. In Afghanistan, in Iraq, that sort of thing was often the prelude to an ambush. It was the sort of thing that often got the other driver shot.

"So what do we need it for?" He kept watching the car as he asked it.

"'It?'"

The car next to them slowed, changed lanes to get to an exit.

"My aptitude. We go shooting, talk about our fathers—the whole guy-bonding thing. Except you already knew all about my dad; you've read my file. So I've got a feeling an 'ask' is coming up."

"It is." Phillips glanced his way. "You know, Blake, I worked with Alia three years before you came along. Two Christmases ago, she spent the holidays up in Stowe, with my family. So I know her pretty well. You've brought out . . . another dimension in her. She's fully smitten."

Blake fingered the window button on his armrest, felt the ridges around it, and looked up. "That a problem?"

"Not at all." Phillips shook his head. "I know quite a few people who met their husbands, their wives, in CIA. Most keep right on working with us after they're married. It's easier, when you have to keep secrets, working with someone who's keeping the same ones. So no; that's not a problem. But I want you to know that . . . that you're valuable to us in more ways than one. Not just as an operative, but as someone special to . . ." He checked his mirror and then glanced over. ". . . to a young lady who is, in a lot of ways, like a daughter to me.

Blake said nothing, listening.

"I won't be cavalier with your welfare, Blake. And I won't use you on anything where the stakes don't justify it."

"I know that. You've got me working on something where the stakes justify it."

"Indonesia? Yes. Asia has extremist groups that could rival al-Qaeda in a few years. How's the prep going for that?"

"Finished the language schools for Dutch, for Bahasa Indonesia. Alia likes that . . . she knows a little Bahasa; her mother was—is—Indonesian. We practice when we're out, when people can't hear us. I still have to take the language school in Javanese, but I'm not expected to be fluent in it. I just have to pass as a Canadian working as an Australian textiles buyer. Have a trip coming up in a couple months to shadow a former MI-6 man at an import/export firm in Canberra, get grounded on the business."

"We're going to have to postpone that trip."

Blake tapped the armrest. "I figured. What's up?"

Driving one-handed, Phillips lifted the lid on the SUV's center console and folded it back. Inside was a flush-mounted pistol vault, the kind you could bolt into your car to carry a handgun securely. Glancing down, he aligned four numbers on the combination lock, opened the vault, and took out a latest-generation iPhone. He touched a dished button to wake it up, tapped in a pass-code, and then—glancing up to check traffic—brought up an image on the screen and handed the iPhone to Blake.

Blake studied the image; it was a man who appeared to be in his mid-seventies: third-world haircut grown out a little too long, a thin, thready beard extending all the way down onto his neck, eyebrows bushy and untrimmed like his beard. The hair and the beard were both streaked with gray, the hair more so than the beard. He was wearing a suit jacket that looked a little bulky at the seams, and although his white shirt was buttoned at the throat, he wore no necktie.

"Muslim country, from the looks of the beard," Blake thought aloud. "Jacket looks like it came from eastern Europe, maybe Turkey. Let me guess: Iranian?"

"Bingo. Colonel Farrokh Nassiri, Iranian Air Force, retired. PhD from MIT in nuclear engineering, bachelor's with a dual major in physics and engineering from Oxford, and now he's supposedly a deputy in their energy ministry, although HUMINT places him as the number-two man in their nuclear munitions program. He's been working with North Korea on delivery systems, and some former Soviets on warhead technology. As you know, Iran has been pretty much in the western world's face on their reactor program. They claimed for years to be developing fission for power plants, but satellite imagery of their infrastructure didn't line up with that. It was pretty obvious they were making weapons-grade plutonium, not the more radioactive sort you'd use in a reactor. So now they're simply saying they're a sovereign nation and they haven't signed any treaties, so we have no business telling them what to do. Their capability isn't pervasive, but it's getting there. Variety of intelligence sources show hardened launch points all over the highlands, Zagros Mountains, principally. The old Soviet shell-game: move your nukes around, keep the opposition guessing where they are. Some of those suspected sites, in Bakhtaran, are just a thousand kilometers from downtown Tel-Aviv. Wouldn't take much of a launch vehicle to strike it. Not to mention you could stand on the border and practically throw a nuke and hit the 447th Air Expeditionary Group at Sather, outside Baghdad. So we have a definite need to know which of those sites are truly launch-capable and which are not. And Nassiri, there, is the man who planned the system. He knows where everything is, when it's scheduled to move, where it moves to, which sites are susceptible to a bunker-buster, and which might require something more."

Blake straightened up. "Something more, as in nuclear?"

Phillips shrugged. "That's one possibility."

"Hard to believe we would do that. It's a threshold no country wants to cross, especially the United States."

"Get to that in a minute." Phillips checked his rear-view mirror and got on the northbound ramp for the Beltway. "SIGINT indicates Iran's president, Mahmoud Ahmadinejad, is back to making his old noise about wiping Israel off the map. We think a one-kiloton strike against Ramat David, on the pretext of evening old scores, is a definite possibility."

"That's crazy." Blake scowled. "That'd start World War III."

"Agreed," Phillips nodded. Sun broke through the clouds overhead, painting the lower half of his face in sunlight. "But from Ahmadinejad's point of view, he's holding a revolver, not a single-shot. If we preempt incompletely, or even if we react, he can launch against Sather, Bagram—lots of American sons and daughters there, and he knows how quite a bit of the public feels about our kids dying in other people's wars."

"Our war eventually. Better to fight it over there."

"I'm with you, but logic doesn't make for good newscasts. Bottom line, Ahmadinejad is a lot like the old Soviet regime. Willing to play chicken with millions of lives. Willing to shake things up. Severely. He doesn't have the ICBM capability to hit CONUS, but he could sure make a mess in the Middle East."

Blake looked back at the iPhone. "So what's the game plan? We going to snatch this Nassiri?"

Phillips shook his head. "Won't need to. Our boy's coming voluntarily."

"That senior a man? Why would he want to bolt?"

Phillips smiled. "You know the old expression, a 'come-to-Jesus talk'?"

Blake nodded.

"Well, Nassiri's had the talk." Phillips changed lanes. Then he glanced over at Blake. "And the man's come to Jesus. Literally."

Chapter Five

The Capital Beltway was creeping into its usual mid-afternoon gridlock and Blake didn't bother Phillips as the DDO drove north, occasionally moving left, into marginally faster traffic. A couple of times, the older man muttered under his breath. Finally he got all the way to the left lane, the one reserved for high-occupancy vehicles. Even there the traffic was moving twenty miles an hour under the limit.

"Wish we could just pack up the government," Phillips said. "The whole thing. Move it out to someplace that's got room. Montana. Wyoming."

"Traffic would just move along with it."

"You're probably right." Phillips glanced over at Blake. "Swipe the screen to bring up the next image."

Blake did as he was asked. The next picture was of a middle-age man with a neatly trimmed beard. He was dressed in a good but not overly expensive suit, and his necktie looked almost exactly like the one Blake got from Alia the Easter before. The man was looking straight into the camera, unsmiling. It looked like the kind of photo you'd shoot for an ID card.

"Middle-Eastern features, but this is an American suit," Blake said. "Recent fashion. He dresses as if he's been here for a while."

"He has." Traffic started picking up and Phillips began changing lanes back to the right. "That's Massoud Shirazi. He was an assistant professor in comparative religions at Tehran University when Khomeni came to power in 1979 and the shah left the country. Shirazi is Christian—his father converted from Islam when the shah was in power and Shirazi was raised that way—and a Christian professor would have had two strikes against him, as far as the ayatollah was concerned. So he and his wife—she was French—went into hiding in a small rural Christian community; house churches, which are against the law in Iran, but are still the fastest-growing religious movement over there.

"Shirazi's plan was to wait it out, seeing as Khomeni was old and in poor health. He knew Hossein Montazari, Khomeini's selected successor, was less of a hard liner. But the ayatollah hung on for ten years, near the end of which the Shirazis had a daughter. Then just before Khomeni died, he dumped Montazari and bent the rules to bring in Khameini: 'meet the new boss, same as the old boss.'

"When it became clear Iran was going to stay hardcore extremist Muslim, Shirazi took what savings they had left and paid to have him and his family smuggled out of the country. He claimed refugee status—naturalized, eventually. He's been here for better than twenty years. Works for us, doing signals traffic analysis."

"You said, 'He's been here.' What about his family?"

"Truck that was smuggling them rolled somewhere in Iraq: wife and daughter both killed. Assets in Iraq confirm that; this was back in Hussein's time. Sharazi made it on his own to Kuwait, then Bahrain. Came here."

Blake looked at the picture, trying to discern emotion in the face. He couldn't.

"Sharazi remains our principal point of contact with the Christians in the Ilam Province of Iran," Phillips said. "One of their people—woman by the name of Zari Nourazar—passes as Muslim and works as an assistant to Nassiri. He keeps a summer house there—it puts him nearer to most of their western launch sites. Nassiri's had issues with a lot of what Ahmadinejad's regime has done over there, took the assistant into his confidence and, long story short, she converted him. He's been a closet Christian for three years now, he can see he's created pretty much a one-target nuclear program with Israel in its crosshairs and from what he's learned in his newfound faith, he has an issue with that. So the man wants out."

"Okay. I take it you want me to go in."

Phillips nodded.

Blake hefted the iPhone. "Shirazi here is our means of communication? He briefs me?"

"Yes. And more than that, besides. He's going in with you."

Blake blinked, turned to face Phillips. "Amos, this guy's got to be fifty years old."

"Fifty-six, last March. But remember, he made it through most of Hussein's Iraq on his own. The man is not without skills."

Blake felt his brow furrowing, stopped it. "How are we getting in-country?"

"This is coming together pretty quickly. We don't have time to do visas through a third nation. We'll drop you in."

"Parachute?" Blake didn't bother hiding his concern. "This guy jump-qualified?"

"He will be."

"Oh, man . . ." Blake looked out his window, then back at Phillips. "Amos, this is going to be interesting . . . Just how are you getting him qualified?"

"Bragg first. Then we're sending the two of you to Yuma."

"Yuma Proving Grounds? The Accelerated Freefall Program? They don't jump you with equipment. And we'll need to carry in civilian clothes, food for the first couple days, enough gear to set up for the extraction."

Phillips glanced up, checked his mirror again. "They'll . . . modify it a bit for us. We have a man, an E-7 with the freefall school. He's a Navy SEAL—did a paramilitary tour with the Agency. We've briefed him. He'll teach our man to jump with gear . . . that and do the night landing."

"We're jumping at *night*?" Blake glanced over at Phillips. Then he nodded. "Of course we're jumping at night. So who's preparing the drop zone?"

"Headman with the Christian group, Wahlid Hensaki. They've had Christian relief agencies drop supplies to them over the years: Farsi Bibles, medicine."

"A supply drop's a lot different from what you're talking about."

"Agreed, and they'll know the difference. In-country missionary named Pardivari trained these folks. He was a former Special Forces NCO who saw action in Panama during Just Cause back in '89 and then Desert Storm the next year."

Blake leaned forward and looked at Phillips. "Let me propose a revised mission plan: drop me in solo, team me with the missionary."

"Wish we could." Phillips shook his head as he said it. "Pardivari's dead: killed in an ambush by the Pasdaran two years ago. So that leaves us with Shirazi; he has intimate local knowledge, speaks Farsi with no accent, and he's the one person we know the locals will absolutely trust. Some of the leaders in the house-church movement there now are the same who were there when

Shirazi left the country. Remember, house churches have been hunted over there for more than two decades now."

"Okay." Blake spread his thumb and forefinger on the iPhone screen, zooming in on the image. "How much time do we have to get ready?"

"Have to snatch Nassiri while he's still at his country house. Six weeks."

"Six weeks!" Blake put his fist to his lips, thinking it over silently. "Amos, my chances are better alone."

"Of succeeding?" Phillips pointed at the iPhone. "Iran hasn't used the law yet, but converting from Islam to Christianity is punishable by death: specifically, by beheading. And Ahmadinejad would love to make an example of a house-church community; he wants Iranian Christians under his thumb, in registered churches. The only thing keeping these Christians away from that is caution. They aren't going to open up to just anybody. A stranger showing up, saying he's from Uncle Sugar? They probably won't play ball. And there's too much to be gained to pass this up. The timing can't be moved—we're looking at a window when Nassiri is at his summer house. Security isn't as tight there. But to get you there, we need Shirazi's connections. There's no other way. He's got to go."

Blake looked at the picture on the iPhone again. "It sounds like we're going to have to work pretty hard to make sure this guy Shirazi survives what will likely be the most exciting thing he has done in a few years. I assume you have complete trust in this man."

Phillips glanced Blake's way. "I do. As for him getting killed, there's that risk, and he's aware of that. But if we get Nassiri, we get current and intimate, firsthand knowledge of the most dangerous nuclear program in the world today. From a cost-benefit analysis, it's worth it. Don't want to sound cold, Blake, but I'd bet Shirazi's life a hundred times over to put Nassiri in a safe house in Virginia. The intelligence is that valuable."

Phillips changed lanes with the Suburban, all the way over to the right lane. He was quiet for a second, then he nodded twice. "The op is risky, and Shirazi wouldn't be my first choice for someone to go in-country with. I wish there was a better way, but we have limited options at this point. That's why you're the right man for the job. I will admit to you I would prefer to use someone I have less personal interest in than you, but this is no time for sentiment. Blake, you're the only man I can trust with this job. I wish there was another option."

He put on his blinker for the Georgetown Pike exit. Then he glanced Blake's way again.

"Like I said, it's worth the risk. Well worth it."

Chapter Six

Mind if I stop at the house?" Phillips made the turn off the Pike into Broyhill-Langley Estates. "Need to drop the rifle off."

Blake nodded. They were on their way back to CIA; bringing a firearm onto Agency grounds would be cause for an all-headquarters lockdown.

They passed by the gates. Blake had not been to Phillips's home before and he was impressed by what he saw: the houses in the area were all set back from the road on manicured, well-landscaped lawns. And the homes were stately— most were done in Georgian or Federal style—and large.

"DDO pays better than I thought."

"Nope." Phillips laughed. "It probably pays just about what you'd think."

He passed a corner and turned into a driveway for a home the equal of its neighbors: lots of red brick and white wood trim, Palladian-style windows above the entryway, and two chimneys on the roof. The clouds were continuing to break, and the sun came out again, washing the house in light.

"I have my dad to thank for this," Phillips said. "Him and my grandfather, really. My grandfather—my dad's dad—died about a year before my dad; left him a farm in Vermont. Dad sold it and, over my mother's objections, put twenty thousand of the proceeds into two little companies he thought might be on their way up: Apple Computer and Microsoft: sheer speculation, totally out of character for him. And after the plane crash, Mom just held onto the stock—know how people sometimes hang onto things that remind them of someone?"

"Sure. With my mom, it was a pickup."

"With mine, it was the Volvo. That and the stock. Guess she felt bad for how she'd griped when he bought it. Six years ago, she passed as well. All this time, she'd been rolling the tech-com dividends back into more shares. My accountant saw the recessions coming, advised me to cash in the Microsoft stock and put the money in CDs. We held onto Apple. Then, three years ago, when the economy tanked, we bought this place for about three-quarters of what it's worth. Could have done better elsewhere, but I wanted to be near the Agency, and Langley real estate didn't get hit as hard as most of the country. So Cheryl and I got this, plus the winter house in Stowe. Paid for the kids' college, set aside trusts for both of them, transferred the rest from CDs into precious-metal mutuals and growth funds. God bless Bill Gates and Steve Jobs."

"Amen," Blake said as they drove past the home to a carriage-house-style garage, connected to the main house by a breezeway.

Phillips stopped the SUV in front of the garage doors.

"Come on in." He got the cased rifle and range bag out of the back and led the way though a screened porch. Past that was a kitchen with a big, built-in industrial-style fridge, an island stovetop, and what looked like a Williams-Sonoma store hanging from a rack above it.

"Who's the cook in the family?"

"Everybody. Want a beer?"

"No, thanks."

"Well, there's iced tea in the fridge. Lemonade, too, I think. Help yourself."

Phillips disappeared through the dining room and Blake opened the refrigerator. It was like swinging open the door to a vault. He found the iced tea and the lemonade, got a glass out of the cupboard—it was an Olympics giveaway from McDonald's, completely at odds with the rest of the kitchen—and made himself a drink, pouring in a little from each pitcher, over ice.

"Making Arnold Palmers?" It was Phillips, back from the den.

"Beg pardon?"

"Half iced tea, half lemonade—that's what they call it. An Arnold Palmer."

"Oh." Blake hefted the glass. "Didn't know it had a name. Want one?"

"Please."

Blake made a second drink—another McDonald's glass—and handed it to Phillips.

"Way my mom always makes it," Blake said. "Sun tea and lemonade."

The two men sipped their drinks in silence, Blake thinking about his mother. She thought he'd been dead for over a year now—that deception was necessary to erase his identity. And while CIA gave him regular updates and assured him she was doing well, she was often on his mind. Blake looked at Phillips over the top of his glass, wondering what thoughts the mention of his mother triggered in his handler.

Blake knew what thoughts they'd triggered in his own mind and he wanted them out of there. He looked out the window again. And almost without thinking, he said, "Wow."

Phillips stepped next to him and followed his gaze. "Wow, what?"

"There." Blake pointed with his drink at the window across the top of the hedge.

It the house opposite, a young woman with long, dark hair was standing in profile, talking to someone. The light in the room was good enough to bring out detail in her face—Blake assumed she was standing in the kitchen as well—and her features were classically beautiful.

She turned to face the window and, if anything, her face became even more attractive. She waved, and Phillips waved back while Blake felt his face redden.

"Neighbor girl?" He asked it to cover his embarrassment, more than anything else.

"That's Leena," Phillips said. "I've watched her grow up these last few years. She's twenty—finishes her bachelor's at Georgetown next June, and then she's off to London School of Economics in the fall."

"Good schools. Must be pretty smart."

"Valedictorian for her high-school class. National Merit Scholar. Smart as a whip."

"Girl like that must make her parents proud."

"She does," Phillips told him. He paused just a moment before he added, "She was born in Iraq."

The girl stepped out of view and Blake looked at Phillips.

"She immigrated?" Blake knew young Iraqis were lined up to come to the United States and not many got the visa.

"No. She's a U.S. citizen."

Blake waited, knowing there had to be more.

"Her dad goes by 'Sam,'" Phillips told him. "Short for 'Samir.' He's Iraqi-born as well. His folks came here in the sixties, back when everything was rosy with the shah and Iraq was our best friend in the Middle East. Sam became a U.S. citizen his first year in college and met Mirah—that's his wife—at the naturalization ceremony. Turned out she was from Baghdad, not far from where he was born, and they got married the day after he graduated. Then he worked until she graduated, they took turns supporting one another through grad school, and now she's a curator at the Smithsonian and he teaches molecular biology at Georgetown."

Blake nodded. Then he looked at Phillips again. "So how is it that their daughter was born in Iraq?"

"Back in the nineties, Sam applied for an academic visa to teach a seminar in Baghdad that would bracket the time Mirah was due. He took her with him; Leena was born in Akhtar Hospital. Sam's American, Mirah's American, so Leena's American as well. But she's also Iraqi: dual citizenship. That way, if things ever clear all the way up over there, she has a choice: grow up here, where her folks chose to live, or go back there and help make it the kind of place it has the potential to be."

"Impressive." Blake looked at the window again. It was still empty. "Are they Muslim?"

"Pillars of their mosque." Phillips put his empty glass in the dishwasher. "You set?"

Blake drained his glass, put it in the dishwasher as well, and the two men headed back out to the SUV.

"Leena house-sits for us when we're away," Phillips told him as they pulled out onto the Pike. "Feeds the dog and walks him, gets the newspapers off the porch."

"Good neighbor."

"She is. Never accepts a cent for it. So we remember her at Christmas."

That got Blake's attention. "They celebrate Christmas?"

Phillips shrugged. "No tree, no lights. But they come over for dinner. And in case you're wondering, yes; I have the place swept after she house-sits. Never anything untoward. I left documents on the desk once: dummies, of course. Left the door open to the den, had Surveillance put a pin-camera in there. She came in, but only because Sadie—that's our Golden Retriever—was sleeping under the desk. Leena never gave the bait a glance."

Blake said nothing. Another car was next to them, keeping pace with them on the four-lane road, and he was watching it. He hated it that he'd developed the habit.

"My point is," Phillips said, "she's a good kid. And her family: good people. Very good. You know?"

Blake turned his way. "Sure."

"I mean, yes, they're Muslims. They belong to a mosque; they're active in it. They pray. They fast. They support charities. Back when he was in college, I believe Sam even made the trip to Mecca, crossed the hadj off his bucket list. But Sam believes sharia law is an anachronism. He refused an offer to teach in the UK because the university was in a town that recognizes the Arbitration Tribunal. Sam and his wife both have doctorates and they want their daughter to get her PhD: an American family that wants their kid to do well. They just have a different belief set."

Blake paused a moment, not sure how to reply.

"Okay," he finally said.

"And I think that, here in this country, probably in a lot of countries, families like Sam's are the vast majority among Muslims: probably over 85 percent. Sam and I have talked religion plenty of times, and he readily admits he has to approach his faith with a filter, remember that the Qur'an was written nearly fourteen hundred years ago, and read it accordingly. What's the word?"

He thought for a moment, then nodded as he remembered. "Hermeneutics."

"Sure." Blake watched the car next to them. It was slowly falling behind, which relieved him. "Same as the Bible. We don't kill witches today and if your teenage son mouths off to you, you don't take him out to the gates of the town to have the elders stone him."

"Much as I'd like to, sometimes." Phillips reached forward and turned the air-conditioning up; the Washington sky was blue and cloudless and the sun through the windows was warm. "But the thing is, not all Muslims feel the way Sam does. You know that; we had you embedded with al-Qaeda last year. Muslim terrorists justify themselves with the Qur'an; they can find plenty of mullahs who agree with them. And Mahmoud Ahmadinejad ups the ante."

"How's that?"

"What do you know about 'al-Mahdi'?"

Blake thought for a moment.

"It's Arabic for 'the guided one,'" he said. "He's supposed to be appointed by Allah to rule the world. This is a prophecy, but not strictly from the Qur'an. This comes later. Shi'a and Sunni have different views on him. Shia believe he is a direct descendant of Muhammad who went into hiding about a thousand years ago . . ."

"In AD 931," Phillips said.

"Yes. That sounds right. Anyhow, they believe he was here once and will come back, while Sunnis—those who believe in him at all—say he hasn't appeared at all yet."

"Like the disagreement between Christians and Jews on the subject of the Messiah."

Blake looked at the DDO. "Yes. Exactly what I thought, first time I heard it."

"Well, Ahmadinejad subscribes to the 'hidden' point of view. Every member of his cabinet subscribes to it as well. And I mean 'subscribe' literally; each one has signed an oath saying he believes Muhammad al-Mahdi, the son of the eleventh Imam, is descended directly from Muhammad and went into hiding when he was five years old. They call him the 'twelfth Imam,' and Ahmadinejad would do anything to make sure al-Mahdi comes out of hiding in his lifetime."

Blake turned in his seat, as much as the seatbelt would allow. "But both Sunni and Shi'a believe there is nothing man can do to cause the appearance of the Mahdi."

"True, but the prophecy does describe the conditions under which the Mahdi appears, doesn't it?"

Blake thought for a moment. Then he fell silent, because they turned left off the pike onto the long drive into CIA headquarters and Phillips was slowing for the guard shack. Both men showed their identification cards and there was a pause while the guard ran Blake's military ID—his fake military ID—on the computer. It came up as approved and Blake wondered, as he always did, if it was still a felony to gain entrance to the CIA fraudulently if the fraudulent identity was provided to you by the CIA.

They rolled forward, Phillips put his window up, and Blake spoke. "He comes back in an even-numbered year . . . which would be an odd-numbered year on our calendar. There will be death in Iraq and a fire in the sky. There will be chaos in the Middle East . . ."

He slowed, the realization coming to him.

"Oh man." The thought almost literally took his breath away. "You mean . . . ?"

"Exactly." Phillips pulled up next to Blake's red Jeep Wrangler. "Ahmadinejad would absolutely love to force the hand. Create chaos in the Middle East. Cause the nuclear conflict that puts fire in the sky over Iraq."

"That's . . ." Blake couldn't finish the sentence. "*Insane*" seemed insufficient, given the scope of what Phillips was suggesting.

Phillips turned to face Blake. "This isn't somebody who's worried about causing World War III, my friend. This is somebody who *wants* to cause it."

Chapter Seven

The onions were brown-braised in beef stock, the mushrooms sauteed in butter.

Alia set them aside, took the casserole from the oven, removed the top and, slipping one oven mitt off, used a fork to test a piece of beef. Browned on the outside, it flaked easily, yet was still moist.

"Hmmmm . . ." She resisted the urge to taste it. She knew it would be good, but wanted to wait until the vegetables were added and the sauce was ready.

Alia set a sieve above a saucepan—a blue Le Crueset, tan-white on the inside, that she almost never used, because she was afraid to scratch or mar it. Car payments and steep Georgetown rent left little money for luxuries, especially on a government assistant's salary, so the saucepan was an extravagance: the best piece of cookware in her collection. Using the mitts, she poured the boeuf bourguignon into the sieve and then set the casserole aside to cool. After a couple of minutes, only beef and bacon were left in the sieve. She washed the casserole out with hot water and returned the meat to it, then topped it with the onions and the mushrooms.

Already, it smelled wonderful.

The sauce settled in the saucepan enough for most of the fat to rise to the top. Alia skimmed that off, put the saucepan on the stove, and brought it up to a simmer. She studied the cookbook for a moment and then dipped a spoon into it. It coated the spoon like oil on a dipstick, and she smiled. Tasting it with her eyes closed, she opened her eyes, added a pinch of salt, tasted again, and then poured the warm sauce slowly over the meat and onions and mushrooms, the saucepan heavy in her mitted hands.

She covered the casserole and looked at the clock on the stove: five forty-one and Blake said he would be over at six. She got out her stainless-steel stockpot, filled it halfway with water, and put it over high heat.

Fifteen minutes later, the noodles from the stockpot were resting in a sieve and she was bringing the casserole up to a simmer on the stovetop.

There was a knock at the door.

Alia quickly basted the meat and vegetables, wiped her hands on her white chef's apron, took the apron off, and checked her reflection in the stainless-steel edging of the stovetop. She couldn't see much, shrugged, and answered the door.

Blake was wearing what he always wore on weekends: a plaid shirt, a slightly faded pair of Levis, and running shoes.

"Hey, stranger." Alia kissed him on the cheek.

He looked past her to the little dining room table, set with real china, the candles burning.

"Whoa. I'm underdressed."

"Don't be silly. I'm wearing jeans, too. Sit. Want wine?"

"Thanks, but I was outside all day. It'd give me a headache. Have tea?"

Alia nodded and got a pitcher of iced tea from the fridge. It was sweet, a taste she'd acquired over the past year: the cost of dating a Virginia country boy.

"Can you pour? I have to baste this one more time."

"Sure." Blake poured the tea into stemmed water glasses, went back into the kitchen to help, and then backed out as Alia came walking through carrying the steaming casserole.

"Smells great. What is it?"

"*Boeuf bourguignon.*" Alia pushed the accent, trying to make it sound as French as possible.

"I'm definitely underdressed."

"You're definitely saying grace. Now, before it gets cold."

Blake did as he was asked after taking his seat. Beaming, Alia spooned the beef, vegetables, and sauce over hot egg noodles and handed the plate to Blake. He took it and sat it in front of him.

"No," Alia protested. "Try it."

"You don't have a plate yet."

"This is my first foray into *Mastering the Art of French Cooking*. Humor me."
Blake picked up his fork and tried a taste.

"Well?"

Black cocked his head, looked up at the ceiling. "Got any . . . Tabasco?"

Alia sagged.

"I'm kidding!" Blake took another taste. "This is . . . amazing. Really. Nicely done, All."

"You're not just saying that because I spent all afternoon cooking it?"

"Well, I would." Blake paused with his fork halfway to his mouth and just inhaled. "But . . . wow. Try it yourself. I'll bet they aren't having this good a dinner at the White House tonight."

Alia tried to keep a straight face, then beamed. She put some noodles on her plate and moved the casserole nearer. "How was your day?"

"Interesting." Blake paused and lowered his fork. "What do you know about the twelfth Imam?"

The serving spoon clattered against the ceramic casserole and Alia set it down. She could feel the color draining from her face.

"Oh, Blake . . ." Her voice was barely a whisper. "They're sending you to Iran."

Chapter Eight

You don't just sign up to become a Special Forces soldier. The screening process is rigorous, and even then, most candidates wash out during the Assessment phase of training. During Assessment, soldiers are required to operate as a singleton, which is the opposite of the teamwork focus they are bombarded with from the first day they enter Basic Training or Boot Camp. Then they experience a very stressful and fatiguing set of tasks over several weeks, including an obstacle course designed to weed out anyone who is claustrophobic, bothered by heights, or lacking in upper body strength, endurance, or balance skills.

The only area where Massoud Shirazi even came close was endurance: the man ran at least two marathons a year and trained for them rigorously. But despite that, Massoud remained an office worker, rather than a warrior, an individual who had no business in fatigues.

The first time he got to the top of a jump tower, Massoud's knees were literally shaking. He was sweating, despite the coolness of the morning.

To his credit—and Blake's amazement—Massoud jumped on command. But Blake was skeptical.

"THIS IS GOING TO be tough for him but we'll keep training and hope he becomes more confident," he told Phillips after one early morning training session. "Even in Special Forces, HAHO jumps are something only a select few people do with any regularity. And Airborne school is a prerequisite just to be a Special Forces candidate. This guy deserves a lot of credit for his perseverance but I've got to tell you: he is not excited about the idea of screaming through the sky at 120 miles per hour. I've seen guys like him before. This is just not their environment. But most of them overcome it; let's pray he does."

"Give him time."

They were at a Waffle House outside Fort Benning, Georgia, a busy, noisy restaurant where a man in uniform talking to a man in an L.L. Bean jacket wouldn't merit a second glance and where a person could recite aloud the secret formula to Coca Cola and not a soul would overhear.

"We'll see how he does on the 250-foot tower tomorrow," Blake told Phillips. "It is a guaranteed attention-getter for someone with a fear of heights. Then we take a ride in an airplane. In Airborne, you train for two weeks before they put you on a plane. Our schedule calls for Massoud to make his first jump at Day Four. We are going to have to work him pretty hard with a couple of long days to build his confidence before we take him to Yuma. Candidly, this is going to be risky. But from what you tell me, we don't have an alternative."

Phillips looked up, smiled at the waitress approaching with more coffee, and shook his head. Then the smile left his face and he looked Blake in the eye. "You're right. We really don't have any at this point. We have to move quickly to get this guy out during a pretty short window. I wish things were different, Blake, but sometimes you have to do what you have to do. And this is one of those times. That's exactly why you are 'the man.' Give me your assessment of the odds."

Blake blinked. "Odds?"

"Of making it."

Blake shook his head. "I don't deal in odds. I figure this is like every operation I've been on, the enemy and the weather always get a vote but we don't let that stop us."

He pushed his plate away.

"Look, Amos . . . this guy is not going to be as ready as I would like but with a little luck and some Divine intervention, we'll get him on the ground in one piece. If he freezes, I go it solo. If he crashes and burns, we execute a contingency plan—get the SEALS in there and pick him up. Then we are back to the solo thing again."

Blake paused for a moment and looked his tablemate squarely in the eye. "Hey, Amos: listen. I know it's a risky op. It's beyond risky, but let's stay positive."

Phillips looked down momentarily as if he was searching for words. He cleared his throat and looked up again.

"I know," he said. "You're right, but I hate doing this to you. I know you are the best we have, but I also realize I am saddling you with a huge liability. But thanks for the way you are handling it."

Blake started to speak, stopped, and finally just looked at Phillips, his hands open.

Phillips signaled for the check. "My friend, you have more than done your duty for your country. You've been shot up, patched together, run through a ringer, dropped in to live with scumbags, and nearly killed, what? Three times? Four? You don't have to do this. You can refuse the mission and not a soul will think the worse of you for it. For that matter, you can bail right now and kiss the Agency good-bye, and no one will think less of you for that, either. You've more than done your share. Leave us, go back to the Army, and the director and the president will make sure you're on a fast track for promotion."

Phillips looked Blake in the eye. "But before you make any decisions, know this: Shirazi volunteered, POTUS has given him the green light."

Phillips reached into his jacket, took out his iPhone, and keyed in a passcode. Then he opened his mail program and keyed in another code. A message came up, all caps, and he turned the little smartphone around so Blake could read the screen.

It was from the director's address.

"'Amulet' is your mission," Phillips told Blake. "And I don't have to tell you who 'POTUS' is."

Blake nodded his head slowly. "'President of the United States.'"

Phillips slid the iPhone back to his side of the table, cleared the screen, and put it in his pocket. "This is extremely high-stakes, my friend. If we get Nassiri out, we can target specific sites, either sabotage or air strike, and short-circuit Iran's nuclear capability. But if we fail, either we have to strike Iran generally, or stand by and do nothing while they launch against Israel, a nation that's been our ally ever since it was created. Either way, the Middle East takes a header off a cliff and pulls the rest of the world down with it. The Administration's not about to let that happen and they need to know we're taking every step to ensure this mission's success. That means sending as small a team as possible, the better to stay covert, but also sending in as much local knowledge as we can. And what that adds up to is a two-man team: you and

Shirazi. I realize Massoud's no Green Beret. He's not even the equal of a grunt fresh out of Basic. But he knows the people we're working with in-country, he's got ground knowledge, and the president wants to make sure we have every advantage. So he's got to go and I appreciate your giving him every advantage you can."

The waitress dropped off the check and both men stayed silent while a family of four—mother, father, and two small boys—passed the table. One of the little boys saw Blake's fatigues and made a gun out of his thumb and forefinger. Blake did the same and the kid grinned.

Blake looked at the family, settling in three booths away. The little boy grinned at him again.

"Amos . . ." Blake said softly.

Phillips looked up.

"Yes, Blake?" He grinned. "You going to say something heroic now, as if I have insulted your courage?"

Blake leaned forward slightly, placing both hands on the table as he came within whisper range of Phillips. "You know I am not going to walk away from this kind of thing. We're talking the fate of a nation, here. Not our nation, but that doesn't matter. We're going to need more than my help to do this. We're going to need God's help. But we will pull this off."

THE TRAINING WENT ON. Several times, Shirazi hesitated—on the jump tower, in the doorway of the plane during practice jumps. Once, Blake had to push him. They did night jumps, several of them, then they progressed to HAHO—high altitude/high opening. But they never practiced HAHO at night. After conferring with the Airborne specialists, Blake concluded it was so dangerous for Shirazi that he would only ask him to do it once, on the actual mission.

And while Blake grew no more hopeful about Shirazi's chances of success, he did develop a grudging respect for the man. Blake remembered something he'd once seen on the tailgate of a pickup truck, of all places. It was a quote attributed to John Wayne: "Courage is being scared to death but saddling up anyway."

Blake doubted John Wayne ever said that. In college the research librarian at Hampden-Sydney often said "just because something is repeated on a hundred Web sites doesn't make it a fact." And a couple hours of research convinced Blake the saying, while memorable, probably hadn't come from the Duke. But that didn't prevent him from admiring it.

He had to admit it certainly applied to Massoud Shirazi. Heights terrified the man. One evening, he admitted to Blake that, although he flew to Europe and the Far East whenever his work required it, for domestic travel he always checked Amtrak first and took it whenever it was time- and cost-effective.

The admission came during a rare introspective moment with Shirazi. The man had his wallet open and was looking at a picture. It was a child of two, maybe three, holding a stuffed bear.

He and Blake were sitting at a table in an empty classroom at the Jump School, filling out Shirazi's logbook, and Blake looked at the open wallet.

"Your daughter?"

Shirazi nodded.

Blake looked again. "But not one of your wife?"

Shirazi shook his head. "I have no need. Anytime I want, I can close my eyes and picture my wife's face. But my daughter—time and time again, I find myself thinking of her. Wondering what she would look like today, you know? What she would look like had she made it here, to America."

"Got to be tough."

Shirazi put the picture away. "God is taking care of her. Now, let us speak of tomorrow's training."

THE PREPARATION WENT BEYOND putting Shirazi through accelerated jump school. It included one trip Blake made alone to McMaster University in Hamilton, Ontario. An associate professor in the anthropology program there was a former master corporal in Princess Patricia's Canadian Light Infantry Regiment: the sniper cell. And when one of his former officers called asking a favor for another sniper—one who was about to embark on a covert mission and needed the identity of a Canadian graduate student as his cover—he agreed to not only work with Blake, but to put him up at his house.

"IT TOOK HIM ABOUT thirty seconds to figure out my real name isn't Edward McNamara," Blake told Alia when he got back. They were having lunch at the Boston Market on Chain Bridge Road—Alia was a sucker for the chicken potpies.

"Lucky guess?"

"No." Blake was having the meatloaf. "Snipers are a pretty small community. And while not all of them join the veterans' groups, those who do tend, as a group, to know those who don't. No 'Edward McNamara' ever worked as a member of a sniper team, or as a sniper in Special Ops. At least not one my approximate age. But we talked shop almost as soon as we met, and we exchanged tricks: things like leaving your ammo sitting out in the sun to warm it up, make the load hotter, lengthen the useful range. So he knew I trained as a sniper, that I've worked as one in the field. That left only one possibility: that the Eddie McNamara identity was false."

Alia peppered her chicken potpie. "He have a problem with that?"

"Not at all." Blake dipped a fork of meatloaf into a small puddle of ketchup. "The master corporal did a great job of showing me around, going through faculty directories, and generally backgrounding me. Gave me a few books to ground me in what an anthropologist studying the Achaemenid Empire would be looking for in modern-day Iran. Said he understood entirely about the name and he hopes someday I can come back and tell him who I am."

Alia ate her potpie in silence for a moment. "I hope his expectations are not too high because I don't think he's going to see that happen."

Alia's face was serious as was her tone when she spoke again. "You have done more than most for your country already, Blake."

Blake looked at her, studying her face, silent.

"This is sounding so . . . thrown together." She shook her head. "And there is no dishonor in sitting this one out."

Then she looked up. "But I'll support you, Blake. I will be with you either way you go."

Blake put his own fork down. "I've accepted the mission."

Tears began to fill her eyes as she looked directly into his.

"I love you, Blake Kershaw." Alia took a breath. "And I am proud of you. I already knew what you were going to say. It's who you are. As much as I want to begin a life with you, I want more to see you follow the plan God has for you and I believe this is what God wants you to do. It's strange, Blake, but I believe there really is some important reason why you have been chosen for this. And it goes beyond your skill and experience. Really, Blake, I think there is more to this than you are aware of right now but I can't discern what that is. Anyway, I will be praying for the man I love with all my energy."

Her eyes were full of tears now but Blake knew they were not tears of sadness. He had known Alia long enough to recognize when she was weeping tears of joy and pride.

They were coming from the one person who meant the world to Blake. So he laced his hand gently on top of hers and leaned forward slowly to kiss her lightly on a tear-dampened cheek.

"I love you, Ali."

They sat for a moment just staring into each others eyes before Blake spoke again.

"Ali, there are people in Iran who are putting it all on the line for this. This woman who's gotten close to Nassiri, Zari Nourazar, is probably risking her life."

Alia spoke softly, "Then she is blessed to have you on her side. Now you go, Blake. You do this and you come back to me. Our time will come eventually. I believe that. It will come and we will spend a lifetime together. But now, you must do this."

Chapter Nine

Blake Kershaw knew that, somewhere in the foothills of Iran, a drop zone was prepared for their landing and fires were lit in oil drums. The drums were arranged in an arrow, pointing into the prevailing wind. Difficult to see from ground level until one was right on top of them, those barrels would be visible for miles to an approaching parachutist.

But Blake couldn't see an arrow. He couldn't see a single barrel. And he knew he wouldn't; Shirazi and he had opened better than 14,000 feet too low.

Blake was a veteran of dozens of HAHO jumps. He'd become expert at trimming out the canopy, adjusting the trim tabs for maximum glide. He knew he could milk every last inch of distance out of the parachute.

He had no such illusions about his partner. The Iranian was barely jump-qualified; it took written orders, straight from the director, just to get the CIA flight crew to agree to put Shirazi on the airplane. The other man did not have the finesse to trim the canopy for maximum glide. And Shirazi hadn't jettisoned his gear, so he was dropping heavy.

They'd been under canopy for less than two minutes and already Shirazi was gliding level with Blake. He could see the strobe blinking; the other man hadn't even dropped his helmet.

Blake swallowed. All things considered, it probably wasn't such a bad thing Shirazi still had his helmet.

"Massoud."

"Yes, my friend." The older man's voice had regained some strength.

"Dead ahead. Maybe seven kilometers. See the surf line?"

There were two seconds of silence. Then, "Yes. I see it. Can we make it?"

Blake checked the altimeter: 2,340 feet. It was well within the glide range of their canopies, but that assumed an expert parachutist. Shirazi was anything but. "Remember how we showed you to use the canopy brakes?"

"Yes," Shirazi answered. "For a short-field landing."

"You got it," Blake told him. "I want you to pump the brakes."

"Pump?"

"Pull them: over and over and over."

The strobe had definitely dropped lower than Blake.

"But that will slow me."

"It'll keep you aloft. Pump 'em."

The strobe began to fall aft of Blake. But it also continued to drop beneath him.

Ninety seconds passed. Blake dropped below a thousand feet; he couldn't see Shirazi's strobe anymore. But he could see the surf line, a distant, waxing and waning gray-white brushstroke in the starlight.

And he could see something else. Above the surf. He just wasn't sure what.

He looked off to the side, allowing his peripheral vision, the more light-sensitive parts of his eyes, to come into play. And now, he could see what was above the surf.

A cliff. For hundreds of kilometers along the Iranian coast, the shore was dunes sloping to a gentle beach. But they were coming straight in at the rare headland that ended in a cliff. That was something they'd never considered in the planning; the plan was never to land on the beach.

Blake turned his head: still no sign of the other man.

"Massoud! Turn! Turn hard left! Now."

No answer.

"Left steering line! Pull! Hard!"

Now Blake was turning himself. He could dimly make out the other man's parachute, nearly two hundred feet below him.

"I cannot." Shirazi's voice was barely audible above the rising crash of surf. "The water . . . All this gear."

"Ditch it when you hit! You can do it. Turn! *Turn now!*"

He knew even as he said it the situation was falling apart. Blake craned his head back, over his left shoulder. Massoud's parachute continued to glide, straight in, toward the shore.

Blake pulled hard left on his own steering line. It caused the canopy to side-slip, losing altitude, but that did not matter; the cliff-top was still better than 150 feet beneath his heels as he crossed over it. He continued the left turn, completing a one-eighty, and then brought himself level just before his boots touched down on Iranian soil. The canopy collapsed behind him in the light onshore wind and he quickly shed his harness, dug into one of his bellows pockets, and pulled out an LED flashlight.

"Massoud?"

There was no answer.

Blake ran to the edge of the cliff, dropped prone on sparse sea-grass, and aimed his flashlight beam down, toward the sea.

The beam found a fluttering sheet of black nylon and he followed it back to a twisted figure on a sloping rock shelf, about thirty feet below. It was Shirazi. And he wasn't moving.

Chapter Ten

The cliff was steep, but not vertical. Still, much of the rock was loose, the night was dark, and down-climbing is more difficult than climbing, so even with his Special Forces training, it took Blake nearly five minutes to reach his partner.

The surf, a hundred feet below in the night, thundered like a rhythmic avalanche. It wasn't until he was almost on top of him that Blake could hear Shirazi groaning.

The other man's strobe, shattered on impact, was dead.

Worse still, the Iranian's right leg had done little better.

The older man's jumpsuit was wet with blood from the right knee on down and Blake could see the splintered fibula sticking out through a tear in the suit. Holding his tactical flashlight in his teeth, he cut away Shirazi's risers and balled the parachute up, placing it under the older man's head.

"My leg. I . . ."

Blake transferred the flashlight to a ledge. "I see."

Working as carefully as he could, he removed the rucksack from Shirazi's legs and opened it, pulling out the first aid kit. "Hang tight. We'll get some morphine into you."

"No!" The Iranian's eyes came completely open. "I must be awake. I must tell you . . ."

"Relax." Blake opened his bellows pocket, got out the black case containing the satellite phone. "I'll make a call to Langley, they'll relay to the sub. Two hours, tops, we'll have a SEAL team here, get you stable, evac us both."

"No." Shirazi grabbed Blake's wrist; his grip was surprisingly strong. "We cannot call off the mission. This . . . this is our only opportunity to get Nassiri out of the country. There will not be another."

"I know." Blake gently pried the other man's fingers off his wrist. "But you aren't going anywhere but to a hospital. You can't travel." This was what Blake had most feared. Now the mission was going to have to be aborted. He could not go on and leave this man behind.

Shirazi took a breath. "I understand that, my friend. But there are things I have not told you. You must continue this mission without me. I know I cannot travel, so I ask you, my friend. Please . . . kill me."

Blake fell silent for a moment while he absorbed the man's request. Then he shook his head. "Not happening, my friend. I'm calling the SEALs."

"Listen!" Shirazi sat up partway. "Nassiri's assistant. Her name was changed. When she was born . . . the first two years of her life . . . it was 'Nasrin Shirazi.'"

"That's . . ."

"That's right. My name. She is the little girl . . . the picture I showed you."

Blake studied the man's face in the glow of the flashlight. "Massoud, your daughter's dead."

The older man shook his head. "My wife and I were worried about taking Nasrin with us when we fled the country. We did not know how dangerous it might be. Another family in the church, the Nourazar family, had a daughter born with a heart-valve defect. It was getting worse; she needed surgery or she would be dead within six months. And here in Iran, the hospitals are run by the state; the Nourazars feared the scrutiny. The girls looked so much alike they could pass for twins, so we made a pact. My wife and I would take Zari with us when we fled—for her, the risk was worth it—and Nasrin would stay here; the Nourazars would say she was their daughter."

Shirazi groaned and took a breath. "We would get Zari to a hospital in England or America, get her help, and then once we knew the way was safe, we would let the Nourazar family know, and they would follow with Nasrin."

He paused, his breath becoming ragged. "It was Zari who died in the crash. . . . And then, once I reached America, word came that the smugglers who'd helped me had been caught. The way out was closed. . . . The Nourazar family thought no ill of me; they knew my wife and I tried our best. They raised our Nasrin as their own daughter. . . . And two years ago, Mrs. Nourazar died in a house fire. Zari—my Nasrin—was away, working. Since then, I have worked night and day to find a way to get her out. And now . . . now God has opened one."

"But Massoud . . ."

"Listen to me!" The Iranian's voice became strong again. "If you cannot think of my daughter, then think of the mission. If we do not extract Nassiri, we do not obtain the locations of the active launch sites. And Ahmadinejad will use them. You know he will. He has targeted Israel. He will kill hundreds of thousands of people. He will start a war that could end it all.

"And besides . . ." Shirazi's voice grew weaker again. He looked up at the cliff face. "This is the only chance. This country, it becomes more like a prison each day. The special police units, the Pasdaran—their numbers increase every month. Even now, to take someone out involves great risk. By next year, even later this year? It could be impossible. But you can do it. Even by yourself. I have seen you; you are cunning, my friend. You can find the people of the church, get to Nassiri."

"Massoud . . ."

The older man struggled up to a sitting position, put his hand on Blake's shoulder. His voice became a whisper. "You are a warrior, my friend. To pay one death, so millions can live? You know that this is a bargain. It is right. So I beg you: get Nassiri out. Save my daughter."

Massoud took a deep breath. "Kill me. I am ready; kill me now."

Chapter Eleven

For Blake, the worst thing was he knew the older man was right.

Amos Phillips had said as much back in Washington. The intelligence that came along with Farid Nassiri was easily worth the price of a life. It was the kind of information for which any reasonable intelligence agency would place dozens, or even hundreds of lives at risk. It would save many lives and prevent a world war.

He thought about it as he placed a tourniquet above Shirazi's knee. Extraction would take two, three hours, minimum. Make it four by the time the Iranian was in the submarine sick bay. After that much time, Shirazi might lose his lower leg. But the break was not a lethal wound. It would not kill him.

Meaning that, if this mission was to succeed, Blake would have to.

Under his civilian clothes, Blake had a sidearm, a Springfield Armory XD(m) with a full magazine of nine-millimeter hollow-point ammunition. But with him shouting directions to his partner, their arrival had been considerably less than stealthy. He couldn't risk firing a shot on top of that.

He felt the other man's body in the dark and found the left strap to Shirazi's parachute harness. Upside-down on the left shoulder, each man's harness was equipped with a sheathed fighting knife, useful for cutting away entanglements if they fell into trees or power lines. Blake silently unsnapped the nylon sheath and drew the knife.

Blake put his arm around the older man and drew him close, as if comforting him. He bent the Iranian's head forward, opening a gap between the vertebrae. He found the horseshoe indentation at the base of the skull and put the blade-tip against it.

Blake thought about it. He thought he could accomplish it with one quick push, both hands. He'd have to thrust the blade all the way in: separate the spinal column at the base of the skull, stop the heart, and interrupt respiration. It was as close to an instantaneous death as he could accomplish on this remote cliffside without making some noise.

Blake took a deep breath. He knew what he had to do and he did not want to do it. He remembered a piece of Scripture: "*. . . take this cup away from me.*"

Shirazi shook within his arms and gasped.

Blake looked down at the man. He hadn't moved the knife. Not a bit. "What is it?"

"Arrh . . ." Shirazi grimaced, holding his abdomen.

Blake switched on the flashlight, unzipped the Iranian's jumpsuit, and pulled up the shirt and jacket he wore underneath. The older man's abdomen was distended, the skin striated, black marks growing larger.

"What is it?" Shirazi wheezed and groaned.

"You're bleeding internally," Blake told him. He shifted the flashlight and looked in the other man's eyes. "Looks as if you ruptured your liver. Bad bleed: there's . . . there's nothing I can do here to stop it."

Shirazi smiled, took a ragged breath, and patted his hand. "Then . . . God has done the job for you. But I felt the knife-tip, my friend. You were ready. . . Thank you."

Massoud shivered and groaned again. "So cold . . ."

Blake held him, set the knife aside. "It won't be long, Massoud. I'll stay with you."

The older man's eyes closed, then opened again.

"Promise me," he said. "Whatever you do, you will get my Zari out of Iran. Will you give me your word on this?"

Blake squeezed the other man's hand. "I give you my word."

"Thank you." Shirazi looked up at the dark sky. He smiled. "Every night, I have prayed to God that someday I would come home, that I would die in Iran."

The smile left his face and he shivered again, shivered the length of his body, despite the warmth of the Iranian night. Ten minutes later, he fell still.

There was no time for mourning. Blake put the flat of three fingertips against the man's neck and felt for a pulse.

Nothing.

He unzipped Shirazi's jumpsuit, slid a hand inside his shirt, and checked again, this time in his armpit.

Still nothing.

SYSTEMATICALLY, BLAKE SET ABOUT "sanitizing" the body. He used the fighting knife to cut away the parachute risers, put a breadloaf-sized rock in the fabric of the canopy, and hurled the unfurled fabric as far seaward as he could. It vanished almost instantly in the darkness, but a second later, he heard a faint splash between the crashes of the waves hitting the base of the cliff.

The parachute harness was next. Then he stripped off Shirazi's jumpsuit and did the same with his own, putting the satellite phone and a small Magellan GPS atop Massoud's rucksack. Tying the jumpsuits to the harness, he filled the empty parachute pack with several pounds of rocks, and then threw everything out to sea.

That left only the body.

Blake thought about that as he searched the dead man's pockets, making sure nothing was left behind that would identify him as an American. The sea was the logical solution for the body as well, although a body would be hard to sink—and would probably not stay sunk for long. The Arabian Sea was warm; bacteria would grow and bloat the intestines, bringing the dead man to the surface, if the sea life didn't pick him apart first. Someone would find him on the shore, or on the rocks.

And then what?

Probably nothing, Blake decided. An anonymous man falls off a cliff and drowns in the ocean: the sort of thing that only stays news for a day. The jumpsuits and the parachute were on the sea bottom and would stay there. It was a viable solution.

He looked at Shirazi's corpse. The man had a family . . . a daughter. She might want to reclaim her father's body someday, give it a Christian burial.

Blake played the flashlight over the ledge and found what he was looking for: a place where the rock was undercut enough to stuff a man into it. He dragged the Iranian's body there and pushed, shoved, and rearranged it until it was nearly all the way beneath the rock of the cliff. For the next fifteen minutes, he gathered stones and walled Shirazi's body over, creating a blanket of rocks to discourage seabirds—the only wildlife likely to reach such a remote place.

To Blake Kershaw, prayers for the dead were simply consolation for the living. He believed a man's state with his God had to be decided by him, when there was still breath within him. So when the final stone was in place, he didn't hesitate. He swung the rucksack onto his back and made the climb back to the top of the cliff.

THE GPS PLACED THE landing zone eight miles inland. Blake glanced at the sky: the constellations told him he had about four hours before dawn and four hours of stealthy walking would be about right to put him at the drop zone.

If the church group was following instructions, it would be empty. But the landing zone was remote and rural, chosen because it was both within range of a parachute and isolated enough no one was likely to stumble upon it.

It would be a good place to lay up during the day; the group had instructions to come check the landing zone twenty-four hours after the initial ETA. And if they didn't show, his mission plan required him to call the mission and proceed to an extraction point on the coast.

Blake got the bearing from the GPS and looked up.

A gray-white smudge appeared on the dark horizon in front of him. It got brighter. Two brilliant points of light appeared.

Headlights.

Blake looked to either side. He was still out of range of the approaching vehicle's lights, but not for long.

The clothing he was wearing was appropriate to a college professor in the field; khaki pants and a canvas shirt. Both were about the color of the surrounding terrain, but neither could even remotely be considered camouflage.

A darker place appeared against the horizon to his left, and he moved there. It was brush: low shrubs of a palm-like plant, and he got behind them, shed his rucksack, and slid the pistol from the holster to the inside of his waistband, thumbing the safety off.

The vehicle groaned and whined nearer and stopped near the top of the cliff. It was a Jeep: the older military style. One man got out and Blake saw green pant-legs: a uniform of some sort—police or a beach patrol.

"Who was the one who called this in?" The man asked the question in Arabic, which was not that unusual for western Iran. Not all Iranians spoke Farsi as their primary language.

"Fisherman," the other man told him. "Lives down the shore. He was rowing back from checking his nets and said he heard voices in the sky near here: not Arabic and not Farsi."

The first man laughed. "And this is why they send us out here? Because some drunk of a fisherman is hearing angels in the sky?"

He walked to the cliff's edge. A flashlight blinked on, then off again.

"There's nothing here," the first man said. He hesitated, and Blake saw the outline of the man turn in his direction. "Hold on. Wait a minute."

The flashlight winked on, then off again, straight at Blake. He stiffened and willed himself to melt into the earth.

The uniformed man walked nearer, kept walking until he was standing just three feet away. Blake canted the pistol up, began applying pressure with his trigger finger.

Above him, the man's head was leaned forward. It was difficult to tell in the dark; it seemed as if he was looking straight at Blake.

Blake couldn't understand what he was waiting for. He crept the trigger back a millimeter.

There was the sound of a zipper, then liquid began to splash on the ground, not a foot from Blake's face. The smell of ammonia filled the air around him. He heard the zipper again, the man began to walk away, and Blake relaxed the pressure on the trigger.

"There," he heard the man call in Arabic to his companion, "now you can hit all the ruts and potholes that you want. I swear, a trained baboon could drive better than you."

"You can always walk," his companion replied.

"Oh, shut your mouth and drive."

The Jeep wheeled around and drove away, its square red taillights bouncing and growing smaller and nearer together until they vanished over the rump of a small hill.

Blake got up, slid the pistol back into its holster, and swung the rucksack onto his back.

He looked down at the shrub.

"Not a bad idea," he muttered aloud.

He unzipped and relieved himself on the same spot the Iranian policeman used. Then he zipped up and began walking inland.

Chapter Twelve

Special Forces soldiers do most of their fighting in teams, but every Special Forces soldier also receives extensive training in operating solo. Much of that training is aimed at helping the individual escape the enemy and either rejoin his unit or get back to safer ground. What Blake was doing was the opposite: heading toward his enemy, to take an asset out from under his enemy's nose.

It wasn't his first time. But it made him feel no less odd.

Blake avoided roads. That much was elementary—one of the first things a soldier learns when it comes to evading the enemy. But by the time he was an hour away from the sea, the vegetation had all but disappeared, and the ground was the subtle, close-to-level terrain of desert hardpan. Rocks dotted the landscape, but the occasional tire track was enough to convince Blake that not all vehicle traffic in this part of Iran was confined to the roads. Obviously, among those Iranians affluent enough to afford four-wheel drive, a few had the extra money necessary to buy a decent off-road GPS as well.

And it went without saying the Iranian Revolutionary Guard Corps—known by Iranians simply as "The Guard," or *Pasdaran* in Farsi—would have been equipped with military-caliber GPS and four-wheel drive. Ahmadinejad's regime took in a hundred million dollars in oil sales a day and the Pasdaran was a close second behind the nuclear program in Ahmadinejad's list of pet projects.

So Blake kept his ears open for the sound of engines approaching, and did a continuous horizon-to-horizon scan as he walked, studying one area of pitch-black landscape for a second, shifting ten degrees, and studying the next.

Near the end of the second hour, the terrain began to roll again, and as he neared the crest of his third rise, he heard voices, mostly Farsi and some Arabic.

Blake dropped to a crawl and edged forward.

Peering around the side of a truck-tire-sized boulder, he looked down on a slope that ran perhaps an eighth of a mile to a dirt road. On the road were two vehicles—a medium-duty truck with a canvas awning covering its load and what appeared in the darkness to be a Renault Sherpa 2, a military utility vehicle originally designed for the French military.

"I don't have a crowbar," a man in a flat-topped hat was saying in Arabic to a group of men in fatigues. "I drive a truck. I have socket wrenches, a jack, an extra fan belt. Why would I carry a crowbar?"

"Bring me a hammer," one of the uniformed men called back. He said it in Farsi, but Blake understood just enough to follow. And by the man's tone, Blake took him to be an officer.

A man came running up and handed the officer a small sledge. The man crawled into the back of the truck—as he did this the lights from the Sherpa caught him and Blake noted with a certain amount of disgust the Iranian was wearing a green beret.

There was the sound of pounding, of wood breaking.

"Here now," the driver called. "That's my load. I have to deliver it."

The Pasdaran officer came out with something rectangular in his hand. "Your bill of lading says nails. You call this nails?"

"I don't know anything about that. They told me when I picked it up that it was nails."

The officer swung whatever it was and caught the driver in the face. There was the sound of heavy plastic shattering, and the driver was knocked to the ground and then jerked back to his feet by some of the Pasdaran.

"You need a notebook computer, my brother?" The driver's voice was thick, as if he'd lost a tooth or two. "I'll give you one. I'll give all of you one."

"Really?" The officer sounded interested. "What are they worth?"

"A thousand American dollars in Ilam."

"Then we will add attempted bribery to the smuggling charge: that and attempted escape."

"Brother, you are mistaken. I never tried to escape."

"Then how did you get wounded?" The officer pulled a semiautomatic pistol from his holster and fired a single round.

For a moment after the sharp crack of the shot, everything was silent. Then the driver leaned forward, gripped his side, and began to scream.

The officer approached the driver, his pistol extended. "You want another?" Immediately, the driver's screams subsided to a moan.

The officer nodded at the truck. "Put a box of those in our vehicle before the impoundment team gets here. And put a bandage on him before we transport. I don't want blood in my vehicle."

Blake back-crawled away from the crest of the hill. Then he got to his feet and vectored east, only turning north again when the lights of the Pasdaran vehicle-stop were just a lighter smudge off to his left. From what he'd seen, it was clear the Iranians made intercepting contraband their mission for the evening. They'd showed no signs of high alert, no indication they even suspected their country had been infiltrated.

The sky was lightening just a bit, not enough to completely wash the stars away, but enough to give him a better view of the surrounding landscape. Blake got out the GPS, regained his bearing, and picked up his pace, moving across the desert at something between a fast walk and a trot. Now that he had enough light to avoid stepping off into a wadi or tripping over a low boulder, he could afford to make haste, and he needed to. During the light of day, the safest thing was to lay up at the rendezvous point, so he wanted to be at the drop zone by dawn.

WHEN THE GPS SHOWED him within half a mile of the drop zone, Blake could see it clearly in the pre-dawn light: a low, treeless hill that looked to be as long as two football fields. As tan as the desert around it, its flat top was about forty feet higher than the surrounding country. That would allow anyone on top of it to see intruders approaching long before they got there.

Blake crouched low as he approached and climbed the gentle slope that way. When he got to the top, he began to circle the big crest of the hill and within five minutes found the circular footprints marking the ground where fifty-five-gallon drums had been set alight to provide the previous evening's directional arrow. But that—and some broad, vaguely disturbed ground that

Blake assumed was caused by a vehicle dragging brush to obscure its tire tracks—was the only indication someone had been there.

Blake searched the horizon, turning slowly until he could see a truck passing on a road about a mile and a half to the east. Five minutes later, it was followed by a tan military utility vehicle—no doubt the Pasdaran intent on another contraband stop.

That cinched it. He set down his rucksack, got out an entrenching tool, and dug a trench big enough to hold a man and a backpack. He anchored a tan square of camouflage netting over it with heavy stones, and then scattered dirt and sand over it until it was indistinguishable from the desert ground around it.

As the sun crept over the brink of the desert, Blake slithered backward into his makeshift shelter. The netting provided shade and the desert sand would help insulate him from the coming heat of the day. Combine that with the view and the trench was nearly a perfect "hide"—a place from which to watch the road, and the ground between the road and the hill, between catnaps.

THE DAY PASSED, THE traffic on the road sporadic. The sun was setting, the shadow of the low hill reaching out toward the road, when Blake saw a brown jeep-like vehicle racing eastward, running much faster than most of the traffic he'd seen during the day. As he watched, it turned off the road, a long cloud of dust rooster-tailing behind it, and aimed straight at his hide.

Off to Blake's right was a boulder about the size of a sofa—something he'd noted in the morning as he selected his hide. And the approaching vehicle was still in sunlight, meaning the hill he was on was backlit. If he wanted to move, Blake had to do it now, before whoever was in the vehicle got the sun out of their eyes.

The pistol in his hand, he raced across the hundred feet between the hide and the boulder, and threw himself to the ground behind it just as the car crossed into shadow. Pistol before him in a two-handed prone grip, he watched over the sights as the vehicle drew nearer.

In less than a minute, he was certain it was headed for the hill. He gripped the pistol more tightly, pressing the grip safety all the way flush, ready to fire.

The vehicle—Blake could see now it was a Pushpak, a smaller SUV made in India—slowed as it neared the base of the hill, drove partway up, and turned broadside, pointed to Blake's right. A man, bearded, wearing the flat cloth cap of a hillsman, stepped out of the vehicle, both of his hands visible on the roof of the vehicle. He looked straight at the place where Blake sited his hide. Then he turned, brown eyes blinking once, before looking directly at the boulder that all but obscured Blake.

The man at the vehicle cupped his hands to his mouth.

"*De oppresso,*" he shouted.

Blake recognized it: it was Latin for "the oppressed."

Setting aside his pistol, he made a megaphone of his own hands.

"*Liber,*" he called back. It meant, "free them."

And then he stood, putting his pistol back on safe, because "*de oppresso liber*"—"to free the oppressed"—was the motto of the United States Army Special Forces.

"Hormoz Pardivari?"

The other man nodded.

"You know," Blake said as he walked nearer. "You're supposed to be dead."

"I know for a fact that I will be, unless we get on the move," Pardivari said, shaking Blake's hand. Despite his distinctively Middle-Eastern appearance, the man spoke English like a Southerner, with a low-country accent. "There's a full guard unit about to come up our hindquarters . . . about ten klicks behind me."

Chapter Thirteen

Trouble with your partner?" Pardivari asked as he drove.

"He got in trouble on the jump, dropped through our opening level, busted up when we landed short. I'm sorry; he didn't make it."

"I never knew him, even though several of our group did." He glanced Blake's way. "So if he opened low . . . I take it you did, as well?"

"I didn't think he'd open, otherwise."

The missionary shook his head. "That's admirable, but scary, partner. Looks like I'm working with you now and it's important we get this old boy Nassiri out of Iraq; I've been working with these house churches here about five years now and they're like family to me. Ahmadinejad launches, this whole part of the world is going to turn into one piece of fused glass, and I don't want that happening to my people. So promise me right now that you'll put the mission first."

"You've got it." The silence was uncomfortable. "So how is it you're not dead?"

Pardivari laughed. "*Times* of London sent a freelancer to interview me a couple years ago. Iranian by birth, same as me. I was supposed to meet him at an empty house we sometimes used as a supply cache and because we had never met before, we both agreed to bring passports, credit cards and whatnot, establish identity, you know? He got there first, and the Pasdaran must have gotten wind we used the place sometimes, because they left a passive device—bomb in a briefcase. He must have thought it was a message from me, opened it; I heard the explosion when I was still a full click away."

Pardivari tapped a compass mounted on the dash. They weren't going back to the road, and they didn't have their lights on either, despite the gathering darkness. "It wasn't much of a bomb, but it did a number on him: hands gone, face gone: metal fragments in his chest. He must have died instantly. Things

67

were getting hot for me, anyhow—I'd been debating pulling out, just so I wouldn't endanger the various churches I was working with. So I switched my documents with his and then beat feet out of there. Authorities got there about fifteen minutes later, found the body. Here in the Middle East, they don't bother testing for DNA when they've got a passport. I doubt they even ran his blood type. So that put me off the grid, bought me a few more years in the mission field."

Pardivari steered expertly around a hole Blake barely saw in the gathering darkness. They weren't doing much more than twenty miles per hour, but still it was faster than Blake would have risked driving without the lights. Obviously the man knew the country.

"They told me you were a missionary and former Special Forces," Blake said. "But nothing else. Like I said, CIA lists you as dead. What group were you with?"

"Seventh," Pardivari said, not looking away from the windshield. "Stationed in Panama: we were part of Task Force Blake . . . Operation Just Cause."

"Sure." Blake nodded.

"We held the bridge at the Pacora River, kept the Panamanian Defense Force from breaking through. Got the bronze star with V, got promoted to E-6. Thought I was all that and a bucket of chicken, you know?"

Blake smiled. He hadn't heard the expression in years.

"I stayed in for about three years after that," Pardivari said. "But the peacetime Army seemed mostly to me like waiting. Then one day, I was talking with my pastor—I'd been a Christian for years—and he said field skills like what I had, that and the ability to speak Farsi like a native, could be a real blessing in the mission field. So I went to seminary and here I am."

Blake suspected there was more to it than that, but he left it; he'd just met the man. It was full-on night now and Blake could no longer even make out Pardivari's face. But the missionary drove steadily, glancing at the compass every minute or so.

"And how is it you speak English like a good old boy?"

Pardivari laughed. "My parents worked at a hospital in DC for a while and then began touring with UNICEF, supervising relief efforts. Kept them in the field a lot. So when I hit seventh grade, they sent me to Valley Forge. You know it? Military school in Pennsylvania?"

"Little West Point."

"That's what they call it." Pardivari smiled. "I'd learned English from a British tutor and had me this posh accent. Sounded like Hugh Grant. Between that and looking like Ali Babba, goes without saying: I didn't fit in. So, they had me bunking with a kid from Charleston and I learned to talk like him. Even spent a couple summers at his house when my folks were traveling. Turned me into a genuine hadji redneck."

He glanced Blake's way and smiled. "But don't worry. My Farsi and my Arabic don't have a hint of Redman or monster truck in 'em."

Blake laughed. He'd already decided he liked Pardivari.

They rode in silence for about ten minutes, then the missionary asked, "Don't hear much about pop culture on Iranian TV; Springsteen have a new album out yet?"

"Springsteen? You mean Bruce Springsteen?"

Pardivari nodded.

Blake shrugged. "I wouldn't have a clue."

"Man, kid." Pardivari shook his head. "How young are you, anyhow?"

He checked his watch. "We can't make much time, driving cross-country like this. Probably have to lay up at sunrise, do all our traveling at night. Iranians have aircraft that can detect heat signatures, but they don't fly 'em much. So as long as we travel lights-off, we're pretty much undetectable. Only problem is, it's slow."

"Understood."

"That'll give us time to talk about the mission, though. And the first thing you need to know is you have to stay under cover. Your legend . . . you're a Canadian professor, is that right?"

"Yes. Jeffrey Walker. Professor of anthropology."

"Then that's who you are to everyone you meet. Everyone except me and Zari. There's one other member of the group in the know, but you'll never meet him. He's laid up, dying of cancer, and he's the one who has the satellite internet connection—it was him in contact with Massoud. The rest of these folks, they're good people, but this is Iran. People like to talk. House churches are more close-lipped than most, because we have to stay under the radar, but still, if the Pasdaran takes anybody in, starts grilling 'em, it's better if they don't have anything to say, you know?"

THE EASTERN SKY WAS beginning to gray when Pardivari turned off the heading he'd been following. They crossed about half a mile of open desert and drove down a slope into a wadi—a dried-up creek bed. The missionary followed the wadi for a mile and then stopped at a bend. The wadi was about twelve feet deep at that point, and there was a cave in the outside of the bend, about four feet off the ground.

The two men stashed their gear into the cave and then came back and covered the little SUV with camouflage netting. They went up to the cave and sat in the opening while the eastern sky turned pink.

Pardivari handed Blake a packet. "Imagine you've seen one of these before."

Blake laughed. It was an MRE—the military "meal, ready-to-eat."

"Got a bunch of these in a relief drop about six months ago. Turkey goulash. Every single packet is turkey goulash. Me, I like it, but the rest of the folks can't stand it."

"Fine by me," Blake said. He poured a little water from a canteen into the heating sleeve and slid it into the packet, set it aside to warm itself. "This Zari . . . the one who's the assistant to Nassiri: what do you know about her?"

"She's as much nurse as she is assistant; the old man's arthritic. Her family goes back to the beginnings of the house churches here—all these families come from Muslim backgrounds, originally. Her mother died a few years back. Her dad's the one who's been communicating with Massoud. He doesn't have much time left; maybe a month. But don't worry. She's solid. I know everything there is to know about her."

Blake picked up his MRE. It was hot.

He wondered if he should tell Pardivari the one thing he didn't know about the young woman.

It seemed like a complication that they didn't need to have right now.

He ate his food.

Chapter Fourteen

They slept through the day, the earthen walls of the cave keeping the air around them bearable, if not cool. When the sun was low enough to put nearly the entire wadi into shadow, Pardivari went out and opened the windows on the SUV.

"Like an oven in there right now," he said. "Need to let some heat out. You hungry? We got us a treat. MREs, boy: turkey goulash!"

Blake laughed and accepted the pale tan plastic package. "How many of these you eat a week?"

"Not many. Only when I'm on the move, like this, and I don't get out and move unless I have to. Mostly I stay with my church folks. They eat a lot of rice . . . chicken and goat. That sort of stuff: your standard Middle Eastern menu. Far as I'm concerned, this here's a little taste of the old days, back when I was a green beanie."

Blake set part of the ration aside to heat. "What about home? You ever miss it?"

Pardivari stepped out of the cave for a second, gauged the height of the sun, and sat in the entrance. "Suppose I do, sometimes. Lot of what I miss isn't there now. My folks had me after the time when most people are done raising kids; they both passed back while I was still in the Army."

He slid his food out of its cardboard container. "If why I stay here is what you're gettin' at, I guess the work is the main thing. It's the best-kept secret in Western media that Christianity is the fastest-growing religion in the Middle East. Here in Iran, Ahmadinejad tries to keep a herd on that by permitting a certain number of churches and then controlling what they can do, and how. That's where the house churches come from. It's like the underground was in occupied France, only it all revolves around faith. These people put their lives, their livelihoods, their homes, and their families on the line every time they gather to pray. I can't help but admire that . . . makes me want to do what I can to help them."

Pardivari fell silent. "I'd better get the engine started. This old girl runs pretty good when she's warmed up, but she stalls pretty easy when she's cold. Like me, I guess; the older you get, the longer it takes to get the aches and stiffness out, so you can start movin'."

He nodded at Blake's MRE package. "We'll take those with us, bury 'em an hour or two out. This here cave's a pretty good hide; I might want to use it again sometime."

THEY DID JUST THAT, swinging off-course and stopping to bury their waste after two hours of driving in the dark. They used the stop to re-fuel as well, replenishing the vehicle's tank from a jerry can of diesel. Then they were back on the move, Pardivari driving the little SUV at a pace barely faster than a man could run. The terrain turned more stony and the missionary was wearing night-vision gear. Even with it, he had to swing off-line frequently to avoid patches of boulders.

Blake didn't talk. He could tell from Pardivari's frequent glances at the compass that the missionary was doing the math in his head, calculating the deviations from their heading and then adding the degrees back in to put them back on course. The lack of conversation and the rocking of the Pushpak had their effect and after half an hour or so Blake nodded off.

He woke when the vehicle swung abruptly to their right and accelerated. Blake sat up and reached back, taking the pistol out of its waistband holster. He looked at Pardivari. "What's up?"

Pardivari swung off between two truck-size boulders.

"Chopper," he said. "On our six."

He threw the Pushpak into neutral and yanked on the emergency brake. "Better bail."

The two men ran away from the SUV and took cover behind a smaller group of boulders. Blake could hear the rotor noise from the helicopter now. He located it and saw the running lights. As he watched, a searchlight stabbed down from the approaching aircraft, swept the ground for five seconds, and then winked out again.

"They onto us?"

Pardivari shook his head. He was still wearing the night-vision gear. "Don't see how. We're headed toward the village, but I've swung east, to avoid Ilam— capital of the province, good-size city. No one knows we're taking this route except me."

The pitch of the noise went up as the helicopter bore down on them. The searchlight came on again and swept the empty ground between their patch of boulders and the larger rocks, where the truck was hidden.

"Worked," Pardivari said as the helicopter raced by, not two hundred feet off the ground, rotor noise dropping in tone as it passed. "Those big rocks soak up lots of heat during the day. They're still radiating it; masks the signature of the jeep, if they're using thermal."

He watched the helicopter as it flew northwest. "That's a Toufan. Attack helicopter: Iran began building them, couple years ago. Vahidi, the defense minister, worries about tanks coming out of Iraq . . . or across Iraq."

Blake cocked his head, listening.

"More coming," he said. "Not the same type. Different rotor noise."

This time it was a group of five helicopters flying in a loose V formation. They were flying nearly a thousand feet higher than the Toufan, but following the same course.

"Hueys?" Blake asked.

Pardivari rocked his hand. "Bell 214s. Like a Huey, only bigger. Holdovers from back before the revolution. What they use when they have to move troops in a hurry. Five of them can carry seventy people plus crew . . ."

He looked to the south. "More coming."

Another flight of five helicopters swept over.

"You said seventy troops apiece?" Blake asked.

"That, plus two flight crew per chopper."

Blake did that math. "Wow. That's . . ."

"You got it," Pardivari told him. "A full company of air cavalry."

"Is it common for them to move troops like this?"

Pardivari stood up, scanning the southern horizon with the night-vision goggles.

"Not common at all. Like I said, the Bells date back to the time of the shah. Iran has a good refit program—so good they can pretty much build a 214 from scratch if they need to. Your oil dollars at work, don't you know. But ten of them is probably about a third of what they have operational right now. So this? This is pretty major."

They began walking back to the SUV.

"You know what bothers me the most though . . ." Pardivari said as they got to the Pushpak.

"What's that?"

Pardivari pointed northwest.

"Them boys are all headed in the same direction as us."

Chapter Fifteen

This time Blake stayed awake as they drove. The desert night was cold, but they kept the windows open on the Pushpak, listening for approaching aircraft.

No more came. And this time, as the eastern sky grayed, they kept driving. The stars were winking out when they dropped off the desert onto a two-track path, and by the time the sun was peeking over the horizon behind them, Blake could see it reflecting back from the windows of a car driving on a road about three miles ahead of them.

He was just about to comment on it when he heard the *chirrup* of a cell phone.

It was Pardivari's. He fished it off the dash, looked at the caller ID, and put it back on the dash, still ringing.

"Not planning on answering that?"

Pardivari shook his head. "It's Zari. Won't expect me to answer. Iranian intelligence has been known to selectively monitor cellular traffic, particularly cell-phone calls made away from the bigger cities. That call's a signal. Just to let me know to get ready with the other phone."

He pulled to the side of the two-track dirt road and got another phone, about the size of a household cordless phone, out of the glove box. The two men stepped outside the SUV and Pardivari pulled up the phone's antenna; it was stout, and nearly as long again as the phone.

"Satellite phone . . ." Blake observed. "Let me guess; Thuraya?"

"Yep." Pardivari nodded. "Government doesn't monitor these. They use a pretty good commercial encryption algorithm: too sophisticated for Tehran to decode, and even if they could, they'd only get half the conversation. You have to be out in the open to get a clear shot at a satellite, but everybody in the oil business uses them, so they don't attract much notice."

"Smart." Blake had seen the Thuraya phones before in Iraq and Afghanistan. They didn't have nearly the global coverage of the Iridium phone in his rucksack, but they worked all over the Middle East, as well as Europe, most of Africa, Russia, and even India. And because rural Iran lacked cellular coverage—and that included most of the oil fields—Pardivari was right; the Thuraya phones were used by businesspeople and even oil-field roughnecks all over the Middle East.

The satellite phone rang, a low polyphonic chirp, and Pardivari answered it in Farsi. It was a language Blake knew only minimally and he stepped aside and watched the distant highway, letting the missionary talk.

A minute later, Pardivari was next to him, powering down the satellite phone.

"Change of plan," he told Blake. "Troops in the village: platoon strength."

"They onto us?"

Pardivari shook his head. "Doubtful. Zari says they aren't questioning anyone, aren't going house to house. Nothing like that. They've just stationed themselves at the crossroads and they're checking the papers on anyone who drives through."

He slid the antenna back into the phone. "They do this every once in a while. There are a couple of missile launch sites not far from the village. Sometimes it means they're moving missiles from one launch site to another. And sometimes it's a readiness drill."

The two men got back into the SUV.

"Readiness drill?" Blake asked.

"For a missile strike," Pardivari explained. "Troops secure all ground ingress to the launch sites and other key locations. To prevent people like us from messing with them."

He started the Pushpak.

"So we divert," Pardivari said, "to the Warshowskys."

"Warshowsky? What sort of Iranian name is that?"

Pardivari grinned. "It ain't."

Chapter Sixteen

Vladimir Warshowsky was a Russian Jew, fled to Iran back in 1943," Pardivari said as he drove. "Guess he figured it was best to get his tail out of Dodge while Stalin still had his hands full with Hitler. Old Vlad was the original multitasker: sold diamonds most say he smuggled out of Russia, used money he got from that to get started in import/export, mostly oil field equipment under the shah. Later on, he set up pretty much the lion's share of the telecommunications infrastructure for the country. Made some major bucks, put together a villa here, away from the cities, and then he died back in the seventies. Now his son, Boris, has the place and runs what's left of their business."

Blake steadied himself against the door as Pardivari turned the Pushpak off the paved highway and down a berm onto a dirt road. "A rich Jew and Ahmadinejad let him stick around?"

Pardivari glanced his way. "That's a long, roundabout story. Old Vlad had a brother who drank the Kool-Aid when Stalin was in power: thought of Vlad as a common criminal because he was running diamonds out of the Soviet Union. Vlad's son, Boris, had a kid—two kids, actually, but the one I'm talking about is the boy, Anatoly. Anatoly was an undergrad at the American University in Paris when his great-uncle paid him a visit, convinced him to come do his graduate studies in Leningrad. Boris about disinherited the kid; old Vlad risked life and limb to get the family out of Russia and here Vlad's grandson was going back there willingly. But the Russian side of the family took Anatoly in. He got a doctorate in nuclear physics and a master's degree in mechanical engineering, and when he came back to Iran, it was 'hail the conquering hero' as far as the administration here was concerned. In less than five years, he's become a major muckity-muck in both the nuclear energy and nuclear munitions programs."

Blake cocked his head. "He's Jewish and he's helping to arm a country that wants to annihilate Israel?"

"Anatoly Warshowsky comes from a Jewish family." Pardivari waved his right hand like he was wiping a table. "But as for him being Jewish? Personally, I think being raised by Jews in a Muslim country turned out to be a zero-sum game for Anatoly. And from what I can tell, the great-uncle was pretty much agnostic. Anatoly had a big falling-out with his father over it. Not that Boris was all that religious to begin with, but Anatoly wanted nothing to do with it. Even heard he changed to a Muslim name."

Blake straightened up a little. "And we're going to his house?"

"Not quite." Pardivari laughed. "We're going to his father's place. I don't believe old Boris has said ten words to Anatoly since the kid got back to Iran. I know for sure the boy's never set foot in the villa since he got back home. He's a grown man now, nearly thirty. Zari says she's seen him at Nassiri's summer house and he didn't even act like he recognized her. And of course, she couldn't approach him; it's not that kind of culture. Still, it's something because Zari used to go to the Warshowskys to study with their daughter and she and wonder-boy were always running into one another. Odd that he'd make strange with her."

Blake almost laughed: "make strange" was another expression from back home.

The missionary shrugged. "Silver lining is, especially since Anatoly got back, Ahmadinejad has taken a hands-off approach with the Warshowsky family. Of course, they don't have the import-export business anymore, but then again they don't need it, you know? The family's invested in everything you can think of . . . and probably quite a few things you can't. So the kid's in cahoots with Dr. Strangelove, Boris and his family have their own Fort Apache out in the sticks, Boris doesn't talk to his kid, the kid acts like they aren't even kin, the government leaves Boris and his people alone, and that's pretty much the way it goes."

THEY DROVE FOR NEARLY an hour, then Pardivari crested a small hill. Far off to their right, Blake saw a small collection of buildings, all the same light-beige color, which seemed nearly white in the blazing morning sun. All were

built in a style that seemed more appropriate to a Tuscan vineyard and surrounded by a wall the same color as the buildings. A crushed-gravel road,
bordered by tall poplars, led to the broad gates.

Pardivari turned onto the road.

"The Warshowsky's house is in this village?" Blake asked.

Pardivari laughed, a deep, booming laugh.

"That 'village,'" he replied, "*is* the Warshowsky's house."

As they neared the gate, a man stepped out into the road, his hand out in
the universal "stop" signal. The Pushpak came to a halt, and the man, stoop-
ing to peer into the open driver's side window, went into a broken-toothed
grin and shook Pardivari's hand. Blake heard the Farsi word for "welcome,"
and then they were moving again.

"One of the members of my church," Pardivari explained as they passed
through a courtyard and then into a long, barn-like structure.

"He didn't recognize the vehicle?"

"I never drive the same car for long," Pardivari said, slowing as a man
crossed in front of them with a wheelbarrow. "Another of our group, in another
house church, goes to Tehran and buys old cars, old trucks, brings them back
here, rebuilds the engines, transmissions, whatever they need, and then sells
them for a profit in Ilam. If one's a four-wheel-drive, he loans it to me for a
while and I drive it until he gets the next one done. It's a good plan. As I am
not supposed to be alive, no one ever sees the same vehicle long enough to
know it. My friend gets a test driver—like on this one, when we swap vehicles,
I'll be telling him about how it stalls when it's cold."

The building was part horse stalls, part garage, and part storehouse, and
Pardivari passed out of the back of it and parked at the rear of the main house.
A covered stairwell led down to a cellar and the two men took their rucksacks
and headed down it. They emerged into a basement room that was bare except
for a table and a couple of cots with fresh sheets on them.

A woman, stout and in her forties, emerged from a hall and kissed Pardivari
on both cheeks. There was a brief conversation in Farsi and then she turned to
Blake.

"You are Canadian, then?" Her English had the thick remnants of a Russian
accent.

"Yes, ma'am."

"I am Olga and you are welcome in this house. I apologize for my husband; he travels to Switzerland now, where we use bank."

She glanced from Blake to Pardivari and then back again. "When Hormoz brings people here, they usually do not wish to be seen, so please, stay in cellar. I, myself, will bring you food, and there is bath just across your hall. Leave your clothes in there and I will have someone wash."

"Thank you, ma'am, my name is . . ."

"Shhhh." She touched his lips with her finger. "I have no doubt that the name you are about to tell is false—the work done with the church, it must be secret, yes? But even that I do not need to know. Please, make yourself at home."

She looked around the room. It was bare except for the cots, the table, two chairs, and the men's rucksacks. "No Bibles this trip?"

Hormoz shook his head. "Not this trip."

"Well then." Olga swiped her hands against each other, as if she just finished a piece of work. "Whatever it is that you do this time, be careful, yes?"

"Thank you, ma'am," Blake told her. "We will."

AT PARDIVARI'S INSISTENCE, BLAKE got cleaned up first. The restroom was simple; an anteroom with a table, where he left his clothes, and beyond that, a deep-basin sink and a squat-toilet in a small adjoining room. But it was spotless, the towels were thick Turkish cotton, and the water was hot. He washed, using a big white brick of homemade soap, changed into a clean set of clothes, and when he came out of the inner room, his old clothes were gone from the table.

"Come on," Pardivari said, motioning to a steaming bowl and a huge loaf of dark bread. "Dig in. Olga just brought it down."

The bowl was lamb stew, thick and spicy, full of turnips and onions, the bread was a thick rye, and it was as good a breakfast as Blake ever ate. He was just finishing when Pardivari came back out of the washroom.

"I need to go outside, use the Thuraya, check in with Zari," the missionary said. "Go ahead and relax. I'll be right back."

Blake sat down on one of the bunks and leaned against the wall. The room was plain and windowless, and if it was not for the good meal he just had, and the thickness of the towel he'd just used, it could easily have passed for a jail cell.

He closed his eyes and did the math. There was a seven-and-a-half hour time difference between Iran and the East Coast. It would be the middle of the night in Washington; Alia would still be fast asleep.

Blake imagined her leaving the office the evening before. He wondered where she'd had dinner. There was a Japanese restaurant she liked to get take-out from. Or she might have stopped for sashimi on the way home from Langley. That was her favorite dine-alone option. Blake didn't eat sashimi—it looked too much like bait.

Then again, she could be taking another trip into *Mastering the Art of French Cooking.* She'd been looking at stock pots the weekend before he'd left for mission prep in Yuma. He thought of her with a smudge of flour on her nose, and the image made him yearn to be back with her.

He pushed the thought out of his mind. He'd known too many men in Iraq, in Afghanistan, who'd let their heads live back home, rather than where they were. And that was how a man got hurt. Sometimes, that was how a man got killed.

Blake knew the best way to make certain he got back home to Alia was to stop thinking about her until he was back home with her. It was counter-intuitive, but it was true. So he thought about the mission: about getting Farrokh Nassiri out of Iran alive and well.

The door opened and Pardivari came back in.

"We're on for tonight," he said. "The ministry only keeps two guards at Nassiri's house. Same two guards for the last four months: Artesh—regular Iranian infantry. And they stay outside at night, keeping an eye on the road in front. Nassiri was barely walking when they first got there—he twisted an ankle—and he's kept up the act ever since. I mean, he does have arthritis; he's had it for several years, but he's ambulatory. The guards don't know that—the old man's got them convinced he's a semi-invalid. He and Zari are going to leave out the back at midnight tonight. They have a couple hundred meters of open ground to cover, all of it out of sight of where the guards sit, and then they follow a wadi for about four klicks. It'll be rough on the old man, but Zari says he can do it. We'll be waiting for them with the Pushpak and a truck I'll borrow and off we'll go. Nassiri has a study right off his bedroom;

the guards are used to not seeing him until midday, when the whole household usually has a meal together. Any luck, we'll be halfway to the sea before they know anything's wrong. We've got a lot of Pasdaran around the village right now, but we can be out of range of them in four or five hours. If we want to make good time, we'll need to keep traveling when daylight comes, but it's worth the risk."

"Sounds like a plan," Blake agreed. "So long as we hit the sea at night, I can have people waiting for us."

"One of my church members—the mechanic—is going to stage the other truck and wait for us. Both have license plates taken off wrecks in Tehran; neither one can be traced back to him."

Blake thought the plan over. It was simple, it involved a minimum number of people, and had a minimum number of places it could go wrong.

He reached into his rucksack and brought out a cling-wrapped bundle of twenty 500-euro notes. "Get this to your mechanic friend, will you? There's a pretty good chance he's not going to see his trucks again."

Pardivari hefted the bundle. "Ten thousand euros? You could probably get ten of his trucks for that."

"He's taking a risk for us." Blake looked at his watch. "Midnight's twelve hours from now. Let's get a full eight hours' worth."

"Sounds right by me."

And without another word, both men stretched out on their cots and fell asleep: the sleep of men who were accustomed to resting under pressure.

WHEN BLAKE WOKE, HE knew in an instant he hadn't been asleep a full eight hours. A glance at his watch confirmed it was only half that.

He glanced at the other cot; Pardivari was gone. And there was no light showing under the washroom door.

Slipping his pistol out from under his pillow, he slid the slide back a fraction of an inch, caught a reassuring glimpse of brass in the chamber, and padded barefooted to the door leading to the stairs.

The stairwell was empty. Blake made his way up, placing his feet only on the outside of the steps, got to the door, and pushed it ajar very slowly.

Pardivari was out there, talking with someone. And despite Blake's care in opening the door, the missionary turned.

"You're up," he said. "Good. Step out; we're clear."

Blake pushed the door open further. "What's up?"

"We have a problem." The voice was feminine, Iranian-accented English, and almost melodic.

Blake stepped out and turned toward the voice.

Blake Kershaw was a man trained to be unfazed by the unexpected. But the young woman standing there pushed all that by the board. She was about one head shorter than he was, the modest dress she wore could do little to hide the fact she was athletically slender, and a fall of dark brown hair framed a face with delicate features and brown eyes, full and expressive, and right now were showing concern.

"The Pasdaran came to the house three hours ago and changed our guard," she said. "They took away the two army men who were there and left a group of six: five enlisted men and a captain. I don't know any of these people."

"And tonight's the new moon," Pardivari added.

Blake nodded. That was one of the key elements in choosing the date for the mission; it was the last completely moonless night before Nassiri was scheduled to leave his country retreat and go back to Tehran.

"We cannot go ahead with the plan," the young woman said.

Even at a second glance, she was amazing to look at. Blake had to clear his throat.

"I take it you're Zari Nourazar," he said.

She nodded. Her hair rose and fell in one dark brown cascade.

"And your father . . ." Blake hesitated as he said that word. "He is dying of cancer?"

Zari blinked. "He is."

"When the Pasdaran arrived, did you give them tea?"

Zari cocked her head. "Farrokh still pretends to be Muslim. And even if he did not, it is the culture . . . Yes. Of course I gave them tea. Chai tea."

"And did they all drink it?"

"They did."

Blake looked down at the ground for a moment. It was not his habit when he was thinking, but he didn't trust himself to look this young woman in the face and think clearly.

"If your father's cancer is that far advanced, he must be experiencing considerable pain."

"Almost always." He could hear the hurt in her voice.

"And his medication is more frequent?"

"Yes."

Blake thought. He looked up at Pardivari. "But he's been active enough to communicate on the computer, so I take it he's not on an IV."

He looked at Zari. "His pain medicine: is he taking it orally?"

"Yes." She nodded again, her brow furrowed. "We live away from the city and I cannot be with him except for a few days a week. So he did not want to use needles. He uses capsules."

"And the medicine within the capsules; is it water-soluble?"

"It is." She looked puzzled as she said it. Then her eyes brightened and she smiled. "Ah! I see . . . Yes—it is!"

Chapter Seventeen

Farrokh Nassiri walked the length of his summer house's old tile-floored kitchen, turned, and walked it back again. He leaned on his wooden cane and then walked nearer to the young woman at the sink. Low sunlight slanted in through the western window, painting both them and the room the color of amber. The man looked older than his seventy years: his posture stooped, as if by a great weight. His lips moved wordlessly, his brushy eyebrows knitted close together with concern.

"If they discover what you are doing here . . ." he began in Farsi. He stamped his cane as he paused. "I . . . cannot bear to think what the Pasdaran would do to you."

Zari Nourazar turned a knob on the propane stove, struck a match, and lit it. Then, without looking at Nassiri, she filled a teakettle with cold water and set it on the burner. Lifting off the top of the pot, she lowered in a cheesecloth bundle of anise, orange peel, ginger root, cinnamon bark, and other spices.

"My daughter," Nassiri said. It was a form of address he had used more and more with Zari over the last month, and he touched her shoulder as he said it. "I cannot allow you to do this thing."

Zari turned the knob on the stove, bringing the burner to its highest setting. She straightened up, looked Nassiri in the eyes, and held the gaze until he blinked and looked away.

Zari bent down slightly to look him in the face again. "Do you truly think of me as your daughter?"

The scientist nodded mutely.

"Farrokh," Zari said softly, "throughout history, men have stood by and let madmen do as they would, because they were afraid that, if they acted, their families might suffer. And in the end, almost invariably, those men lost everything, including their families. You must not make that same mistake. You cannot protect me by letting this thing go forward. You must act."

The teakettle rattled softly as the water within it warmed.

"Think," Zari urged him. In Farsi, the word was very nearly a hiss. "If you do nothing, no one will know which launch sites are the real targets. Then all the sites become targets: this entire province and then some. When Israel strikes—and sooner or later, unless we act, they will have to strike—then you will die. I will die. My church will die. Everyone I care for will be wiped from the face of the earth. Is this the sort of favor you believe I want from you? And even if the Israelis don't strike first and this madman we call our president fires his missiles first, the Israelis will retaliate. The entire country will still be destroyed. We must all take risks to save Israel and our own people. It is God's will, Farrokh. So let us do as God has directed."

Nassiri blinked.

"Perhaps I am not thinking of you," he said. "My wife is gone now eight years. You are all I have left, my daughter. Perhaps that is what I am afraid of. Perhaps I fear being alone."

She looked at him. One side of her mouth lifted slightly in a half smile.

"Other men, perhaps," she said. "But you? You are the bravest man I know, grandfather."

He straightened, blinking. It was the first time the young woman had used such an endearment with him.

"You would never be afraid for yourself," Zari told him. "And you need not be afraid for me."

A puff of steam rose from the teakettle's spout. Zari reduced it to a simmer and added black tea to the pot.

Nassiri said nothing as the young woman set out six tea glasses, putting milk, honey, and just a touch of vanilla into each one.

She took a pill bottle out of her apron pocket, counted out a dozen white tablets, and began crushing them into powder with a mortar and pestle.

"Phenobarbital," she said to the scientist. "These are 500-milligram doses. The usual dose is 200 milligrams or so, but my father's pain is too severe for that. I figure I will give them 1000 milligrams each."

Nassiri picked up the bottle and rattled it. There were still tablets inside. "Maybe you should give them more."

Zari shook her head. "I read the physician's reference on this. Too much can cause coma, pulmonary edema, acute renal failure. I mean to render them unconscious, not to murder them."

She measured the powder out into the glasses. Then she put a measured spoonful of sugar into each tea glass.

"The drug is bitter," she explained to the scientist. "The sweetness will cover the taste."

Using a potholder, she took the top from the teapot and lifted the cheese-cloth, setting it in the sink. Then she strained the tea into the six glasses. With the milk and the honey, the chai was the color of *café au lait*.

Her dark blue *hijab*—the traditional woman's head covering of Muslim society—was on a chair-back at the kitchen table and she picked it up and put it on, careful not to let a single strand of hair show. She looked in the mirror as she did this and saw that Nassiri had turned away while she covered her head, a remnant of modesty from the years he spent in Islam.

When she finished, the face in the mirror seemed like a doll's face to her. Living in a Iran, she wore the hijab every time she ventured outdoors since her adolescence, and yet she still was not used to it. To her, it was like an animal's collar around her neck.

Zari arranged the tea glasses on an engraved stainless-steel salver, setting them with the handles facing out. She looked at Nassiri pointedly.

"It is your home," she said. "I cannot speak to them. It is *haram*."

The compressor on the refrigerator thrummed to life, as if growling in response to the Arabic word for "forbidden."

"Farrokh," Zari whispered. "You must do your part."

The scientist nodded his head—the gesture was almost a bow—and left the kitchen.

THERE WAS A STONE patio off the dining room of the country house and five of the six soldiers were gathered there at the outdoor table. Two of the men had field-stripped and cleaned their sidearms and were putting them back together. The other two were in conversation with their captain, who looked up as Nassiri stepped out into the gathering dusk.

"You have eaten?" Nassiri asked in Farsi.

"Thank you," the officer replied. "We have. We have brought rations enough for a week, and when the rest of the company arrives, they will run meals out to us three times a day."

"It seems like so much trouble. The other two men simply ate in my kitchen. And I was accustomed to them. They were no bother."

The officer looked up. Unlike his men, whose faces were covered with what was nearly a five o'clock shadow, his beard was full but neatly trimmed and his eyes, full and brown, should have seemed expressive but looked suspicious instead, as if he was examining anyone he spoke with, looking for the lie. Now, he gazed with that expression at Nassiri.

"The other men were regular infantry," he said. "Members of the Artesh, the Islamic Republic of Iran Army."

He said it as if it left a bad taste in his mouth.

"My men," he said, "are specialists—Army of the Guardians of the Islamic Revolution."

He said it that way, the formal name, rather than *Pasdaran*—"the Guard."

"We are trained in security." The captain spoke as if he was educating an underling. "And we will billet, sir, on your grounds, and not in your home. I think it best my men not grow too . . . too familiar with your household."

Nassiri nodded. "As you wish."

"Another thing," the officer added. "When you go out from now on, please tell me first. I will detail two men to go along with you."

"Even to the village?" Nassiri laughed. "I am in no danger there."

"You are an asset of the republic, sir. You have knowledge that must be protected. If this intrudes on your privacy, I am sorry for the inconvenience." His voice didn't sound as if he was sorry at all. "But I am afraid that it must be so."

Nassiri nodded. "As you think best. But now, if I cannot give you a meal, at least let me give you tea."

He opened the door behind him. "Zari, bring it."

"Colonel, that will not be . . . ." the officer began. Then he saw Zari's face and fell silent for a moment.

"Tea . . ." He looked directly at Zari as he said it, met her eyes with his. "Tea would be very pleasant."

Zari looked at Nassiri. The officer was practically leering. And she was not a member of his household. In a deeply Muslim culture, it was a discourtesy bordering on insult. Nassiri nodded and she began to give the men their tea.

"Hospitality is not the same as alms-giving, as *zakat*," Nassiri said, as if he had not seen the slight. "It is not one of the five pillars. But still, it is the custom. It is the manner of my house."

"And a fine custom," the officer said. He sipped his tea. "It is quite sweet."

"I take it sweet in the morning and at night," Nassiri said. "I think it makes a good beginning and a fine end to the day. And it is Zari's specialty."

Picking up on the cue, Zari smiled back at the scientist.

"Well then," the captain said, lifting his tea glass. "It is a custom we must adopt. Drink up, men."

The patio was surrounded by a gated wall and the gate opened, revealing a man a full head taller than the rest, with shoulders so broad they very nearly spanned the opening.

"Sergeant," the captain said, "you are just in time. Join us for tea."

"Thank you, sir, no. I am here to detail two men for the first guard, sir."

"There will be time for that in a moment." The captain's tone made it clear he was not accustomed to giving instructions twice. "Our host is offering us his hospitality. Join us and drink your tea."

"Sir." The big man accepted a glass. In his hands, it looked very nearly like a thimble, and he drained the warm glass in three sips.

"Sit, sergeant," the captain said. "You will have your detail after we have finished here."

He took another drink of his tea and looked over at Zari again, letting his gaze linger for nearly a minute. Then he turned to Nassiri. "You are right about the sweet chai," the captain told him. "It is quite calming."

BLAKE AND PARDIVARI SET their rucksacks in the back of the Pushpak. As they did, there was a distant rumbling and lights came on in the building behind them.

Olga Warshowsky came out with a small bundle wrapped in muslin.

"Bread for your journey," she said. She looked back at the house. "Finally we have lights again. We had to bring man out from the village to mend generator. I am sorry you had to get ready in dark."

"You have been very kind to us," Blake told her. "And we appreciate it. Thank you for opening your home to us."

The woman's face softened. "Zari and my Nadia would meet here to study when they were girls. Her father, Mr. Nourazar, would arrange for some of the tutors. My Boris arranged for others. And sometimes Anatoly would study with them as well . . ."

Her voice trailed off for a moment. She cleared her throat.

"After Khomeni," she continued. "There was less and less education for girls here. Islam frowns on it, and besides, in the years after shah, many girls had to work, and others married young—some as young as twelve. And for a girl in the teenage to study with a boy, as they did in our home? Under *sharia*, it would be considered . . . what is word? Sacrilege. It would be sacrilege. But we wanted our children to have opportunity, and they did. Zari learned English and French. Not English like mine, not English like bad movie, but real English. It was even our hope we would find way to send her to Europe, to study with Nadia. The two were Christian and Jew, yet they were like sisters. How I wish they could have . . . have grown up together."

"What happened?"

Olga's eyes welled with tears. "It was year my Nadia turned nineteen. She was in Tehran. She told us she was going there to get student visa for the following year, but now we know she was going to take part in a protest against . . . how do you say it? The violence: domestic violence against women—great problem in this country. The protest attracted attention. Too much attention. A crowd gathered, angry men. Rocks were thrown. My Nadia was struck. She was in coma for a week. Then she died. She never woke up, never regained the consciousness."

The moment that followed was so silent Blake could hear a moth buzzing against the light near the door.

"I'm sorry," he said.

"As am I." Olga put a hand on his shoulder. She almost whispered what came next, "I should have been there. I should have been there with her."

She took a breath. "Enjoy the bread. And whatever it is you do this evening, if it helps someone resist the crazy man who runs this government, this country, then my hopes and my prayers go with you, young man. Take with you the blessing of this house."

AT THE FRONT OF the house, in the courtyard outside the barn, a diesel mechanic was stowing his tools into the back of a twenty-year-old Mercedes van. It was late; he'd missed prayer and—far worse in his mind—he had also missed his dinner. The woman in the villa offered him dinner, but that was unthinkable. He would never accept a meal from a Jew.

Of course, he did not say that. These people paid their bills promptly, and the generator was not the only diesel engine on their property. They had two trucks, and the man, whom the mechanic did not see on this trip, owned a new Mercedes that, in truth, was too sophisticated for the mechanic's self-taught skills. But he knew enough to do the preventive maintenance on it, and while the Jews drove their vehicles into town for tire rotations and tune-ups, the bill for repairing the generator more than justified the half-hour drive out to the villa to work on it.

He thought of his older brother, a sergeant in the army. That the mechanic should have enlisted as well was a constant source of argument between them. The brother said that if he enlisted, the mechanic would no longer have to worry about where his next paycheck was coming from; he would have a steady job and perhaps some man would consider him dependable enough to give him a daughter in marriage. The mechanic always countered that at least he chose his own hours, and besides, the older brother had been hoping for a promotion to an officer's rank for two years and it had not happened yet.

And paydays like today's made the mechanic think his was the right decision.

The mechanic slid his long toolbox into the back of the van. It caught on something before it was all the way in and he could not see what; the light in the back of the van burned out the week before, and he hadn't bothered to replace it.

Cursing under his breath, he climbed into the back of the van, felt around, and found the trouble-lamp cord the toolbox was catching on. He pulled it loose, yanked the box the rest of the way in, pinched his thumb, and jerked upright, muttering in pain.

Just then, a little SUV came growling out of the barn. Had the mechanic not mended the generator, it would have passed by in darkness, but because he made the trip out and did his job, the light in the courtyard was burning and the driver's face was illuminated briefly as he drove by.

In the shadows within the unlighted van, the mechanic forgot all about his thumb and sat, stunned.

Immediately he began to doubt what he saw. It was only a moment, the light was tricky, and besides, everyone knew the man he thought he just saw was dead.

Wasn't he?

He thought about it as he closed the doors on the back of the van, walked up to the driver's door, got in, and started the old van's engine. The valves tapped for a few seconds until the oil got flowing to them; what was that saying about the shoemaker's children having no shoes? Then the engine quieted down and he put the van in gear and drove out of the courtyard and past the night-shadowed poplars.

Before he turned out of the drive and onto the road, he stopped, closed his eyes, and pictured again the face he glimpsed behind the wheel of the little SUV. It sure looked familiar. It looked exactly like someone he'd seen years before. But everyone knew the man he was thinking about was dead: killed in that explosion two years before.

The diesel mechanic turned on the radio and music, scratchy and streaked with static, came out of the one working speaker. It was that singer Arash and the mechanic listened for a moment and then turned it off. Arash lived in Sweden, and Ebi, before him, lived in Canada and then Spain. What was it with all these Iranian pop singers? They all talked about how they loved the Persian culture and then they all lived elsewhere. And in cold climates, no less. How did that make sense? It didn't seem very patriotic to the mechanic.

Then again, the mechanic was never all that patriotic. He'd avoided going into the army by getting village elders to claim his skills as a mechanic were needed at home. But he thought of himself as someone who would fight if it came to that. If the Israelis came, if the Americans came, certainly he would fight them.

He thought about that as he drove. And he debated about the face he saw. Certainly, he could have been mistaken; it was not as if he saw the fellow every day, not as if he was familiar with him. He had only known him in passing.

But the driver of that SUV sure looked like the man he was thinking of.

Digging into his pocket, he pulled out his cell phone, thumbed in a speed-dial number, and listened as it rang once, twice, three times.

After four rings, it went to voice mail. That was fine; if the mechanic was wrong, it would be easier if he just passed the information along to a machine, rather than having a conversation with his brother.

He listened to the recorded greeting, then the beep, and he laughed and said, "What? Are you out chasing women? This is your brother, and listen, this may be nothing, but then again it might be what finally gets you that third-lieutenant star you've been looking for. Do you remember that American missionary the Pasdaran were chasing a couple of years ago? The one the newspapers said was blown up in that abandoned house? Well, maybe it is because my eyes are tired, or perhaps it is my hunger, because I worked past dinner tonight, but I swear I just saw him leaving that rich Jew's house. It was not twenty minutes ago, as I was finishing my work there. He was driving a little SUV, not a Toyota. One of those Indian SUVs. The Hindustan ones. And I swear it was that missionary . . . what was his name? Pardivari: that's it . . . Pardivari."

THE CELL PHONE IN Hormoz Pardivari's pocket rang and he answered it, listened for a moment, said, "Good" in Farsi, and hung up.

"That was Zari," he told Blake. "Our friends are taking their nap. We'll make one quick stop, pick up the other truck, and then go."

Blake nodded. They were coming into the outskirts of the village and he was glad for the beard he started when he was first told about this mission. In the darkness, the Pushpak looked like any other old vehicle in the province, and its occupants—two bearded men—looked like any other men who might be out in the early evening.

Pardivari took an alley and stopped behind a squat, square building. Next to it was a twelve-year-old Toyota Land Cruiser, the model that looked vaguely like an older Jeep Wagoneer.

"I take it," Pardivari said, "a good old boy like you can drive a stick?"

Blake smiled. "Since before I can remember."

"The keys will be in it, then. Follow me, and I'll take us up to the old man's house."

Blake hopped out, got into the Toyota, and noted that no light came on when he got in. He reached up and found the open ceiling lamp, its bulb pulled.

Appreciating that small touch of stealth, he pushed in the clutch, turned the key to the first notch, waited until the glow-plug light winked off, and then turned the key the rest of the way. The engine rumbled to life immediately, pulsing testimony to the mechanical skill of Pardivari's church member. He pulled the lights on and followed the little Pushpak down the stone-strewn alley and out onto the dirt road.

Blake shifted from first to second and then from second to third, and stayed there, the condition of the road never allowing them to go fast enough to shift into fourth.

They turned off that road onto one that was graded better, but twisted and turned often to get to the top of a small plateau. When they reached the edge, he saw the lights of a house below and the road began to descend, once again twisting down a series of switchbacks. Three minutes later, they were pulling up to the house. It was much smaller than the Warshowsky's villa, but larger than a typical Iranian home, particularly out here in the provinces. Date palms were growing in front, and while folded white muslin was staged at the foot of each tree, none had been covered against the cool of the evening. A woman in a headscarf was waiting among them with a flashlight in her hand. The headlamps picked her out; it was Zari.

"Farrokh is inside," she said, coming closer to the trucks. "Gathering his things."

"We can't take much," Blake said as he stepped out. He had his jacket off, the Springfield pistol ready in his hand, a penlight clipped into his shirt pocket, and the Iridium phone in his pocket. "We have to travel light."

"He knows this."

Blake turned to Pardivari. "Stay here with the vehicles and watch the road. I'll fetch Nassiri and then we'll get on the move."

"I'll come with you," Zari said. "To show you the way."

They followed a path to the back of the house and passed through a door-size gate into a patio. There was a fountain playing there; the lights were on, and it looked nearly festive except for the men in camouflage fatigues. All were slumped, gape-mouthed. Blake stopped next to one with four stars on his shoulder.

"Pasdaran captain," he said. He looked at Zari. "You're right; they were definitely tightening the screws."

She nodded and led him into the house. He smelled vanilla, spice, and the scent of wood polish. The place was furnished well, although not ostentatiously; there wasn't even a television in the living room.

They found Nassiri in the study, watching a line grow across a small gray box on his computer monitor. The box changed to a confirmation message, then he pulled a card reader out of a USB port on the side of the computer, popped the SD card out of it, put it into the flap in the back of a small Moleskine notebook, and buttoned the notebook into his right-hand shirt pocket. The man looked gaunt and even older than his picture.

"Are you ready?" Blake asked him in English.

Nassiri nodded. "May I also bring this?"

He held up a black book. Even with his limited Farsi, Blake could see it was a Bible.

"Certainly, Colonel."

The older man smiled. "My friends are welcome to call me Farrokh."

"Thank you, Farrokh. We'd better go."

Blake led the way out onto the patio, then through the gate and onto the path that led to the vehicles. They were putting Nassiri into the Pushpak when Zari bent close to him.

"Grandfather? Did you bring your medicine?"

The scientist smiled, patted his pocket, and then rolled his eyes.

"We can get him medicine when we get down to the ship," Blake told her.

"He is on blood thinners. For his heart. He needs them every day." She looked at the house. "It will only take me a minute to fetch them. We can go back, though the kitchen."

Blake nodded once. "I'll go with you."

The Iranians were still slumped at their seats in the patio, the splashing of the fountain the only sound. Blake followed Zari into the kitchen, where she picked up a pillbox with the days of the week marked on it in Arabic, put it in a canvas bag, and then opened a cabinet and added a couple of pill bottles to it. She got a water bottle out of the refrigerator and put it in the bag as well.

"All right." She put the bag on her shoulder. "We can go."

They left the kitchen, went down the hall, and out onto the patio. The six Iranians were sprawled, still in exactly the same positions they'd been in earlier.

Blake followed Zari, stepping around the unconscious Pasdarans' legs. They were just passing the fountain when he glimpsed it: movement in the far edge of his peripheral vision.

He turned and saw the largest of the Iranians, the big master sergeant, bringing up a KL, the banana-clipped Iranian-made copy of the Russian AKM. "Down!"

He shouted it in English and shoved Zari between the shoulder-blades, toppling her forward. At the same time, he hit the deck himself, only it wasn't the deck; he hadn't made the turn yet, so he went over the knee-high wall and into the fountain, falling face-first into three feet of water. In a flurry of bubbles, it enveloped him.

Even underwater, he could hear the metallic clatter of the KL firing on full automatic. He held onto the piping on the bottom of the fountain and listened: loud percussive noises, like hammerheads striking bricks, sounded from all around him. It was the 7.62-millimeter rounds striking the walls and central armature of the fountain.

He waited until the firing paused and then came out of the water, gun-hand first, grip-safety squeezed flush, pulling the trigger as the Springfield pistol pointed center-mass at the big Iranian. The XD barked three times in rapid succession, and the big sergeant, who had stopped to change magazines, dropped as if to take a knee and then plunged forward, hitting his head on the marble table-edge as he fell.

Water streaming from his hair, his shirt, and his trousers, Blake stepped out of the fountain and put a hand under Zari's arm. She was trembling, obviously shocked by what just happened.

"It's over," he told her as he pulled her to her feet. "Are you hit?"

She began to answer in Farsi, then switched to English. "I . . . don't think so. Do you see . . . ?"

Blake turned her around and looked her over. It felt oddly intimate to be doing that, and he blinked the thought away. "You're good. Let's go."

"I gave him so much," she said as they ran around the side of the house. "How did he wake?"

"He was a big guy," Blake told her as they turned the corner. Then he raised his voice, "Hormoz, it's us. We're clear."

The missionary was halfway from the truck, a big folding knife flicked open in his hand. He stopped and stared at Blake's dripping clothing. "What happened?"

"One of 'em woke up. This place is remote, but not that remote. Those shots are going to draw attention. And I'd hoped we'd have a few hours before the colonel, there, was discovered missing. We're going to have to lay up."

He looked at Zari. "What do you think? Can we go back to the same place?"

Zari was still a bit dazed. She hesitated for an instant and then dug into the canvas bag and pulled out a cell phone. "I will call Olga."

Chapter Eighteen

I can drive," Zari said, getting behind the wheel of the Land Cruiser.

"You know how?"

She glanced sidelong at him. "Yes. I know. Iranian women don't drive. But when we were fourteen, my friend Nadia and I taught ourselves in one of her father's trucks. We used to go out at night, with the lights off, so no one would see us. She and I . . ."

Her voice trailed off.

"I know," Blake told her as she cranked the engine to life. "Olga told me about Nadia."

"Then she must like you." She glanced his way as she said it. "Olga is a very private person. So was Nadia. But Nadia could be outspoken when she saw something wrong; it was something I loved about her. It is something I love about Olga, as well."

Turning on the penlight and holding it in his mouth, Blake took the Iridium phone out of his pocket and opened the battery cover, taking the battery out. Drops of moisture glinted back at him. He extended the antenna, pried off the keyboard, and shook it to get the excess moisture off of it. He pulled out the tail of his shirt to dry it further, but it was useless; the shirt was still soaking wet.

"Here." Zari took off her hijab and handed it to him.

"Thanks." He dried the phone carefully and then looked closely at the display. He saw what he feared; condensation was already clouding it.

He looked at the girl as she drove. The widows were open and her long hair was moving in the wind, her face softly lit by the glow of the instrument panel. She turned, caught him looking, and smiled.

"You look half-drowned."

"I didn't want to fall on top of you."

"I wouldn't break."

"That's not what I was worried about. I was afraid you'd move and spoil my shot."

Her face straightened. "That soldier. Did you . . . ?"

"Kill him?" Blake nodded.

Instantly, her face clouded. "It is my fault. I should have known to give him more of the drug. He was larger than the rest."

Blake shook his head. "To give him more, you would have had to give them all more. You had no way of knowing who would drink what. And what was sufficient to keep a man of his size down might have been enough to stop the hearts of all the others."

She looked uncertain.

"Zari," Blake said, "if I hadn't killed him, he would have killed us. That, or captured us. And that man up there . . ." he nodded toward the taillights they were following—". . . if we don't get him out of the country and debrief him, a whole bunch of people are going to die. Thousands. Maybe more. People not in uniform. It was well worth the price."

"I know this." She swallowed. "It is just . . . it is not a price I am . . . accustomed to paying."

"I know." Blake touched her shoulder. "I hope that never changes for you."

They reached the edge of town, drove a short distance out, and then the taillights ahead winked out. Zari leaned forward and turned her lights off as well. Then she swung the wheel and the Land Cruiser bounced through a ditch and onto barren ground.

"Short cut?" Blake asked.

"Something like that." She was smiling again. "I showed this to Hormoz last year. It is the way Nadia and I used to drive when we took the Warshowsky's truck to town at night, when we were girls. It is open country: some rocks, and one shallow wadi, but we know where they are. We follow this and it brings us up behind their villa. They used to keep goats and there is a gate there where they could go out to tend the herd. A 'back way,' is that the way you say it?"

"That's right. And you're sure you know where you're going?" He noticed her shifting up into fourth gear.

"Do not worry. I could do this with my eyes closed."

Blake peered through the windshield at the moonless night. "I'd say that's pretty close to what you're doing now."

THEY DROVE IN DARKNESS for twenty minutes and it was obvious Pardivari knew the country as well as Zari; his brake lights never came on—not once. Then Blake saw the glow of the villa in the distance. As they drew nearer, a white oblong appeared in the back wall—the open gate. And in it was the figure of a person: someone not too tall, not too slim. From a hundred yards out, Blake recognized Olga Warshowsky.

She stood there and watched as they drove up and killed the engines. Zari was the first to the gate, and the two women put their arms around one another like mother and daughter. Then Blake stepped into the light and Olga looked up at him.

"Ma'am," he said, "I am very sorry to impose on you again."

"Do not sorrow. You make welcome here. You are friend of Zari? Then you are always welcome here. All of you."

Pardivari came up, helping Nassiri over the stony ground. They passed wordlessly through the gate and headed for the doorway to the cellar.

"That man," Olga said to Blake. "He is the man who makes the weapons. The rockets. The missiles. Yes?"

"He is," Blake told her. "And he is coming with us, to tell people where they are, so they can never be used against Israel."

Olga's eyes grew wider.

"You are welcome," she said. "Always welcome in this house."

THEY ASSEMBLED IN THE cellar and Olga was waiting to take Blake's wet things as he came out of the bathroom, changed into dry clothes.

"You wish to eat?"

"No, ma'am." Blake looked at the Iridium phone, lying on the table in pieces. "But could I get a long pan, like a bread pan? Filled about halfway up with rice?"

"You wish to eat rice?"

Blake shook his head. "No, ma'am. Not cooked rice. Uncooked. Dry. About halfway up the pan. And a sheet of tinfoil, if you have it."

The woman looked confused, but she nodded her head. "I will bring."

Five minutes later, she was back with a bread pan half-full of rice, and Blake put the disassembled phone in it and then shook it until the damp parts settled into and disappeared under the white grains of rice.

"When I was growing up," Blake explained to the four people watching him, "my mother would put rice into salt shakers during the summer, to keep the salt from sticking. Dry rice acts like a desiccant, absorbing moisture. When you wet electronics like this, it's not the water that kills them. It's the power, shorting across the wet components. So when I took the battery out, I removed that problem. Army taught us to use silica gel beads in a plastic bag to revive a wet GPS and the like, but I figure, in a pinch, rice will do."

He pinched a square of aluminum foil over the top of the pan.

"Take a week to do it right, but by morning it will be dry enough to make a call. Hopefully. It doesn't need to last long."

Zari and Olga retired to the residence upstairs. Blake took his Springfield pistol out of his waistband, dropped the magazine into his open hand, cycled the round out of the chamber, and began to strip the weapon.

"I have endangered you all," Nassiri said. "I am very sorry to have put you to this trouble."

"You're a very brave man," Blake told him. He set the slide, the barrel, and the recoil spring on the table before him, and began stripping the frame. "And you're doing a very brave thing. It's our privilege to assist you, sir."

He turned to Pardivari. "But, come morning, everybody and his brother in the Iranian army is going to be out looking for us and they are going to be shooting, not talking. Running to the sea won't work. They'll take us out before we're halfway there. We need a Plan B. West of here is the mountains; what's east?"

"East?" Pardivari scratched his beard. "It's just desert."

"Desert we can drive to?" Blake took a cloth from the side of the table and began drying the wet components.

Another scratch of the beard. "The vehicles we have? Sure. They can make it out there."

"Got anyplace out there that's open enough to land an aircraft?" He looked around the room.

Pardivari stepped into the hallway and came back with a small oil can. "Aircraft? You mean like a helicopter?"

"Like a helicopter. Yes." Blake accepted the oil can and began wiping a thin coat onto the bare metal parts.

"I have a place we've used for airdrops. Not as remote as what we had set up for you to land at, but it isn't more than three-and-a-half hours, tops, from here."

Blake nodded. "Sounds perfect. You have lat-long on it?"

Pardivari smiled. "Degree, minute, and second."

"Then . . ." Blake tore a strip of cloth, threaded and turned it through the pistol barrel, and pulled it through. "We just might still be in business."

Chapter Nineteen

Captain Rahim Bahmani woke to a splitting headache and a bright light being shined in his left eye.

"Are you mad?" He asked the question in Farsi, pushing the penlight away.

"Stop that, Captain. Let me do my work."

The voice sounded familiar. Bahmani looked to the side of the light, blinked the fogginess away, and saw a face, lightly bearded. It was someone he knew from his youth. Someone he went to school with.

The regiment's doctor. That's who he was. But he wasn't supposed to be here with their team.

Bahmani pushed the penlight away from his eyes.

"Leave me," he grumbled. "And just what are you doing here? I did not request you."

The captain struggled to rise, got halfway up, and was hit with a wave of vertigo. He dropped back to his seat, fighting nausea.

"No, you didn't," the doctor told him. The two men were the same rank, so he addressed him as an equal. "The police called us when they saw your vehicles here. What happened?"

Bahmani blinked again. The sky above the courtyard wall was pink with the coming dawn. Dozens of bullet holes pock-marked the far wall of the courtyard and water ran from a crack in the fountain and pooled on the floor before trickling out the far gate. Medics were tending to some of his other men. And two enlisted men were lifting a stretcher on which a body had been covered with a light nylon tarp.

"Who is that?"

"Your master sergeant. He was shot while changing magazines and by someone who knows how to shoot: twice through the heart and once between the eyes."

The captain felt his jaw go slack. He looked at the doctor. "What . . . who did this?"

The doctor crossed his arms. "It was our hope you could tell us."

Bahmani leaned forward, put his hands on his knees, pushed himself up to a standing position, and ignored the wave of nausea until it had mostly passed. He took a faltering step and then another, stronger.

"Nassiri's woman," he said. "She gave us tea to drink."

"She did? Did she offer it?"

The captain shook his head. The nausea returned and then left. "She only served it. It was the colonel who offered it."

He looked around. "They are gone?"

The doctor nodded. He crossed his arms again. "So what is this, Rahim? A kidnapping, or a defection? My men tell me the closets are still full of clothes. Nassiri's suitcases are in the guest bedroom, untouched."

"I think I have a way to tell."

Ignoring the doctor's protest, Bahmani staggered into the house and then the kitchen, the captain following him.

"He keeps medication," he said. "I made an inventory when we arrived."

He opened the cupboard and checked one shelf, another. Then he turned.

"It is gone," he told the captain. "If he showed that much foresight . . . then I think Nassiri left this place of his own free will."

He looked at his watch. "We had the tea less than six hours ago."

"It took us a while to bring you around. I had to send a man back to regiment to get the proper drugs. We received the report of shots being fired and arrived within twenty minutes. When he saw Nassiri was not here, the lieutenant in charge called for blocks on all the roads within thirty miles. Nassiri has not shown up at any of those checkpoints."

Bahmani squeezed his eyes closed and rubbed his temples with his hand. "Then they knew the shots would put us into high alert. They are still nearby."

He drew himself to a standing position. The sky had become a noticeably lighter shade of pink.

"My friend," Bahmani told the doctor, "I need to pursue them. They were lost on my watch. I need to find them."

The doctor furrowed his brow. "Are you certain you are fit enough? Can you find them?"

"Fit enough." The Pasdaran captain took his beret from his shoulder epaulet and squared it on his head. "And if I cannot locate the colonel, I will locate the woman."

"Be careful, Rahim. You may want to call for more assistance."

"Not just yet." Bahmani started for the door, put his hand on it, and looked back. "And when I find that witch who drugged us, she will tell us where to find Nassiri. I am absolutely certain of that."

Blake Kershaw stepped outside the basement room, crossed the walkway, and opened the narrow back gate to the compound. The high desert landscape was just beginning to blush with the first light of dawn. He walked to the vehicles and checked the sight-lines in all four directions; Pardivari and Zari had chosen well: the two SUVs were in a shallow depression not visible from any highway, and they were close enough to the compound wall that they'd be hard to spot from the air.

He stood, listening. A bird called in the distance and nearer to the house a goat was bleating to be milked. But he could hear no engine sounds—no aircraft of any kind and nothing approaching on the roads.

Blake went back into the villa, stopping after he stepped inside to let his eyes adjust to the darkness.

The bread pan he borrowed from Olga was sitting against a wall that felt slightly higher in temperature than the others when he checked them the night before. He put his hand on the surface of the rice; it was noticeably warm.

Pardivari came in from the main house and handed Blake a cup of hot chai.

"You know," the older man said. "Both Zari and I have the Thuraya phones, if you want to use one of those."

Blake shook his head. "This one uses a special encryption: non-commercial. The number I'll be calling won't even pick up for another phone. I have ways of calling in the clear, but it's time-consuming. And even though your phone might be more secure than most, I want to spend the absolute minimum time possible on the air."

"Makes sense." Pardivari looked into the bread pan. "Think you got all the water out?"

"No." Blake reached into the pan, took out the main body of the phone, and blew the rice dust off before examining it. "I'm pretty certain I did not. It takes about a week to do it right; I'd never try charging it like this. But there's no condensation on the screen. Hopefully it's good enough to make a call. How long a drive is it to that landing zone you told me about?"

"From here? Three hours, taking our time. Two-and-a-half, if we push it."

Blake snapped the keyboard back on the phone. "Local sunset's about what time tonight? Six-forty?"

"Give or take."

"You good with leaving about eight, then? Making the drive in the dark?"

"Only way I'd suggest doing it, partner."

"Okay, then."

Blake walked outside, where the phone would have a clear shot at any available satellite. He looked at the blank display, closed his eyes for several seconds, and opened them again. Then he extended the antenna, held it vertical, and pressed the button in the lower left-hand corner of the keypad.

For one long moment, nothing happened. Then the display came alive with the search icon. This went on for nearly a minute and Blake inspected the antenna before looking at the display again. As he did, the search icon was replaced by a single word: "Iridium."

Meaning the phone had acquired a satellite.

He keyed in "00," then "1"—the country code for the United States—then "703" and a phone number and pressed the key on the upper right-hand corner of the pad. Then he put the phone to his ear.

"Authenticate," he said. "Slap-shot. I say again, slap-shot."

Blake listened for a moment, then replied, "My comms unit is damaged. It may fail; please take this down and repeat. . . ."

And for the next two minutes he spoke without pausing. Then he listened while his agency contact repeated the message back to him.

"Very good," he said. "We will . . ."

He stopped and looked at the display. It was blank again.

Pardivari came out of the house and stepped next to him. "Did you get through?"

"I did." Blake held the phone next to the missionary's ear.

Pardivari scowled. "What's that whine?"

"The capacitor dying." Blake opened the back of the phone, took the battery out, and sniffed at the case. "Phone's fried. But I gave them Plan B. And Plan A is still in effect; the SEAL team will still come ashore tonight; it just won't be for us. I gave them the GPS coordinates, and they're coming in to retrieve my partner's body."

"Never leave one behind," Pardivari said. He nodded; the nod of a man who knew the special culture of elite warriors.

"Let's get as much rest as we can," Blake told him. "We can sleep in four-hour shifts. You go first and I'll get my gear squared away in the back of the truck. I'll wake you up when it's your watch."

HALF AN HOUR AWAY, a Pasdaran sergeant drove a desert-camouflage Safir tactical vehicle, very similar to an American military Jeep, except for its four headlamps. He stole a glance at the captain in the passenger's seat. Rubbing his thumb on the steering wheel, the sergeant drove in silence for a kilometer. He didn't know this officer; he was simply told to pick him up at the home of that retired colonel, Nassiri, and take him into the village.

This captain looked as if he was in a foul mood; his clothing rumpled, his eyes bloodshot, his face fixed in a frown. The man looked as if he had been out on an all-night drunk, but for an officer of the Guard, that was unthinkable.

The sergeant drove another kilometer. Then he cleared his throat.

"Excuse me, captain, but I . . ."

The captain held up a hand, palm out. "Not now, sergeant. I am thinking."

"Yes, sir. My apologies, sir."

The captain looked at his watch. "How much longer before we are there?"

"No more than ten minutes, sir."

"And we already have a squad inside the house?"

"Yes, sir. They radioed that they had it secured just before I picked you up."

"Very good."

"Thank you, sir. I was going to say that . . ."

"Later, sergeant." The captain shook his head curtly. "I told you; I am thinking."

108 // William G. Boykin and Tom Morrisey

"Sorry, sir." The sergeant swallowed and drove, rubbing his damp hands against the wheel. He kept his eyes on the road, trying not to look in his passenger's direction.

WHEN THEY GOT TO the house, Bahmani was out of the jeep and on his feet before the vehicle had fully stopped.

He scowled. The home was small, squat and rectangular, very similar to those on either side and differing from them only in the small ramp that led to the front door and the air-conditioning unit laboring in the window. It looked like the home of a businessman who made perhaps a fraction more than his neighbors; it did not look like the home of an anarchist.

The corporal at the door stood aside to let him in and the captain stood in the main room of the house for a moment, blinking to let his eyes adjust to the dark. When they had, he could make out a man in a wheelchair, flanked by two Pasdaran enlisted men.

Bahmani stepped nearer. That the man was very ill was obvious; his skin appeared grey, and on his close-shorn head there were the blotches of small sores. His clothing appeared too large for him, like a child dressed in an adult's clothing, and he was breathing from a nasal cannula attached to a green cylinder of oxygen on the back of his chair. He looked so gaunt he could have been forty or he could have been ninety—Bahmani really couldn't tell.

"You are welcome to my home," the man said. "May I offer you tea?"

A kitchen opened onto the main room and Bahmani took a chair from it, turned it around backward, and sat that way in front of the man, less than half a meter between them.

"Your daughter," Bahmani said, "already gave me tea."

The man said nothing, but Bahmani was certain he saw the glimmer of a smile.

"I would like to repay her hospitality," Bahmani told him. "Where is she?"

"Zari?" The man in the wheelchair shrugged. "She came to see me yesterday. Why? Is she in trouble?"

"Yesterday?" Bahmani gestured with an open hand at the wheelchair. "Who cares for you, attends to you?"

"Zari works, so I have a day-nurse," the man said. He smiled. "She is provided to me by the state. She should be here now, making my breakfast, but I imagine she saw your men and got frightened. That is the specialty of the Guard, is it not? Frightening innocent people?"

"Watch your tongue, old man."

"I forget myself." The man in the wheelchair smiled again. "You are my guest."

"I do not have time to play games." Bahmani took a deep breath, exhaled it through his nose. "You will tell me where your daughter is."

The man said nothing.

"Now." Bahmani unholstered his pistol and put the muzzle against the other man's forehead.

The man in the wheelchair smiled. "You cannot frighten me with heaven, my friend. If I knew where my daughter was, I would happily die before telling you. I have cancer in my lymph nodes, cancer in my lungs, my stomach, my bones, and my brain. I have pain no man could imagine. Every morning, I pray to God to take me, if that be his will. I have no plans that go beyond next week, because my doctor tells me there is a very good chance I will be gone from this Earth by the end of next week. I look forward to that time. I pray for it. But it is as I said: I do not know where she is."

"Think about this carefully, old man. I can make this very hard for you."

"Hard?" The man in the wheelchair laughed. "For three years I have fought this cancer, Captain. Pain is like an old friend to me. Break my arms, if you will. I have very little further use for them; to be deprived of them for a week is nothing but an inconvenience. Besides, it would take very little, I imagine, to kill me now. And that, as I said, would be a release."

Bahmani looked up at the Pasdaran corporal nearest him. "Have you searched the house?"

The enlisted man straightened. "Sir. He has a hospital bed in the bedroom, with a bar for getting in and out. The only thing unusual is his computer: a laptop. The hard drive has been removed."

Bahmani looked at the man in the wheelchair. "And where might that be?"

"In the burning barrel out back. I removed it from the machine, drilled holes through it with an electric drill, smashed it with a hammer, and then had my daughter put it in the barrel when she burned the week's trash."

The man gave a little shrug. "As I said, I will be dead soon. And I wish to protect my privacy, once I'm gone."

Bahmani stood. "Take him back to headquarters."

"Don't bother locking up," the man in the wheelchair said. "Let my neighbors come take what they will. If you move me, if you make me travel, I will not be coming back here. You may be certain of that."

PARDIVARI WENT TO SLEEP on one of the cots and Zari came in about half an hour later, carrying bowls of hot barley for their breakfast. Nassiri, the colonel, was in the bathroom, washing up, so it was just Blake and Zari in the outer room.

"I'm sorry about last night, the courtyard," Blake said as he accepted a bowl.

"It was my fault. If I'd remembered Farrokh's medicine in the first place, none of that would have happened."

"Don't say, 'if.' It happened and it's done. Start thinking about how it might have gone in this business and it's a sure ticket to crazy. And in a way, it was good; had that man come around without us noticing it, they could have mounted a search while we all thought we were in the clear. Still, I'm sorry you had to be there for that."

Zari bowed her head, then looked Blake in the eye. "If you had not shot, that man would have killed us both. Or worse."

Blake nodded and tried the barley. It was mixed with milk, like an oatmeal, and sweetened with brown sugar. It tasted much better than it looked.

"We leave tonight, after sundown," he told her. "But have your things ready as soon as you can. If things turn bad, we may have to leave with a moment's notice."

The girl nodded as she set out the breakfast things for Nassiri.

"Your father," Blake said. "Are you okay with leaving him?"

"My father and I said our good-byes last night," Zari told him. "There is nothing more for us to do. He will be dead soon and he and I both know that."

Blake ate his barley and looked at the young woman as she tidied the table. In the soft morning light, she was beyond pretty. She was radiant, beautiful.

He wondered how to tell her that her real father was already dead: that he had died in Blake's arms not four days earlier.

Again, it didn't seem the time. Blake ate his barley.

THROUGHOUT THE MORNING, BLAKE kept watch, checking on the vehicles every hour, and walking the perimeter of the walled compound. Olga sent a couple of servants out to the drive to trim around the bases of the poplars and he noticed they were taking their time, stretching every now and then as they scanned the road in front. It felt good, knowing his were not the only eyes on watch.

After four hours he ate lunch, a curried lamb stew, then he washed the bowl and utensils, refilled the bowl with stew, and woke Pardivari. Ten minutes later, Blake was on a bunk, sound asleep.

THE PASDARAN SERGEANT WAS getting on Bahmani's nerves. All day, the man lurked in the background, always on the periphery of the captain's vision, like a child afraid he will be overlooked when the sweets are passed out.

Bahmani ignored the man and left the temporary office the regiment set up in an unused school building. He went down the hall and stood outside the classroom they'd appropriated for interrogation, looking in through the wire-reinforced glass set into the door. Nourazar, the woman's father, was in his wheelchair with his oxygen on one side of a plain table, his eyes half closed, not speaking. Bahmani's colleague, the doctor, who was also the unit's specialist in interrogation, was sitting on the other side. He had a notebook in front of him, but he was not writing in it.

Bahmani rapped softly on the door. The doctor looked up, saw him, left his seat, and came to the door. Glancing back at the sick man, he stepped out into the hall, closing the door behind him.

"How's it going?" Bahmani did not bother with formalities.

"Nothing so far, Rahim." The captain's Farsi had a slight accent; it reminded Bahmani of his childhood.

"Then persuade him."

"I don't know, Rahim." The other captain rubbed his unshaved chin and looked back into the room through the window in the door. "We check vitals when we have these . . . conversations. If they drop too low, we don't use chemicals. We haven't given him a thing and his vitals are already so low that, were we administering them, we'd have to stop."

"Then break a finger, a toe."

"The man's eaten up with cancer. He's in so much pain already, I doubt he'd notice."

"Take him off his pain drugs, then."

The other captain shook his head. "I cannot tell for certain without hospital equipment, but from the color of his eyes, his skin, I would say he is in almost complete renal failure—virtually no kidney function. Were we to take him off, the drugs would stay in his system for days, maybe longer. Probably longer than he has to live."

Bahmani took off his beret, rolled it, and tapped it against his palm. He looked in the window; the sick man appeared to be sleeping. "So what if his vitals are low? Why not use the chemicals anyhow?"

"He could die. He *will* die."

Bahmani rolled his eyes. "My friend, he is dying as we speak. The only loss is if he dies without telling us where his daughter has gone . . . where she has taken Nassiri. Use the chemicals. Get some good out of this old goat while he is still upon this Earth."

"I'll have to get the drugs." The doctor turned to go.

Bahmani looked in the classroom window and then he pressed on the door and went inside.

The room smelled faintly foul, like dried urine, unwashed bodies, and the beginnings of corruption.

"My friend, if you tell us where she is, I will not harm her."

The man in the wheelchair did not move.

Bahmani went to his side and sat on the table, leaning close to him, speaking in his ear. "She will not be charged. She will not spend a single hour in custody. I will let her go free. You have my word on this, as an officer of the Guard."

Still no reaction.

Bahmani took a breath. "By Allah's name, I swear this."

Nourazar did not even open his eyes.

"You idiot." Bahmani's voice was almost a shout. "If I have to go looking for her, she will suffer. She is young, a beauty; I will question her and then I will give her to my men. Every single one of them. Over and over again. She will long for death."

Nourazar did not move. Bahmani cupped the man's chin. Drooled spittle wet his palm and he wiped it on Nourazar's shoulder. He lifted one of the man's eyelids with his thumb; all he could see was the white of his eye and a small crescent of iris.

Bahmani leaned back, his arms crossed, scowling. He was still leaning like that when the other captain—the unit's doctor—came back in.

The doctor took Nourazar's pulse. Then he took it again and opened the sick man's eyes, inspecting them with a penlight. He took a small folding knife from his pocket, opened a thin blade, and danced the point up and down the sick man's bare forearm.

"He is unresponsive," he told Bahmani. "This man is in a coma."

"Can you bring him out?" Bahmani asked.

"He has a very faint pulse. The shock of the stimulants will almost certainly stop his heart."

"I don't care. Bring him around."

"OLGA MADE US A salad."

Blake opened his eyes and sat upright on the cot.

"Greens from her garden and cheese," Pardivari said. "I told her we had a lot of traveling ahead of us tonight, that we didn't want a heavy meal that could make us drowsy."

"Good thinking. Did you tell Nassiri?"

"He ate already. He and Zari are out by the vehicles, walking."

"Hasn't said much, has he?"

Pardivari shook his head. "He's in second-guessing mode, thinking about what he's walked away from."

"Then it's good that Zari is with him. She's someone familiar who can reassure him, tell him that he's done the right thing."

"No doubt."

Blake went to the bathroom, washed his face and hands, and came out to the simple wooden table in the outer room. The salad was in a large ceramic bowl on one side of the table. And on the other side was a semiautomatic rifle with an open wooden stock that looked like what you'd put on a target model, and a barrel and forestock that were faintly reminiscent of an AK-47. It had a telescopic sight with a long, corrugated rubber eye-cup, a leather sling, and while there were some dull spots where the bluing had rubbed thin, it looked brand-new in every other respect.

Blake stood, looking down at it. "Is that what I think it is?"

"*Snayperskaya Vintovka Dragunova.*" Pardivari pronounced the Russian flawlessly. Then he grinned. "Dragunov sniper rifle. The old one: wooden stock, Soviet proof marks. Genuine Cold War Soviet shooting technology."

"Where'd it come from?"

"Old man Warshowsky got it from a friend, a colonel in the Red Army, before he and the family beat feet for Iran. He left it to Boris, who's had it in the bedroom closet ever since. Olga says he's never shot it. But someone else has." Pardivari held up a folded sheet of yellowed paper. "The Dragunov's a rebuild. This is the armorer's report from when the weapon was rebarreled. My Russian stinks, but I know enough to tell the scope is zeroed for 200 meters, and it holds minute-of-angle accuracy at that distance. I stripped and oiled it and looked it over. Bore is clean as a whistle and not a spot of rust anywhere on it. I've seen Romanian-made examples and plenty of Western knock-offs, but this is the first one I've seen that's the real, original deal. There are collectors who'd give an arm and a leg for one of these."

Blake picked up the magazine lying next to the rifle. He pressed down on the top cartridge and it moved only a millimeter or so.

"Mag's full. Ten rounds, right? They any newer than the rifle?"

Pardivari laughed and shook his head. "I seriously doubt it. If Boris never shot it, he hasn't ever had a need to feed it. But when Olga saw all we had was your pistol, she thought we could use some firepower. And I suppose she's right; you know what they say about pistols."

Blake nodded. "'They're a good thing to have so you can fight your way back to a rifle.' Man . . . but this thing is what? Forty years old? Or more? A lot could have happened to knock it out of zero in all that time. And who knows if the primers are even viable in that ammo?"

"It's a gift horse." Pardivari nodded at the bowl of salad. "I'll say grace, and let's dig in."

TWO INFANTRY MEDICS RUSHED past Bahmani's open office door, walking double-time toward the improvised interrogation room.

Stifling a curse, the Pasdaran captain got to his feet and followed them. Sure enough, the door to the interrogation room was wide open and his friend, the doctor, was kneeling.

The sick one, Nourazar, was on the floor with his shirt open, his oxygen bottle and wheelchair pushed to the side. His entire body quivered as one of the medics held a pair of defibrillator paddles to his chest. The doctor checked for a pulse and said, "Again."

There was the whine of the unit charging and then a thunk, like the snap of a spark, only louder and deeper, and the man's body nearly jumped from the floor. But when the doctor checked for a pulse a second time, he shook his head.

"This is useless," the doctor told Bahmani. "He's not coming back, Rahim. His body is wasted by the cancer. There is nothing here to revive."

"All right. We are done, then." Bahmani nodded at the lifeless body. "Were you able to pull him out of the coma?"

"For a minute. Maybe less."

"Did he say anything?"

"Yes."

Bahmani crossed his arms and waited. "And?"

The other captain looked up at the ceiling, then back at Bahmani. "He told me that he blessed us . . . and that he forgave us."

Bahmani stared at him. "That's it?"

The other captain looked back into the room, at the medics stowing their gear, the lifeless body lying there like a discarded rag.

"Unbelievable." Bahmani stormed back to his office. His driver, the sergeant, was still waiting there, by his door. Bahmani stopped and glowered at him.

"By the prophet's beard! I am beyond weary of this, sergeant. Out with it and then leave me alone!"

"Sir?" Even with the single syllable, his voice nearly cracked.

"You have something you want to say. You've had something you want to say all day. You have hung closer to me than my shadow. So tell me; what is it?"

The man shuffled. He'd been bursting to speak for hours and now he was obviously tongue-tied. He swallowed and took a deep breath. "It could be nothing, sir. But my brother phoned me late last night. He saw something."

"'Something?' That is what he saw? 'Something?'" The captain didn't bother hiding the sarcasm in his voice. "A pity you can't be more specific."

The sergeant gulped. "There was a missionary here two years ago, sir. An American . . . Christian . . . Proselytizing. We had a report he was killed."

"Yes. Yes. I was in Tehran then, but I saw the report. He fell for a trap. So what of it?"

The sergeant swallowed again. "My brother swears he saw him. Last night."

"Well, then, make a report . . ." Bahmani stopped. "Wait. This missionary. His name was . . . Pardivari. Is that right?"

"Yes, sir!" The sergeant brightened. "That's the one."

"The one intelligence said was . . ." Bahmani almost said the Farsi for "commando" here, but he caught himself. ". . . American Special Forces?"

"Was, sir. He left it and came here."

"Think, sergeant." Bahmani leaned toward the other man. "Think carefully. Exactly where did your brother say he saw this Pardivari?"

THE PUSHPAK AND THE Land Cruiser were packed, not that there was all that much to carry. Blake and Pardivari were taking everything they'd brought with them, but only to get it out of the Warshowsky's compound; they wanted to leave no sign of themselves behind. Nassiri and Zari brought little but a change of clothes, medicines, the colonel's Bible, and a small leather attaché the old man would not let out of his sight. At Pardivari's suggestion, Blake added thick woolen blankets to the back seats of both vehicles; if they got to the landing zone early and had to wait, the desert night could be bitterly cold. And to that meager collection, Blake added the Dragunov sniper rifle, placing it across the blankets on the rear seat of the Toyota, its chamber clear, but a full magazine locked into place. Then he and Pardivari reduced the tire pressure on both vehicles to half normal. It was an old Middle Eastern trick—Pardivari said there would be some deep, loose sand near the end of the drive, and partially deflated tires would have much better traction.

Now Zari and the colonel were outside; the sun was about to set, and the colonel's arthritis did better if he walked and moved every hour or so. Blake and Pardivari were indoors, at the plain wooden table, with an ordinary Farsi road map spread out on the tabletop.

"You can't see it on this map, but there's a wadi a few klicks west of here," Pardivari was saying. "It's not like most of the wadis in the Middle East. This one's more of a gully. It's narrow and it's got really steep sides most of the way; steep enough a man might have a problem if he had to climb out. But there's a place where the bank is broken down about here . . ." He tapped on the map. ". . . and we can get into it there, then follow it north for a while before it finally turns east. It's plenty deep enough to hide a vehicle and I've cleared the bigger stones out on the earlier trips, running out to pick up my mission air drops. Should hide a lot of our heat signature too, unless a helicopter's right on top of us. Lots of Pasdaran and regular Iranian army here now, what with the readiness drill, but they aren't local. They don't know the country, and this wadi's not on most maps. We've got a good chance of getting to the landing zone undetected."

Blake looked at the map. "Has Zari done this drive before?"

"Sure has. Not for a while, though."

Blake rubbed his chin. "I was hoping to put her and Farrokh in the lead vehicle, let us follow. Pasdaran wouldn't know where to ambush us in open country, but they might follow tire tracks. That means any trouble would come from the rear. I was hoping to have you and me in back, with the weapons."

Pardivari shook his head. "She wouldn't find the wadi entry, not even with the night vision goggles. Let's put you with the weapons with her, in back, and I'll take Nassiri with me, in front. Still have a tail gunner that way."

"That's what we'll have to do." Blake nodded. "Just remember though, if anything happens, I'm expendable and the girl's expendable. But Farrokh has to get to that LZ in one piece. Absolutely. You understand?"

"I read you."

The door opened and Nassiri and Zari came in. Blake looked back at the map, but found himself looking up again. He remembered what he just said, about the girl being expendable. He hoped he could remember that, if the time came.

"Full dark is about half an hour away," he told them. "We'll start the vehicles up in about forty-five minutes, get them warmed up, and leave in an hour. Farrokh, you'll ride with Hormoz, and Zari, I'll ride with you and keep watch for anyone trailing us. Hormoz has the only night-vision equipment, so Zari, you'll want to ride fairly close to him, keep him well within sight. It'll be tough, because there won't be a moon until near sunrise and even then it would just be the thinnest sliver. Hopefully by that time, we'll be well out of the country."

He looked Zari in the eye and thought once again about what he'd told Pardivari. "You good with driving?"

She nodded slightly, not breaking his gaze.

"All right then." He folded the map and handed it to Pardivari, then went to the back door and opened it. The gate in the compound wall was still ajar and he could see the sun was fully set. The sky was already deepening into dusk. "Let's double-check that we've picked everything up here then. We don't want to compromise Olga by leaving any . . ."

"You must go!"

Blake stopped in mid-sentence. All four of them turned to the door leading into the main house. It was Olga Warshowsky, wearing an apron, flour on her hands. Her eyes were wide with fear.

"It is Pasdaran!" She waved both hands, shoulder high. "They are coming! They are coming down drive! They are here! Go! Go now!"

Pardivari took Nassiri by the elbow and began half-guiding, half-pushing him out of the room. Blake did the same with Zari.

"Keys are in the truck," he told her.

"Wait." She turned to the Russian woman. "You come too."

"*Nyet.*" The older woman stamped her foot. She switched to Farsi. "I will not give my house to those devils."

"Olga, please. Boris is in Switzerland. He's safe. You can meet him there."

"I will be fine, but you must go now." Olga turned to Blake.

"Take her," she said in English. "They come! Leave! Is best for us all."

"She's right; with or without her, we can't be here when they come in." Blake took Zari by the wrist and she resisted for a moment only, then followed him.

Pardivari and Nassiri were already in the Pushpak, the engine running. Zari got into the driver's side of the Toyota and Blake took the passenger's seat. The girl turned the key and the engine caught immediately.

"I follow Hormoz, yes?"

Blake pointed west. "Just drive. We can fall in behind him later. Go."

Both vehicles lurched into action, side-by-side, and Blake watched the dust rise behind him. He shook his head; had it been fifteen minutes later, it would be too dark to see, but now it was like a plume of smoke, pointing to them as its source.

"Fast as we safely can," he told the girl. "We've got to put some distance behind us."

He looked over at Pardivari, who grinned back at him as the vehicles ran two abreast. Then the Pushpak fell behind them. Blake leaned out the window to look.

The little SUV was rolling to a halt.

"Stop the truck; Hormoz is stalled out."

Zari did as he asked and Blake stepped out into the darkening evening. It was the hardest time of day to judge distances, but he figured the Pushpak to be fifty meters behind them, the compound gate two hundred meters beyond that. Behind them, he could hear the starter churring as Pardivari tried to re-crank the engine. Blake leaned back into the truck.

"He's flooded. This is going to take a while. Crank your wheel right and turn us broadside to the house. Put it in neutral and leave the engine running."

She did what he said without question and when she was stopped again, he walked around the truck and took the sniper rifle out of the back. He racked the bolt and it snapped forward, chambering the top round in the magazine.

"Get out and hunker down behind me, Zari."

She looked at him. There was just enough light to see the question on her face.

"Now, Zari. I'm going to go up here, by the hood. If the Pasdaran comes out of that gate, I doubt they're carrying anything that can shoot through an engine block."

She got out and Blake put his left arm through the rifle sling, as if he was about to put it on his shoulder, and then twisted it so it was snug against his upper arm. He leaned forward, chest against the fender, resting his elbows on the hood, still warm from a day in the sun. He rested his cheek lightly against the open stock's raised comb, and put his eye to the scope's long, rubber eye-relief cup, settling the reticle of the sniper scope on the open gate just as a shadow crossed from the courtyard behind.

Someone stepped through the gate. It was just a flicker, not enough for Blake to see if it was friend or foe. Between the compound and Blake, the Pushpak engine cranked, caught, and died again.

Blake was just wondering if the shadow was really a soldier when he saw a five-spoked spark of brief, orange muzzle blast. Less than half a second later, there was a crack overhead as the round passed high, still supersonic.

"He's raw," Blake said, more to himself than to Zari. "Not firing aimed shots."

He searched with the scope for where the fire came from. Night had fallen quickly, and the wall of the Warshowsky compound was just a long black block. He could not make out the shooter.

Two more sparks blinked and died, the report of the shooter's rifle arriving half a second later. There was no more crack of bullets flying overhead. The Pushpak's engine was still cranking.

"He's not shooting at us anymore," Blake said. "He found the other truck, and he's targeting them. Cover your ears."

Now the muzzle-blast was regular, three-round orange bursts in the sniperscope and Blake centered them easily on the top chevron of the reticle as the crack of the distant rifle reached their ears. Blake only half-heard his adversary shooting and no longer heard the Pushpak's starter at all. Breathing slowly, deliberately, he quieted his racing heart, felt his pulse against the fender, and focused on the dim, dark image in the scope. His heartbeat slowed. The rifle in his hands was zeroed for two hundred meters and he estimated his target to be fifty meters farther out than that, so he lifted the reticle ever so slightly high.

And as he remembered that, he also remembered what he had in his hands was a forty-year-old weapon with forty-year-old ammunition, a weapon that had not had a round through it in decades and could have had its scope knocked out of alignment by nothing more than being moved around in a closet. He didn't even know if it would fire.

"Lord, please," he said aloud. "It has to . . ."

Blake pushed all other thoughts out of his mind, took a slow half-breath, held it, felt for the pause between heartbeats, and slowly pressed straight back on the trigger.

Chapter Twenty

The Dragunov barked, its flash suppressor briefly painting the hood and the windshield of the Land Cruiser with brilliant, orange-white light. Blake felt the familiar mechanical kick in his shoulder and kept the sight on his target, following through.

In the sight, there was one more three-round burst of muzzle flash, pointed upward. Then nothing.

Blake swung the sight left, to the open gate, illuminated by the light in the courtyard beyond. He saw the form of a man passing through it with a rifle at quarter-arms and Blake led the figure slightly and squeezed, seeing only the back half of the distant man's body as he fell.

The next Iranian came charging straight out and Blake aimed high, center mass, and saw him drop half a second after he pulled the trigger. In the silence after the shot, he heard his expended brass hit the truck's windshield and bounce and roll across the hood to the ground. Half a second later, the sound of the third soldier's scream reached them. It only lasted a moment.

The Pushpak's engine cranked again and caught, the engine revving twice.

Now the Iranians were being cautious. He saw two of them peering out from either side of the gate, just their heads, one low and one high. Blake sighted on one and then the other, practiced the movement twice, and then did it for real, firing at either end of the tiny arc. The two distant figures fell toward one another, one soldier landing on the other. These two did not scream.

The Pushpak's engine noise drew nearer.

"He comes," Zari said behind him. "Hormoz: he is moving again."

"Okay." Blake kept the scope on the open gate. Following the contour of the vehicle with his knee, he began moving toward the front bumper. "As soon as I tell you, get in and be ready to follow him. Don't touch the brakes."

Still following the outline of the vehicle with his leg, he walked next to the front bumper and then, once it ran out, crossed back toward the passenger door. The gate was still just a blank rectangle of light in his scope. The optics were so good he could make out the texture of the house's wall through the gate. There wasn't so much as a shadow moving; no one was trying to follow the five men who already came through. To make sure the Iranians continued to keep their heads down, Blake fired one last round through the open gate.

"Okay." He jumped in the Toyota and shut the door. "Gun it."

Zari drove like someone accustomed to the desert, picking up speed smoothly, with a minimum of wheel-spin. Blake turned and watched the back gate to the Warshowsky compound; there was still no movement and he noted with satisfaction that the dust behind them was dark; Zari was keeping her foot off the brake.

Blake watched until the distant gate was just a distant dot of light. Then he turned and settled in his seat. It took him several seconds to pick out Pardivari's SUV, bouncing and rocking in the darkness just ahead. But Zari followed the lead vehicle's every move, driving less than fifty feet off his rear bumper.

Blake glanced back again. "How far to the wadi?"

"At this speed?" Zari kept her eyes on Pardivari's vehicle as she spoke. "Ten minutes. Maybe less."

"Let's hope for less. We're going to have everything in this district with boots, wheels, or wings following us . . . just as soon as those folks back there make a radio call."

"They probably think we are trying to make the Iraqi border. That, or drop down and go back to the village to change trucks and try to get on the highway, head for the sea. The wadi will take us north and then east, and east is the direction they will least expect us to take."

"That's what we're hoping." Blake admired the way she grasped it.

The Land Cruiser lifted, dropped, and then lifted again as they crossed a dip in the terrain.

"Thank you." Zari glanced his way, just for a moment. "What you did back there . . . you kept us—Farookh and me—from being captured. That was very brave."

"It's my job. And you did well."

The young woman drove in silence for several seconds.

"What," she asked, "will become of Olga?"

Blake checked the desert behind them. It was dark, empty as far as he could see.

"That depends on what story she tells them. If she says we forced our way in, threatened her . . . if she's convincing, maybe not much of anything happens. Maybe house arrest."

Zari glanced his way. "You do not believe that."

"I hope it."

He could see her blinking back tears in the starlight as she drove.

"She needs our help," Zari said. "She is in danger. We must go back."

"Zari, you tried to convince her to come with us. She refused."

Now the tears were running down her face. "But they have her. And we have guns."

"We have two guns," Blake agreed. "And they still have the rest of an infantry squad back there at the compound; maybe eight soldiers. They've already made a radio call by now, and they probably have a full platoon, probably a full company, inbound for the house. We'd be two guns trying to take a fortified position, held by a superior force. They'd kill us all. And if the man in that truck up there does not make it out of the country, you're talking a war that could easily kill Olga and every other person in this province."

"Yes," Zari said, "I told Farrokh the same thing."

"Then you know what our priorities are."

Zari drove, saying nothing.

"Olga's smart," Blake told her. "If anyone can pull through this, she can."

Zari kept driving. Over the sound of the engine, Blake could hear her sniffling.

He turned and scanned the dark horizon behind him. There was still no light, no sign of a pursuer of any kind.

The Land Cruiser decelerated, its engine growling at a higher pitch as Zari downshifted.

Blake turned, looking through the windshield. "What's up?"

"Hormoz slows." Zari nodded at the vehicle ahead of them. "I am using the transmission to slow as well, a lower gear, so we do not show the brake light. I think we have reached the entry to the wadi."

Blake could barely make out Pardivari's SUV through the windshield. He leaned his head and shoulders out the window so he could see better.

Ahead of them, the shadowed back end of the Pushpak tipped forward nearly forty-five degrees; it looked as if the little SUV was driving off the brink of a cliff. The vehicle hesitated for a moment and then lumbered forward. It was like watching a ship sink into a dark desert sea.

"Well," Blake said. "I can see why not many people know how to get into this wadi."

As Blake watched, Zari drove up to the brink of the wadi. She gradually applied the parking brake until they came to a stop.

"It's okay," he said. "We can follow him."

Zari looked at him. Her cheeks were still wet with tears. "I know. I am giving him time to get clear."

She slipped the clutch and the Land Cruiser crept forward, dipping down steeply. In a moment, Blake had both hands against the dash, bracing to keep himself from crashing face-first into the windshield.

The engine moaned and the transmission whined in protest as the SUV dropped forward.

"Brakes," Blake said, "would be good."

"No. I do not wish to show the lights."

They bottomed and she cranked the wheel hard right. The Land Cruiser tipped a little, and the action nearly threw Blake across the shifter and into her lap. They settled back onto all four wheels with a squeak of springs.

"Sorry." Blake's face was no more than an inch from hers. She glanced his way, moving her eyes only. Even in the dark, she had amazing eyes.

"It is understandable." She looked forward. "Hormoz is moving. To keep him in sight, I must drive."

"Sorry."

"Yes. You said that already."

Blake slid back into his seat and the Land Cruiser began to move forward again.

The night appeared even blacker than before and, leaning out the SUV's window, he could more sense than see the near wall of the wadi. In the dim starlight, everything around him was shadow, but he had the feeling that, were he to lean from the window and stretch out his arm, he could touch the crumbling, eroding earth and sandstone of the wall.

Just ahead of them, he could hear the Pushpak as it ground along the dry stream bed, stones crunching under its tires or spitting to the sides and striking the hard-packed Earth of the gully walls. But he had to glance to the side, using his more light-sensitive peripheral vision, to make out the shape of the little SUV ahead of them, and even then it was nothing more than a rocking, blurred, slate-gray shadow. He settled back in his seat.

"You can see well enough to drive?"

"Shhhh." Zari's head did not turn as she shushed him; at least, he was fairly certain it did not turn. "I must . . . need . . . concentrate."

Blake went quiet and let the young woman attend to her task.

For the next hour-and-a-half, neither one of them said a word. They kept their windows down, and the night air was dusty, but a few degrees cooler than it was when they fled the house. Blake alternated his gaze between the sky in the top quarter of the windshield, the sky above the dark wadi, and what he could see through the dusty glass of the rear hatch.

It was nothing but darkness and stars. Then he saw something; the briefest glimpse of a tiny red light.

"Zari," he said, his voice even and calm. "Push in the clutch, put us in neutral, and let us roll to a stop."

"But Hormoz . . ."

"He's monitoring you in the rear-view. He'll stop with you. Go to neutral, now."

She did and Blake opened the door and stepped outside. The distant red light blinked across the wadi far behind them again. And he could hear the distant *whump-whump-whump* of rotor noise.

Looking up, he could see the brink of the wadi against the star-strewn sky. But when he reached out to touch the wall, his hand closed on thin air. He reached over his head and, just above his head, felt crumbling Earth and stone. Following it, he walked away from the Land Cruiser; he got about five feet before it began to slope downward.

Blake walked back to the passenger-side window.

"The bank here is undercut," he told Zari. "Crank your wheel right and pull in slowly; we want to get the entire hood under the bank if we can. But go slow . . . if this bank collapses on us, we're not going anywhere."

"But Hormoz . . ."

"He'll do what we do. Go ahead."

She did as he asked. He could see the dim, fuzzy outline of Pardivari's Pushpak mimicking their action. In less than twenty seconds, both vehicles were partially hidden by the undercut bank.

"Okay," Blake said, getting back inside, glad there was no interior light. "Cut the engine."

This time she obeyed without question. The sound of the rotor blades drew nearer.

"The back ends of the vehicles," Zari said after a minute. "They can be seen from the air."

"I know." Blake pulled the pistol from his waistband, ejected the magazine, pushed down on the top round to make sure it was full, and slid the mag back into the grip of the pistol. "But all we've seen so far of that helicopter is anti-collision lights. They're not using a searchlight. Artesh—the Iranian army—has night-vision capability, but the newest stuff, what NATO uses, is embargoed. They can't get it here. So they're probably using thermal imagery to look for us; they have that. With the hood under the bank like this, we have a good four or five feet of insulation between us and their equipment. And with the engine shut off, we're not emitting a warm exhaust plume."

"So they can't see us?"

Blake shook his head. Then he shook it again; it was so dark there was no way Zari could see him.

"They can," he admitted. He reached back to retrieve the sniper rifle, remembering he'd already used six rounds from the only magazine he had for it; that left one in the chamber and three in the mag. He reached back and found the two blankets as well. "But they'll have to be at the right angle and they'll need to have the sensitivity set so low they'd be getting a lot of false hits on rocks still warm from the day. We're not completely invisible. But we've lowered our risk of being detected."

"And if they do see us?"

"Then we fight. Stay here." He opened the door and, leaving it opened, scuttled under the overhang and away from the vehicles, the blankets in one hand, sniper rifle in the other.

Blake resigned himself to using vision as little as possible. He remembered what an older master sergeant, a Vietnam veteran, taught him in SERE—Survival, Evasion, Resistance and Escape training: In Vietnam, helicopter gun crews learned to look behind the aircraft, rather than in front of it, because the Vietcong would hide as the helicopter was approaching, and then come out to look up and follow it as it flew away. Against the green underbrush, their faces would show up: "like targets" was the way the master sergeant put it.

In the dark, Blake faced the same dilemma. If he could see the helicopter, then his face was exposed, and his face was a heat source. It would show as a bright white oval to standard military thermal imaging equipment. And while he could mask that with the thick, wool blankets, they would only work for a minute, maybe less; after that, the wool of the blankets would warm from his body heat and he would be visible once again.

He put the blankets in the hollow at the base of the wadi wall, where they would remain as cool as possible, and tucked himself against the wall a few feet away. Then he kept his head down and listened: the helicopter seemed to be crisscrossing the wadi, overflying it as part of a more general search pattern.

Blake shut his eyes, concentrating on the sound. It was only one helicopter; he was certain of that, and the deeper tone of the rotor noise suggested it was a larger gunship. That meant at least a certain amount of armor, heavy machine guns, probably rockets as well, and a crew of three—at least three and possibly more.

He took a breath and listened. Against something like that, the 7.62 millimeter sniper rifle in his hands was like a peashooter. And the 9 millimeter pistol—the firearm for which he had the most ammunition—was even less effective.

Blake pictured their route to this point. Since they'd entered the wadi, Polaris—the North Star—had been visible most of the time, a tiny pinpoint of light about 33 degrees above the horizon, just over Pardivari's SUV as they drove up the wadi. That meant the wadi was still running north-south and had not taken its turn to the east. Since it wasn't on most maps, there was a good chance the crew in the chopper didn't know the wadi eventually turned east; that would make it seem unlikely to them as an escape route. As Zari said, any

Artesh and Pasdaran forces searching this far north would probably assume they were making an oblique run for the border.

The rotor noise approached rapidly, overflew him, and receded, the Doppler effect making the pitch drop as the helicopter passed. He watched the tritium second hand on his watch: a long seven minutes passed and then the helicopter overflew them again, farther up the wadi, just past the vehicles, the rotor noise diminishing. Less than a minute later he heard it pick up in volume again, farther north still, going the opposite direction. Then it died away.

Blake waited. The desert night was as quiet as any environment he'd ever been in. It wasn't like the woods at night back home in Virginia. There were no bird-sounds, no animals calling to one another, no leaves being rustled by the breeze. This far away from habitation, there weren't even any flocks, so no goats or sheep bleated. It was eerily close to totally silent. He heard a soft creak from the direction of the vehicles; possibly someone shifting inside one of them, making it settle on its suspension. It was impossible to be sure.

He thought about the rotor noise and what it told him. Seven minutes between passes going west-to-east, but less than one minute going east-to-west: that meant the aircrew was using the wadi as the eastern border of their search grid, making a turn after they passed it, and then searching the open desert to the west. It made sense; they would see the steep wadi as a barrier, impossible to cross in a wheeled vehicle.

Seven minutes on the dot, he heard the helicopter again, quite distant this time. It flew west-to-east and the rotor noise faded away completely.

Blake watched the luminous second hand circle his watch. A minute passed and he did not hear the sound of the helicopter return. But he did hear something else: the crunch of gravel against gravel.

Footsteps. Someone was walking his way: trying to be silent, and almost succeeding.

Blake opened his mouth to exhale slowly. It was more noiseless than breathing through his nose and the night was so silent he didn't want to risk any sound at all. He lifted the sniper rifle completely clear of the ground and—carefully, noiselessly—aimed in the direction of the footsteps. He kept his finger on the trigger guard, conscious of the fact that both the Pushpak and the Land Cruiser were somewhere off in the shadows, in the background of any shot he might take.

The footsteps came nearer and then passed him, walking further down the wadi. Five feet past, they stopped.

"Hello?" It was Zari. "Are you there?"

"Zari." Blake relaxed. "You should have stayed with the truck; I nearly shot you."

"But the helicopter's gone. Why aren't we moving?"

"The helicopter is past us. It isn't gone. If the search began where they last had contact with us, at the Warshowsky's, then it stands to reason that they'll head back to their start point. I don't want to be detectable when they do that."

"Oh." He could hear her turn to face his voice. "I am sorry. I will return to the . . ."

They both heard it at the same time: the helicopter returning, the rotor noise growing. It wasn't going back and forth; it was running south, coming straight down the wadi. Quickly.

Blake dropped the rifle and, rising, reached out at the shadow that was Zari. His right arm closed around her hip and waist and, reaching up with his left hand to protect her head, he pulled her to the ground.

"What . . . ?"

"Don't move," Blake told her. He reached out, grabbed both of the blankets, and pulled them over the two of them. The rotor noise rose to a palpable thunder and he trapped the far ends of the blanket with his booted feet.

"Don't move a muscle." Zari's ear was less than six inches from his mouth, but he had to raise his voice to say it. "Stay still until I tell you it's safe."

When it didn't seem as if the approaching helicopter noise could be any louder, it grew louder still. The blanket quivered as if trying to fly away and sand flew in under the edges, stinging the exposed skin of their faces and the backs of their hands. Blake pulled the girl nearer to him, trying to protect her with his body, gripping the blankets with both boot-tips and one hand, struggling to keep it from flipping up and revealing their warm bodies to the thermal imagery.

The helicopter thundered over, rotor wash beating down on them, the hurricane of wind reaching them even under the protected overhang. Blake could feel Zari's body quivering against his as the helicopter passed. He held her more closely and she quieted.

Then the helicopter was gone, the rotor noise receding down the wadi. The chopper was flying so low the noise receded in less than a minute. And after it was gone, there was a long moment of nearly total silence, with Blake holding the girl and her breath warm against his cheek.

Blake pulled the blanket down. He could just barely see her face, but they were eye-to-eye, their lips less than a finger's width apart.

"We're safe now," he told her, his voice a whisper. "That was their return leg; they've finished searching here. We can go."

"Yes." Then they got up, Blake retrieved his rifle, and they started back for the Toyota, guiding themselves in the dark by feeling for the wall of the wadi.

When they got there, they could hear that Pardivari already had his engine running, ready to go. Zari started the Land Cruiser as well.

"Look behind you, see where you want to go, and then close your eyes as you back up," Blake told her. "That way you won't lose your night vision when the back-up lamp comes on."

She did it, backing in an arc and then pulling forward a few feet.

"Okay," she told him. "I am in neutral again."

"Keep your eyes closed. I'll watch while Hormoz backs up and tell you when his light goes off."

Blake squinted, but after better than two hours in near-total darkness, the light from the back of the little Pushpak seemed brilliant when Pardivari put it in reverse. The small SUV jumped back, then stalled, and then restarted and came the rest of the way back.

Some of the light reflected back from the front of their vehicle: enough that Blake could see no fewer than three bullet holes in the back of the Pushpak. One was in the bumper and two were in the window and it made him glad he took the shooter out. The man was obviously finding his target; a few seconds more and he had little doubt the Pasdaran rifleman would have killed both Pardivari and Nassiri.

Then the backup light went out, and all Blake could see was reddish-yellow afterimage, his night vision ruined. But it seemed to him that the Pushpak lurched again as it started forward. He wondered if its drivetrain was damaged.

If it was, there was nothing they could do; they'd just have to drive it until it dropped, push it to the side, and cram everyone into the Land Cruiser.

"Okay," he told Zari. "We're good. Hormoz is on the move. You can open your eyes and follow him."

She put the Land Cruiser in gear and Blake could feel them start to move again. But feeling was about the only dependable sense he had; except for his peripheral vision, he could see nothing but amorphous blobs of afterimage. So he settled back, closed his eyes, and waited for his night vision to return.

For the next five minutes, there was nothing but the growl of the engine, the low whine of the transmission, and the sound of rocks popping out from beneath the partially deflated tires.

"Thank you again," Zari said. "That was stupid of me, coming back to look for you. But the helicopter was gone so long, I thought perhaps you fell and were hurt."

"You couldn't have known. I hope I didn't hurt you when I pulled you down with me."

"You did not," she said. "Actually, it was rather . . ."

But she didn't finish the sentence and Blake wasn't sure what to say after that, so they drove on in silence.

After twenty minutes, the wadi turned to the east. And twenty minutes after that, the wadi walls began to slop back further and further until soon the stream bed was running down the center of something that was barely a depression in the ground.

Now, in order to see Polaris, Blake had to lean out of the window and look over the top of the Land Cruiser's roof, sighting through the tubular aluminum roof rack. And when the wadi began to angle toward the southeast, Pardivari drove straight up the gently angled bank and onto the ground beyond.

Zari followed him. In moments, the noise of gravel disappeared and the dust around them grew thicker; they were driving on sand. But it was open sand, and Zari shifted up until they were running in top gear.

She coughed and then coughed a second time, and Blake shifted in his seat, taking his bandanna out of his hip pocket.

"Here," he said, taking the wheel with his other hand. "I've got us. Knot that around your face. It'll keep some of the dust out."

"What about you?"

"I'm not driving. I can breathe through my sleeve, if I have to."

She accepted the bandanna and brushed his arm a couple of times as he held the wheel and she put the handkerchief on, bank-robber style. Then they drove in dust for another ten minutes until they left the sand and got onto more packed Earth. Things began to settle and with his eyes now accustomed to the dark, Blake saw Zari pull the bandanna down and leave it around her neck, like a cowboy's neckerchief. He could barely see her, but she looked like a woman on an adventure.

She looked his way and then back at the SUV. "Is Hormoz leaving with you?"

"With us?" Blake's lips were caked with dust. He had to wet them to speak. "That's up to him. He's done a pretty good job of staying off the radar for the past two years, but things are going to get pretty hot here, now. I'm hoping he comes back with us."

She nodded and drove without speaking for better than a minute. Then she glanced at Blake again.

"If he doesn't go . . . if he decides to stay . . ." She turned to face ahead, looking through the windshield again. ". . . then I will stay here. With Hormoz."

Blake exhaled through his nose, the dust making a sound as he did it. "Zari, that wouldn't be wise. As far as we know, the Pasdaran thinks Hormoz is dead. They're under no such illusions when it comes to you. You're a wanted woman. Anywhere you go in Iran, in any country that has relations with Iran, that's going to be the case."

She looked straight ahead, giving no indication she heard what he said.

"You knew that when you and your father proposed this, Zari."

"Yes." When she turned his way again, he could see the tears had returned. "Yes, I knew. But I did not know I would place Olga in danger . . . not in danger such as this. When we used her house, I thought no one would know, or if they did, they would hear it later, but it would be all right. Anatoly does not speak to his family, but I understand he takes care of them, keeps the government from troubling them."

She pulled the bandanna up and wiped her eyes with it.

"But this," she said. "This, not even Anatoly can fix. Olga will go to prison. The Pasdaran are animals; they will hurt her to make her talk. She might die. And don't tell me having Farrokh makes it different. You have Farrokh, but Olga will still die. I cannot run away and let that happen."

Blake let her get it all out. He reached over, touched her shoulder and squeezed gently, felt her soften beneath his touch.

"Zari, there's nothing you can do, alone, to change things. If all of us went back right now, the most we could accomplish is to give them four more prisoners. The best thing you can do is come with us, help Farrokh in the debrief, and help move this forward on a diplomatic or a military basis."

Zari shook her head. "We are leaving her. Abandoning her."

"I know it seems that way, Zari. But this isn't the sort of thing you can react to emotionally. If you do, it will blow up in your face and Olga won't be any further ahead."

She looked at him. Even in the darkness, he could see her eyes. "Then what do I do?"

"Get him safely onto the aircraft we're meeting. Get him safely out of the country. Help him understand he's made the right decision. Help get the information he's carrying into the right hands."

Zari drove. Blake couldn't see her knuckles as she gripped the wheel but he knew that, if he could, they would be white.

"Olga knows what we're doing." Blake tried to keep his voice low, soothing. "She decided to help us. She decided to stay. This is not your fault. You did not do this to her."

Zari put her right hand on the shifter, rested it there for a moment, and then struck the dash with the heel of her hand. She sniffed, the sound of a woman trying to weep silently.

"Farrokh will be on the plane," she finally said. Now she did not try to disguise the fact that she was weeping. "We will get him out of Iran. Do not worry; I will help you."

THE COUNTRY BECAME MORE rolling again. In the dim starlight, Blake could see low scrub vegetation dotting the sand-white countryside and Zari steered expertly through it, following Pardivari and mimicking his every move.

They began going downhill, then stayed on the flat for better than ten minutes. After that, it was all gentle uphill for another five, before the land around them began to level out, and the surrounding vegetation thinned out.

Zari began to downshift and Blake sat up. "We're there?"

"We are here." She opened her door. "I must go to Farrokh. He is not accustomed to sitting for so long. His arthritis; he will be stiff."

"Sure." Blake opened his own door and got the sniper rifle from the back seat. Then he went around to the rear hatch, and opened it and grabbed his rucksack. He looked at his watch.

"Hormoz," he called. "Dust-off in thirty minutes. We'd better get all this stuff staged, ready to go."

There was no answer. He turned and looked at the Pushpak; Zari had Nassiri outside and was letting him lean on her as he walked, the pain in his steps obvious. But Pardivari was nowhere to be seen.

"Hormoz?"

Blake turned and walked over to the Pushpak, sitting with its engine off thirty feet away.

As he neared, even in the starlight, he could see the gray-rimmed pocks of bullet holes marking the SUV's side panels. Hormoz was still in the driver's seat, slumped forward. Blake ran the last ten feet and opened the door.

The missionary turned, pain etched on his face. "It's my leg. Left."

Blake fished in his pocket and came out with a small tactical flashlight, pressing the button on the bottom. From his shin down, Pardivari's leg was sticky and wet with blood. And on the floor, nearly a quarter inch of blood was pooled on the floorpan.

"Farrokh doesn't know," Pardivari said. "Truth be told, I didn't know I was hit until we got to the wadi and I went to push on the clutch. And by then, I figured I better keep my mouth shut; didn't want to freak the old man out. He's in so much pain, I don't think he noticed much about me, anyhow. I asked him if he was all right when we got restarted at the Warshowsky's and when the helicopter passed, and he said he was okay both times. But other than that, he hasn't said a word."

Blake lifted the man's blood-wet pant leg and looked at the wound.

"Through and through," he told Pardivari. "But it took out at least part of the bone. We're going to have to splint you before we try moving you. Hang tight."

He ran back to the Land Cruiser, got his rucksack, and ran it back. What he had inside wasn't anything like the medic bag one member of a Special Forces team would always carry, but it had what he needed: a bottle of hydrogen peroxide, gauze squares, a squeeze bottle of sterile water, a blood-stopper bandage, a pair of surgical snips, and an air splint.

"Okay," he told Hormoz. "I've got to turn you so your legs are outside the door."

"Sounds painful."

"I'm sure that's an understatement. Here goes."

Blake reached in and lifted Pardivari by both knees, the missionary groaning in agony as he did it, but pushing up with his arms to help at the same time.

"I'd give you morphine, but I need you awake."

"Understood. You don't want me dropping off into shock."

Blake held the flashlight in his mouth while he used the surgical snips to cut away the man's boot, his stocking, and the lower half of his pant leg. Then he emptied most of the hydrogen peroxide onto the shin and foot, used three of the gauze squares to wipe most of the blood away, rinsed everything with sterile water, dried it with gauze, checked to make sure the bleeding had slowed, and wiped everything with bacitracin cream. He wrapped the blood-stopper bandage with its coagulant surfaces around the wound and then, admiring the missionary's stoic silence, slid the air splint over Pardivari's foot and tugged it almost all the way up to his knee. Then he blew into the air splint until it was firm and inflexible, stoppered it, and checked it for leaks.

When he looked up, both Zari and Nassiri were looking down at what he was doing.

"Will he be all right?" Zari asked.

Pardivari laughed. "Little darlin', I'm afraid I won't be taking you dancing anytime soon, but I'll live."

"I did not know," Nassiri muttered.

"He didn't want you worried," Blake told him. "Here: you two keep him company for a few minutes while I empty out the backs of the trucks."

They did and in less than five minutes Blake had their few belongings stacked in a small heap in front of the trucks. He kept his rucksack separate; he'd need it for what was coming next. Then he squatted next to Pardivari's door.

"We'd better all be on our feet when the dust-off comes. They see anybody sitting in a vehicle, they might think we've been captured, being used for a trap. Just keep all your weight on me and your good leg. I'll walk you up to the fender."

"You got it."

Blake was fully prepared for him to black out when he stood up; he'd lost a lot of blood. But Pardivari merely grunted.

"You are one tough old bird," Blake told him as they walked to the front of the truck, where Blake half-sat him against the fender.

"One of those two things is true." Pardivari laughed and then he groaned.

"You keep talking to us, you hear? Don't doze off."

"Doze off? Y'all kidding? We're havin' an adventure here. This here stuff's exciting."

Zari and Nassiri joined them and for two minutes, the four were clustered and silent, as if gathering in prayer. Blake assumed that was what the others were doing; he was. Then Blake made a quick check of the wind direction. There was a slight breeze coming from the west—not enough to have any impact on the landing of the incoming aircraft. He reached into the side pocket of his rucksack and fished out a small red filter for his penlight. He knew a military aircrew was going to expect a " SAFE TO LAND" signal from the ground. He placed the filter on his light and tested it by blinking several times in rapid succession.

Then he heard it: a low drone, almost like the sound of a distant semi traveling down a country highway.

Within seconds, the others heard it as well. They turned toward it and Pardivari winced as he did, but the sky to the west was black, interrupted only by the low shadows of the distant mountains and the stars. Blake steadied the wounded man to keep him on his feet.

Then they appeared: two dim, adjacent circles of pale green, growing larger in the western sky. As the four of them watched, the circles became squat and elongated, slowly transforming into ovals. Nassiri uttered a single word in Farsi, something Blake didn't understand.

"What did he say?"

"'Aliens'," Pardivari said. "He said it looks like aliens."

"He's pretty close," Blake told him. "They're Marines."

Chapter Twenty-One

The sound of the approaching aircraft changed. It was a throbbing, pulsing thunder now, like a helicopter, only faster and higher in pitch.

Blake pulled the flashlight from his pocket. Then he turned to the others, "Cover your faces the best you can, okay? It's going to get pretty dusty."

"What is it?" Nassiri asked.

"It's a V22," Blake told him. "An Osprey—tilt-rotor aircraft. It keeps its rotors forward, like an airplane's propellors, when it's cruising, but tilts them overhead, like a helicopter, to hover. They have selectable landing lights; they'll use infrared here. They lit up the rotor tips just so we can see we'll be clear of them when they come in."

The green circles were nearly parallel to the ground now and the noise was growing.

"Listen up," Blake said. "When they land, let them come to us. I've got the rifle stashed with our things, so they don't see any of us holding a gun. But they're deep in a country where they aren't supposed to be, so this might become a little rough. Just go with it and let them get us on board. When they land, it'll be too loud for us to talk."

"All right." It was Zari. She moved to the side and he could see she was bent forward over the vehicle's hood, writing something.

Blake nodded. He then pointed his flashlight in the direction of the incoming aircraft and began blinking a series of rapid blinks to indicate it was clear to land. It was standard field procedure for situations in which the ground had no voice communications with the aircraft.

Now the twin green circles were parallel to the ground, even canted back slightly, very close, and they could discern the dark shape of the aircraft, almost like one of those boxy commuter aircraft, only with the two huge thiryt-eight-foot rotors whirling above it. It settled ground-ward and then hovered in a great cloud of stinging dust, the green rotor tips nearly obscured by the dust storm. The aircraft turned until the cockpit was facing away. Then the pitch of the rotors changed and the dust moved off to either side—it was oddly similar to the old movie, where Charlton Heston parted the Red Sea as Moses. As the dust cloud parted, they could see straight into the red-lighted interior of the aircraft and the first thing Blake noticed was the gunner on the ramp, standing ready behind a deck-mounted .50-caliber machine gun. Behind him was a cluster of men in camouflaged combat uniforms, one of them holding a rifle with an oversized hand guard and a long curved magazine; it took him a moment to recognize it as an H&K infantry assault rifle, a recent issue for the Marines.

That man and one other, carrying an M4 carbine, sprinted down the ramp of the Osprey and out to either side, panning the area around them with night-vision goggles. Then, weapons to their shoulders, they approached the group, the M4 covering them while the Marine with the H&K let his weapon hang by a shoulder lanyard, flipped up his night-vision goggles, and pulled a pocket computer and a flashlight from the upper pocket of his uniform. He directed the flashlight beam onto Blake's face, then Nassiri's, and signaled thumbs-up to the man with the M4. That man let his weapon hang by its lanyard as well and both reached out to guide the four of them into the aircraft.

WHEN THE MAN WITH the small rifle took Zari by the arm, his grip was gentle, yet firm. She looked at Nassiri and he nodded and came along with her as well, limping heavily from hours of sitting on arthritic hips, his old leather attaché gripped tightly with both hands.

Zari stooped as they passed the pile of rucksacks and bags and picked up her overnight bag—the only bag she'd brought along. The soldier guiding her shook his head and said something, but she pretended she didn't know what he wanted, which was not true, and that she could not hear him over the noise of the engines and the rotor blades, which was true. She was banking on him being too much of a gentleman to physically remove the bag from her shoulder, and as it turned out, she was right. He shook his hand side-to-side—the universal sign language for "forget it"—and led them onto the aircraft's ramp.

The metal beneath Zari's feet vibrated, as if the aircraft resented being on the ground. She looked back at Nassiri and offered the old man her hand, guiding up and past the Marine who kept both hands on the deck-mounted machine gun, looking past them into the swirling dust and darkness beyond, all business.

Zari had never been on a submarine, but she imagined that the inside of the V22 was something like a submarine. The overhead and parts of the walls were crammed with pipes and tubing and the deck was dotted with D-rings set into hollows. Canvas seat bottoms were folded up against the bulkhead on either side and the entire thing was dimly lighted in red, which she knew was combat lighting, being used to preserve the nocturnal vision of the crew.

The man guiding her steered her over to the side, and a pair of uniformed crew passed her, carrying Hormoz between them; Hormoz winked and gave her a thumbs-up as they passed. They laid Hormoz on a litter secured against the bulkhead and the man guiding Zari folded down two of the canvas seats and pointed at them, lifting the shoulder harnesses as he did.

Zari helped Farrokh into a seat and guided his arms through the straps of the harness. His eyes wrinkled with pain; it was obvious his arthritis was troubling him greatly. Still, he released the leather attaché only long enough for Zari to strap him in. Then he gripped it again. Zari pantomimed giving him a shot in the arm, after which she placed her hands together and put her head against them, closing her eyes for a moment to convey the impression of sleep. Farrokh nodded emphatically.

There were three men bent over Hormoz. One was strapping him into the litter, and another was hanging an IV bag for the needle they already placed in and taped to his arm. The third uniformed man was taking a blood-pressure reading and after he'd written it down, Zari tugged on his sleeve, pointed to Nassiri's pain-contorted face, mouthed the word "arthritis," and repeated her pantomime for a shot to make him sleep.

The man held up one finger, turned to the man hanging the IV, and wrote something on a plastic slate and showed it to him; the other man nodded.

The man Zari went to—he looked young, like a teenager—took Farrokh's pulse, blood pressure, and temperature, and wrote them all on a cardboard tag. He gave Farrokh an injection with a pen-like hypodermic device, checked his watch, wrote something else on the cardboard tag, and tied it onto one of

Farrokh's shirt buttons. He put a plain noise-suppression headset—the kind of thing a person would wear to go shooting—on Nassiri and offered a second set to Zari. Then the young man tightened the seat harness around Farrokh and went back to Hormoz.

Zari glanced to either side. Everyone was back on the aircraft now, and the American agent, the one masquerading as a Canadian professor, joined the people clustered over Hormoz. She remembered huddling with him under the blankets as the helicopter flew down the wadi, and felt a moment of dizziness and warmth.

Already, Farrokh's eyes were closed in sleep, his arms wrapped around his leather attaché. Zari opened his shirt pocket, took out the small Moleskine notebook he had there, undid the elastic strap, and opened it exposing the pocket in the back cover, where he'd put the SD card.

Zari did not remove the card. She didn't even touch it. But she took from her blouse the note she'd written on the hood of the SUV, put it next to the media card, replaced the elastic strap, and buttoned the notebook back into the old man's shirt pocket.

There was a hand on her shoulder; it was one of the Marines. He motioned at the seat next to Farrokh, and she sat in it, put her overnight bag under her seat, and slipped the padded harness straps over her shoulders. The man's lips moved; Zari assumed he was apologizing for being so close, because he put a waist-belt across her lap and tightened both it and the shoulder straps until they were beyond snug.

Zari nodded her thanks and the man got up and walked to the front of the aircraft.

Zari looked around; everyone was busy with one task or another. The man with the big rifle was talking into a boom microphone attached to his helmet and the American agent and three of the crew were bent over Hormoz. There was only one person near the loading ramp now, the person manning the machine gun.

Zari looked at the American agent. He was turned away from her now, and she waited a moment to see if he would turn, if their eyes would meet. And when he did not turn, she slid her hands up her shoulder straps and slowly, stealthily, began to loosen them.

BLAKE WAS STILL ALERT and attentive. He didn't make the rookie's mistake of relaxing once he was aboard the aircraft, because the fact remained the aircraft was still deep inside a country where it was not supposed to be. He'd relax once he was in US-controlled airspace.

Still, he'd been glad to see Zari allowing one of the Marines to strap her into a jump seat. With what she said about the Warshowsky woman, there'd been a moment he thought she might not come along. But now, all hands were present and accounted for and, while Pardivari was the worse for wear, they were all alive and headed for a much safer place.

He was pleased to see the flight crew was bumped up to include two Navy hospital corpsmen and a trauma surgeon. And the team knew what they were doing; they stabilized Pardivari and secured him for transport quickly and effectively, and one of the corpsmen was continually logging his vitals while the surgeon prepared a detailed brief on a ruggedized notebook computer.

Blake bent over Pardivari and squeezed his hand. The missionary grinned back and winked.

A Marine corporal tapped him on the shoulder and showed him a clenched fist on an open palm: *sit*.

Blake nodded, began walking aft, and stopped.

One minute before, Zari had been strapped in next to the physicist. Now the seat next to the old man was empty.

He looked both directions, blinking in the dim red light. There was no sign of her.

Zari was gone.

Chapter Twenty-Two

Blake took one step to start sprinting for the rear ramp. A large hand grabbed him by the shoulder, stopped him, and wouldn't be shaken away.

Ready to fight, Blake turned. Facing him was the gunnery sergeant who was first off the Osprey. In his free hand, he was holding out a David Clark intercom headset; he shook it at Blake, and Blake put it on.

The gunny reached out and worked a switch on the side of the headset. Instantly, the noise level dropped to a tenth of what it had been, the engine sounds still present, but much lower in both volume and tone. Then the gunny keyed his helmet microphone. "Sir, AWACS has three rotorcraft inbound on us, four minutes out. Rotor return says they're quick—probably Super Cobras. Iran's got a few of those."

"But the girl . . ."

"Ran past my corporal on the ramp, aft. He tried to grab her, missed, and she only stopped once. He said she was waving like she was shooing us, telling us to fly away. My corporal couldn't leave his gun; that's written in stone. I was about to go after her myself when the pilot told me about the AWACS call. We've got no choice, sir; we have to leave, and I need you strapped in."

Blake sagged and nodded his assent. He folded down a jump-seat and slumped into it, threading on the harness. "She take a vehicle?"

The gunny nodded. "Corporal saw her leaving through his NVG, sir. Heading west. I've advised the captain and he's going to swing wide and go east for a minute after take-off. That should get all three aircraft following us and keep the heat off of her."

The gunnery sergeant looked aft, where the ramp gunner was clipped off to a thick nylon strap running to his harness, and forward, where the medical team was seated and strapped in near their patients. He sat across from Blake, slid into his shoulder straps and waistband, tightened both with three swift motions, and keyed his mic, saying, "Clear."

The Osprey rocked upward. The feeling was like being in an oversized car on a Ferris wheel, going slowly skyward. Then the entire fuselage dipped forward.

What happened next was unlike anything Blake ever experienced in a helicopter. The V22 did not simply take off; it shot up and forward simultaneously. Blake had the impression that some enormous hand loaded them into a slingshot and launched them skyward.

"More used to helicopters, sir?" The gunnery sergeant leaned in the direction of travel as he spoke.

Blake nodded.

"V22 is a little different." He put his hand to his helmet, listening. "Inbound choppers are a minute out and closing. Don't worry; a Super Cobra is pretty quick, but there ain't a helicopter on Earth that can catch an Osprey."

Then the cabin lighting dimmed until the combat illumination was practically nonexistent. Up forward, one of the corpsmen switched on a red penlight for a moment while he checked something, and then switched it off again.

The aircraft heeled left until it was almost on its side; Blake could feel himself hanging in his harness. After that, he had the feeling he was lying on his back, and then they were level again.

Blake thought through the two turns. The first, the gunny said, would be to the east. "Are we headed south?"

"Yes, sir. We're with VMM-263, the Thunder Chickens, based in Al Asad—the few left, supporting the Iraqis. But the border just west of here is too hot to run straight back. So we'll fly to the Gulf, drop down to the deck, and go nap-of-earth into Iraq before we pop up to refuel."

"Refuel?"

"Yes, sir. Al Asad's far enough away we'd be on fumes before we got there. And we're not going back to Al Asad, anyhow. Our orders are to take you to Cyprus—Akrotiri."

Blake nodded. Akrotiri was a Royal Air Force Base, but CIA used it for years to launch and recover U2 flights.

The Osprey banked full left and then full right, then nosed down.

"Cobras getting close?"

"Close enough." The gunnery sergeant reached into his pocket, took out a round tin, and put something in his mouth. Blake had to smile; the evasive maneuvers were enough to make most people airsick, but the gunny was chewing tobacco.

"Captain's not running at full cruise," the Marine said around his chaw. "Lower speed makes us look like a fast helicopter. Keeps the Iranians from ID-ing us; lots of countries have fast helicopters. But we got enough of a head start that we'll outrun 'em easy, even throttled down. And the—"

He stopped talking and put a hand to the side of his helmet, making a better seal against his ear with the headset. "Hang tight: missiles inbound."

The Osprey tilted up; it felt like at least a forty-five degree angle. Looking back, past the Marine manning the deck gun, Blake could see the lights of a small village; it was like he was looking straight down at it. Then the lights dropped away as the pilots nosed over and went full left rudder. The fuselage pulsed six times in rapid succession and, although Blake could see nothing but dark sky through the open rear ramp of the aircraft, he knew they were firing flares and chaff into empty sky beneath them, creating false targets for the air-to-air missiles. He remembered reading something about the V22's engines having infrared suppressors to reduce their heat signature. He hoped he was remembering correctly.

It was a frustrating place for a warrior to be: strapped helplessly into a seat in the bucking, banking aircraft. His firearms were strapped under cargo netting with his rucksack behind the cockpit. And even if Blake had them, the gunner at the rear ramp had not yet fired a shot. The missiles were coming from aircraft too far away to be reached with firearms.

Then, after one more turn, the Osprey settled back into straight and level flight.

Blake assumed the pursuing helicopters had broken off their attack. The gunnery sergeant wasn't saying anything, though. He just took an empty plastic water bottle out of his pocket, spat tobacco into it—in the dim combat lighting, it looked black—and put the bottle back into his pocket.

The Osprey nosed down again, stayed that way for half a minute, and then began to buck up and down, like a roller coaster on a wavy track.

"We've got more visitors; a flight of Saeghehs," the gunnery sergeant said. "Like an F-18, only built here. They're still a good ten minutes out of missile range, so the captain's taken us down to the deck. We have terrain-following capability; puts us in the ground return on their radar, makes us harder to find."

"How close to the ground are we?"

"Trust me, sir; you don't want to know."

Blake could tell, just by the sound of his voice, that the gunnery sergeant was grinning. Turning the bezel on his watch, Blake aligned the luminous hack mark with the minute hand.

For nine minutes, the Osprey bumped and jumped, following every dimple on the ground below. Blake wondered about Pardivari; the ride was unsettling enough without a shattered lower leg. If the docs gave him enough intravenous fluids to offset his blood loss, Blake assumed they also gave Pardivari a sedative, the same as with Nassiri.

The old man looked asleep, his head forward over his attaché. As Blake watched, Nassiri's fingers moved, getting a tighter grip on the briefcase; whatever was in there, Nassiri's instinct to protect it was so great he wasn't about to let go, not even while he was knocked unconscious by the drugs.

The minute hand on Blake's watch was just creeping up to the "10" on the bezel when the Osprey rocked side-to-side, as if hit by a great gust of wind. Half a second later, there was a roar Blake could hear even with the noise-suppression headset on and, through the open rear ramp, he could see four blue-orange ovals of flame, rapidly diminishing in size.

"They're friendly," the gunnery sergeant told Blake. "Air Force F-16s. The Iraqi border juts a tad east here, so the captain slipped us over into Iraqi air space and AWACS dispatched a welcoming party. Iranians won't follow us here, not with our own fighters aloft. They know if they put so much as a wingtip over the border, we'll light 'em up like it's New Year's Eve."

And that was the end of the drama. Still flying nap-of-the-earth, the Osprey made a long, slow, left-hand turn. The bumping and bucking stopped.

"We're over water?" Blake asked.

"Yes, sir. We turn here, reenter over Kuwait, stay low until we're in Iraq and well out of the range of Iranian radar, and then pop up for our refuel. Excuse me, please, sir."

The gunnery sergeant got up and helped the ramp gunner secure the machine gun. Both men stepped back, the gunny operated a control on the bulkhead, and the ramp whined itself closed. The noise level dropped—although not enough to warrant removing the headset—and regular fluorescent lighting came on in the cabin.

Blake blinked at the change in light level. With lights, the cabin looked smaller, not nearly as cavernous; everything was olive-drab green, with stenciled warnings and identification painted on the various pipes and aircraft components.

Both Marines sat opposite him and strapped in again.

"We got about another twenty minutes of bumpy," the gunnery sergeant said. "Then we'll be well out of radar range for any station in Iran and we can go back to a good cruise level. Right now, Iran knows somebody came in and mowed their lawn, but they ain't sure who, and this'll keep it that way."

"They'll accuse us," Blake said.

"Of course, but we'll deny it. These Gulf countries don't want this maniac to have nukes either. So the best we can hope for is that the Iranians consider it was one of them that snatched this fellow. They can't tell from the radar what kind of aircraft we are, so there is no American signature. The flight deck tells us they're picking up dummy radio traffic from the Iraqi air-traffic-control stations in the area, challenging unidentified aircraft. The Iranians monitor Iraqi air traffic control. It may add a little credibility to our denial."

"It may."

The gunny grinned. "Gotta love the politics."

And the rest of the flight was just as the Marine said. There was another twenty minutes of roller-coaster while the Osprey hugged the terrain across Kuwait and southern Iraq, followed by a long, smooth climb to altitude, and ten minutes during which everyone stayed belted in while the Marine aircraft met up with a Navy tanker for a mid-air refueling—an operation Blake knew was nerve-wracking difficult at any time and that he couldn't even fathom doing in the dead of night.

Once they were refueled, the Osprey climbed to its optimal cruising altitude of 15,000 feet and sped up to 350 miles per hour. The Marines and Navy crew members unstrapped and attended to duties around the cabin; the Navy doctor and corpsmen huddled over Pardivari while they removed his air splint, recleaned his wound, replaced his dressing, and monitored his vitals.

Nassiri was still sedated, his mouth open as he slept.

There was nothing for Blake to do. So he tried to do what he always did during down time on a mission, he tried to fall asleep. But his mind would not cooperate. He had but one thought, Zari. He promised a dying man he would bring the man's daughter out of Iran, and he had failed. It was the first failure in his career. But that was not what bothered him most. He could not stop wondering what would become of Zari. Would she be captured, tortured, raped? Would she be killed?

He forced himself to think of the one thing that always comforted him. The woman he loved, the woman who saved his life on a previous mission—Alia.

Chapter Twenty-Three

Blake was back in the wadi, holding the woman close under the blanket, protecting her from the sand and rocks being blasted in by the helicopter as it overflew the dark wadi. Her hand was in the small of his back, drawing him nearer to her trembling body, and her breath on his cheek was sweet and warm. Blake's hand was on her head and as the sound of the helicopter faded, he breathed the clean scent of the woman's hair. It smelled hauntingly familiar.

Somehow, even in the darkness of the night and the shadows of the wadi, Blake could see the woman's eyes as she opened them and they were beautiful, moist with tears.

Blake's eyes were adjusting to the darkness now and he could see her whole face. And as he did, his heart skipped a beat.

It was Alia.

"You can't be here," he told her. "It isn't safe."

She said something in Farsi and, while Blake spoke the language sparingly, he could not follow what she said.

"We have to get you back," he told her. "We need to get you home, to Washington."

Alia shook her head ever so slightly and touched a finger to his lips, shushing him. She cupped her hand to his cheek, her skin warm against his face. Then she pulled the blanket away from them.

The stars above were the brightest Blake ever saw, a spray of white across the blue-black velvet of the desert sky. Alia arose; she was wearing a white linen dress.

"No," Blake told her. "Get down. The helicopter . . . it's coming back. I can hear it."

Alia smiled, shook her head, and began to walk down the center of the wadi.

Blake tried to get up. He could not. Something had him by the shoulders; it was pinning him to the ground. He shook, trying to free himself from its grasp, but he could not break free. And now the sound of the helicopter was getting louder. He could see its marker lights—red and green and white—as it wheeled over the far end of the wadi and came directly toward them.

"Down!"

His voice was drowned in the thump and roar of the Iranian helicopter as it approached. A spotlight came on and stabbed down, a narrow cone of blue-white light, brilliant, turning Alia into a diaphanous shadow between him and the approaching chopper.

"Alia!"

She turned in the light as if dancing slowly on a stage. Arms spread wide, she began to run, away from Blake, and toward the helicopter, and still he was pinned, as if bound by strong restraints to the earth. He fought them, but he could not break free.

Alia was swallowed by the light. Blake could hear her: she was laughing. But she was little more now than the dimmest of shadows in the growing, blue-white light. Now Blake saw one thing more: the yellow-orange starbursts of automatic weapons fire.

Blake tried to shout, but he could not make a sound.

CLAMMY, SHAKEN, BLAKE GASPED awake. He was still in the cabin of the Osprey, but could hear a new whine in the background noise; the nacelles were being tilted to put the rotors overhead, in the hovering position. They were landing.

The white fluorescent lights were still on and two of the Navy medical team members were with Pardivari, taking down his IV bag and getting him ready to be moved, while the third checked Nassiri, who appeared to still be heavily sedated, his head sagging and his mouth partly open. The two Marine flight engineers were up and moving as well; the gun mount was gone from the tail ramp and when the Osprey settled on its landing gear, the gunnery sergeant threw a switch on the bulkhead and the hatch opened in the back. The ramp settling down to meet a tarmac illuminated only by blue taxiway path cones and a distant row of sodium vapor lights.

Two military ambulances pulled up in the darkness outside, and Blake remained seated while they took Pardivari out on a gurney and brought in a wheelchair to fetch Nassiri. He followed them out, getting into the left side of a Land Rover Wolf, driven by a young female corporal, her blonde hair back in a bun.

"Good morning, sir." Her voice sounded like London. "The wing commander asked me to take you to the officers' mess. Fancy a clean-up first?"

Blake looked down at his khaki shirt and patted it; dust flew up in a small cloud. "Thanks. I think that would be in order."

They drove to an outbuilding where, after some directions—"Just inside and first door on your right, sir"—he found a towel, socks, underwear, a jumpsuit, and a shaving kit waiting on a bench outside a bank of lockers. He showered, left his beard untrimmed, brushed his teeth, and put on the jumpsuit, which fit surprisingly well. Then he walked outside, where the same corporal waited.

"Sure I'm dressed properly for the officers' mess?" Blake had eaten with British officers before.

"Quite sure, sir. This hour of the morning, I'm reasonably certain you'll be the only one there."

The corporal was right. The only ones in the mess hall were a steward and a cook, and if either one objected to being called to duty three hours earlier than usual, they didn't show it. Within a minute, Blake had fresh coffee in front of him. Five minutes later, it was butter and scones. Ten minutes after that, it was a full pilot's breakfast of sausage, scrambled eggs, beans, and stewed tomatoes. The steward even found a fresh bottle of Tabasco sauce when Blake requested it. Blake interpreted that as meaning a considerable number of Americans still deployed to and through Akrotiri.

He was allowed to eat his breakfast in peace, but when the steward promised more coffee, it was delivered, not by the steward, but by a slender man in his thirties, dressed in a light blue Tommy Bahamas camp shirt, tan linen trousers, and boat shoes. His sun-bleached hair was just long enough to suggest he was probably not military, and at his temples, thin lines of white implied that he spent much of his time outdoors, wearing sunglasses. He had pale blue eyes and an easy smile and said, "Good morning, lieutenant," even though Blake wore no rank insignia on his jumpsuit.

"Good morning, sir." Blake allowed the man to pour him a fresh cup of coffee. "You're American?"

"Canadian. Grew up in Sarnia, Ontario, served with the Royal Canadian Dragoons, went to school, got my commission, and got tapped by MI6." He produced identification and offered it to Blake. "Which, Amos Phillips tells me, is roughly similar to your own background, although he told me only your rank and not your name and I'll not ask it; although my name, as you see there on the card, is McKay—Patrick McKay."

"Good to meet you, Mr. Mckay." Blake shook McKay's hand and returned his ID. "What can I do for you, sir?"

"The question is the other way around. Amos has asked us to render all possible assistance. His brief said you would be in possession of a Colonel Farrokh Nassiri, whom we have under guard in a secure wing of the hospital, although he still hasn't awakened from the sedative your medical crew gave him. The other fellow is under sedation also. I take it he's the one who went in with you—Shirazi?"

"No, sir. Massoud died from injuries received in the jump. The man with us is a missionary, a former Special Forces sergeant named Hormos Pardivari. He helped get Nassiri out."

"Sorry to hear about Shirazi." McKay wrote something in a small black notebook. "And that makes Pardivari the one I need to talk to you about. The round he took shattered his tibia pretty badly; about the only thing our base hospital could do for him is amputation, but your Navy doctor did a good job of stabilizing him, so we don't think such extreme measures advisable just yet. Our doctors think they can get him stabilized, at least enough to travel up to Landstuhl Regional Medical Center, in Germany, where they're far more experienced in GSW and trauma treatment. So we're outfitting a C17 right now to fly the three of you up to Ramstein Air Base, which is right across the autobahn from Landstuhl. They'll take . . . Pardivari over in an ambulance and you and Nassiri will have a direct flight back to the States. It'll be waiting when you land."

McKay smiled and closed his notebook. "So how else can MI6 be of service to you?"

Blake thought for a moment. "Sir, can you get me a clean notebook computer? I'd need one with a full battery and Microsoft Word installed. That and a USB jump drive?"

"I can do you one better than that. The C17 has 120 outlets and your other transport will have airlines-style power points. I'll pull you a fresh laptop with Office from stores, power cords for both options, and an eight-gigabyte flash drive. Anything else?"

Blake stirred cream and sugar into his cup. "When do we leave, sir?"

McKay nodded at Blake's cup. "Just as soon as you finish that coffee."

THE C-17 GLOBEMASTER III heavy-lift transport is the titan of Air Force jet aircraft. Its cargo cabin is eighteen feet wide, wide enough to accommodate an M1 Abrams main battle tank, and eight-eight feet long, which is long enough to carry four Blackhawk helicopters.

The Globemaster carrying Blake, Nassiri, and Pardivari to Germany was set up for medical transport, with six banks of three stretchers apiece against each side, plus bulkhead seating for twelve at the rear of the aircraft, nearest the load ramp. Blake was belted into one of those seats, a MacBook Pro on his lap.

"Coffee or a juice, sir?"

Blake looked up. The woman, part of the eight-person medical team aboard, had short-cropped red hair and a pleasant face.

"You don't have to wait on me, lieutenant."

"I'm not waiting on you, sir. I'm on my way to the galley to get an orange juice for myself."

Blake smiled. "Then an orange juice for me would be great."

The young woman returned with two small plastic bottles and cracked the top on Blake's before handing it to him.

"Sorry," she said. "I'm used to doing that."

"Well, I appreciate it. And I'm sorry we're taking up your entire airplane for just the three of us."

"Nothing to feel sorry about. We were on our way back from Ramstein when we got the call to divert to Akrotiri. The air crew appreciates the extra flight time and once we get back to Balad in Iraq, this bird is going in for minor overhaul and we all rotate back Stateside. So one extra mission is a good thing, particularly since we've all been told to record this flight as a dead-head—if anybody asks, we're supposed to tell them we went back to pick up urgent medical supplies that came in just after we departed for Iraq."

She smiled and sipped her juice.

"And you're wondering just what the three of us are up to that justifies rearranging Air Force flight schedules?"

"I am wondering." She smiled again. "But that's not why I'm talking to you; I know you can't tell me. I just wanted to stop by because . . . well, if it's important enough to divert a quarter million pounds of airplane, then it's obviously important to our country. And neither you nor your friends came aboard with the standard military paperwork. That puts you off the grid. So I wanted to say, 'Thank you.'"

"'Thank you?' For?"

"For going off the grid." She reached out and took his empty juice bottle. "For taking whatever risks you've taken, or are taking. It's a complicated world. Our country needs guys like you."

"Well . . ." Blake had long since learned to gracefully accept compliments on his work. Ever since college he could talk to pretty girls without becoming tongue-tied. But he hadn't had much practice at doing both at the same time. "Thanks for the juice."

"My pleasure. If you need anything else . . ."—she pointed up—". . . just push the button for the flight attendant."

Blake grinned; there was no overhead button.

He spent the next ninety minutes on the notebook computer, writing up his after-action report, including everything: Shirazi's injury, his revelation that he was Zari's father, his death, Pardivari's appearance and assistance, the details of removing Nassiri from his summer house, the Pasdaran arrival at the Warshowsky compound, Olga's probable capture, the drive up the wadi, the V22 flight and its attack by the Iranian Cobras, and the decision to transport Pardivari to Landstuhl.

Blake went through the report one more time, checking to make sure he'd left out no important detail, ran a spell-check, and saved the document onto a flash drive no larger than a thick stick of gum.

He ejected the drive and zipped it into the chest pocket of his jumpsuit, powered down the computer, closed it up, and returned it to its neoprene case. He took his seatbelt off, stood up, and walked forward, where the stretchers were. Each one had a thin nylon-covered mattress on it, a pillow with a disposable slipcover, and a folded blanket strapped atop it. Some of the stretchers were filled with heavy nylon Pelikan cases, but except for the two occupied by Pardivari and Nassiri, the rest were empty.

"Want to grab a rack?" It was the lieutenant who brought him the juice.

Blake looked at the lieutenant, at the nearest empty stretcher, back at the lieutenant, and laughed.

She had a redhead's tendency to blush easily. "Okay, that came out wrong. But if you want to grab some shut-eye, sir, go right ahead. Just put the lap-belt on over the blanket. The deck's hard; you don't want to roll off onto it."

"Well, thanks. I appreciate that."

Five minutes later, Blake was asleep again.

WHEN BLAKE WOKE, IT was to a light hand on his shoulder, gently shaking him.

It was the redheaded lieutenant.

Blake sat up. "We landing?"

"Soon, sir. But the older gentleman woke up a few minutes ago. I helped him to the lavatory, walked him back and forth a little, and gave him some flurbiprofin; it's nonsteroidal: helps with inflammation and pain, without dulling the senses."

"Thank you." Blake didn't tell her that, until he had Nassiri on a plane headed States-side, he was really hoping to keep the old man's senses dulled.

"Sir, he's asking about someone. Someone named Zari?"

Blake undid the lap-belt and swung out of the stretcher. "I'll talk to him."

He found Nassiri sitting in one of the seats near the rear of the huge cabin. The man was still dressed in the same dusty clothing as when he boarded the Osprey. Blake settled into the next seat.

"How are you feeling? Any pain?"

"A little." Nassiri shrugged. "But better than most days. They gave me something new for it."

"We're taking Hormoz to an American military hospital in Germany. They can care for him there. We will have another plane waiting for us there, to take us to America. We can get you a shower, a change of clothes before we go. You'll feel better." Blake was careful not to say who "we" were.

Nassiri met his gaze. "I cannot find Zari. Where is she?"

Blake looked down at the deck, collecting his words. Then he looked Nassiri in the eye. "She tricked us, Farrokh."

"Tricked? How?"

"She had the medics put you out, for your pain . . ."

Nassiri nodded three times. "Yes. Yes. I know. I remember. What of it?"

"She was worried about Olga. She told me and I thought I'd convinced her there was nothing we could do. But then when you were unconscious, and our backs were turned, she unbuckled and ran out of the aircraft."

Nassiri's eyes narrowed. "And all of you men did nothing? No one went after her?"

"We got a radio call. Iranian gunships were inbound, only a few minutes away. If they caught us on the ground, they would kill us all and then go after her, kill her as well. The only way to keep them from doing that was to take off immediately, draw their attention, get them to follow us . . . and distract them, to keep them from following her. It was close; they got off some missiles. We had to evade."

Nassiri said nothing, his lips set thin.

"Farrokh, sometimes the bravest thing is the wrong thing. If I'd thought we could have gotten her out by running after her, I would have. But I couldn't. There wasn't enough time. I would have been signing her death sentence. You are an air force officer; you know what I'm saying is true."

Nassiri's face softened. He nodded once. Then he put his hand over his face.

Blake stood and walked away. He understood the Middle Eastern culture well enough to know that an older man would not want a younger one to see him weep.

But that was not the only reason he walked.

His mission was to get Nassiri back to the United States. But his promise was he would get Zari out as well.

He thought it through. Had he shaken off the gunnery sergeant's grip, had he run after Zari, and let the Osprey take off without him, he was certain CIA and MI6 would have gotten the old man to Washington. And with him and his training, he could probably have gotten her out of the country.

But his orders said otherwise. And Blake Kershaw was a soldier; he followed orders.

It should have been cut and dry. But it wasn't. He felt he'd failed; failed Massoud and failed Zari. Had it gone the other way, regardless of whether Nassiri got to the CIA or not, Blake would have failed his country.

The big airplane began to bank. There was the distinctive low whirring sound of screw-drives extending the huge jet's flaps.

Blake found a seat well away from Nassiri and strapped in. The lieutenant came and sat next to him.

"Everything okay?"

Blake pointed over at Nassiri. "Can we get my friend a shower in the ready room and find him some clothes his size?"

"Sure. I'll make a call while we're taxiing. Anything else?" She had a very pretty smile.

"No. I think that'll about cover it."

The big airplane tilted ever so slightly nose-high and they heard the chirp of the tires kissing the runway. Twenty seconds later, the jet engines whined in reverse thrust and the C-17 slowed. Less than half a minute after that, they felt the aircraft turning onto the taxiway.

The lieutenant unbuckled her seat belt. "I'll go make that call. And, sir?"

Blake looked up as she stood. "Yes?"

She put her hand on top of his. "I meant what I said. Thank you."

Chapter Twenty-Four

Ulysses S. Grant went to great lengths to avoid allowing another man to see him unclothed. Blake remembered reading that in Civil War history; while there were generals who bathed next to their men in streams as they found them, Grant always had his baths drawn in a canvas tub within an enclosed tent, even at the height of summer, when the practice must have been stifling.

Colonel Farrokh Nassiri appeared to be a man of similar sensitivity. So, after printing out his after-action report and faxing it to Phillips at Langley, Blake changed into the civilian clothes brought to him—jeans, a polo shirt, and running shoes—and then took up station outside the ready-room lavatory to guarantee the old man his privacy.

Nassiri didn't take long. In less than fifteen minutes he emerged, hair still damp, dressed in a white shirt, tan slacks, and a pair of soft brown loafers.

"They'll have breakfast for you on the plane," Blake told him, and the old man simply nodded and followed him out to the tarmac.

The CIA jet was a Gulfstream V, small and white in the predawn light, indistinguishable from any other corporate jet, even on the inside, where the cabin was accented with polished maple, and the seating was cream-colored leather. It came with a crew of four: pilot, first officer, and two cabin attendants, a young man and a young woman whom Blake knew would also be highly trained field agents. He could tell both were armed with pistols in waistband holsters that were supposed to be concealable. His training taught him to look for the small telltale signs of a concealed weapon. In their case, they were either very inexperienced at hiding their weapons or they were not trying to hide them at all. He knew the Agency was not careless.

The Gulfstream was laid out simply: two sets of well-padded, reclining seats facing one another just aft of the cockpit, a sofa facing a long credenza just behind that and, at the back of the cabin, the lavatory, a small galley, and jump seats for the cabin crew to use during takeoff and landing. Nassiri sat facing forward, visibly pleased at the comfort of the seating, his briefcase lying in the seat next to him, and Blake sat opposite, facing him.

"Your colleague, Hormoz," Nassiri asked as they taxied, "he is well? He will recover from his wounds?"

"I hope so, sir," Blake told him. "He wasn't conscious when they offloaded him. Even though they gave him blood in Akrotiri, he looked gray. I spoke to the medical team and they told me his sort of wound is usually highly surviv- able if it's treated right away. But he drove in the dust for three hours after he was shot, he lost a considerable amount of blood, and the bullet took pieces of sheet metal and cloth in with it; enough to start an infection. He's started to run a fever, which is not a good sign; they're giving him IV antibiotics to fight that. The flight surgeon told me, if it was his call, he'd amputate. And even if they do that, it's going to be touch-and-go for a while."

"Your friend is a good man." Nassiri looked out the window at the pink eastern sky. "I am very sorry to have caused him such trouble."

"Colonel, I'm sure he'd do it all over again in a heartbeat. Your motives are good. You're doing the right thing."

Nassiri shook his head. "So much pain, so much turmoil. And for what? For me? I am the one who caused the trouble you try to stop."

"Better you, sir, than someone who would not have second thoughts about it."

The Gulfstream made the turn onto the base of the runway and began accel- erating down the runway. In fewer than twenty-five seconds it rotated—sunk back on its main landing gear and lifted its nose wheel free of the runway— and five seconds later it leapt skyward, retracting its gear as it climbed.

From his rear-facing seat, Blake could easily look out the oval, oversize cabin window and see the Landstuhl hospital across the autobahn from the air base. He closed his eyes.

"You pray for your friend?"

Blake opened his eyes. "I do."

Nassiri opened his briefcase and took out his Farsi Bible. "It says here, in the book that you would call 'Matthew,' that when two or more pray together, the Christ has promised that he will be there with them. Let me join you."

And the two warriors, the old and the young, leaned toward one another and joined hands.

THE GULFSTREAM CLIMBED TO its cruising altitude of 43,000 feet, the rising sun flooding the cabin with light that was first pink, then golden, then brilliant white. Then the pilot turned the aircraft on a course due west, over the Atlantic, and the early morning sunlight crept forward, painting the bulkhead, before disappearing entirely.

The two cabin attendants—both were blonde-haired and blue-eyed and looked enough alike to be brother and sister—came forward, opened a hatch on the cabin wall, and unfolded a table between the two men. Chai tea was served, triangular *sangak* bread sprinkled with sesame seeds was brought on a salver, and then the young woman set a small ceramic soup tureen before Nassiri. She lifted the lid and his eyes lit up.

"*Kaleh pacheh!*" He looked at Blake. "How is this possible?"

Blake grinned. "Landstuhl treats a few Afghani and Iraqi Coalition soldiers whose wounds are too severe for local hospitalization and the medical center maintains a halal kitchen for them. I thought you might want familiar food, at least for this breakfast."

Nassiri shook his head, smiling. "Every weekday evening, when I was a boy, my mother would make kaleh pacheh and my brother and I would have it the next morning, a hot breakfast before we set off for school. For me, it is, ah . . . what's the phrase?"

"Comfort food?"

"Exactly." Nassiri looked over his shoulder, for the cabin attendant. "Where is she? We must have her bring another bowl, so you can try some."

"No, please." Blake shook his head and held up his hand. "I had my breakfast in Akrotiri, while you were asleep. The soup is for you. I'll just have a little sangak."

"You Americans!" Nassiri laughed. "Why is it you become squeamish at the idea of a little sheep's head soup?"

"It's not just the head," Blake said. "It's the lower legs, too. Thus the name *kaleh pacheh*; it means 'sheep's shins;' am I right?"

Nassiri looked surprised. "Then you've had it before?"

"And enjoyed it," Blake told him. "Many times. But this, as I said, is for you. Just for you. Please."

The old colonel tried a spoonful, closed his eyes, and shook his head slowly. "Excellent. Ah, my friend, this brings back memories."

He bent over the bowl, from time to time dipping the bread into the bowl.

"When I was a boy," Nassiri told Blake, "this was how we ate our breakfast, with just the sangak to use as ladles. And afterward, we would drink the rest of the broth. The school I went to was run by Westerners, and they made us use forks and spoons, but when I told my mother about it, she said, 'Do at school as they teach, but I tell you, this very morning, the shah himself is eating his kaleh pacheh with sangak and nothing more.'"

He shook his head at the memory. "But then again, this is a fine, new white shirt and I have people to meet soon, so perhaps I had best use a spoon, eh?"

For the next two or three minutes he ate with gusto, but then he shook his head, his expression grim.

Blake cocked his head. "Is something wrong with the soup?"

"No." Nassiri looked down at the tureen. "The soup is wonderful. But what am I thinking? Here I am, dressed in clean clothes on this fine airplane, and feasting on a warm meal, and my Zari—who is like a daughter to me—is somewhere back there, in the desert. She cannot go home, not to her home or mine, because the Pasdaran will be watching them. And she cannot go to the house of the Jews, because surely they have captured the woman, Olga. So my Zari is alone and cold in the empty desert this morning, while I reminisce over hot soup."

He set his spoon aside and leaned back in his seat, blinking back tears, his weathered face suddenly fragile.

"What," he asked, "have I done?"

He picked up his Bible again, opened it at a place near the back, and put on a pair of reading glasses.

"You're reading Matthew?" Blake asked.

The old man nodded.

"Please, read it aloud."

Nassiri looked up. "You wish me to translate?"

"No. Read it as it is written there. Let me hear how it sounds in Farsi."

"Of course." Nassiri pushed his glasses back on his nose and cleared his throat. As the airplane flew west, away from the rising sun, the small, close cabin was filled with the words of the living God.

Chapter Twenty-Five

Flaps extended, the Gulfstream V descended over Northampton and banked as it passed over Norfolk; looking across the cabin and through the windows on the other side, Blake could look straight down at two Aegis-class cruisers in for refit in the Navy yard. The aircraft came out of its bank and nosed up as it slowed.

Nassiri looked through the window next to him at the waters of the Chesapeake. Then he turned.

"You have fulfilled your mission," he told Blake.

"Nearly."

"By day's end you certainly will have. And you have done well. When you take me to those who will . . . who will interview me, then you will be free of any further responsibility for me."

Blake waited.

"But I have one further thing to ask, my friend," Nassiri told him.

"Ask it."

"Zari," Nassiri told him. "Will you return? Will you find her? Will you take her out of danger and bring her here?"

Blake was silent. He had already made that promise once and he had not kept it.

"If I can," he said, "then I will."

"You can." Nassiri leaned forward. "You must."

Blake said nothing.

"I know," Nassiri said. "You are a soldier, a man at arms. I do not know how well you followed the Farsi, but in the book I read to you just a few hours ago, there was the story of a soldier, a centurion. Your life is as his was, as he explained it to the Christ: 'I am a man under authority, with soldiers under me. I tell this one, "Go," and he goes; and that one, "Come," and he comes.'

And because you are a soldier, my young friend, your life and your time are not your own. You must do as you are ordered. But I will make it easy for you to return to Iran, to find Zari."

Blake studied the other man. "How will you do that?"

"I have information your government needs, and I shall share it."

Blake nodded.

"But I will not share it," Nassiri said, "until my Zari is safe and here with me. I will not share it until you return, and get her out, as well."

Blake could not reply. If he did, it would begin an interview, a negotiation and an interrogation, and doing so was not his mission. He understood from his training that the relationship between the interrogator and the subject had to be carefully cultivated, that in an amicable debrief, the exchange was a delicate dance that had to be conducted according to careful plan. If Blake tried to persuade or sway Nassiri, he knew he could disrupt that plan; disrupt and possibly damage it.

"Please," Nassiri said, "do not misinterpret my intention. I love Zari, but not in the sense that a man loves a woman. She has cared for me. She has led me to the truth. I married once, my friend, when I was young. It was wonderful, and it ended far too soon; my wife died in childbirth. It was the most painful thing I ever experienced, losing my wife and our child, both in one day. I never remarried and never knew the joys of family; not until Zari. She is like the daughter I never had, the family I never had. On this point I am adamant; I will not lose my family again."

Blake studied the man's face. Nassiri's eyes were wet with barely restrained tears.

There was the whine and mechanical clump of the landing gear lowering into place.

"We're getting ready to land," Blake said. "Better check your seat belt; make sure it's snug."

Nassiri gave him a long, silent look and tugged on his belt.

THERE WAS THE BRIEFEST glimpse of the golf course at the edge of the naval air station. Then they touched down and the male attendant brought Blake a note.

"From . . . my superior at Langley," Blake said. "It looks as if we need to have you checked over here by the flight surgeon on base. He says it's just a matter of procedure; a doctor has to examine you in order to continue the prescriptions you're on. Going now will keep you from having to come back to a doctor later."

Nassiri shrugged. "I was a pilot in my youth; I have had my share of experience with flight surgeons, none of them pleasant. Medical examinations are encounters that rob a man of his dignity. But, of course, I can understand the necessity. I suppose another time will not matter to me one way or the other."

The plane rolled to a stop, the door opened, and an armored Humvee was waiting at the bottom of the steep, folding stairs. A second vehicle was behind it. Inside the black sedan were two security personnel in business suits. Blake was not sure whether they were CIA or Naval security, but he knew their task . . . keep the old colonel safe. Nassiri looked around after he got into the vehicle; like most people, he obviously expected the interior to be much larger and did not realized how much room would be taken up by the drivetrain tunnel.

They drove a short distance over to the infirmary, where Blake and Nassiri followed a hospital corpsman to an empty office followed by the armed guards from the sedan. The corpsman had a tablet computer for taking down Nassiri's medical history.

"How much time will you need?" Blake asked him.

"A complete physical, sir? Two hours for the exam. Four hours total, if we do the blood work-up. That's if we expedite everything, which we've been told to do. I can call you a car, get you a ride to the officers' club, and come get you when we're finished, if you like, sir."

"No. I'll wait right here, thank you." Blake looked at Nassiri as he said it, and the old man nodded; he understood Blake would keep watch until the old scientist reached his final destination.

"Whatever you'd like, sir. Please, make yourself comfortable, and, Mr. Nassiri . . ."

"It's 'Colonel Nassiri,'" Blake said.

"I'm very sorry, sir. Colonel, if you'll follow me to the examination room, I'll take a history and get some vitals, and then the commander will see you."

"Let us get this done with." Nassiri patted Blake on the shoulder. "My friend, I will see you just as soon as they are done with their pinching and their probing."

Blake went to the door and watched Nassiri and the corpsman go down the hall to a door with a multicolored placards above it. The security people followed closely behind, not letting Nassiri out of their sight. He'd just gone back to sit behind the desk—it looked like the most comfortable chair in the room—when there was a knock at the door. And when he turned, Amos Phillips was standing at the threshold.

"I was wondering when you'd show up."

"I thought it best not to appear when Nassiri was present." Without comment, Amos handed Blake his Agency identification and key card: the one with the Edward McNamara identity. "In situations such as this, it's better not to introduce extraneous personnel. Which is what I've come to talk to you about; I'd like you to deliver him to his debrief."

"Sure."

"I'll have a Sea Hawk ready to take you when you're all finished here."

"Take us to . . ."

"A safe house in Virginia. It won't take long: an hour and a half, out and back. The pilot knows where he's going."

"Okay." Blake pulled the chair out from behind the desk and held a hand out to it. "We have time for you to sit. He's not coming back for at least two hours."

Phillips looked at his watch. "Want me to run and get you some lunch, first?"

Blake shook his head. "The lab work will take a couple hours after they finish examining Nassiri. If we can find a secure way to do it, I was thinking of taking Farrokh over to the officers' club for something while we wait."

"We've brought people through here before; I think I can arrange something that would work." Phillips ignored the desk chair and settled into the guest chair. "I read the after-action. I was sorry to hear about Massoud."

"He still laid the groundwork. There wouldn't have been a mission without him."

"And Nassiri's assistant: Massoud's daughter. I didn't see that coming."

"Nor did anyone, with the exception of Zari's nominal father. And from what I understand, he's dying . . . he's probably dead by now."

"So Nassiri has no idea."

"He doesn't." Blake rocked forward in his chair. "Nor does Zari. But there's a complication. Nassiri is . . . fond . . . of Zari. He loves her. It's not an affair. Nothing like that. But he feels . . . paternal toward her. Protective."

Phillips rubbed his chin. "And she flew the coop before the Osprey took off, so now he wants us to go back and get her."

"Close." Blake tapped the arm of the chair. "He wants *me* to go back and get her."

"Not going to happen." Phillips scowled. "If we'd known Pasdaran was going to be at that level of alert, that the guard was changing at Nassiri's summer house, we never would have sent you after him in the first place."

"Good thing you did, though. Things appear to be heating up over there. Nassiri is a good man to have in our pocket at a time like this."

"But my point," Phillips told him, "is that we can't in all conscience send you back now. They're not only on alert; they're a nest of hornets, and you, my friend, have strolled on in and whacked 'em with a stick."

Blake clasped his hands atop his head, looked at the ceiling, and then dropped his hands to his lap, meeting Phillips eye-to-eye.

"Amos, I promised Massoud I'd get his daughter out."

Phillips peered at Blake over the top of his glasses. "That was a promise you fulfilled when you got her to that landing zone and put her on the V22."

"No, I didn't promise to get her *to* anything. I promised to get her *out*."

Phillips glanced behind himself, making certain they were alone. "Blake, there's a large and ethical difference between extraction and abduction."

"There is." Blake shrugged and shook his head. "But you could argue that Zari made it possible for us to abduct Nassiri when she had the corpsman put him out. She made it impossible for him to protest . . . impossible for him to resist. And that's essentially the same thing as taking him against his will."

"Blake . . ." Phillips scratched his head. "I feel for you, my friend. I really do. But you don't know where Zari Nourazar is. Your three points of contact over there were her father's house—where the communications came from, Nassiri's house, and the Warshowsky compound. We know the last two are severely compromised and it's a very safe bet that the first is as well. You don't know where to find her, buddy."

"But I know what she's trying to find."

Phillips waited, his eyebrows raised.

"Olga Warshowsky."

"Who the Pasdaran likely have in custody and are not going to let go of anytime soon."

"But if I find her . . . eventually, I find Zari."

Phillips sagged. "You know I can't possibly tell you to do that, Blake. I'm not going to order you back to Iran."

"I know."

Phillips pushed his glasses up. "We have the best man in the business running Nassiri's debrief. He's been doing this all the way back to the Cold War. I'm confident that, within a week, maybe less, he'll know everything Nassiri knows."

"That would solve one problem," Blake said.

Phillips nodded. "One is better than none."

Nassiri emerged exactly two hours after he'd gone into the examination room. The commander conducting the physical made a call to get Blake and Nassiri into a private room in the officers' club, and after a late lunch of roast chicken and a long walk to limber up the old man's arthritis, they came back, sat with the doctor, got no unexpected news, and walked out to the waiting Humvee with a small plastic bag containing eight bottles—enough medication to see Nassiri through the next six months. The security personnel stayed within a few steps of Blake and the old man during the events of the afternoon, even though they were on a secure US Naval base. Blake appreciated the diligence. He understood the Iranians would do anything to get their top nuclear scientist back.

He wondered how good Iranian intelligence was and how long it would take them to know for sure the United States had him. The Osprey extraction, keeping the speed down so it looked like a helicopter and then fleeing over the sea . . . all of these had been done to allow for the possibility that it might have been another Middle Eastern nation, trying to delay the Iranian nuclear program.

Blake doubted the Iranians believed it was anybody in the neighborhood.

The Humvee took them straight out to the flight line, where a UH-60 Seahawk was waiting, its rotors turning. The helicopter looked a lot like a Blackhawk and, in fact, was a variant of the same model, only the Seahawk was equipped with a FLIR turret ahead of its nose, for low-visibility operation.

Inside, the Seahawk was almost identical to the Blackhawks Blake had ridden in, right down to the spring-suspended seats with their shoulder harnesses. He and Nassiri took the outboard seats facing forward, next to the doors, while the two armed security people boarded on the seats facing them and the rear of the helo. The flight engineer checked their harnesses before sliding the door closed.

The takeoff was like a Blackhawk as well, a moment of suspension, followed by a pronounced tilt forward, the springs of the seats squeaking from the movement against the background of the turbine whine. Then they were aloft and gaining altitude, the helicopter turning like a weathervane as the pilot found his heading: west by northwest.

Virginia Beach and the busy tidewater region unreeled far beneath the window on Blake's right. He saw ships in dry dock being attended to by cranes, and farther away, on the Chesapeake, fishing boats and freighters making their way, leaving trails of frosty white wakes on the deep blue water. It was a typical busy day in America, a day when people attended to their industry, when probably not one person in a thousand suspected that, somewhere in the Middle East, a lunatic was getting ready to press the button that would annihilate an entire nation.

After ten minutes of flight, the city began to thin out, the strip malls and neighborhoods and warehouses giving way to fields: corn, soybeans, and the old Virginia staple—tobacco. The houses here were farmhouses, tucked away at the end of long, curving drives, reached by curving roads as they followed the silver threads of rivers and the sinews of hills. There were tobacco barns and henhouses, oftentimes quite distant from the farmhouses, and the riverbanks were crowded with trees.

Half an hour out, Blake saw Richmond on the horizon to his side, the downtown buildings nestled against the banks of the River James. Suburbs cropped up and thinned out again, and then they were back in the country-side. A farmer was pulling a flatbed trailer with a tractor and Blake caught the flash of the western sun on the man's eyeglasses as he looked up at the passing helicopter.

They crossed interstates—I-95 and then I-85—and Blake began to follow their progress more closely, because this was country he knew well.

Sure enough, as he gazed to the left, out Nassiri's window, he saw the open green spaces of Camp Pickett, the Virginia National Guard base, with its build-ings for vehicle maintenance. The pilot altered course to the northwest and Blake recognized the terrain of the battlefield at Sailor's Creek, where Robert E. Lee fought one final battle before accepting the inevitable and surrendering to Ulysses S. Grant. The battlefield was only a few miles from where Blake lived when he was attending college at Hampden-Sydney; he remembered riding his Harley on the same country roads on which Lee's army marched and seeing houses along the way where the farmer owners had never replaced the plank siding, so the homes still bore minié ball scars from nearly a century-and-a-half before.

The Appomattox River wound beneath them and then they were banking over the iron trestles of High Bridge, another antebellum landmark Blake knew well.

Now he knew where they were going. The helicopter followed the old, abandoned, Civil War-era rail right-of-way, and then banked into a pasture with a lake beyond it.

At the edge of the field was a wooden utility pole with a bright orange wind-sock atop it, in the center of the pasture a hundred-foot circle had been finish-cut down to lawn height, and at the edge of the circle an elderly man of medium height, with a beard, was clutching his porkpie hat and his garnet-and-gray warmup jacket in anticipation of the rotor blast. A small John Deere Gator four-by-four was parked just behind him. And next to the old gentle-man was a German shepherd.

Blake smiled as he saw him.

"Amazing," he said aloud. "The old man is still in the game." Blake thought for a moment, wondering how many times the old warrior stood vigil as a helo approached a remote landing zone. Blake did the math: the man he was looking at had to be eighty-eight, his service went back to World World II—the jungles of the China-Burma-India Theater with Merrill's Marauders and he obviously never even considered retirement.

The helicopter settled into the center of the mowed circle, the pilot killing the engines as soon as they'd settled fully onto the landing gear. Blake climbed out of the helicopter and helped Nassiri out. Then the two of them walked to the man and the waiting vehicle.

"Colonel Nassiri," Blake said, "I'd like to introduce you to a very good friend of mine, General Samuel V. Wilson. General Sam, this is Colonel Farrokh Nassiri."

"I have been looking forward to making your acquaintance, Colonel," General Sam said. "Has this young man taken proper care of you?"

"He has done more than that, General." Nassiri smiled, obviously warmed by the old man's Virginia charm.

The German shepherd bumped its head against the Iranian's thigh, and he smiled and scratched the dog behind the ears.

"Max is telling us he's checked you over and you have passed muster, Colonel."

The Iranian gave the dog another scratch. "I am flattered."

General Sam turned to Blake. "Can you stay and join us for supper?"

Blake noticed the general did not use his name—neither his given name nor his cover name. "Thank you, sir, but the helicopter is going to take me straight to Langley; I have a debrief to conduct."

It was a half-truth. His report and his conversation with Phillips was debrief enough. But Blake knew it was important for General Sam's relationship with Nassiri to be one-on-one, with no distractions.

General Sam patted Blake on the shoulder. "He's all business, this one."

The general watched as the flight engineer put Nassiri's overnight bag and his prescription drugs into the back of the Gator and then he turned to the scientist. "Sir, you have had a formidable journey and I have a light supper awaiting us. What do you say we get to that and then we can make you comfortable and let you rest?"

"I would appreciate that, General." Nassiri shook Blake's hand. "Thank you, sir. Perhaps one day I will know your name. For now, I will simply remember you as my friend."

"Take care of yourself, sir."

"I shall." Nassiri kept hold of Blake's hand a moment longer. "Please . . . remember what we discussed."

General Sam and Nassiri got into the Gator and, with a last wave to Blake, the general started the little vehicle and drove toward the lake with Max in hot pursuit. The roof of a cabin showed above the trees. Behind Blake, the pilot brought the Seahawk's turbines up to speed and they caught with a sound halfway between a roar and a whine.

He stepped aboard the helo and strapped in, and they lifted off and headed east, toward Washington.

Chapter Twenty-Six

Straightening her desk, Alia looked again at the e-mail Amos Philips forwarded to her earlier in the day: the CIA deputy station chief in Tel Aviv was out on maternity leave and the person who'd been filling in was called home to Texas to attend to a dying parent. That left three weeks of the deputy station chief's leave to be covered; the station chief asked Amos for a suggestion and Amos suggested Alia.

Sorry I didn't discuss w/you earlier, the note from Amos read. *Was trying to get to a meeting, something not on my calendar. But this would be excellent experience and you wouldn't be gone long. I think you should do it.*

Alia looked at the original e-mail; they needed someone in the post by the end of the week. If she was to take the assignment, she'd have to leave in the morning.

The morning. Blake was still deployed. It left her torn: the Tel Aviv assignment sounded intriguing; it would be her first time back in the Middle East since she left it when she was in her teens. But Blake and she had seen little of one another while he was training to go to Iran and, as far as she knew, his Indonesia assignment would still be coming up. That left her only a couple of months in which to see her fiancé and she was hesitant to shrink that window even further.

Alia leaned back in her chair. For the umpteenth time, she wondered why she allowed herself to fall in love with a man whose identity was destroyed and who was apt to go off to the ends of the earth on a moment's notice. Now she was considering going off to another end of the earth, herself.

Was this relationship really meant to be?

There was a buzz and a click at the outer office door; someone was coming in, using a key card. Yet when Amos left, at mid-morning, he said he would be gone for the day.

Puzzled, Alia rose from her desk and walked into the small outer office. The door swung open.

And the love of her life stepped through.

"Blake!" She covered the space between them in one step, throwing herself into his arms. With both hands, she pulled his face to hers for a kiss.

It was a long kiss and when they came up for air, Blake told her, "If I didn't know better, I'd think you weren't expecting me."

"I wasn't." She kissed him again. "I knew we sent a plane and an aircrew to Europe, but I didn't know they'd returned. I thought you were still in Iran."

She leaned back and looked up. "Did you send us an after-action report?"

"This morning. Before dawn, your time."

Holding his hand as if she was afraid to let him go, Alia pulled Blake into her office and checked her Outlook files. "I don't see that Phil got anything . . . wait. Here it is. He pulled it off the server and put it into his local files. It was about half an hour before I got to the office."

She smiled. "That explains that. You got Nassiri, brought him back safe and sound?"

Blake nodded.

"Fantastic!" Alia studied Blake's face. "But you don't look fantastic. What's troubling you, sweetheart?"

"Maybe," Blake said, "you'd better read the after-action report."

ALIA BROUGHT THE DOCUMENT up on the screen and began reading. When she got to the part about Massoud's death, she looked and said, "Blake . . . I'm so sorry." But he just pointed at the screen and said, "Please—keep reading."

Alia read the report and when she was finished, she looked up.

"You want to go back."

Blake nodded. "Nassiri came here at a cost. I killed six soldiers to get him here. He said he won't talk unless I go back and get Zari."

Alia looked at the screen. "That's not in the report."

"He told me after I filed it. But Amos knows. He met me at Oceana, and I told him."

"What did he say?"

"That the situation is too hot for him to order me back in."

Alia looked at him, the silence so deep she could hear the hushed murmur of the air-conditioning vents.

Blake took a breath. "All, I promised her father. I promised a dying man."

Alia touched her knuckles to her lips, and looked at the report again. "Who's at the safe house? Who's conducting the debrief?"

"General Sam."

Alia's face fell. "Blake, he's good. He was good before you and I were born. Do you honestly think he won't be able to persuade Nassiri to share his information?"

"I'm sure he will, but I don't know how long it will take." Blake sat on the edge of the desk. "Iran was ramping up their military presence around the launch sites. Something's going down, sooner rather than later. I can feel it. And again: I promised her father. I promised the man as he was dying in my arms."

He stood up. "I've got money saved. I'll fly to London, go from there to Istanbul, and then on to Tehran."

"That won't work." Alia's fingers flew over her keyboard. "If Amos saw you, back on American soil, standard procedure is he closed the mission. Your passport won't exist on any system when you try to board a plane or enter a country. It will . . ."

She paused. "That's weird."

"What?"

"Your mission. It's still open. Passport, credit cards, challenge codes. Everything's still operational. In fact, it's flagged to stay open. Amos wouldn't make a mistake like that."

"Maybe it's not a mistake." Blake sat on the desk again, brow furrowed. "Amos never said I couldn't go back. He said he wouldn't order me. Maybe he left the door open so I could still go, but it would remain deniable."

He pushed his hair back from his forehead, thinking.

"No." Blake shook his head. "It doesn't make sense. It's not practical. Amos would never let me go completely black as far as the Agency is concerned. There'd have to be somebody on the ground in the Middle East; someone in the know I could reach out to for comms and support."

"Oh," Alia said. "Wow . . ."

She switched her screen to Outlook and showed him the e-mail Amos forwarded to her. "Date-stamped late this afternoon . . . which would be after he met with you."

Neither of them said a word for a moment, the sound of the air-conditioning seeming to grow louder.

Blake finally broke the silence.

"This is going to be dangerous," he warned Alia. "You're heading to ground-zero: Tel Aviv is the probable target."

"I know." She typed rapidly, moved her mouse to put the arrow on the "Send" button, and clicked it. "But I just accepted."

Blake stared at her. Then she shook his head and smiled.

"You," he said, "are amazing."

"And don't you forget it." She leaned toward him.

"Okay." Blake kissed her. "I still have the passport, the credit cards, and all but ten thousand euros of the money I started with. Can you do me a favor and book me on Comair tonight out of Reagan or Dulles, whichever one works, London first, then whatever change I have to make to connect into Tehran?"

She nodded, settling back into her chair, her fingertips on her keyboard.

Blake stood. "I have to get home and pack: Canadians and Americans are close enough that the clean clothes I have at home will work."

"Weapons?"

"Not this trip. Too many airports. But see what you can Google on Iranian archaeological sites and e-mail me the links to my home account. And one other thing . . ."

Alia looked up, ready to take notes.

He kissed her, again, softly. "I love you."

She held his hands. "I'll do e-tickets. You can go straight from your apartment to the airport. You'd better get moving."

She said it, but her hands were still out, as if to hold him, when he pulled away.

"I love you," she called after him to the closing door.

Chapter Twenty-Seven

OUTSIDE FARMVILLE, VIRGINIA

General Sam's guest room was thoughtfully arranged: a bedroom with a queen-size bed, a walk-in closet, and a sitting area; a bathroom with shower; and an anteroom equipped with a sofa, a desk and chair, and a small table with two chairs near the window. Simple clothing—blue jeans and Dockers, a variety of shirts, and a light Carhardt jacket—had been purchased, all in Farrokh Nassiri's size, and there were writing materials waiting on the desk.

Leather briefcase in hand, Nassiri walked down the short hall to the dining room, where General Sam was laying out the dinner things.

"You do not have to wait on me," Nassiri told him.

The old general smiled. "Normally I have a housekeeper who helps when I have guests. But for a visit such as this, it's best it just be you and me. Mrs. Murphy will still come, but only while we are out. In fact, she made the dinner we are about to enjoy."

Nassiri looked on the wall nearest him, which displayed two certificates. One was for the Army award for valor, the Distinguished Service Cross. He had to walk nearer to read the writing on the second one, and it surprised him. "You are a pastor?"

"I am a preacher." The general set his table with cloth napkins, china so thin it was nearly translucent, and crystal stemware.

"The date is very recent."

"Yes," the general agreed. "My church has offered to ordain me several times—I serve from the pulpit when our pastor is away. And last spring, I accepted. I am a veteran of World War II and the Cold War and president emeritus of a men's college and the sum of those two elements is that my friends tend to congregate around one of two extremes—young men who want marrying and old men who want burying. Ordination grants me a higher degree of function on either occasion."

He laughed as he said it, and Nassiri did as well.

"Please," the general said, pulling back a chair, "join me at table."

After Nassiri was seated—his leather attaché on the floor next to his chair—General Sam took his seat.

"We may not have been stationed in the same places," the general observed, "but our backgrounds appear to be similar."

"I don't know about that," Nassiri said. "I saw your decorations. You served with honor on the field of battle. In my career, at least lately, I have done little more than provide the technology that leads my nation nearer to misery. I imagine that must offend a man of your sensibilities."

"Over the millennia," he told Nassiri, "men have always complained about how technology has robbed battle of its dignity. A century ago it was the machine gun. Half a century before that, it was the rifled musket and the minié ball. When the Spartans made their stand at Thermopylae, they were armed with short swords, shields, and lances, and Xerxes threatened them with the technology of the time. He told them his arrows would be so numerous they would block out the sun, to which one Spartan, Dienekes, had a famous retort."

"I remember," Nassiri said. "He shouted back, 'Excellent! Then we shall fight in the shade.'"

Both men chuckled.

"And the Greeks almost proved Dienekes's bravado to be right," General Sam observed. "Until they were betrayed, they succeeded in holding back Xerxes and his thousands with nothing more than like-minded warriors standing shoulder-to-shoulder with resolve: the classic Grecian defense . . . the phalanx."

"You know, General," Nassiri said with a slight grin. "Xerxes was a Persian: probably an ancient ancestor of mine."

"Oh, yes, Colonel. I am quite aware of that." The general returned the slight grin. "'*Molon labe.*' So perhaps we had best turn to topics other than battle. But first, let me lead us in the blessing."

DINNER WAS EXCELLENT: GRILLED chicken in marinade, sliced thin and plated cold over fresh greens and croutons, French bread with salted butter, and bowls of chilled berries and sliced melon for dessert. It was a light meal, perfect after a long, hard day of traveling.

Over General Sam's protest, Nassiri helped the old man clear the table. When they had finished with that, the general looked down at Nassiri's attaché, still sitting on the floor next to the Iranian scientist's seat.

"The door to your room is equipped with a very serviceable lock," the general said. "But after your journey, I want your sleep to be as restful as it can be. My study is equipped with an excellent Mosler safe my father once owned. It took four men to carry it in there and it is impervious to tampering or fire. May I offer you its use for your valuables?"

Nassiri thought for a moment and then nodded. "Thank you, General Wilson. That is very kind of you."

They went to the study, where General Sam dialed in the combination, opened the safe, and then stepped out of the room.

Nassiri looked into the safe. It contained two handgun cases, portfolios full of what he assumed were stock certificates, velvet jewelry bags, and a tidy stack of banded hundred-dollar bills. He thought about how he had been clutching his attaché all day and it humbled him: this American, who he just met, left him alone with his valuables.

Nassiri set his attaché in the safe. He unbuttoned his shirt pocket and took out the Moleskine notebook. Remembering the media card, he checked the notebook's back pocket.

The card was still there, but so was something else: a folded sheet of paper. He opened it and saw Farsi script.

> *Grandfather, I write this as the plane is coming and I know you will be distressed when you wake and I am not there. Please do not be. My absence is of my own doing and I go only because, were I to go to America with you, I would be haunted for the rest of my life by the knowledge I left Olga behind. Each of us has a task ahead of us. I must go to Olga and save her, and you must go to America and save our people and our country. Please do as you have intended and, if God so wills it, I will see you in America once Olga is out of harm's way. Z.*

Nassiri read the note twice, put it back in the notebook, set the notebook in the safe, closed the door, lifted the handle, and turned the dial. He stepped out into the hall, where the general was waiting.

Nassiri looked General Sam in the eye. "When do we talk?"

The general patted his shoulder. "I want you to rest and in the morning, when you rise, we will have a light breakfast: poached eggs and toast, if that is all right with you. Then I would like to show you the property. The deer come from the woods in early morning and if you fish, there are bass in the lake. After lunch you can rest and read; I know you have brought your Bible. So tomorrow night we can talk. Or the next morning, if you would rather retire early. But right now, the important thing is to rest. Is the room to your complete satisfaction?"

"Yes," Nassiri told him. "It is excellent."

"Then good night, Colonel. I am thoroughly enjoying your company."

Chapter Twenty-Eight

ILAM PROVINCE, IRAN

The large room was arranged with six lights on tripods, all aimed at a single scarred metal chair in the center, and on the chair was Olga Warshowsky. Her sixty-four-year-old body was naked, her ankles taped to the outside of the chair legs, her arms bound behind her with plastic zip-strips, a painful arrangement that forced her to sit only on the forward edge of the chair. She was drenched in sweat, her damp hair stuck to one side of her face. She squinted, trying to discern the man seated at a table beyond the lights.

"Please," she begged the unseen Pasdaran officer. "Cover me."

Captain Rahim Bahmani wanted a cigarette, but he had men in the room with him, and Pasdaran officers were not supposed to use tobacco. It irritated him even more than the obstinate woman in front of him.

"You are right to be ashamed," he told her. "You are ugly. Look at you; you have a body that looks like a goatskin full of rice. Now, again: who took Nassiri?"

"I told you. I do not know."

"They were in your house, woman."

"They broke in, forced their way in. They looked desperate. My husband was not home. They had guns. I feared for my life, for the lives of my people, my servants."

Bahmani looked down at a tablet. It had very few lines written on it.

"We know the girl's name," he said. He read it from the tablet, "Nourazar. Zari Nourazar. Are you sitting here and telling me you have never heard of her?"

"I have heard of her," Olga told him. "It is a small village. I have heard of everyone here. Rumor has it she is a Christian. I am a Jew. We have no use for one another."

"And even less for a Muslim, I imagine. You know, woman, we are talking to people around the village right now. If we find out you are lying, well . . . let me assure you that, long before you die in prison, you will wish you were dead already."

"Please," the woman begged. "Let me up. I need a toilet."

"Toilets are for people who tell me the truth. You are less than a person and less than truthful. Do what you need to right where you are. You could not disgust me more."

Bahmani pushed back from the table, signaled to the doctor, and the two men stepped out into the hall.

"Give her more," he told the doctor.

"She is already on both scopalamine to weaken her resolve and methedrine to keep her awake. The two drugs are not compatible, Rahim. If I give her more of either, she could have a stroke, or a heart attack, or both."

Bahmani blinked. "And I should care about this . . . why?"

The doctor crossed his arms. "The villagers tell us her husband is a powerful businessman. Very powerful. The local police have orders to leave them alone. It is why we do not beat her; she cannot be marked."

"The man is a Jew."

"And that changes nothing. Somehow, he has connections."

Bahmani looked through the small window into the door. The woman appeared to be sobbing and a puddle had formed beneath her on the floor.

"Well, her story hasn't changed. So tell me, doctor: is she telling the truth?"

The doctor looked in as well. "Maybe. But the fact that her story is so consistent . . . that bothers me. Most people will embellish, elaborate, when they retell a true story. But lies? Some people, when they tell a story often enough, can convince themselves they are telling the truth. It's very rare, but it happens."

"Well?" Bahmani took two steps, turned, walked back, became aware he was pacing, and stopped. "Is she one of them?"

"To tell, I would need to run a functional MRI, see her brain reacting as she spoke to us. There is no such equipment anywhere in this province."

"Then give her more drugs."

The doctor raised his hands, dropped them. "I tell you, it's not safe. This is not like that man, the cancer patient. This woman is not all alone; she has family to be considered. And we have been questioning her now for sixteen hours. If you don't let her rest, she'll become catatonic. I'm warning you."

"A little longer." The captain walked back into the room, picked up a bucket of water, stood at the edge of the light, and threw it at the sagging, nude woman. She sat up, gasping from the shock, water dripping from her hair.

"Tell me what I need to know," Bahmani told her. He sat. "Pardivari. Was he at your house?"

"I do not know that name."

"Speak," Bahmani hissed. "If you do not speak soon, then I will cease to be kind."

Chapter Twenty-Nine

Blake Kershaw arrived in Iran as most first-time Western travelers arrive; amazed by the clean, modern, and very nearly state-of-the-art expanse of the airport, twenty miles southwest of the capital.

Unlike most first-time Western travelers, though, Blake was versed in the background of this particular airport. Although ground was first broken on it in 1979, it did not open until twenty-five years later, and even then it was subject to wild political swings: some Iranian-owned commuter airlines refused to land there until the Turkish holding company that ran it was replaced by the managers of Iran Air. Even then, the IRGC invaded and held the airport in its first days, reflecting the government's general paranoia about any part of the country open to the outside world. And soon after Imam Khomeini International—that was what they called it—opened, both the British and the Canadian governments warned their citizens against travel in and out of it, citing fears the runways were not built to accepted international standards and could very likely be prone to sinkholes and collapse.

So the airport in Iran was an elaborate facade, hiding a national infrastructure both inadequate and corrupt.

Still, to Blake's eyes it appeared refreshingly modern, right down to the immigrations officer who ran his Canadian passport through a reader and got the response that it was both genuine and current—which it absolutely was not. He looked at the yellow slip and visa, both of which appeared in order, although only the yellow slip was.

"Mister Walker?" The immigration agent pronounced the last name "wahl-ker."

"That's right." Blake pushed his fake glasses up on his nose. "Actually, it's Doctor Walker. But Mister is fine . . . or, uh, Jeff."

He tried to affect just the right amount of nervousness, because anxiety is common at immigration halls, particularly those in third-world countries; if he appeared too blasé, it could single him out.

"I am sorry, doctor. You are a physician?"

"Oh, no." Blake pushed his glasses up again. "I am a professor at McMaster. Anthropology."

"I see. And you are here, professor, on business, or on pleasure?"

"Business. I'm here on business."

The agent made a note and looked up. "And what is the nature of your business?"

"I am here on behalf of UNESCO, consulting on an archaeological excavation."

"Ah," the agent smiled for the first time. "Persepolis, yes?"

"No." Blake shook his head. "The only work being done with Persepolis is in laboratories; that site is completely excavated. I'm here for Tappeh Sialk, the World Heritage Site. The government has requested UNESCO's help in stabilizing the resource."

He deliberately fumbled and opened the leather, courier-style bag he was carrying. "Would you like to see the letter from UNESCO?"

"No, professor," the immigrations agent said. "That is quite all right." Which was what Blake expected him to say; the bag, in fact, contained no such letter.

The agent stamped Blake's passport, scribbled in a date in day/month/year order that showed his visa valid for six months, and pointed to the doorway leading to customs, an action entirely unnecessary, because it was the only exit in the hall.

The customs agent was considerably less cordial. A burly man with pock-marked skin showing above his beard, he said something in Farsi, and then in Arabic, and when Blake pretended to understand neither, he repeated the command in English: "Your bags. Open them. All of them."

Blake complied and the customs officer immediately fixed, as Blake had known he would, on the large bag containing a construction-size stadia rod, a transit and tripod, and a laser rangefinder.

The customs officer picked up the rangefinder, uncapped it, and looked through it. "Is camera? Video?"

"No. It's a rangefinder. For measuring distance."

"How does it work?"

"With a laser."

"No." The customs agent set the instrument aside. "No laser."

He began to go through the rest of the bag.

"But I need that," Blake told him, feigning concern. "It is for my work. I must have it to measure the site. I am an archaeologist."

The customs agent shook his head. "Is laser. Not allowed."

"But it's not harmful. It just measures things. Like from here to the wall."

The customs agent crossed his arms. He leaned forward. "One hundred dollars."

Blake blinked, pretending to be surprised. "I beg your pardon?"

"To bring the laser into Iran," the agent said. "Is one hundred dollars."

"Oh." Blake brought out a wallet. "Of course. Is Canadian okay?"

The customs agent huffed and peered down into the wallet. "Euro, then. One hundred euro."

Blake opened the wallet wider, hesitated, and the agent plucked a hundred-euro note from it. "Is good. You can go."

The deflection worked exactly as Blake knew it would. Focused on the rangefinder—which was technically legal to own in Iran, but obscure enough to demand the formal bribe known as *baksheesh*—the customs agent did not check either of Blake's other two bags, including the one with fifty thousand euros stuffed into the toes of a pair of running shoes.

Blake exited the hall, scanned the ragtag band of seedy men in ill-fitting suits standing there, found the one with the hand-lettered cardboard displaying, "WALKER," and raised his hand, walking over to meet the Iranian, who smiled.

ALIA, WHO GREW UP in Egypt, knew as they were hastily arranging the trip that renting a car, in the sense one rents a car on most business trips, was essentially impossible in most Middle Eastern countries. One can hire a car, but it invariably comes with a driver.

For most travelers, that is not an issue. In the Middle East, the daily cost of a car, with driver, is far less than one would pay for a rental car in most

Western nations, and the driver will be familiar with the area, as well as with local road etiquette which, in the case of Iran, is essentially nonexistent.

But for Blake, an Iranian national at the wheel wouldn't work. And because the mission needed to be deniable, Alia couldn't use any of the few dependable local assets CIA had in Iran. So she did the logical alternative.

She bought him a car.

It turned out to be extremely simple to do. She went to the Web site of Pars Khodro, the company that manufactures Nissans under license in Iran; the site was all in Farsi and Arabic, but Alia, fluent in both languages, quickly navigated to the company's dealer list. She located a dealer in Iran and telephoning through a Canadian-prefixed number, claimed to be from a Toronto travel company specializing in Middle Eastern business travel. Speaking in Arabic, she told the dealer her client was foolish enough to think he had purchased a car from a broker, but the broker turned out to be fraudulent—a crime so common in Iran it was laughable.

Her client would be arriving within a day, she told the dealer, and he needed a vehicle when he arrived.

The dealer did what Alia expected, claiming his stock was all sold, but that she could have a new Nissan Roniz—the local version of the Xterra—for only twice the already inflated going price.

Alia, long accustomed to haggling, promised future business, and eventually talked the dealer down to only one million rials—about one hundred Canadian dollars—over the retail price, agreed to wire the money from Banque du Canada, and arranged for an airport pickup, to boot.

And that was the smiling Iranian.

"I am Mister Farid," he said, smiling, taking Blake's bags. "I will drive you to your car."

THE DEALERSHIP TURNED OUT to be a construction-style trailer on a razor-wire fenced lot near the outskirts of Tehran. A mechanic had a sedan up on a portable lift next to the trailer and two dozen vehicles were parked inches apart at the back of the lot, so close that only the door of the outermost would open, which Blake assumed was a precaution against theft.

The Nissan Roniz SUV was sitting in front of the trailer. It still had the white protective plastic film on its hood and fenders. The seats inside were covered in plastic, there were cardboard mats on the floor, and a white block of Styrofoam protruded from the space where the radio was supposed to go.

"Professor Walker!" The man who came out of the trailer was wearing a necktie with a knot as big as his fist. "You are a fortunate man. We have for you a new Roniz."

Blake shook his hand. "Why is there plastic all over it?"

"So you can see the newness!" The man handed Blake a key. "Please. Inspect your car. We are very honest."

Blake got in, turned the key, and started it. Then he looked at the dealer. "The odometer says it already has 10,000 kilometers on it."

"Yes!" The dealer smiled. "Of course. I have driven it myself."

"But my university paid for a new car." Blake didn't care, but he knew the professor he was masquerading as would.

"Is new!" The dealer pointed at the plastic film.

"It is used. Someone has driven it 10,000 kilometers." He got out and looked at the tires. "These are worn."

"Aha. . ." The dealer nodded. "My brother, a Nissan made in Iran is not the same as a Nissan made in Canada. Here, we drive a little, fix a little, drive a little, fix a lot . . . all the fixing on this one is done. It is better than new! Trust me. You are very, very fortunate here. We are very, very honest."

Blake looked at him, hands on his hips, and finally nodded. "All right. Can someone take all the plastic off?"

"But of course!" The dealer barked orders in Farsi at the mechanic, who left the sedan on the lift and began pulling film from the SUV. Then the dealer turned to Blake. "Come! I have coffee. And the papers to sign."

The papers turned out to be only two. Then the dealer produced a third. "And for the number plate, the registration, of course it is ten million rial."

Blake had never licensed a car in Iran, but a thousand dollars American seemed steep to him. And again he reacted as his legend would.

"My university agreed on a price. They wired you the money. It was supposed to be everything."

"It is only ten million." The dealer cocked his head and smiled. "For a car, ready in a day, it is not bad, no?"

"Tell you what." Blake leaned close. "The rental for you driving my car is one thousand rials a kilometer. Only ten million. Then we are all square and I don't have to tell my university and their travel agency what you did."

The dealer hunched a bit, apparently trying to figure out what "all square" meant. Then he smiled. "But of course. We wish you to be happy. We are honest here. Very, very honest."

TEN MINUTES LATER, BLAKE stopped the Nissan at the side of the road, put his iPhone on the dash, where it had a view of the sky, and activated the GPS.

It took it a while to acquire the satellites. And as it did, Blake heard the thunder of rotors.

He got out of the Nissan and looked at the sky. Three tandem-rotor helicopters—they looked to be CH-47s, Chinooks in desert camouflage—were passing to his right, northeast to southwest, climbing as they flew.

They were heading in the same direction as him. He wondered if they were headed the same place. It was possible. It happened the last time, and it wasn't good.

The screen on the iPhone changed. It fixed its location and he tapped in a destination: Ilam province. The screen changed again, zooming out, and showing him a route.

Blake put the little SUV in gear. He had several hours of driving ahead and he was tired of the college professor masquerade.

It was time to get down to business.

Chapter Thirty

Major Zudi Maberi watched the three CH-47s, the second flight of the day, recede toward the southwest. Like all the Chinooks in service in the Iranian military, they dated back to the time of the shah. And like all of the Chinooks in service in the Iranian military, they were kept flying by reverse-engineering: like Soviet Russia during and just after the Second World War, Iran generally preferred stealing technology to developing it—or persuading others to develop it for them.

It was a hallmark of a regime that operated on the principles of sloth and entitlement. Iran was sitting on an ocean of crude oil: more oil than Iraq, and more oil than Kuwait. The life expectancy of its reserves was more than a century—enough to outlast anyone in the government and enough to outlast their children.

That removed any need for ingenuity. Ahmadinejad and his ministers knew they could use oil money to hire virtually any expertise they desired and the promise of oil to coerce other nations to cooperate with them.

Then again, at twenty-nine years of age, Zudi Maberi would not have a major's *ghope* on his shoulder, were it not for Iran's dependence on imported technology. And the tailored uniform he wore would not be that of the Quds Force: the most elite unit of the Iranian military, used by Ahmadinejad in much the same way Hitler used the Waffen-SS.

Maberi knew it was a fact that did not sit well with the regular Artesh officer next to him. And Maberi did not care.

"The helicopters are clear," he told the other man. He said it in Arabic, rather than Farsi. "Bring in your trucks."

"Brother," the other said. His Arabic was halting and unpolished. "That sounded suspiciously like an order. We are the same rank."

"Major," Maberi replied, "you received your ghope two years after I received mine. And you are what? Forty-five? It is quite likely to be the last ghope you receive. So yes, Major, that was an order. Bring in your trucks. And do it now; I am on a schedule."

The other man reddened and stomped off. But within three minutes, heavy-duty military trucks were arriving at the open rear ramp of the huge Russian IL-76 jet transport sitting on the tarmac.

A forklift began offloading pallets of metal cases into the trucks. Maberi paid them little mind; he had an entire team of Quds Force enlisted men, plus the seven-man Russian flight crew, to attend to that. His attention was fixed on the two men on the observation deck at the base of the control tower. One wore a Quds Force general's uniform. The other wore a light-colored suit, but no tie, and a sparse beard. Even at a distance, Maberi recognized him.

Mahmoud Ahmadinejad.

The two men were watching the unloading process and making no attempt to disguise it. Maberi considered giving them a wave, or even a salute. He did neither. He just watched them and, after a minute, Ahmadinejad walked off to his waiting cohort, and the general took a call on his cell phone. Then the senior officer started down the exterior stairs to the deck.

Maberi watched the general get into a KM410, the Iranian knockoff of the old military Jeep. The driver and the general exchanged words, and Maberi was not surprised when the vehicle began to head his way.

He saluted as the general got out and held the salute until it was returned.

"Zudi," the general said in Farsi. "You had a pleasant flight?"

"And successful, sir." For the general, Maberi used the language of his childhood: Farsi, which was every bit as good as his Arabic. "Everything arrived in perfect condition; the guidance systems and the detonators."

"The president is very impressed that you will be able to accomplish this upgrade without removing the missiles from their launch platforms."

"The Shahab 3 is designed so it can be worked on in the field. They are a very robust system; our bunkers are needed to protect them from conventional weapons, not the elements. The cluster warhead is easily removed and we already have the nuclear warheads built from a Russian design under their engineers' supervision in place in the field, ready to be lifted on. All we needed for the warheads from Russia were the detonators."

The general smiled and shook his head. "I am still amazed we were able to bring them in. The Americans have been very . . . obstructive."

"That uproar was over completed missiles. You show a picture of them on television and people are easily outraged. The detonators don't look so obviously lethal. And the guidance systems look like nothing; they look like something you'd find in your computer."

The general scowled. "I understand the detonators. We have the enriched uranium, thanks to our facilities at Fordow, and the Korean team we brought in was able to make the warheads here, but not the detonators. But why change the guidance system? I thought we already had a system accurate to within 150 meters."

"It is, when it works." Maberi rubbed his chin and felt the unfamiliar growth of beard, something he had to start before returning to Iran. "Our Shahab 3 design is an adaptation of an older Korean missile. We have upgraded it several times, but the reliability of the guidance system has been a continuous issue; you're as apt to hit Tehran as Tel Aviv. With our friends in Russia, we've adapted one of their designs—very rugged and very reliable. The accuracy falls off to about 500 meters, but with a nuclear warhead, that's quite acceptable. And it really adds no time to upgrade the guidance system. It sits just beneath the warhead, which we're changing anyhow."

"Well . . ." The general watched the forklift load a pallet onto a truck. "It's your field. You should know."

He glanced sideways at Maberi. "I got a call from an Artesh colleague. Apparently the major working with you here feels insulted."

"He should." Maberi smiled. "Were I forced to accept a post in Artesh, rather than Quds Force, I would feel genuinely insulted as well."

The general shook his head slightly. "Zudi, you have spent most of the last nine years in Russia. That is almost a third of your life. You know how Iranians feel about foreigners."

"I am Iranian." Maberi glowered as he said it. "I was born in this very city. Who has said otherwise?"

"No one has. And the president himself recommended your last promotion. But treat them like your countrymen, Zudi. We are all on the same side."

"Yes, sir." Maberi almost said it under his breath.

The general watched another pallet go onto a truck. "You have been briefed about Nassiri?"

"I have." Maberi blinked and looked the general in the eye. "I cannot believe it was a defection. It was he who facilitated the alliance with the Koreans. Without him, we would not be where we are today. He must have been taken."

"His assistant, Zari Nourazar . . . I understand she was quite a beauty."

"I never met her." Maberi watched the truck drive away as another came to take its place. "But Nassiri would not betray his country for a woman. I worked with the man. It was four years ago, but I worked with him. He is a hero of the revolution."

"Perhaps you are correct, but he is gone and with him missing, our state of readiness and the current locations of our active launchers is seriously compromised. I understand the usual time to accomplish these upgrades is two weeks. Is that correct, Zudi?"

"It is, sir. The work itself is fairly simple, but there is calibration that has to be done and all of the electronics must be thoroughly tested."

"We need them ready in 144 hours, Zudi. Can you do that?"

"Six days?" Maberi removed his Quds Force beret, ran his hand back though his thick, dark hair, and replaced the beret. "Yes. At least at the primary sites, the six in the Zagros Mountains. I can redeploy the teams headed for the outlying sites, send them to the Zagros, have the men work around the clock in shifts. I'll catch a helicopter to Tactical Air Base 28, in Ilam, so I can supervise. But trust me; it can be done. My men were all trained in Russia; they know their tasks. I can have six missiles converted and ready and the other six we brought—I won't be able to convert them to the nuclear munitions, but the guidance upgrade can still be accomplished."

"Six is enough." The general's face was suddenly somber. "Make it so. The president wants to use these missiles before we are permanently denied the ability to do so. We launch in one week, at midday."

Chapter Thirty-One

OUTSIDE FARMVILLE, VIRGINIA

The two old warriors sat beside each other on the second-story porch of General Sam's log cabin. Bullfrogs were beginning their late afternoon cacophony. It blended with the sounds of the crickets to create what seemed to Farrokh Nassiri's ears an exquisite music, a sort of natural symphony.

The lake before them was perfectly calm except for the occasional bass braking the surface in pursuit of a dragonfly, or a small bullfrog making the fatal mistake of trying to cross through the big bass's territory. The old Iranian watched it all and thought of Zari . . . wondered where she was and what she was seeing. He wondered if she was safe.

General Sam broke the silence. "My friend, how about a ride around the lake and up through the woods? This time of day brings the fauna out; deer, and fox, and woodchucks. It will do you good and I can tell you a bit more about the Battle of Sailor's Creek. It was a Civil War battle fought on this very spot. I don't get many visitors here since the Cold War ended, so my storytelling skills could use a little polish. Would you allow me to practice them on you?"

The Iranian looked silently at the general for a moment as if trying to force his mind to focus on what he had just been asked to do. Then he smiled and responded.

"Yes, my friend. That would be a nice way to spend the remaining hour . . . before dark consumes this lovely Virginia woods."

"Good. I'll bring the Gator up straight away."

GENERAL SAM WALKED CAREFULLY down the steps to the porch, taking care to hold onto the handrail. He followed a path of paving stones and disappeared around the corner of the house. Less than three minutes later, he was at the bottom of the steps, the little John Deere's engine growling at idle.

"Max and I await your company, if you are not afraid to ride with an old driver," General Sam quipped. "I'll warn you, though. I have been known to occasionally get this thing stuck in the low places."

The Iranian scientist moved to the steps and, like the general, held the handrails as he negotiated each step to the awaiting vehicle. He seated himself in the passenger seat and said nothing. The general eased it into gear and they started down the path around the lake. Max, the German shepherd, trotted along beside as if this were the highlight of his day.

As they neared the far side of the lake, a small flock of a half dozen turkeys scrambled across the trail. They flew off through the woods as the Gator got close.

Nassiri shook his head. "What magnificent birds."

"We are in accord," the general said. "Benjamin Franklin thought the turkey had the perfect character to be America's national bird."

The Iranian scientist nodded. He didn't reply.

They rode a little farther and Max took the lead as if to say, "You old guys are too slow." A deer jumped from hiding and Max gave chase.

Nassiri followed him with his eyes. "Will he come back?"

"Oh, yes." The general chuckled. "He is just showing off for you."

They sat for a moment awaiting Max's return. General Sam leaned forward on the Gator's wheel.

"I was in Iran during the time of the shah," he said. "I spent several weeks there when I was doing some work for the Department of Defense. I enjoyed my time there, but I have not been back."

"So you know my country." Nassiri's face broke into a smile. "Where did you go?"

"Oh, I was in Tehran most of the time, but I spent a couple of days out at Merhebad Airbase. I was there to discuss the future of our intelligence cooperation with the shah's government. Your country was a key region for collection against the Soviets. In fact, my friend, your country was, for many years, the closest ally the US had in the region. Did you know Iran has voted with the United States in UN votes more than nearly any country in the world? I am saddened by what the current leadership has done to Iran."

"Yes." Nassiri nodded slowly. " Yes, you are quite correct. It is sad what has happened in Iran since the return of the Ayatollah Khomeini in 1979. He was supposed to be the savior of our people and our culture. But he became a brutal dictator who abused and enslaved the masses. Most of the population there now lives in fear. And today his disciples want to spread their sharia law across the globe and to destroy Israel. They must be stopped."

He paused briefly and stared for a moment into the open meadow next to the Gator and then turned back to General Sam.

"I know your government needs the information I have in order to do just that: stop them. But I cannot contribute to the death of my own daughter and that is what my Zari is to me: a daughter. If you fire missiles or drop bombs, the places where that will be done is too close to where I believe she is hiding."

General Sam nodded and patted the steering wheel.

"Colonel, you are a man of honor and I understand. I believe there is an effort underway right now to see that your Zari is reunited with you. If my hunch is correct, the man who has gone to save her is the best we have. After all, he brought you here against the odds."

"Then it will all be for the best," Nassiri said.

"Then it shall."

Chapter Thirty-Two

Thirsty. Zari was so thirsty. The roof of her mouth felt leathery, her tongue thick. She had a headache from it and from time to time she became dizzy.

She had been living in the Land Cruiser, hiding in the wadi during the day, because a woman at the wheel of a car would draw too much attention in daylight. At night, she drove enough to see her father's house was still occupied by Pasdaran and that the road leading to Nassiri's summer home was practically an armed camp.

But the Warshowsky compound, despite its gate being shut, was dark. At least it was dark on the night after their escape, when she finally gathered the nerve to drive by it.

Now it was the second night and she had found no water in the wadi, not even when she scraped in the earth. Her thinking dulled. She stumbled when she walked more than a few feet. And the Land Cruiser was down to its last few liters of fuel. So she drove to the back of the Warshowsky compound and crept to the back gate.

It was locked.

Zari stifled a moan. She needed water. She forced herself to think.

Of course. When she and Nadia were girls, when they used to sneak out in the evening, they always hid a key.

Where? Where did they hide it?

Zari knew and she did not know. It was as if the thirst robbed her of some of her senses. She leaned against the wall next to the gate, keeping herself on her feet. She prayed and she looked to the stars as she did.

Then she saw the lintel.

That was it. The lintel over the gate was a beam of thick, heavy wood, and Nadia found a crack in it, just big enough to hide a key.

Raising herself on her toes, Zari felt in the dark and found it, a rounded bit of metal that felt like the edge of a coin. She worked it back and forth until it loosened and then she drew it out. The key.

Praying the Warshowskys had not changed the lock in all those years, Zari felt for the lock and put the key in. She tried to turn it, but it would not budge.

She did not weep because she had no tears. Her body was consuming every bit of moisture within it. She tried turning the key the other way. The lock resisted for a moment, then it opened.

Moaning in a combination of joy and the pain of dehydration, Zari pushed the gate open and stumbled the few feet to the door leading to the secret basement room. It was unlocked and she made her way down the steps in the dark, one step at a time, felt her way in the dark and found the door to the bathroom. Her hands fell upon the tap in the sink, and she turned it. Water, cool and fresh, splashed in the darkened sink and Zari lowered her face to it and splashed it on her dusty lips. Pushing her hair out of the way, she drank, each swallow returning life to her parched body.

ONE HOUR LATER, ZARI had bathed. She was still afraid to turn on any of the room lights, for fear of calling attention to the compound, but by the light of a small candle, she made her way to the room that had once been Nadia's.

Zari was banking on the fact that Olga was sentimental, and she banked correctly. Nadia's mother had saved her clothes; they were no longer in the closet, but they were boxed away in cedar boxes in her room, and Nadia and Zari had always been the same size. She found a blouse and a skirt, and put them on.

With her thirst slaked, food was the next order of business for Zari. She found her way to the big main house's kitchen, opened the refrigerator, fumbled to find the switch that turned the light back off, and used her candle to select what was left of a round of roast beef and carry it to the big wooden kitchen table.

She found a butcher's knife and carved off a slice of beef, rolling it and eating it cold, just as it was. It was sprinkled with cracked peppercorns and there was horseradish on the crust, and she was certain she had never tasted anything better. She sliced off a second thin slice and rolled and ate it cold as well.

Zari was just carving a third slice when she heard it; the creak of the wood floor underfoot.

First she froze, feeling the hair rise on the back of her neck, feeling dizzy, her stomach tight and queasy. She grabbed the knife, peering into the shadows from whence the sound came. Then she pinched the wick of the candle, and pushed silently back from the table.

Holding the butcher's knife before her like a sword, Zari squatted, turning first one way and then the other. She imagined Pasdaran closing in on her, the grasp of huge, hairy hands on her wrists, her ankles, her neck. She imagined a rifle aimed at her in the dark.

Summoning her courage, she spoke, in Farsi: "Who is it?"

No one answered.

"I have a gun," she lied. "I'll use it."

Still no answer.

"Olga?" Zari asked hopefully.

"Miss Zari?" It was an old man's voice: Farsi, but with a Russian accent.

A small flashlight came on in the hallway leading to the kitchen. Zari hissed and pointed her knife at it, but the man aimed the flashlight at himself and the old woman at his side.

The knife drooped from Zari's hands.

"Nikolai," she said. "Kristina."

Zari began to weep tears of relief. She knew these people from her girlhood, from her visits with Nadia.

The old man and woman were the Warshowskys' housekeepers. They came with the family from Russia as teenagers and kept the house and its grounds for three generations of family. Now they were old, and mostly they oversaw Iranians that they hired from the village, but they lived at the compound; it was their home as much as it was the Warshowskys.

Zari put her hand out to her side. The room began to spin around her. She heard footsteps coming toward her and felt hands, old but strong, catching her as she fell.

WHEN ZARI AWOKE, SHE was in the basement room, where a table lamp cast a roomful of light.

"It is all right," the woman, Kristina, said to her in Farsi. "This room has no windows. It was built for times such as this. Rest. You are exhausted."

"Olga," Zari said. "Is she here as well?"

Kristina shook her head. "No, child. She is not."

Zari tried to sit up. She became dizzy again and allowed Kristina to push her back to the pillow.

"The Pasdaran took Mrs. Olga," Nikolai, the old man, told her. "We were in town, buying salt and flour, and we saw the trucks here from the road so we drove by. We hid in the village with a family that works for us and I drove by every few hours until I saw that the Pasdaran had gone. We came here, but first we talked to the people in town. They told us someone saw the soldiers taking Mrs. Olga into the old school, that they have her there. So we came here, closed and locked the gates, and we dare not show a light near the windows."

Zari raised her head. "How many Pasdaran?"

"Twenty or thirty," Nikolai said. "Too many, dear child. That is why we are here. There is nothing we can do. There is nothing you can do. We cannot save her."

Chapter Thirty-Three

OUTSIDE FARMVILLE, VIRGINIA

The bald eagle soared a hundred feet above the circle of the woods-fringed lake, banked, and wheeled about. It folded its wings against its body and dropped like a white-headed bullet. Then, just when it appeared certain to crash into the waters of the lake, it opened its wings, flared, flipped its yellow talons forward through the surface, and came up with a small bass. Turning the fish head-forward for better aerodynamics, the great bird picked up its tempo and flapped heavily for the sky.

"Magnificent!" Farrokh Nassiri watched the eagle as it disappeared over the trees on the far side of the lake. "And this is the eagle that prevailed over your beloved wild turkey to become America's national bird. Is that correct?"

"It is." General Sam Wilson chuckled as he said it. "As you can see, both species have their merits. The turkey is practical. The bald eagle . . . awe-inspiring."

"And awe won out?"

"Doesn't it always?"

Now it was Nassiri's turn to laugh. But his laughter died away quickly. He turned on the seat of the small, utilitarian, off-road vehicle, and looked at his host.

"General, I dreamed last night of my Zari . . . in Iran."

The general said nothing, listening.

"Zari is a generous person," Nassiri said. "Perhaps it is her faith; perhaps it is how she was born. Perhaps it is both. I have never known her to be selfish."

"She sounds," said General Sam, "like a fine young woman."

"She is." Nassiri nodded. "And if she knew what I have been doing, keeping my information away from you, I know what she would say of that. She would say I am being selfish."

General Sam examined the sky above the lake. It was blue and cloudless.

"What of you, my friend?" He did not look at Nassiri as he asked it. "What do you say?"

Nassiri sighed.

"I say . . ." His voice was barely a whisper. "I say it is time for us to leave this beautiful lake to the eagle and go back to your house. In your safe I have some materials and I have need of them."

THE GENERAL DIALED THE combination on the heavy old Mosler safe and turned the handle down, releasing the bolts.

"There you are, Colonel." The general moved to the doorway. "I'll just step outside and give you some privacy."

The Iranian nodded his thanks and the heavy oaken door clicked shut.

Nassiri slid the leather portfolio out, then retrieved the small, black Moleskine notebook. He slipped the elastic band off the cover and opened it, flipping pages all the way to the pocket in the back. He took the slip of paper out, shook his head when he recognized Zari's handwriting, and read the brief note twice. Then he shook the SD card out into the palm of his hand, secured the elastic band around the cover of the pocket-size notebook, closed and locked the safe, picked up his materials, and opened the office door.

He found General Sam in the kitchen, making coffee.

"General," Nassiri said. "This is a beautiful home, with splendid country around it, and you have been a gracious host."

The general spooned coffee into a filter. "I trust, Colonel, your visit here is only beginning."

"It will not be necessary, sir. Everything you are looking for is here."

Nassiri put the portfolio and the SD card on the kitchen table.

"In the portfolio," he said, "are maps, site schematics, spreadsheets detailing the fortification of launch sites, complete plans for our Shahab 3 missile, including the latest upgrades, and a thorough down-to-the-minute timetable for the upgrade protocol. The SD card is the high-capacity version: thirty-two gigabytes. It contains everything I just described to you, in digital form."

General Sam picked up the SD card. It was smaller than a postage stamp and weighed about the same as a business card. He looked up at Nassiri. "Would you mind if I copied this?"

"It is my gift to you, sir. It is yours to do with as you will. I have no further need of it."

"Thank you, sir." General Sam put the card back on top of the leather portfolio. He poured a cup of coffee for each of them. "There's cream and sugar here. Why don't you make your coffee as you like it and then we can retire into my study?"

Nassiri smiled. "You are a wise man, General."

"I am complimented. Why do you say that?"

"Because this . . ."—Nassiri patted the leather portfolio—". . . could be a ruse, disinformation to make you think Iran is at a greater state of readiness than she actually is. It could be a feint, to convince America and Israel to make a first strike, which would incite anger among Iran's Middle Eastern neighbors. And by speaking with me, you hope to determine what I have here: a fabrication or genuine intelligence."

General Sam added a little milk to his own coffee. He looked up.

"Yes, Colonel," he said, "I have a responsibility to my country and that is exactly what I hope to do. Why don't you gather up your materials and go make yourself comfortable? I'll put some of this coffee into a carafe and join you momentarily."

General Sam ran hot water into an insulated, stainless-steel carafe, and set it aside so the water would warm it and help it keep its temperature longer. The cabin was built so the bedrooms and the kitchen all faced east, toward the lake, and the old soldier looked out the window.

His cabin was at approximately 37 degrees north in latitude. He tried to remember the latitude of Tehran—it was about 35 degrees north, if he recalled correctly. And some parts of Iran extended even farther north than Virginia. So by looking due east, there was a good chance he was looking in the direction of his protégé, a young man whom he sent, albeit indirectly, into harm's way. And from what Amos Phillips told him, Blake's young lady was in Israel, so she was at risk as well.

Blake Kershaw, Alia Kassab, Zari Nourazar—the general did the math: if he added all of their ages together, the number was still less than the number of years he'd spent on Earth. And it didn't matter if Iran launched first or if America and Israel orchestrated a preemptive strike; either way, there was a very good chance all three of those young lives would come to a very violent end.

He thought back to the last time he'd been in combat and then to his Cold War days, when he'd last been in harm's way. It was long before Blake Kershaw was born.

It didn't seem fair.

But General Sam was a general. He had made hard decisions before: decisions that put excellent people—friends good and dear—in the path of almost certain destruction. He accepted and willingly carried out orders that had likewise put himself at great risk. It was the nature of soldiering.

General Sam had long been a Christian and he believed in the prescience of God and the omnipotence of God. But he also believed God gave man free will and that quality was distributed without bias, available equally to saints and to madmen alike.

He emptied the hot water out of the carafe, filled it with coffee, and switched off the coffee-maker. Then he walked down the hall to his office, praying as he went that, in this case, the wills of the madmen would not prevail.

Chapter Thirty-Four

Blake Kershaw had only been to the wadi near the Warshowsky compound once and that was in the dark and on the run. But like most Special Forces soldiers, he had excellent spatial memory. Time, distance, heading—these created a two-dimensional image in his mind, and in the late afternoon sun, he headed off-road across the rugged desert uplands of western Iran, and after two hours of driving, found the wadi his group used in their escape just a few days before.

He was on the opposite side of the wadi from the Warshowsky place and the gully walls were steep, but he reasoned that, if the ground sloped enough to allow entry on one side, someplace along the way, it would allow entry on the other.

He found just such a place within half a kilometer of where they entered two evenings before and he put the Nissan close against the wadi wall and parked it.

Blake had no camouflage netting, but earlier that afternoon, at a bazaar in the middle of Iran, he'd found two dun-colored nylon groundcloths, one large enough to place beneath a family-size tent and the other small enough to cover a man. Using rocks as anchors, he rigged the larger tarp over the Nissan, putting wrinkles into the fabric to break up the outline of the vehicle. Then, putting the smaller groundcloth, several bottles of water, and a pair of binoculars into his rucksack, he set off across the barren country on foot.

He wore civilian clothes, but they were khaki in color, appropriate for an archaeologist in the field and a nearly perfect match for the sandy terrain he was crossing. His boots, also perfect for his archaeologist cover story, made short work of the seven or eight miles between the wadi and the Warshowsky compound.

Blake stopped when he was first within sight of the place. He could see a vehicle near the back gate; using the binoculars, he identified it as what he thought it would be—the Land Cruiser.

There was a road far off to his right, so he began walking to his left, checking the terrain behind him to make sure it was higher ground and crawling when it was not, to avoid skylining. Every hundred meters, he would stop, sweep the country to either side of him with the binoculars, and then check the compound for signs of occupation. But the windows he saw were dark and he heard no engine sounds—no generator running and no vehicles.

After two hours of circling, he came to the road, watched it for five minutes for signs of approaching vehicles, and crossed it, staying low, because the ground on this side had no hills beyond it. An hour after that, he crossed the road again and began to work his way back where he had begun, well to the rear of the compound.

It was getting near dark now, the sun low above the western mountains. From 500 meters away, Blake saw the back gate open. He lowered himself prone on the sandy soil and put the binoculars to his eyes.

It was an old man, a man Blake remembered from the workers tending the trees along the drive the week before. As Blake watched, the man shielded his eyes with his hand and searched the open ground in each direction. He shut the gate behind him. Then he got into the Land Cruiser, started it, and drove along the wall of the compound, turning the corner.

Blake waited several minutes. The vehicle did not appear on the road in the distance, not on either side of the compound. That meant it was being moved around to the front, presumably to bring it in through the front gate.

Blake thought for a moment. The old man had merely shut the gate; Blake did not see him turn a lock.

It was worth a try.

Staying low, Blake sprinted the half kilometer to the back gate of the compound and tried lifting the latch. It moved easily.

He opened the gate a crack. He could see a plaster wall marred by a single bullet hole—the bullet he remembered putting there just before they fled into the night.

Slipping through the gate, Blake closed it behind him. The door leading down to the basement room was just a few feet away, but he still wasn't sure of the situation.

The house's second story was inset from its first, a flat terrace running all the way around it. And the angled top to a cistern came within six feet of the terrace's edge. Sprinting silently, Blake used the cistern cover to jump for the edge of the roof, which he caught with both hands. Mantling up and over it, he crawled to a place where he was at an acute angle to any window, yet could still see the broad, shallow courtyard before the rear gate.

In less than a minute, the old man appeared, locking the rear gate and trying it. He said something in Russian and a woman's voice, also elderly, responded. There was the sound of a door closing and then nothing.

The sun was setting on the western hills. Blake drank one of his water bottles and assessed the situation. The rear gate was locked; Blake assumed the front was locked as well. And whoever they were, the two old people knew enough to bring the Land Cruiser inside and hide it.

Blake crawled to the edge of the roof, lowered himself from it, and silently dropped the five feet to the ground. Carefully, walking in the rolling, heel-to-ball-of-foot gait he learned in the woods as a child, he found the door to the basement room, opened it noiselessly, and slipped inside.

He went down the steps one at a time, walking only on the outsides of the risers.

The room was mostly dark, the only light coming from the anteroom of the bath, where a door had been left partially ajar. But no sound came from the bathroom and Blake deduced it was being used as a night-light.

There was one form asleep on one of the two cots, and Blake waited for his eyes to completely adjust to the lower light before he approached it.

Long, dark hair cascaded down one side of the pillow.

Zari.

Kneeling, Blake put his hand around and over the young woman's mouth. Her body stiffened.

"Shhhhh," he whispered. "It's me."

Zari turned to him, eyes still wide with fear. Then she saw his face and they relaxed.

"You?" She blinked herself more fully awake. "You did not leave? You did not go to America?"

"I did," Blake told her. "Farrokh is there now and safe. But I came back."

"You shouldn't have."

"I had to."

Zari's eyes narrowed. "Why?"

Blake took a knee next to the cot. "Zari, when I first came, I had a partner with me. He was injured on the jump in and he died."

"Yes." She nodded. "Hormos told me."

Blake studied her face. "That was your father."

And for the next ten minutes, he told her the entire story: how the two families exchanged daughters, how the pipeline collapsed when it became time to smuggle Zari out, how Massoud Sharazi stayed in touch with the house church, and the promise Blake made to the dying Massoud.

Zari blinked back tears. "So all these years I was living with people I thought were my parents . . ."

"They still were," Blake told her. "They raised you as their child, loved you as their child. That makes them your parents. You just had another father, that's all. One you never knew about."

"And one who died the same week as the father who adopted me." Zari leaned nearer, looking Blake in the eye. "That is . . . that is so . . ."

But she could not finish the sentence. She simply bowed her head and nestled it between his chin and his shoulder, and he held her, lightly and gingerly, rocking her slightly as she wept.

After five minutes, she excused herself and went into the bathroom. Blake heard her blow her nose. Then water ran for half a minute and when she came back out, the tears were washed from her face.

"So," she said, sitting next to him on the cot. "You have returned for me because of your promise to a dying man."

"Yes," Blake said. "That's part of it."

She looked at him, searching his eyes. "And the other part?"

Blake leaned forward, elbows on his knees, hands folded, studying the worn, tiled floor of the basement room.

"You're a brave woman, Zari," he said, then looked her in the eye. "I couldn't spend the rest of my life wondering what happened to you—whether you made it okay. You knew the odds were stacked against you and you came back anyway? It takes a special kind of person to summon up that sort of courage. I couldn't ignore that. I couldn't start this fight and then leave you alone to finish it."

Her eyes were welling with tears again. It wasn't what Blake wanted.

"Besides," he added, "Colonel Nassiri is just that: a colonel. He ordered me to return for you. In my heart, I am still a soldier. And that's what soldiers do. We follow orders."

She reached out, took his hand, and rubbed the calloused knuckles with her thumb. There was the soft sound of a sniff and when she looked up again, her eyes were clear, the tears all gone.

"Then that is good," she said. She looked around the small basement room. "That is very good, because this house . . . it has need of a soldier."

An hour later, Blake, Zari, and the old couple were sitting around the simple wooden table in the basement room. Blake listened as the old man explained about Olga being held by the Pasdaran at the school.

"How large is the school?" Blake asked him.

The old man thought.

"Two offices, six classrooms, and an entry hall off the first floor," he said. "And there is a basement, open the length of the school except for the pillars holding up the first floor."

"Fine." Blake looked at the three of them. "I need to go look at it. I need to see a map that shows me how to get there. I need clothes, so I will look like a hillsman. And I need a vehicle, something small and common."

"There is a motorbike," the old man told him.

An hour later, wearing the long jacket, loose trousers and flat woolen cap of a common hills person, Blake was on a rickety, whining 125cc Suzuki dirt bike, heading into the village. There were soldiers gathered around a medium-duty truck near the outskirts of town, but they paid him no mind as he rode by.

It was full dark now, the Suzuki's headlamp painting the road ahead in a swatch of yellow-white light that increased and decreased with the sound of the engine.

The school was long and narrow, about fifty meters long by twenty wide, and the Pasdaran staged their trucks nose-in all along one wall, very near the wall; Blake assumed they did it that way so they could hear if any of the vehicles were started.

There were two guards at each of the two doors and lights were burning throughout the building. But that was all Blake could see. Paper had been taped over all the windows and he could not see in. He had no idea where Olga was being kept or questioned, or where the Pasdaran would congregate.

Disappointed, he rode the whiney little dirt bike out of town. But when he got within a mile of the Warshowsky compound, he stopped.

The lights were on. The generator was running; he could hear it in the distance. It was a mistake Zari and the caretakers would never make.

Hiding the motorcycle in the ditch, Blake worked his way up the long drive, using the poplars as cover. He risked a look into the open front gate.

His heart fell. A tan Safir tactical jeep, an Iranian military vehicle, was parked in the forecourt of the compound.

Working along the walls, Blake stepped in through the gate, ducked low, and got to a window of the house. Through it, he could see part of a hall and the dining room beyond. Zari was sitting at the table and a man in uniform was looming over her. Blake recognized the uniform: Quds Force, as bad as bad news got in Iran. And the man wore a major's insignia.

There was no other sign of soldiers. But Blake couldn't trust things to stay that way for long. As far as he knew, there could be a full company en route as he waited.

Blake scrambled into the barn and felt along a wall of tools. He found a long screwdriver, its tip fairly sharp. It wasn't much, but in the hands of a Special Forces soldier, it was more than enough.

He ran through the barn and to the rear of the house, entering through the basement door. He had not been in the upper part of the house before, but he knew where the stairs were and made his way up by feel.

The door at the top of the stairs opened to a kitchen, awash with light. Dropping to his stomach, Blake thought for a moment—kitchens meant knives. But he didn't want to make noise finding one, and he didn't know if he even had the time.

He could hear voices, Farsi, down the hall. Crawling down it, he got where he could see into the dining room. Zari, he could see, was weeping. And the major was turned enough that Blake could see his Farsi nameplate on his uniform. It read, "MABERI."

The major was pacing. Blake waited until the man was turned away from him. Then he launched himself into the room, leaping like a runner sliding into second base and striking the man behind the knees with both feet.

It worked. The Iranian major collapsed and Blake was on him in an instant, jerking his head back, the screwdriver tip under his jaw, pointed up at the soft tissue. He gathered his strength: he would need to drive it up, through a layer of muscle and into the thin part of the cranium, just behind the roof of the mouth.

"No! No! Stop!" It was English and someone had hold of him.

Blake hesitated. He looked up. It was Zari, pulling on his arm, her eyes wide.

"Let him go," she pleaded, and Blake relaxed his grip. The Iranian major slumped, still dazed, and Zari knelt at the man's side, holding his head.

"Do not harm him," she told him. "This is Anatoly . . . Anatoly Warshowsky."

"What?" Blake looked at the Quds Force uniform. The man was coming around.

"That's right," the man said in perfect, London-accented English. He rubbed his head and squinted at Blake. "I am Anatoly. I'm Olga's son."

Chapter Thirty-Five

Nestled at one end of the cabin's loft, General Sam's communications room was spartan by any definition. It held an old wooden desk chair made a bit more tolerable with the addition of a buckwheat-shell-filled cushion and he sat on that under a bare lightbulb with a chain switch. Before him was a simple folding table, the rectangular kind that one might expect to encounter at a church social. And on the table, at the end where the general sat, was a fax machine. It was an older model, the sort with a telephone handset nestled on one side, and it used thermal paper to print, although the general had, in fact, never received a fax on this particular unit. He used it for sending only.

More modern models had been on the market for years. But the reason the old fax remained in service was that it had been thoroughly reengineered by CIA technicians twenty years earlier. It transmitted a highly encrypted signal and that, together with the highly secure line to which it was connected, made it far more secure than any computerized method of file transfer.

The general had the contents of Farrokh Nassiri's leather portfolio in his hands: better than half a ream of standard-size typing paper containing every pertinent detail of the Iranian launch sites in the Zagros Mountains. And atop it were the twelve pages of notes General Sam himself typed up on an old IBM Selectric typewriter, a Cold War-era machine that, like him, still soldiered on after literally decades of service.

The information was worthless unless shared. And if shared, it had the potential to take thousands of lives, to change millions of lives . . . to alter nations.

General Sam had been at this crossroads before, but it didn't matter how many times he had been there. It never became any easier; it was a terrible responsibility.

His mind went back to something he often said in his classes: "To be an effective leader of men, you must know your men. You must live among them and earn their trust, their respect, and in doing so, you will likewise respect them. They will take on a new dimension in your eyes, the dimension of comrades, of people you would gladly die for. And that is why the mantle of leadership is so heavy because, when the time comes, rather than dying for them, you must sometimes order them into harm's way, and ask these men— men who have become to you like brothers, like sons—to give everything they have and risk dying for a cause."

Somewhere in Iran, Blake Kershaw was doing just that. And while General Sam had not ordered him to return, it was General Sam who first recognized the potential in what was then a student, a Special Forces soldier who was attending college while he recovered from wounds acquired in combat. The young man had already paid for the freedom of others with his blood; he owed no debt for his liberty. But when General Sam asked him to consider risking his life once again for his country, Blake Kershaw accepted without hesitation.

Honor, glory—the young man had no need for more of that. His devotion to country was indisputable. He deserved a wife, a home, babies, and the gentle reward of the freedom for which he's so often fought. But instead he was alone in a strange land, and the machine General Sam was about to put in motion had the capacity to crush the life from him.

Not for the first time, General Sam wished he could change places with him. The general was an old man; he had enjoyed all life had to offer. But such wishing was fantasy and he knew it. He remembered an old English proverb and he whispered it aloud: "If wishes were horses, beggars would ride."

Seventy-two hours. That was the window General Sam calculated the United States and Israel had in which to act: roughly seventy-two hours. And he could waste no more of it. He bowed his head, prayed silently for the young man halfway around the world, and fed the first stack of paper into the fax.

THE SHEET-FEEDER WOULD ACCEPT only twenty-five pages at a time, requiring the general to tend the machine for better than an hour. Finally, the last of them disappeared into the feeder slot and passed through the machine before ejecting onto a stack at the other end.

General Sam waited three minutes and finally heard a conformation tone, verifying a successful fax. Pushing with his heels, he rolled the desk chair to the other end of the folding table, where a nondescript black telephone sat. Like the house phone in a hotel, it had no dial or keypad. That was because it had no need of one; as soon as the general picked the handset up, the phone on the other end of the line began to ring. It was picked up on the third ring.

"Good evening, Mr. Director," General Sam said. "I trust I have not disturbed you. I apologize for the lateness of my call."

It was the hospitable thing to say. In truth, General Sam had awakened this director of the Central Intelligence Agency at much earlier hours, as he had awakened several generations of Agency directors over the previous four decades.

"The documents I just sent you; I assume they are being examined by your Middle East desk? Very good, sir. And the digital version of this information is on its way to you by Agency courier; you should have it by the top of the hour."

The old soldier listened for a moment, nodding out of habit. He touched his hand to his chin as he spoke and sat up a bit; his beard was an addition of recent years and sometimes, particularly late at night, he forgot he had it.

"Sir," he said after a minute, "what Nassiri has been outlining for me is a situation of the gravest consequence. The nuclear capability of the Republic of Iran is much more significantly advanced than our most recent briefs would have suggested. According to the timetable included in Nassiri's documents, the western launch sites—those most likely to be used in a strike against Israel—would become fully capable in just two weeks' time. But he believes his disappearance might trigger an advanced timetable. He says that, by transferring technicians from the outlying launch sites, the most critical locations could work multiple shifts and be ready much quicker."

He listened again for a moment and then replied. "A week, sir. They could be ready as soon as one week from this morning."

This triggered a much more lengthy reply, and General Sam leaned forward as he listened.

"Sir," he finally said, "thanks to your technical team, my study is equipped for Layered Voice Analysis, the latest version. Colonel Nassiri was not aware of its use, but the results over several hours of conversation indicate that he is, beyond the shadow of a doubt, telling us the absolute truth. And even without the technology, I would be convinced of his veracity."

There was a muffled scratching at the door. The room was small enough that General Sam could turn in the swiveling desk chair and, without taking the handset from his ear, let Max in. There was a dog bed under the desk, where the German shepherd turned once and then settled into it.

"Sir," General Sam said, "I have done this for many years—more than I care to remember. It doesn't get any easier. Colonel Nassiri is a sincere and passionate man who wants to do the right thing, but he carries a deep burden. His caregiver stayed behind in Iran and the colonel is tormented, knowing he may cause the death of the person he loves most. I understand his grief because, as you know, the young man I brought into our fold has returned to retrieve her, and he entered the country in a fashion meant to afford us a certain degree of deniability. But even though I have great compassion for these young people, I agree with you; this mission is far too important to allow our sentiments to disrupt it. The only thing I ask is that you give Blake Kershaw as much time as you possibly can."

Chapter Thirty-Six

Few people ever see the inside of the White House Situation Room. And among those who do for the first time, the usual reaction is that it is much smaller than they would have imagined. Approximately fifty feet long by thirty feet wide, the average elementary school classroom compares favorably to it.

But the size of the room is deliberate. The Situation Room is only used for highly classified discussions, and those invited there are limited to the select few who can be trusted to keep the nation's secrets.

For this particular meeting in the small hours of the morning, only six of the twelve seats at the large mahogany conference table were taken. The eight additional seats at the wall held nothing more than hats and briefcases, and the four large flat-screen monitors built into the wall were dark—no one was joining the meeting by secure video teleconference.

The door opened, there was a brief glimpse of the Marine standing guard outside, and all six men stood as the president entered the room.

"Good morning, gentlemen." All six men sat as the president took his seat at the head of the table. He looked to the other end and nodded at the director, CIA. "Skip, you called this party. Is everyone up to speed on what we discussed?"

"Yes, Mr. President. General Wilson has been able to obtain some extremely specific target data on Iran's Zagros launch sites. We've also learned that their program has accelerated considerably and they will achieve full strike capability as early as one week from today."

The president looked to his left, the secretary of state. "What's the prognosis for a diplomatic solution, Andy?"

The secretary of state shook his head. "It's business-hours over there and we've already protested through channels, citing the increased helicopter traffic

216

to their launch sites. They're claiming it's a readiness drill . . . but they're also invoking sovereignty and asserting their right to pursue any defense capabilities they desire."

"Which is the same as confirming they now have nuclear capability," the national security advisor added.

The president looked pointedly at the director of National Intelligence, who nodded his agreement, and then the entire room went silent for a moment as that truth settled in.

"All right." The president tapped on the table with a gold Cross pen. "As I understand it, we will need to hit at least twelve of their western facilities to have a significant impact on their strike capabilities. Is that correct?"

It was the secretary of defense who responded. "Mister President, as we see it right now, that is the minimum. That should reduce any immediate threat and set the program back at least twenty-four months. We are planning in real time as General Wilson's documentation is analyzed. Even assuming the minimum—that they'll be at readiness in a week's time—we are confident we can complete the planning and execute a strike better than seventy-two hours before they reach that point."

"And the Israelis? What are they planning?"

"Sir," the secretary of state said, "they have the data as well. We gave it to them this morning as you directed. The latest cable from our embassy in Tel Aviv indicates they also deem an air-strike prudent and they would like a coordinated operation. They want to take one target set and have us hit the others. They also would like US tanker support since aerial refueling remains a chronic shortfall for them. State told them we have their requests under consideration, but we have not agreed to anything yet, and I don't believe Rubin has either."

"That's correct," the secretary of Defense said. "We have asked them to stand by, but we made no promises. In fact, our analysis is they are not really sure whether we plan to strike or whether we are simply giving them the data so they can strike. Their request for a combined operation is as much a matter of prodding on their part as an indication they wish to participate in our plans."

The president leaned back in his chair—it was a dark, upholstered swivel chair, the same as every other chair at the table. He crossed his arms and rolled his lips in, then exhaled.

"To say this stinks is an understatement," he said. "If we strike preemptively, we start World War III. If we wait and let Iran strike first, it's still World War III, only it's them starting it and not us."

"But if they start it," said the director, CIA, "Israel gets nuked. Thousands of civilians die. If we start it, we take out their launch-site personnel."

"In the first strike, you're right," the president agreed. "But what happens in subsequent waves is anybody's guess. There's no way we keep this surgical. And the thing I keep coming back on is the reliability of the source. How confident are we on the intel? Could it be this Iranian colonel is feeding us bogus data? Is Iran trying to goad us into a strike? A sympathy move to get the neighbors back on their side?"

"I . . ." Both the director, CIA, and the director of National Intelligence began speaking at once, and both men stopped just as quickly. The director, CIA nodded, and the DNI continued. "Sir, we have the best man in the business working him. Sam Wilson has had his hand in the intelligence community for decades and he believes in our source. General Wilson also used the voice-analysis technology on him—our source was not aware of this, by the way—and he showed no degree of deception at all. My sense is Colonel Nassiri is 100 percent legit. I would bet my reputation and future on his reliability."

"Well Winston," the president observed, "that is exactly what you are doing; we all are. Were I Ahmadinejad, I would have deduced by this time that Colonel Nassiri has gone over to our side. I'd move to negate the value of his intelligence. Could they have moved the launch sites?"

"Highly unlikely," the secretary of Defense said. The data shows the only sites suitably hardened are those currently housing the launch vehicles."

"And his move to negate the value is the acceleration of his timetable," added the director, CIA. "He's doubled up his technical teams at the Zagros sites. Our satellite imagery confirms this. The pattern of activity is consistent with what we know to be their prelaunch routine, which we have seen them do in numerous exercises. The difference this time is they are moving more quickly and we have several HUMINT reports that all say this is for real. The target is unquestionably Israel. We assess they only have six warheads but they will launch multiple missiles to confuse the Israeli air defense. They will have to guess which ones have the nukes. We believe this is the real thing, sir. They plan to launch on Israel."

"Admiral?" The president turned to the chairman of the Joint Chiefs of Staff. "Can we be assured of knocking out the sites? And if so, what is the risk to our aircraft and crews?"

The Navy admiral folded his hands and leaned forward, elbows on the conference table. "This operation is not without risks, as you already know, Mr. President. The Iranians are equipped with some fairly sophisticated air defense weapons they bought from the Russians and from Belarus. Our assessment is we can defeat them, but there is always a risk. As far as taking out the sites, yes; without question, we can do that. I would like to recommend a combined strike with the Israelis. That reduces the number of our aircraft we have to put in the air and consequently the risks. But we can go it alone if needed. It just means we may have to use two carriers to launch the strike. That's a defensive measure, Mr. President; we will need to keep some readied aircraft onboard and in reserve, to protect the fleet from the Iranian Air Force."

The president looked at the secretary of Defense, his eyebrows raised.

"Yes, sir," the secretary said, taking the cue. "I agree with Foster; this should be a combined strike. I am not sure how Shannon feels about that."

Shannon, the secretary of state, rubbed his forehead. "This is a tough one, Mr. President. We are inviting even more condemnation from the Muslim world if we bring the Israelis in on this thing."

"It's their country in the crosshairs," the president observed.

"True enough, sir. But in the long run, we may be increasing the support for the jihadists. You know, reinforcing their propaganda that we are anti-Muslim and pro-Israel. On the other hand, it may be time for us to make a strong statement to the Russians and the North Koreans that we can only be pushed so far and this is the end of the line. If we wait for them to strike Israel, our credibility as an ally will be zero throughout the world. Everyone knows we have been Israel's shield and her protector since 1948."

The secretary sat back in his chair. "I think the right answer is to go with the combined operation and give the Israelis a target set. We are going to need to show the evidence that the Iranians were preparing to strike Israel when we launched the strike. We may be able to turn this to a positive if we emphasize the fact we were protecting a longtime ally as well as the rest of the Middle East. The Saudis have just as much to fear from Iran as the Israelis."

The president seemed to slump a little.

"Yeah," he said. His voice sounded stronger than he looked. "I agree. I wish there was another way to solve this. But there doesn't seem to be. Do any of you want to offer an alternative?"

He paused and looked around the room. Every eye met his and every head slowly shook side-to-side.

"Well, then . . ." The president put both hands, palms-down, on the conference table. "I guess that makes it pretty straightforward. Admiral, Rubin . . . order the launch and make it a combined operation. Give Israel some targets and tanker support, but whatever you do, keep those tankers out of Iranian airspace. And all that leaves is time; how quickly do we need to move? When do you think the Iranians are planning to launch their strike on Israel?"

The director of National Intelligence fielded the question, "Sir, based on previous exercises and other intel we have on them, our analysts say we have about seventy-two hours if we want to be certain of hitting them before they are fully capable. Our people could do it a little quicker but that would be outside the Iranian's normal sequence and that would foul them up. When it comes to servicing their launch vehicles, they are very precise and predictable."

"All right then." The president put his pen in his pocket. "Let's make it seventy-two hours from now, and Admiral, you can turn them into the wind. Bring me the order, Rubin, and I will sign it immediately. Start developing a media plan and get some diplomatic cables ready to be sent to key embassies just as soon as the strike is underway."

He looked around the room. "Folks, this is the decision I prayed I would never have to make. Come to think of it, it might be wise for all of us to spend a bit of time in prayer. May God bless those brave souls who will fly this mission and those who support them."

He stood. "You all have a lot to do, gentlemen. Let's get to it."

Chapter Thirty-Seven

Despite Anatoly's assurances no one would trouble the compound while a Quds Force vehicle was in the forecourt, Blake, Zari, and Anatoly gathered in the basement room, where no windows could give away the fact the house was occupied.

"The estrangement from my family was my father's idea," Anatoly explained. "He approached me with it the summer I was seventeen. I was born here after the shah was deposed, but even I could see Khomeini was gradually strangling our family's businesses. We had money in reserve, out of the country, but we were not what my grandfather came here to be; we were not free men and we were losing the ability to control our own destiny."

He paused and rubbed his leg where Blake struck him.

"I had very high scores in maths and science." He said it that way, using the British colloquial form for mathematics. "And all through my teen years, my parents sent me to London during the summers for advanced tutoring. I was very fortunate. By the time I was seventeen, I not only understood chemistry, trigonometry, calculus, and physics at the university level—I could easily have taught them, as well.

"My father and I understood this was my family's one hope. Iranians have a deep distrust of anyone not born here and the country was arming up: building munitions factories, reverse-engineering the arms we purchased while the shah was in power and, even then, pursuing a nuclear capability. Iran's leaders were going to need scientists who could help them do that. So while I was at the American University in Paris, I staged a falling-out with my father and later went to Russia to get both my PhDs. While I was there, I petitioned with the Iranian embassy for a name change. Now, other than a few people here, such as Zari and Nikolai and Kristina, who knew me when I was young, and a select few people high up in the government, no one knows that I once was—and remain forever in my heart—Anatoly Warshowsky."

He looked at Zari as he said it, and Blake did not miss the warmth in the smiles they exchanged.

Anatoly took a sip of water. "From the beginning, my plan was vague. My father simply wanted me high enough in the government to protect our interests. As time went on, I came to believe my only way to help us and our country was to get close enough to Ahmadinejad to eliminate him from the picture . . . to assassinate him. That was why I accepted a Quds Force commission. But the government wanted to leverage my knowledge to advance their nuclear program, so I have stayed in Russia much of the last seven years and I began to seek a different route."

He looked into his water glass and then looked up. "Then, earlier this year, an emissary from the Russian president approached me. The president's mother is my father's second cousin, and my father had sent word through her about his growing concern over Iran's nuclear program. The emissary and I met and he arranged for me to be the point man on the project to upgrade Iran's medium-range missiles from conventional warheads to nuclear and to redesign the guidance systems . . . but the components we would manufacture in Russia would be deliberately defective: inert detonators and sabotaged guidance systems. All are good enough to pass a cursory inspection, but none will function if they are actually launched. Those are being installed at critical launch sites all around the country as we speak."

"They're no good?" Blake sat up a little more as he said it.

"They are worthless."

"And does Nassiri know this?"

Anatoly shook his head. "Until what I've heard this evening from Zari and from you, I've never been completely certain where Colonel Nassiri's sympathies lay, so I never took him into my confidence."

"Your mother." Blake clasped his hands under his chin. "Is she aware you and your father staged the falling-out?"

"We are a Jewish family, old chap." Anatoly smiled. "Of course she knows. But she is a strong woman. I do not believe she would give me up."

"Not willingly," Blake agreed. "But let's not be confident it can't be forced out of her. What about your contacts higher up, the ones who know your full identity?"

"I have not heard a word. Strange as it seems, the local Pasdaran seems to be keeping a lid on the fact they have my mother. I think the officer in charge is trying to pull a rabbit out of a hat and salvage his career."

He looked at Blake. "Nassiri is in the West?"

Blake nodded. "In America: he's being questioned by one of our best people."

"That's what I'm afraid of." Anatoly sighed. "If he gives up the location of the active bunkers and he doesn't know the missiles will not detonate . . ."

"He opens the door to a preemptive strike." Blake nodded and thought for a moment. "Israel is the country that's most at risk for a strike from Iran. We need to share your information with them. Otherwise, given the high state of readiness, the increased military presence here on the western side of the country . . . they'll launch against every active site to protect themselves."

"And the whole Middle East will go right off the edge of a cliff," Anatoly said. "It might not be exactly the way Ahmadinejad planned it, but in the end, it's exactly what he wants to see happen. The man wants war for the sake of war. I'd hoped Iran would launch first, that the missiles would fail and the entire nuclear program would be called into question, setting the country back for a period of months, maybe years, and bringing international condemnation."

"Buying some time," Blake observed.

Anatoly nodded. "In these situations, it's generally the best one can do."

He looked at Blake. "How do we proceed?"

"Our first concern is your mother." Blake put both hands on the table. "Not just because she's your mother, but because, if she reveals you're still loyal to your family, then everything you've accomplished is in jeopardy."

He looked at the other two people at the table. "We need to get inside that old school building. We need to know where she's held, how many men are there, where they are."

"That's me," Anatoly said. "I'm a Quds Force officer. I'll have no trouble getting inside."

"This is going to be hard," Blake warned him. "I'm certain they're torturing her."

"All the more reason," Anatoly told him, "to move quickly."

FIRST THING IN THE morning, Anatoly pulled up in front of the old school, leaving his Safir parked at an angle in front of the main entrance. An enlisted man rushed forward, no doubt to tell him he could not park there, and then stiffened when he saw the Quds Force insignia and the major's ghope on his shoulder.

Anatoly glared at him. "Where is your commander?"

"He is inside," the guard at the door said. "I will take you, if you'll sign the log."

Anatoly turned his glare to the second man. "Are you negotiating with me, Corporal?"

"Sir!" The man's Farsi had the accent of the rural east. "No, sir. Please. Come with me."

Two Pasdaran stood guard at the door of a classroom. Anatoly brushed past them and went inside.

He fought to keep his composure at what he saw. His mother, wearing nothing but the rag of a slip, was bound to a chair. Lights shone around her and a Pasdaran captain was speaking to her.

"Woman, we have covered you as you asked. We are not unreasonable. Tell us about the people who took Nassiri."

Anatoly saw his mother raise her head. He made certain he was behind the lights, where she could not see his face.

"Told you . . ." His mother muttered. "Broke in. They broke in. I do not know . . ."

A Pasdaran captain with a medical insignia stepped to Anatoly's side.

"Major," the doctor told him. "You are just in time. We are about to apply a little pressure."

Two soldiers entered, carrying between them a large plastic tub. They set it in front of Olga. Then they lifted her chair, with her in it, and set it down so the front legs of the chair and her feet, which were bound to it, were in the tub. Anatoly heard his mother gasp.

Restraining himself, he turned to the doctor. "What is in the tub?"

"Ice water," the doctor told him. "The local people tell us this woman is the wife of some important businessman with connections in Tehran. We are avoiding anything that leaves a physical scar. Ice water is used in medicine in something called the 'cold pressor' test—it feels brisk and nearly refreshing at first. But in three minutes' time, it will have activated every nerve ending in her legs. The pain is unimaginable. You can take any soldier from this unit, put his feet in there, and in five minutes he will be weeping like a baby."

Anatoly's mother began to moan.

"Stop this," he ordered the doctor.

The doctor motioned to the men, who lifted Olga back out.

This caused the captain at the table to turn. "What is this?"

"In the hall," Anatoly ordered him. "Both of you."

They stepped outside and the captain who'd conducted the interrogation positively bristled. Then he saw Anatoly's rank and the Quds Force insignia on his sleeve and his face went ashen.

Anatoly pointed in the direction of the interrogation room. "What have you learned?"

The captain blinked. "I didn't know the Quds Force was . . ."

"I know," Anatoly said, raising his voice. "You sought to conceal this from us. What has she told you?"

The captain looked at the doctor and then back at Anatoly. "Nothing."

Anatoly looked around. "How many men are in this building?"

The captain blinked. "Forty. Most are billeted in the basement, the end under the entrance."

"So you have forty men questioning one old woman and she has told you nothing." Anatoly shook his head. "Why are regular Pasdaran conducting this interrogation? Why were my people not brought in?"

The two captains looked at one another. The one who'd been doing the questioning straightened and cleared his throat. "Major, we are trained in such matters. The doctor, here, has had special schooling in the necessary drugs for . . ."

"For convincing a college student to tell you where he has hidden a cache of subversive literature," Anatoly said, interrupting him. He noted the man's ashen look and decided to press his luck a little.

"Captains," Anatoly asked, "who authorized this? Who is your commanding officer?"

Neither man said a word. But the one not a doctor was the one who seemed to be sweating the most. Anatoly turned so he was facing only him.

"Let me guess," he said. "You're the one who lost Nassiri, aren't you?"

Bahmani blinked.

"Oh, yes," Anatoly said. "Trust me, Captain; you are the talk of Tehran. And my second guess would be that, if your commanding officer knows you have been in pursuit of the anarchists who took Nassiri, you have not yet told him you managed to capture this one. Is that the case here?"

The captain looked up at Anatoly. He nodded, once.

"Captain . . ." Anatoly put his hand on the man's shoulder. He wanted to strangle him, but he settled for giving him a pat. "You have had this woman now for how long? Two days? Three? And what has she given you: nothing? Don't you think it would be best to hand her over to me? So I can take her back to Tehran and let the professionals take over? We can say she was just captured today. Your name will be completely in the clear. And this victory will offset—somewhat—the fact that the colonel was taken away from under your very nose. It is your best move at this point. Do you not agree?"

The captain named Bahmani nodded. It was barely visible, but it was a nod.

"Major?" It was the doctor addressing him. "Where is your truck? And your detail? Did you bring a detail?"

Anatoly could have kicked himself. Of course they would expect him to use a detail of men to transport an important prisoner. And of course, if he had none of his own, the next step would be for them to offer him one. The last thing he needed was six armed Pasdaran walking out the door with his mother and him.

"No," he told the captain. "I only came by because I heard you had taken a prisoner. I'll have to arrange transportation from TAB-28 to TAB-1, have a detail there to meet us. It will take some time."

He tapped the doctor on the chest. "I am holding you personally responsible for this woman's health, Captain. She is of no use to Quds Force if she is dead. Or a basket case. Take her out of here and feed her, let her rest. Get her ready to travel, and I shall be back."

He turned to go.

"When, sir?" It was the doctor asking. "When will you be back?"

Anatoly looked at his watch. "This evening. At dark."

ONE NINE-MILLIMETER PISTOL AND an assault rifle.

Blake Kershaw walked through the semidarkness of the Warshowskys' stables.

A single pistol and a rifle was what Anatoly told Blake he had with him, in his vehicle. Yet Blake estimated the body of men in the building to be very close to company strength.

They were outmanned and undergunned, both.

So as soon as Anatoly left, Blake and Nikolai, the old caretaker, began to look around the compound for anything they might use as weapons.

"You must have needed to move Earth for the foundations of this place," Blake said. He was speaking Russian, which delighted the old man. "Have you ever done any blasting here?"

"We have." Nikolai's eyes brightened. "Come."

He led them into a storeroom off the stables and opened a metal locker.

"Three years ago we blasted rock in a quarry not far from here, to get gravel for the drive," he said. "See."

Blake looked into the locker. There were about a dozen crimp-style blasting caps and what looked to be about twenty-five meters of waterproof fuse.

"Where's the dynamite?"

Nikolai shook his head. "We used it all. Boris said we should only buy what we need, that it is dangerous to store."

Blake nodded. "Hot climate like this, I'd say he's right. Dynamite would sweat. Too bad, though. We could have used it."

They continued to look through the stables. There were bags of feed for the chickens and the goats, bags of lime for the fields. He opened a door on a stall. It was stacked with plastic bags of ammonium nitrate fertilizer.

Blake thought for a moment.

"The generator I heard running last night," he said to Nikolai. "What does it run on? Gasoline or diesel oil?"

"Diesel. The tank is nearly full. We operate it daily, to charge a bank of batteries for the night, but Kristina and I were afraid to run it after the Pasdaran came. We didn't want to attract attention."

"Okay," Blake said. "Let's get a wheelbarrow. And we're going to need some garden hose and a tub: either porcelain-coated steel or plastic."

ANATOLY ARRIVED HOME HALF an hour later to find the two men working in the barn, stirring a strong-smelling concoction in the bottom half of a heavy plastic barrel. Several empty plastic fertilizer bags were stacked next to the barrel.

"Prills and oil," Blake explained to him. "Five quarts of diesel fuel mixed with a hundred pounds of ammonium nitrate fertilizer—prills—yields a very effective medium explosive. It's used a lot in mining because it's cheap, and back on the farm, it's what we used to blast out ponds, to provide water for livestock. It's not anywhere near as delicate as dynamite. You can pound on it, drop it, even set fire to it, and it's fine. But if you detonate it with a small explosive like these blasting caps . . . we can level that entire building, if we need to. We'll mix it, rebag it, and have a substance that works great as a shaped charge."

Anatoly straightened up, impressed.

"Before we go, we have other matters to attend to," Blake said. "The missiles: we need to know when they intend to launch. Are you privy to that?"

"I get constant updates," Anatoly told him. "The missile upgrades are going smoothly. Late this afternoon, I should have hard information."

He shook his head.

"What?" Blake asked.

"All these years of work," Anatoly said. "I am glad this country will not harm Israel . . . cannot harm her. But I am no nearer to my original goal. I've never had the opportunity to eliminate Ahmadinejad . . . ."

He blinked as he said that and then bowed his head, obviously deep in thought.

Blake looked up at him. "Tell me what's on your mind."

"When we launch . . . there is a protocol. One hour before a launch, even during a launch drill, Ahmadinejad, all of his ministers, the entire Supreme Council . . . they go to a hardened bunker. They'll do it this time, for sure."

"Do you know where it is?"

"A fuel depot near Qom. One of the tanks there has a dome of reinforced concrete in its bottom and the bunker is constructed beneath that. I don't know which tank it is, but I'm quite familiar with the location of the depot."

Anatoly cradled his chin in his hand. Then he shook his head. "But I must be in my place at TAB-1, Mehrabad, when we launch. I am required to be there, to oversee the prelaunch protocol."

He punched his fist into his open palm.

"Let's think about this," Blake said. "This fuel dump; are you familiar enough with it to provide latitude and longitude?"

"Certainly."

Blake thought some more. "All right. I'm assuming that, with your work, you keep a line of communication open between you and Moscow."

Anatoly nodded.

"And as it was the Russian president who contacted you . . ." Blake thought a moment more. "You have a way of contacting him?"

Another nod.

"Then you need to reach out to him and I need to reach out through CIA." Blake tapped on the table as he spoke. "I think I can convince the US to stand down, but Israel? We need to get messages to the Israeli prime minister, each through our own channels. Individually, we might not carry enough weight to stop Israel from launching. But if both the United States and Russia speak out, we have a chance."

Anatoly turned to leave. "I'll make the call immediately."

"Wait."

Anatoly looked back. "What is it?"

"When you came of age, Anatoly, did you have a bar mitzvah?"

"Did I have . . ."Anatoly scowled. "Yes. My mother insisted. Why?"

"So you read and write Hebrew?"

"Yes." Anatoly nodded slowly. "In fact, it's been a consolation to me while I was away. At night, I would transcribe scripture and write commentary on it. I never brought it here, of course, but in my flat in Moscow, I have journals full of it, and . . ."

"I need you to write me something," Blake said, cutting him off. "Now."

"Certainly." Anatoly cocked his head. "Why?"

"If we play our cards right," Blake told him, "we might be able to do more here than buy time. This might—just might—be the end game."

Chapter Thirty-Eight

At forty-nine floors, the Azrieli Center Tower is the tallest building in Israel, a cylindrical shaft looming high above Tel Aviv.

For a couple of reasons, that made it an ideal location for CIA's Israel Operations Group staff. The first was that the building's roof was an ideal location for communications antennae. The second was that security at the tower, it's adjoining skyscrapers, and the shopping mall below was extremely tight, provided by the Israeli military. The word among the staff was the government was able to rent the office space cheaply early in 2002, after the September 11 attacks drove down the prices for high-rise office space.

Alia Kassab normally would have enjoyed a short-term posting as CIA deputy station chief. It was excellent field experience, the staff was warm and welcoming, the shopping and restaurant variety within walking distance of the office was amazing and, from her office on the building's western side, she had an excellent view across the city, all the way to the Mediterranean Sea. It was much nicer than being in the US Embassy where most CIA personnel worked. But the task force she was part of was set up in the Azrieli Tower because of the escalating crisis with Iran and the need for additional security.

Busy as she was, her thoughts since leaving Washington were with Blake. His return to Iran, while not prohibited, had not been sanctioned either, and they'd been able to arrange little of the support he normally would have.

Sitting at her desk after lunch, she awoke her computer screen, keyed in the passcode to bring up her desktop, and opened Outlook to check for incoming messages.

She gasped.

There were six new messages and two were from an address that bore the suffix of a Tehran internet provider, an address the Agency kept in reserve for operatives to use when sending e-mail from the field.

The subject line was in Arabic: EQUIPMENT YOU DESIRED. And the message discussed a used ditch-digger and the price being asked for it.

Alia ignored both of those. The message was prewritten by experts in CIA's cryptography division; there were hundreds of such messages and now that this one had been used, it would never be used again. It contained nothing of importance—it was simply a vehicle to carry the important elements of the e-mail, which were two Windows Media Player videos. One was a walk-around, showing the exterior of the ditch-digger and the other showed the control panels and the seat.

These, also, were prepared by CIA cryptography.

When she first started with CIA, Alia took the classes and training required of all members dealing with operations—even administrators. And one of the things that fascinated her most was steganography.

Steganography is the art of concealing a message within something else. Its first use was by the Greeks, who, during the long siege campaigns of ancient times, would sometimes shave the head of a slave, tattoo a message there, and then allow the hair to grow back. The slave would travel to a general in the field, who would have the slave shaved, and then read the revealed message.

The videos were a twenty-first century version of the same technique. Alia activated a program on her computer and imported the two video files.

Video files are relatively large. That gives them enough volume to do what Blake did with a special CIA app on his iPhone: strip out every hundredth bit of information and replace it with a bit from another computer file. Now, on her computer, Alia stripped away all the data except the bits Blake implanted. These recombined into a single file the computer recognized as a JPEG image, which it brought up on the screen.

The screen was completely gray and the program compensated, auto-matically increasing the contrast by nearly 90 percent. The result was a black-on-white image: a sheet of tightly composed, handwritten Hebrew.

Alia scowled. She didn't read Hebrew.

She processed the other file and it yielded another handwritten page. This time, her heart melted: it was Blake's handwriting, the familiar printing that looked very much like the notes on an architect's drawing:

ALIA, THE ATTACHED MESSAGE IS EYES-ONLY, TOP
PRIORITY FOR DIRECTOR OF OPERATIONS, MOSSAD.
HAVE HIM CONFIRM WITH PHILLIPS ONLY IF HE MUST.
REQUIRE PRIORITY EXTRACT FROM IRAN TONIGHT
AND AGENCY WILL NOT HAVE ASSETS IT CAN MOBILIZE
THAT QUICKLY—WILL REQUIRE ASSISTANCE FROM
MOSSAD.

Alia nodded as she read the note, glad she had lunched with the top people at Mossad—Israel's secret service—just the day before.

The message went on:

IF INSTRUCTIONS ARE FOLLOWED TO THE LETTER, EVAC
FLIGHT WILL ARRIVE RAMAT DAVID LATE TONIGHT.
MOSSAD WILL RESPOND AND WILL GIVE YOU ETA. MISS
YOU AND LOVE YOU ALWAYS. B.

She reread the last line twice, tearing up. Then she smiled; tonight—the flight would come in tonight.

She transmitted the Hebrew message as a top-priority communication to the director of operations at Mossad and called to follow it up. The administrator who answered assured her it was received, printed, and placed in the director's hands. Then, as it was eyes-only, Alia followed protocol and deleted the decrypted original from her computer.

She sat at her desk and looked out the window at the distant Mediterranean. Late that night . . . Ramat David Air Base: it wasn't all that long or all that far away.

Alia went on with her work and began to count the minutes.

Chapter Thirty-Nine

The American ambassador to the Russian Federation was from Texas and he had his suits cut Western-style. They were always reserved and never gaudy—he never looked as if he was about to take the stage at the Grand Ole Opry. But his suits had just enough piping and darts on them that no one ever had any trouble telling where he hailed from. And if they did, he always topped off his outfit with a good Stetson hat.

Dressing in that fashion was a decision he first made during his post as an ambassador to Italy. The fashion-conscious Italians considered Americans uncouth—considerably less refined in manners of dress—and the ambassador understood he would only fuel their disdain if he appeared at state events dressed in Gucci.

Then he remembered that America's first ambassador, Benjamin Franklin, faced a similar quandary when he went to France; the French considered the Americans bumpkins and would laugh if they tried to camouflage the fact by adopting the finery of the court. So Franklin, who had always been a city man and dressed in refined, city fashion, adopted homespun and buckskin as his daily attire. He sent letters to his friends on the American frontier and asked them to send him coonskin caps and moccasins. In elegant European parlors, where everyone else was in ruffles and lace, Franklin would show up looking like he was about to go trap a bear, and the ruse worked; that and his wit made him the darling of Parisian society.

The trick worked equally well in the twenty-first century. The American ambassador was known throughout Europe for his distinctive appearance and his lightning-quick mind. Both political parties sent out feelers to see if, after the next election, he would be interested in a post as secretary of state.

And now, the ambassador was taking a seat in the anteroom of the Russian president, settling his Stetson Durango on his knee. Already there were the British and Israeli ambassadors, who shook his hand as he entered.

"So what's this about, boys?" The ambassador smiled, laugh lines crinkling at the edges of his eyes. "I take it neither of y'all have declared war or anything like that."

"My embassy called me as I was on my way over," the Israeli said. "The president has requested a phone conference in five minutes' time with our prime minister."

"Then we shall know soon enough," the British ambassador observed.

The doors to the president's office opened and his chief of staff beckoned them in. Coffee was served and pleasantries exchanged. Then a secretary stepped in and said something in Russian. The president nodded and looked at the diplomats. "Gentlemen, if you'll indulge me, I am about to bring the prime minister of Israel into this meeting on the speaker phone."

The American ambassador noticed his Israeli counterpart lost a shade or two of color in his face but, to his credit, the man said nothing.

The president pressed a button on his phone. "Mister Prime Minister, I have you on speaker and would like to conduct this conversation in English, if that's acceptable to you; with me are your ambassador, as well as the ambassadors of the United Kingdom and the United States."

"Much as I would like to hear us all attempt a conversation in Hebrew, English would be fine." The comment got the chuckle it was looking for. "What can I do for you this fine morning, Mr. President?"

"If you can grant me the patience to hear me through, sir, I would like to start by telling you that the Islamic Republic of Iran is going to launch a missile strike against your nation within seventy-two hours' time."

Both the British and the Israeli ambassadors began speaking at once, and the American ambassador held his hat up to get their attention. "Boys, I've got the feeling there's a few more cards about to hit the table. Let's let the president speak his piece."

"Thank you," the president said. "I wish to further inform you all that, within the last week, Iran has received nuclear detonators and upgraded guidance systems for their Shahab 3 medium-range missiles."

There was a stunned silence. The American broke it by clearing his throat softly and asking, "May we inquire how you know this, Mr. President?"

The president nodded. "We know this because the Russian Federation was the source of those devices."

Again both the British and the Israeli ambassadors began speaking at once. The Israeli went so far as to use the phrase, "treaty violation." And again the American quieted them down, saying, "Please continue, Mr. President."

"The guidance systems we sent are designed to test perfectly in any of the standard test-bed environments," the president told them. "But when subjected to the G-loads of a launch, they will most certainly fail; in fact, we went to great lengths to be certain they will fail. Our data suggests that, in the western sites that Iran would use to initiate a strike against Israel, the missiles will land in desert areas of Iraq and neighboring parts of the Arabian Gulf."

Now the American ambassador felt compelled to speak. "Mr. President, the United States is pleased to hear you are operating with the best interests of the state of Israel in mind. But I feel compelled to remind you that, even though we no longer have a combat presence there, nuclear detonation in Iraq and the Gulf cannot be interpreted as anything but an act of war against Iraq and all Coalition nations."

"I understand that."

The American ambassador's BlackBerry began to vibrate, the distinctive three-pulse signal that indicated a top-priority message. Lifting his hat slightly from his knee to disguise the action, he slid the BlackBerry partway under the brim, opened the incoming e-mail and keyed in the code to decrypt it.

"But as I said," the Russian president continued, "the detonators were supplied by us as well and, while they are the correct weight and appear to be functional, they are not. The detonators are constructed of inert material and cannot initiate either fission or fusion. The missiles will be harmless."

The American again interrupted the silence that followed. "Gentlemen, I just received a priority message from my CIA station chief, and he confirms, independently, everything the president just told us."

"I appreciate this information." It was the speakerphone, the first time the prime minister said anything since beginning the conversation. "But Mr. President, I cannot order Israel to stand down in the face of a nuclear attack, simply on the basis of hearsay. With all due respect, sir, this could be nothing but an elaborate ruse. You admit you have supplied our enemy. What is stopping you from misinforming us to minimize our ability to respond?"

The American ambassador looked at his colleagues. Both appeared ashen.

The Russian president leaned nearer to the speaker phone. "Mister Prime Minister, I take it you have your chief of intelligence with you, listening in on this call. Please do not trouble yourself with confirming or denying this, I know it to be the case. I would like him to corroborate for you the following fact: I have one son and one son only. His name is Mikhail, he is a multirole fighter pilot in our air force and I love him more than anything in this world."

There was a pause.

"My chief of intelligence confirms this," the Israeli prime minister said over the speaker-phone.

The Russian president looked at the ornate Tiffany clock on the mantle.

"Mister Prime Minister, my Mikhail is presently airborne in a Sukhoi prototype, our next-generation multirole fighter. He is en route to Israel as we speak; your radar has not yet detected him because of the aircraft's stealth capabilities. In five minutes, he will activate his fighter's transponder and make himself visible on your air-traffic-control radar. Here is the identification number . . ."

He gave it and the prime minister repeated it back to him.

"That is correct," the president said. "Please clear him to land at Ramat David and once he is on the ground, please identify him by the records in your database and then make him a guest in your home. You may send your family to shelter if you so desire, but I am asking you not to send Mikhail. Please keep him as much in harm's way as anyone in Israel. I am absolutely confident he will suffer no hurt. The missiles will come nowhere near him or any other person living in Israel. That is how you know that what I tell you here is the absolute truth."

"Offering his only son?" It was the Israeli ambassador, speaking in a whisper. "It is like Scripture: like Abraham and Isaac."

"I had a similar thought," the American told him. "Except the story that came to my mind is in the Gospels."

Chapter Forty

The three men loaded the back of Blake's Nissan, setting down a waterproof tarp first, and then stacking the plastic bags that stank of diesel fuel and ammonia. Blake was glad the drive to town would not be long. He put the blasting caps and fuse in last, measured off a foot of fuse, and carried it well away from the vehicle, where he lit it. The result was the same as the first three times he did that test; it took exactly thirty seconds to burn down to nothing.

They put blankets and a pillow into Anatoly's jeep. The sun was setting and Blake took Anatoly by the elbow and led him aside.

"You said you've studied some scripture," Blake said in a low voice. "Have you read Deuteronomy?"

"Many times. Why?"

"When I was a boy, I used to read those books of the Bible all the time. My mother thought I was being spiritual, but I wasn't; I read them for the battle scenes. And I remember the ones in that book better than many of the others. The Canaanites, the Amorites, the Hittites—all of those tribes that opposed Israel, do you remember what God commanded Israel to do?"

Anatoly looked up at the darkening sky and then back at Blake. "He commanded them to destroy them utterly. To leave no man alive."

"Do you know why?"

"But of course. Israel was outnumbered. The nation couldn't leave warriors alive because they could rise up later and overwhelm them."

Blake nodded. "My friend, that's us tonight. There are people in that building who saw your face today, who will be able to identify you. More might see you tonight. We can't have them passing information. If the government gets even a hint you might be anything but the loyal officer they believe you to be, that ordnance you brought in becomes suspect, and this whole thing unravels. The only way we prevent that is to leave no one alive—none of the Pasdaran who might be able to identify you. The official story has to be that you were never there and no one can be allowed to live if he can contradict that. Are we clear?"

Anatoly nodded.

"All right, then," Blake said. "Let's go over the layout of the school one more time and the plan."

THE SUN SET AND the five of them—Blake, Anatoly, Zari, Nikolai, and Kristina—gathered in the broad, enclosed forecourt of the Warshowsky compound.

"Father," Zari prayed, "we ask your blessing and protection this evening. Please bring Olga safely home to us, and if it be your will, protect those now who go to rescue her."

"Amen," Blake said.

Anatoly repeated the prayer, in Hebrew this time, and when he finished, the old man and woman responded with, "Ah-mayn."

Blake turned to Nikolai.

"Grandfather," he said in Russian, "you have worked hard today. Stay here and rest. Anatoly and I can do this thing."

"*Nyet.*" The old caretaker shook his head deliberately: once, twice, thrice. "It is time these pigs learned a lesson and I will be pleased to be one of the teachers. I am warning you; if you leave me behind, I will follow."

"All right." Blake laughed. He looked at his watch and turned to Anatoly. "I have nineteen hundred hours, in seven seconds, six, five, four, three, two . . . mark. So . . . one hour from now: at twenty hundred hours: you know where you need to be."

"Precisely."

Zari stepped between the two men. "I feel I should go, as well."

"No," Blake told her. "Stay here with Kristina and be ready. Someone has to wash and clothe Olga and get her ready to travel immediately, just as soon as we get back. Nikolai and I will need clean clothes as well. The prills and oil stinks to high heaven."

"He is right," Anatoly told her. "You are needed here."

Blake noticed a look lingered between those two.

"You will come back here?" Zari asked Anatoly.

"No. I go straight to the Ilam air base and from there to Mehrabad. We launch the day after tomorrow, at sunrise. If I am not in my place, they will know the launch is compromised."

"Safe travel, then." Zari held him and kissed him on the cheek.

"And you . . ." Zari searched Blake's eyes. "You have never even told me your name."

"It's a secret," Blake told her. Then he looked at Anatoly. "But if we do not succeed this evening, it will not matter. Blake. That's my name. The two of you can call me Blake."

Zari smiled. "Be safe, then, Blake."

And she hugged him. But as they left, it was Anatoly who she was watching.

THEY DROVE SLOWLY TO the village, Nikolai and Blake riding together and letting Anatoly go ahead, not wishing to get there too soon. Both Nikolai and Blake were dressed in the loose trousers and long overjackets of hillsmen. On the floor behind the front seats, they had Anatoly's KL-7 assault rifle and both Blake and old Nikolai brought along butcher knives from the Warshowskys' kitchen.

Butcher knives. It reminded Blake of kids, playing pirates.

They drove through town, past a single truck where three soldiers were looking at a magazine, and down streets empty except for the occasional goat.

A block from the school, they came even with Anatoly's jeep, parked well away, as they discussed. Glancing at his watch, Blake pulled alongside and put the Nissan into neutral.

"I need you to drive, all right?"

The old man nodded.

Blake got out of the vehicle, opened the hatch, climbed into the back, squatted among the bags of fertilizer, and pulled the hatch down so it was nearly closed.

"What a fine truck!" The old man was rocking back in the seat and looking at the gauges.

"When we're done here, you can have it, if you want it." Blake balanced on the balls of his feet. "Let's go past the school. As soon as we are out of sight of the sentries out front, slow down to a crawl and keep to the far side of the street, as close to the trucks parked there as you possibly can."

The old caretaker did exactly as he was asked. Checking both ways along the dark street to make sure there was no sentry among the trucks, Blake opened the rear hatch and began tossing four twenty-five-kilogram plastic bags of diesel-soaked fertilizer onto the soft ground, one bag behind each truck. They landed almost noiselessly and when they were all out, Blake pulled the hatch-back down again and said, "All right. Pick up speed to normal and drive on past. Go about two blocks down, turn around, and park it."

ANATOLY PARKED AT THE near end of the old school building and bullied his way past the two Pasdaran sentries, just as he had previously. He walked through the school building, checked his watch, and marched into the office at the far end, where the Pasdaran captain was at his desk, eating dinner.

The man looked up and actually smiled when he saw the major.

"Is our prisoner ready to go?"

"She is in the holding area." The captain got to his feet, brushing crumbs from his uniform jacket. "May I get her for you?"

"Yes, please. Immediately. I have a plane waiting for her at the air base."

Anatoly watched the man leave and looked around the office. An older-model Heckler and Koch G3 assault rifle was lying on the credenza behind the desk. He walked around the desk, picked it up, made sure there was a round in the chamber, and set it butt-down on the ground next to the door, where it would be partially hidden by a tall table. Then he checked that his pistol was loaded and cocked, and put it back in its holster with the thumb-safety on.

There. He was as ready as he could be. He faced the office door and waited.

THE OLD MAN WAS not happy when Blake ordered him to stay with the Nissan. But eventually he acquiesced, agreeing to drive forward and be ready just as soon as the charges were detonated.

With the blasting caps in his pocket, the coil of fuse in his left hand, the Type 56 rifle in his right, and the butcher's knife tucked into his belt, Blake trotted in the darkness to the next street over, looking for houses in which the windows showed no light.

It wasn't like America. The yards here had broad walls around them, so Blake mantled up onto the wall of a darkened house and, staying down so he wasn't quite as conspicuous, ran silently along the top of it, crossing past the darkened house and the one behind it, and dropping onto the ground across the street from the school. Checking his watch, he looked both ways for sentries, saw none, and went across the street, where he picked up the first diesel-soaked sack of fertilizer.

The trucks were parked exactly as they had been the day before, nose-in against the school, where those inside would hear if anyone attempted to start one. Blake checked the first truck and its deep front bumper was almost touching the plastered wall of the building. He set the bag of fertilizer on it, directly in front of the radiator, wedged between it and the wall.

Voices came from the basement room beyond the wall, and keeping well back, Blake peered down into the well.

Men were playing cards and reading, some lounging on their bunks. Just as Anatoly described, it was a high-ceiling basement: built, no doubt, for assemblies, with the first floor starting about four feet above ground level. The fertilizer charges, placed on the bumpers, would be shaped by a combination of the mass of the vehicle behind them, plus the floor above: that would send most of the energy through the walls, and then down and into the basement room.

Reaching under his jacket, Blake found the butcher's knife and then used the light from the window to find the mark he made on the fuse at six feet exactly. He cut it there, crimped a blasting cap onto the six feet of fuse, cut a small slit on the plastic bag of fertilizer, and slid the blasting cap into the explosive mixture.

He repeated the process with three more bags of fertilizer on three more trucks. He had just placed the last blasting cap when he heard voices, Farsi, down at the end of the building.

Blake climbed up, onto the hood of the truck, laid flat, and watched around the edge of the cab and through the windows.

It was two of the Pasdaran sentries. They must have just been relieved and apparently the protocol was to walk past the vehicles before going off duty.

Blake watched as one of the soldiers glanced around and then lit a cigarette. His companion said something and Blake caught the word, *sharia*. But the smoker waved his hand, made a comment, and they both laughed.

Blake looked at his watch. It was seven minutes shy of eight. The two sentries walked a little further and then stopped. One walked nearer to the truck Blake was on.

Breathing with his mouth wide open, to make the least noise, Blake slid the rifle up and slipped the safety off.

The soldier checked the fuel tank and wiggled the filler cap. Then he checked the ground beneath it with his hand.

It was the prills and oil, Blake realized. The two men could smell the diesel fuel.

They checked the tanks on the other trucks and Blake dropped silently to the ground to keep them in sight.

Ultimately, the taller of the two shrugged and his companion made a comment, which they both laughed at. They turned the corner at the end of the building and Blake raced to his first fuse.

His watch was just coming up on three minutes of and the lighter, an ancient Zippo Blake borrowed from Nikolai, danced into flame on the first light. He lit the first fuse and, walking sideways, moved across the bumpers, lighting fuses until all four were burning. Then he dropped to the ground, crossed the street at a dead run, ran across the tops of the walls once again, and raced down the street, turning at the end of the second block and coming out where Anatoly had parked the desert-tan Safir jeep.

The key was where Anatoly agreed to leave it, atop the left rear tire. Blake slid behind the wheel and started the engine, leaving the transmission in neutral. He checked his watch: in forty seconds it would be exactly twenty-hundred hours.

CAPTAIN RAHIM BAHMANI STOPPED in the hall with his prisoner and spoke to one of the sentries who was just coming off duty. What the man told him was disquieting.

"Hurry along, you cow," he said to Olga. In a way, he wished she had died in his custody. It seemed to him better than having a superior officer—one in Quds Force no less—know he was unable to make a middle-aged woman talk.

And the thing the sentry said still puzzled him.

They got to his office at the end of the building and he opened the door, guiding her inside. The major was standing next to the desk, waiting.

"Here is your prisoner, Major. But I'm confused. My sentry tells me there is no truck outside. Didn't you say you were returning with a detail?"

Bahmani stepped alongside the prisoner as he asked this.

Then he saw it. It was just the briefest flicker, but it was there; a smile. There quickly, and then gone. And the woman's weary eyes were brimming with tears.

"You know her?" Bahmani blinked at the major and then looked at the credenza, behind his desk.

The rifle.

His rifle was gone.

Bahmani reached for his holster, found his gun. But already the other man had his pistol out and the barrel, big and black and menacing, yawned open, straight at Bahmani's eye. As the captain lifted his gun, he actually saw the major's thumb flip the safety lever off, saw his knuckle move as he pulled his finger back against the trigger.

ANATOLY FIRED TWICE AND then pulled his mother toward him, throwing her to the floor behind the desk.

"Open your mouth," he told her in Russian. "Cover your ears. Stay covered. Stay down."

Then he threw himself down as well, covering her body with his.

THE SECOND HAND APPROACHED the top of Blake's watch. He put the Safir into gear and began to ease his foot up on the clutch.

Down the street, the nearest truck bucked and a fireball erupted, painting the street in yellow-orange light, roiling like a mushroom past the roof of the old school. The sound of the explosion thundered all around him as the second charge went off, and when the third charge detonated, the concussion wave from the first reached him, shaking the jeep.

As the fourth charge went off, the roof of the near side of the building was already falling in on itself, and his foot was up off the clutch, the Safir moving forward through the succession of shock waves, the noise of the explosions echoing off the houses up and down the street. Pulling the lights on, Blake drove forward, rifle next to him on the passenger seat. Four blocks down, he could see lights coming toward him: Nikolai in the Nissan.

Blake slowed as he neared the school. Three men were coming out of the toppled front entrance, their rifles at quarter arms; the third one was aflame, but ran as if he did not realize it. All three Iranians saw his military vehicle, ran toward it, and he shifted to neutral and stopped, stepped out, and opened fire with the rifle, dropping all three with a single burst.

BROKEN GLASS STRUCK THE wall above them with the force of a shotgun blast. Anatoly felt as if a truck had been dropped atop him and the air was thick with plaster dust. The explosions were so loud it seemed as if he had not covered his ears at all, but when he took his hands away, he could hear the lick of flames and the sounds of burning men screaming. Somewhere in the distance, he heard gunfire, an automatic rifle.

"Come, Mother." He pulled her to her feet and they stepped over the shredded body of the Iranian captain and out into the hall. Two soldiers—the sentries from this end of the building—were running his way from the lobby exit, and he raised his pistol and shot each armed man twice.

Anatoly remembered the rifle as he pulled his mother toward the exit. It didn't matter; he had his mother in one hand and the pistol in the other. He would have no way of carrying it.

He stepped outside, dragging his mother from the burning building. As they ran from it, he could see the furthest end had collapsed entirely.

The little Nissan had already come to a halt in the street and Nikolai, the old caretaker, had the door open and was running toward him. He had his arms out and his eyes were wide with fear. He looked straight at Anatoly, then beyond him. He opened his mouth, as if to shout.

"Major!" The call came from behind Anatoly. "Stay down!"

A KL-7 barked three times quickly and the old caretaker fell back as if a rug had been pulled out from under him. Anatoly turned.

It was the doctor, face blackened, uniform torn, rifle in hand.

"Major?" He looked toward the street, where the Safir was sliding to a stop.

Anatoly aimed the pistol at the doctor, center-mass, and pulled the trigger again and again until the slide locked back.

BLAKE RAN FROM THE car and knelt next to Nikolai. The old Russian was not breathing and three fingers against his neck found no pulse. Blake pulled the caretaker's jacket open and saw the three entry wounds, all grouped around the sternum. He looked up at Anatoly, shook his head, and then stepped past to pick up the dead doctor's rifle.

"You're covered in dust," he told Anatoly.

"I have another uniform in the jeep."

The man in the Quds Force uniform whispered something in his mother's ear and she nodded. He half-walked, half carried Olga around to the passenger's side of the Nissan, put her in, and closed the door.

Stepping into the rectangle of headlamps between the two vehicles, Anatoly accepted one of the assault rifles from Blake. His eyes looked sad and tired.

"Take care of her," he told Blake.

"You know I will."

Blake got into the Nissan and watched Anatoly drive off, toward the north. He covered Olga with the blanket he brought from the jeep.

When they passed the military truck parked at the edge of town, one of the men was standing atop the cab, trying to get a better view of the flames rising in the distance. The second was speaking into a radio, checking the face of it, and then speaking again. And the third was in the street, furiously waving for Blake to keep moving.

"Buddy, you've got it." Blake muttered. He drove past and out into the darkened countryside.

ZARI STOOD AT THE gate of the compound, heart pounding as she saw the headlamps and heard the vehicle approaching. It flashed its brights twice and she opened the gate, the little Nissan bumping up the gravel drive and through into the forecourt. Pulling the gate closed, Zari followed the Nissan inside.

Blake already had the door opened and was taking Olga out of the car. She barely resembled the person Zari loved as a second mother; the woman Blake was walking toward the house looked a decade older, maybe two.

She and Blake helped Olga into the kitchen, where Kristina waited with water, towels, clothing, and bandages.

"Get her ready," Blake said, stripping off his fuel-soaked shirt. "We don't have much time. Three minutes, we need to be out of here."

Zari saw Kristina settle Olga into a chair and look among the group.

"Nikolai?" She asked it softly, the way a person might say the first word of a prayer.

"I'm sorry," Blake told her in Russian. He shook his head.

Tears streamed down the woman's face, but she kept to her work, cleaning Olga's face and arms.

"Three minutes," Blake repeated, and Zari nodded.

"Yes," she told him. "We'll be ready."

Chapter Forty-One

Born in Britain and educated on three continents, Ari Solomon could speak English in his choice of three accents—posh British, Chicago Midwestern, or Israeli—or in an unplaceable inflection of his own device that he referred to as "Mediterranean Mid-Atlantic." Joining his family after college in Tel Aviv, he willingly complied to the Israeli requirement of mandatory military service and was swiftly trained to be part of *Yehidat Shaldag*, the commando arm of the Israeli Air Force.

After achieving his commission as a lieutenant, Solomon was recruited by the Institute for Intelligence and Special Operations, Israel's secret service, better known as the Mossad. And in that line of business, the young operative had masqueraded as a diplomat in Turkey, a rock musician's road manager in Afghanistan, and an electrical engineer in Egypt. But this day, he was none of those; he was wearing the blue slacks, white uniform shirt, and four-barred epaulet insignia of a commercial pilot—a rating that, as a matter of fact, he also held—and he stood at the hanger door in the gathering dusk and looked both ways on the tarmac.

The air base was famous as being the very first military installation in Kuwait to fall during Saddam Hussein's invasion in 1990. Around the base, the flags of three nations—Kuwait, the United States, and Great Britain—flew, but one flagpole, the main one, bore no standard. It was the pole from which the Iraqis hung the Kuwaiti general in charge of the base after they took it, and no flag had been flown from it since that day. And the empty building that once housed the officers' club still bore the bullet holes received when the rest of the base's officers were lined up against it and shot.

At the moment, though, Solomon was simply looking for anyone nearby who might hear him when he departed from standard procedure and started a Cessna 208's turboprop engine in the hanger, rather than towing it out-side for the start. Seeing none, he re-entered the hanger accompanied by his copilot for this mission, an older man with years of experience flying in the Negev, ferrying archeological teams into remote desert areas. The two men climbed into the airplane's cockpit and turned the radio to the ground con-trol frequency. The copilot reached behind his seat and came up with a short-barreled submachine gun from a small canvas bag. The UZI was standard issue for Israeli military and carried the advantage of being extremely easy to con-ceal. He removed the magazine and made a final check to ensure it was fully loaded.

They waited, props turning, and after five minutes, they heard it: "Cessna India Two Five Seven Niner Bravo, taxi Hotel to runway Twelve Left and hold short."

That was the cue. Running the prewarmed turboprop up to speed, Ari started the engine, released the toe-brakes, and taxied out.

The Cessna, known in the company's catalog as the "Caravan," was equipped with the optional underbelly cargo pod and painted in the bright green livery of the air courier, Gulf Delivery. And on its tail, it bore the Italian tail number ground control just called: I2579B.

Solomon cut across the tarmac, confident the ground controller in the tower, a man who had been receiving regular checks from CIA for years, would ignore the incursion. Taxiing swiftly to the base of Runway 12 Left, he fell in behind another Cessna 208 Caravan, also painted in Gulf Delivery's livery, and also bearing the tail number I2579B.

The two aircraft were duplicates of those operated by a "feeder company," a contract carrier that often delivered aircraft parts and other small freight on behalf of Gulf Delivery. In fact, the feeder company owned a Cessna 208 with that exact tail number, although it was neither of the airplanes holding short of the runway at Ali Al Salem: that particular aircraft was in for major over-haul that month in Turin.

Solomon turned and checked his cargo: four 55-gallon drums of JP-8 avia-tion fuel. Behind the securely strapped drums, three rows of two seats apiece were left in place and beside them, a small 1250-watt gasoline generator; a 120-volt electric pump; a thirty-foot wire-reinforced, ground-able fuel line of the type used for refueling helicopters in forward areas; a tan nylon rucksack;

fifty feet of heavy electrical extension cord; and a lightweight aluminum step-stool were all secured under nylon-strap cargo netting.

"Cessna Seven Niner Bravo, ASA Tower," the tower called, "proceed Twelve Left, cleared for departure, left turn after takeoff."

"Tower, Seven Niner Bravo, roger," the pilot of the other aircraft radioed. "Left turn after takeoff."

Taking a red penlight from his shirt pocket, Solomon checked the extra switch mounted on the instrument panel—the one that would operate the transponder, the radio device that would display his aircraft's tail number on an air-traffic controller's radar screen—and made sure it, as well as his anti-collision strobes and running lights, were turned off.

The other Cessna was fully illuminated—marker lights, anti-collision lights, and landing lights all on—and Solomon made the turn onto the runway behind him and then pulled next to the other airplane, on the side away from the tower.

The next part was the most dangerous. The pilot in the other plane signaled to Solomon with his own red penlight: a single flash. Both feet on the toe-brakes, Solomon ran the turboprop up to 100 percent, the wheel shuddering under his hand, and signaled back: two flashes. Three seconds later, both aircraft released their brakes and began rolling, less than three feet between their wing tips.

Solomon did not look at the runway ahead of him. His entire attention was focussed on the other airplane, mirroring its every movement. After twenty seconds, he lifted his nose gear at the same instant the other airplane did. And ten seconds later, they left the runway in such perfect synchronicity that, to anyone watching in the gathering darkness, it was one plane taking to the darkened sky.

Solomon held position off the other airplane's wing as it did a climbing left turn, and stayed there as it climbed to ten thousand feet in altitude. Only then, when they were sufficiently far away from any ground or airborne radar to still appear as a single plane, did he fall a hundred feet behind and fifty feet beneath the airplane showing its marker lights.

They flew north, into Iraq, Solomon's Cessna still dark, not broadcasting a transponder return. As they entered airspace over Dhi Qar province, the two aircraft descended slowly and steadily to five thousand feet. An hour later, as they crossed into the next province north, Maysan, they dropped another two thousand feet, as low as they could go and still be considered routine traffic.

The Cessnas were the latest models, equipped with the Garmin G1000 glass cockpit, and Solomon turned his attention to the right-hand screen, the multifunction display. He recalled a preset and a route appeared on the moving map, a route that took maximum advantage of the Iranian border radar, notoriously porous beneath five thousand feet. As his flight path neared the pre-plotted route, he donned night-vision equipment. He zoomed in the display. Then, when the two paths intersected, he banked right and put the aircraft into a shallow dive, descending as fast as he could with 220 gallons of highly flammable liquid strapped behind him.

He threaded through the Zagros Mountains at less than five hundred feet above ground level, following the carefully plotted GPS course and following the valleys, beneath the Iranian radar. Emerging over a small plain, he dropped even further, to just a hundred feet above the terrain, a height at which any error would be unrecoverable.

Solomon entered a secondary range of the mountains, again following another chain of valleys. On the computer back in Kuwait, his twisting flight path worked out to be better than four times as long as a straight flight, and it felt like it. He switched tanks to balance out the fuel load in his wings, and flew for another hour before emerging onto a second plain, north and east of Ilam.

Just ahead, directly on his flight path, a series of small glowing dots appeared in his night-vision goggles. Whoever was on the ground knew what he was doing in setting up an expedient airstrip. There it was just as he expected, the standard "Box-and-One" light pattern marking where he was to land. The technique was over forty years old, used mostly by US Special Forces, but it worked well for this kind of stealth operation. Four chemlights marked the first three hundred feet of the usable airstrip, two on each side forming a box, with a fifth light marking the left flank of the strip another thousand feet down. He aligned himself down the center of the box, throttled back slightly, and extended his flaps.

Chapter Forty-Two

KL-7 assault rifle slung over his back, Blake stood next to the light on the left forward edge of the improvised runway and looked both directions. The runway, marked before sundown on the clear and level plain with the chemlights, was crude, not even up to the standards of a country road, but in his times with the Special Forces team, he had marked runways on rougher ground, and they had worked. It all depended on the skill of the pilot, and his message to the Mossad, sent by way of Alia, made it clear he needed a good backcountry pilot who could do a STOL—short takeoff and landing—mission. He blinked his red-lensed flashlight at the sound of the approaching plane, flashing it five times, followed by two.

Then he stepped back to the Nissan and spoke to the three women inside.

"Just stay put when he lands," he told them. "The airplane doesn't carry quite enough fuel in its tanks to get us back to where we need to go, so we're going to need to refuel it. It'll take only a few minutes, maybe fifteen."

He turned to Zari. "If something happens . . . if the military shows up while the plane's still on the ground . . . get out of here. I'll engage, give you time to get clear. Head for Turkey if you can and use the phone number I gave you."

Zari nodded, her eyes somber.

The roar of the approaching turboprop dropped; the pilot reduced power to almost nothing. There would be no landing lights, since they would wash out the pilot's night-vision goggles. The airplane was only fifty feet above the desert. The pilot canted the nose of the plane up as he set the airplane down on its main gear, using the fuselage and the wings to catch the wind and act as an air brake. The nose settled lightly on its gear, the pilot powered the engine back up, and the airplane bumped and rocked its way down the rough runway to the very end, where the pilot brought the airplane around in a broad circle.

When it was back on the runway, pointed into the light desert breeze, he cut the engine entirely, the silence flooding back in on the deserted, improvised strip.

Blake was there by the time the pilot opened the rear cabin door. The two men set about unloading the heavy generator and setting it on level ground. The pilot took the aluminum ladder around to the right side of the aircraft, climbed up, and loosened the cap to the fuel tank. Then he went back into the airplane, uncapped one of the fuel barrels, and threaded the long plastic hose of the electrical pump down into it. He attached the fuel hose and ran the hose under the fuselage and over to the right side of the plane. Then he primed the carburetor of the generator and gave the cord a pull; it coughed and started on the first try. The copilot, UZI in hand, climbed down from the aircraft and moved away from the plane. His task was to provide security for the refueling operation. Blake watched him move into the darkness beyond the Land Rover. No doubt he would remain there in an overwatch position until time to take off.

"All right," Ari said to Blake. It was the first thing he said since landing. "Come 'round with me to the other side."

The pilot had Blake climb the ladder and handed up the fuel hose, on which the fueling valve had been tied open with a length of Velcro strip.

"Open up the fuel cap," the pilot told Blake. "The cap's on a chain, so you don't have to worry about losing it. Just put the nozzle in the tank, keep it there, and check the level every once in a while with your torch. It's not like a car, you can look right into the tank and see the level. It should take the first three drums easily, but I'm not sure it will fully hold the fourth."

"Got it." Blake put the nozzle in. "Start pumping when you're ready."

Less than a minute later the hose moved in Blake's hands, and jet fuel, smelling of kerosene, began flowing into the tank. The first drum didn't seem to make any appreciable difference in the fuel level, but by the end of the second drum, the level of the yellowish liquid rose visibly. By the time they switched from the third drum to the fourth, Blake's forearms were aching, but the fuel was fast approaching the bottom of the threaded filler pipe. Blake took the Velcro strap off the handle and kept the lever pressed by hand, flashlight in his teeth, watching the fuel rise. When it reached the bottom of the short filler pipe, he released the handle and lifted the nozzle out.

"All right," he called down as he screwed the filler cap back into place. "That's it. You're full."

"Just leave the hose on the ground and take down the ladder and lay it down as well," the pilot called back. He cut the power on the generator.

When Blake got back to the left side of the airplane, three of the fuel drums were on the sand outside, rolled well away from the airplane. He helped the pilot wrestle the fourth drum out and laid it, with the pump and hose still attached, on the sand next to the others. The copilot walked in from the darkness and, without a word, climbed into the cockpit and strapped in.

"Right, then," the pilot said. "I've the doors and windows open and the cabin fans are on. We'll run them a bit to clear the smell; jet fuel tends to linger."

He reached back into the airplane.

"And here's the kit you asked for." He handed Blake a large tan rucksack.

"Thanks." Blake reached into his pocket and pulled out an envelope. "A woman from CIA will meet you at Ramat David. Give her this, will you?"

"You've got it." The pilot tucked the envelope into his jacket.

Blake carried the rucksack to the rear of the Nissan, opened the back hatch, got out the women's bags, and put the rucksack in. He carried the bags to the plane and then came back to the SUV.

"All right." He checked the dark horizons as he spoke; there were no lights, no sounds of approaching vehicles. "Time to get on the plane."

The pilot had a little stool on the ground, an odd bit of convenience in the desert surroundings, and Olga smiled her appreciation as the two men helped her aboard. Then it was Zari's turn.

"Here you go," Blake told her. "Safe travels."

She froze on the stool and looked down at him. "You're not coming?"

Blake shook his head. "I have some business to take care of here first."

"But you must come."

"I'm sorry." He shook his head again. "This time, I'm the one who needs to stay behind."

"Folks," the pilot said, looking at his watch. "I'm afraid I have to hurry you along here."

Zari looked down at Blake, blinking back tears. She took his face in her hands, turned it up to meet hers, and kissed him softly on the cheek.

"Thank you," she told him. Then she was gone into the plane, and the pilot followed her with the stool, closing the hatch behind him.

Blake retreated to the SUV and watched, the rifle in his hands, as the turboprop spun up to starting speed and caught with a ragged roar. A small red light came on in the cockpit and the airplane moved down the runway, gathering speed. The plane climbed rapidly for only a few seconds and then leveled out and became a small black shadow, moving against the stars.

By the time it made the turn to head west, Blake was driving away in the little Nissan Roniz, making his way across the desert north by northeast, toward the ancient city of Qom.

Chapter Forty-Three

The three women took seats next to one another, near the front, the two younger women holding the older one, consoling her.

Ari Solomon paid the situation no attention. They were strapped in and they were quiet. That was all he needed.

He exited Iran by a different route than the one he used to enter, again taking two-and-a-half hours to cover ground that would have taken less than half an hour had he gone to a cruising altitude and simply flown point-to-point.

He was thirty kilometers into Iran, still flying nap-of-the-earth, when he saw another aircraft approaching from the north, three thousand feet above him.

Pushing back his headset, Solomon picked up a citizen's-band radio handset, extremely low-powered, with a range of less than two miles.

"Dragon Two, this is Dragon One," he called. "Believe I have you in sight. Please confirm, flash landing lights twice."

On the distant aircraft, a bright white light came on, then off, then on, then off again.

"Confirmed," Solomon called. "Hold course."

He turned back to look at the women. "We'll be climbing very steeply. Don't worry."

The older woman nodded and Solomon gave the Cessna full throttle, pulling the yoke back, toward his chest. The airplane climbed like it was being cranked upward on a cable and less that two minutes later he was in position again, a hundred feet behind and fifty feet beneath the other Cessna, the one marked identically to his.

"We've joined an airplane that just left Balad, the big American airbase to the north," Solomon explained to the women. "To radar, we look like one plane."

He lifted the handset radio. "Dragon Two, go to course."

Together, the two airplanes turned west, climbing together to ten thousand feet.

They flew that way for nearly an hour, then they descended to three thousand feet. Solomon lifted the handset radio. "Dragon Two; confirm?"

"Dragon Two."

Prepare to switch on my mark in ten. Nine. Eight. Seven. Six. Five. Four Three. Two. One."

And instead of saying, "zero," Solomon turned on his transponder and anti-collision lights at the same moment that the other airplane doused his.

A shadow to their left, the other airplane, nosed steeply down.

"Where is he going?" Olga asked.

"We're over Jordan," Solomon told her. "We have a crew there, at a temporary field in the desert; something the Americans arranged. The crew will repaint and remark the plane and, two days from now, it will fly out and go home."

He held his course, watching the moving map on the multifunction display. The airplane icon approached a thin red line and crossed it.

"That does it," he told the women behind him. "We've crossed the border. Welcome to Israel."

ALIA STOOD ON THE tarmac at Ramat David next to the ambulance with its Israeli Air Force medics. Even at midnight, the base was busy, with fighter jets screaming away into the night, and she did not realize the Cessna had landed until it taxied into the pool of work lights the medics set up.

The Cessna's yellow fuselage was unmarred—no bullet holes, no signs of trauma of any sort, and Alia took that as a good sign.

The medics were opening the door just as soon as the engine was cut and they began to bring people out, laying a middle-aged woman on a gurney and wheeling her toward the ambulance, helping an elderly woman toward a waiting wheelchair. Only one of the passengers was walking completely under her own power and she was young, somewhere near Alia's age.

Alia looked past her, into the airplane. Except for the pilot and the copilot, who were setting aside clipboards and leaving the cockpit, the high-winged airplane was empty.

Alia looked around again.

"Blake?" She surprised herself with the weakness of her voice.

"He stayed," the young woman told her. "In Iran."

And then the medics were guiding the young woman to the ambulance as well.

The tarmac seemed to ripple as tears welled in Alia's eyes. Then the pilot was in front of her, looking at the CIA credentials hung on a lanyard from her neck.

"Miss?" His voice sounded vaguely British. "The gentleman in the desert asked me to give this to you."

It was an envelope, a single thing written on the front of it: "Alia." And inside were two sheets of paper.

She opened the first one and sniffed back tears as she saw the simple, precise printing he always used. Stepping beneath one of the worklights, she read it.

EFFECTIVE 2400 THIS DATE, I RESIGN MY COMMISSION AS AN OFFICER IN THE UNITED STATES ARMY, AND AS AN OPERATIVE OF THE CENTRAL INTELLIGENCE AGENCY OF THE UNITED STATES. I DECLARE MYSELF TO BE A PRIVATE CITIZEN, ACTING ALONE AND NOT AS AN AGENT OF ANY STATE OR GOVERNMENT. I VERIFY THAT NO DIRECTIVE HAS BEEN GIVEN TO ME TO CARRY OUT ANY ORDERS OR ASSIGNMENT FROM THIS DATE FORWARD. HENCEFORTH, ANY ACTIONS OF MINE ARE PERSONALLY UNDERTAKEN AND ENTIRELY OF MY OWN VOLITION.

And beneath his signature, he printed his name: BLAKE KERSHAW, LT, USA.

"Oh, Blake," Alia whispered. "What have you done?"

She opened the second sheet. It was his handwriting again:

DEAR ALIA—

I WON'T BLAME YOU IF YOU'RE ANGRY WITH ME. TRUTH BE TOLD, I'M ANGRY AT MYSELF. BUT THERE'S THIS THING THAT HAS TO BE DONE, AND I'M NOT THE ONLY ONE IN A POSITION TO DO IT, AND IF I DO IT

RIGHT, IT'S GOING TO KEEP A LOT OF PEOPLE SAFE, YOU INCLUDED.

IF THERE'S A WAY THAT'S HUMANLY POSSIBLE, I'LL COME BACK TO YOU. I PROMISE YOU THAT. BUT I WANT YOU TO KNOW THAT I LOVE YOU, AND I'VE WANTED TO SPEND MY LIFE WITH YOU. GOD WILLING, THAT WILL BE THE CASE.

PRAY FOR ME, SWEETHEART.

BLAKE

Now her tears were coming unabated, and she blinked, looking around the tarmac.

The two pilots were walking toward a Humvee and Alia ran and caught up with them, putting her hand on the shoulder of the smaller one, the one who handed her the envelope.

"Yes, miss?"

"The man who gave you this." She held up the letter. "Did you give him anything when you flew in?"

"Of course, miss. We gave him everything requested."

"'Requested?'"

"Yes, miss. In the note you sent us: in Hebrew."

Allie swallowed. "And what was that?"

The pilot looked at his copilot and then back at Alia. "Standard recon gear. A tarp, a camouflage net, night-vision goggles, water, a handheld radio . . ."

"Weapons." Alia said. "Did you bring him any weapons?"

"Weapons?" The pilot looked at his copilot again. "Not really . . ."

It was an odd answer and Alia waited.

"Nothing that shoots," the pilot explained. "But the biggest thing we brought him was the designator."

Alia blinked, not understanding.

"You know," the copilot told her. "A laser designator. For guiding in laser-guided bombs."

Chapter Forty-Four

Qom is an ancient city, the center of Shiiite Islam and home to more Muslim seminaries than any other town in Iran. Highly spiritual, it is also highly academic and home to close to a dozen colleges, universities, and research institutes.

As Blake drove along the river, he passed the golden dome and spires of the Ma'sumeh shrine. The place was beautiful, the sort of setting that would look perfect on the cover of *National Geographic*.

But Blake also knew that, five times in the last thirty years, women had been convicted of "immoral relations" in Qom, and given the harshest punishment possible: death by stoning.

He remembered a video of the punishment being administered. A hole was dug, like the hole for a large post, and the woman, dressed all in white and with her hands tied behind her back, was placed in it, her legs and hips in the hole, and her body exposed from the waist up. The hole was filled and the dirt was tamped down around her to hold her firmly, with her torso, abdomen, and all the vital organs of the body unprotected. Then appointees of the court, and often her accusers, would hurl brick-size stones at the victim until she died as a result of either blunt-force trauma or bleeding to death. In the video Blake saw, the white robe of the victim was scarlet by the time she slumped over, dead.

It was the most barbaric thing he had ever seen, grown men cursing and hurling stones at a mere willow of a woman. Alia once told him that, while "immoral relations" was generally understood to be adultery, sharia law contained no actual definition, so the nature of the act was left up to the courts. In one case, a young woman was stoned solely because she was seen leaving her home accompanied by a man who was not a member of her immediately family. In another, a thirteen-year-old girl was stoned because she admitted she was raped by three men. In her case, the court decided to bury her all the way up to her neck, so only her head would be struck by the stones. That would make death come more quickly: a more merciful sentence in the eyes of the clerics on the court.

And then there was the other thing Qom was famous for: the Fordow uranium enrichment facility, where Iran prepared the base materials for warheads with which to attack Israel. It was located just north of the city.

Blake thought about that as he looked back, in his rear-view mirror, at the receding shrine. It didn't matter how many mosques and minarets, how many universities, parks and museums Qom was home to. It was also home to death in doses small and large and attacks upon the innocent by the cowardly. That, in Blake Kershaw's way of thinking, made it the ugliest city on Earth.

He drove hundreds of kilometers out of his way to enter the city from the side nearest Tehran, to the north. That way he would not appear to be coming from Ilam province. The newspapers and the TV stations all along the way were alive with the discussion of a "terrorist attack upon a medical mission" in the west.

Blake didn't mind being labeled a terrorist. If he terrified the people who ran this country, he could not be more pleased and more proud. But the part about it being a medical mission really stuck in his craw.

He drove through the city, confident his dusty beard and the flat cloth cap made him indistinguishable from the thousands of Iranians driving around him, blowing their horns, passing in the center on two-lane roads, bumping up onto sidewalks as the spirit moved them, and carrying furniture, caged animals, and bolts of cloth on the roofs of their vehicles, all secured by ropes and twine that looked ready to break if someone so much as sneezed at it.

The fuel depot was south of the city, near enough that the minarets and blocky, Middle-Eastern skyline of the town was still visible. And it was guarded more heavily than Fort Knox: armored troop carriers were parked at every entrance, even those that were chained shut, and at the main entrance. Construction trucks entered through a sally port, where a soldier walked the perimeter of each truck while another checked the undercarriage from a pit in the ground.

The place was huge. Blake counted the giant fuel tanks as he drove by: there were eighteen by his count, and they occupied an expanse of land nearly four kilometers long. And there was one other thing he noticed: there were no tankers, no fuel trucks—not anywhere on the property. Either the tank farm wasn't active yet, or it was never intended to be active, which made sense. A regular fuel dump would be a fireball if it was attached; it was the last place a foreign government would think to look for the political elite of Iran. But if it was a decoy, it was the largest decoy Blake had ever seen. The place was as large as most airports.

That presented a problem. The laser designator in the rucksack in the back of the Nissan was the Northrop model, made in Apopka, Florida, by the same company that made the famous bomb-sight during World War II and it was the latest design. But in Special Forces, three kilometers was always the guideline the teams were given for working with laser designators. Much beyond that and there wouldn't be enough contrast for the bomb sensor to work with.

That meant, in order to get into a position where his laser designator could reach every single tank in the depot, he would have to be in the center of it.

Driving at normal speed, he watched the apparent movement as he passed the giant tanks, and he saw a second problem; even if he was in the center of them, one or more of the tanks would always be completely blocked by its neighbors.

The depot was more open to its east. It looked as if its designers left room there for future construction. In fact, there was earth-moving equipment traveling around on that end. And most of the completed tanks were clustered in the other half, on the western end.

And the western end had a hill beyond it, less than half a kilometer beyond the razor-wire fence.

So that settled it. Blake couldn't cover all of his bases. He'd just have to play the odds.

HE DROVE A DOZEN or more kilometers beyond the depot before turning off the road into open desert. It was a riskier move than he wanted; during the mid-afternoon, his vehicle and the plume of dust beyond it would be highly visible; from the air, it would probably be seen a dozen miles away.

But Blake saw no aircraft and he reflected on the fact that, because of its clandestine purpose, the Iranians had probably declared the depot and all the air space around it a no-fly zone, conveniently providing a cloak of invisibility for intruders such as him.

He found a stand of scrub vegetation next to some boulders and parked the Nissan there, leaving the keys under the lip of the rear bumper so he wouldn't risk losing them. He left the rifle there as well; a man with a rucksack might be mistaken at a distance as a lost hiker, but a man with a rifle would be a target. Then he shouldered his rucksack and began hiking east.

The nearer he got to the hill, the more careful he became about his approach. When he reached its western edge, the sun was just about to touch the horizon, so he worked into a ravine, where he could be hidden, and drank a quart of water while he waited.

As always, he was astounded by the relative briefness of the desert dusk. An hour after the sun set, the stars were out, and virtually no gray remained in the sky behind him. He put on his night-vision goggles, switched them on, and surveyed the hill in front of him.

Were this a high-security area in a Western nation, Blake's first concern would have been acoustical surveillance; miniature seismographs, networked together to register vibrations as light as a human footstep. Most American military reservations had them; in the better ones, the operators could distinguish between a coyote and fox running between their devices.

But the construction equipment Blake saw earlier made acoustical surveillance unlikely. The vibrations from a road grader or a bulldozer would carry through the ground for dozens of kilometers in all directions, making the listening devices impractical.

So he went about a third of the way up the shallow hill and then started working his way around it, not going any higher to avoid skylining himself to any watchers in the depot.

The hill was draped with ravines, which made the going slow, but increased Blake's confidence. He had concealment less than fifty feet away from every point on his walk around the hill. Still, he walked slowly, kept low against the hill, and stopped every thirty seconds to listen. All he heard was the distant drone of an insect.

When he saw the fence-line of the depot, he began to move higher, but stopped more frequently, checking for watchers beneath the red-lamped hulks of the big fuel tanks. Twice with his night-vision goggles he saw guards walking rounds, also wearing NGVs, and he had to melt into a ravine until they were out of sight.

Finally, at about an hour past midnight, he reached the upper limb of a ravine, a place where he could see the sides of ten of the fuel tanks and the tops of another three. That made thirteen, and it made him think of the way the news anchor on one of the Virginia stations always called that number when announcing the lottery winners: "lucky number 13." Blake didn't give it much thought, because he didn't believe in luck.

Using the darkness while he still had it, Blake got out his camo netting, rubbed it in the earth to get it dusty, and then spread it over his hide. He drank more water and used his range-finding binoculars to measure the distance to the various fuel tanks. All thirteen were within two-and-a-half kilometers, and the nearest one was less than half a kilometer away.

The placard dangling from the radio contained his call-sign, the incoming aircraft's call sign, information on primary, secondary, and tertiary frequencies, instructions for using the headset and whisper—microphone, and a note that the lithium-ion batteries would provide full power for a minimum of eight hours. So he watched the depot until four in the morning, then he turned on the radio, trying the primary frequency. There was no static until he turned the squelch all the way down and even then it was minimal, so Blake kept the earset and its stubby boom mike plugged in, and continued his watch on the depot.

They arrived ninety minutes later, at half-past five: a long motorcade of dark SUVs, an armored personnel carrier at either end. Blake watched as they drove in from the distant sally port and was secretly relieved when they turned his way. Then he watched in amazement as the headlights kept coming until they pulled up adjacent to the nearest fuel tank, the one less than half a kilometer away.

In a few minutes the eastern sky would be so light that it would be risky to use binoculars; the lighter sky could throw a pale reflection against the glass and pinpoint Blake's hide on the hill. But for a few minutes yet it was still safe, and he inspected the men who got out of the cars.

The third car back, he spotted him: short dark hair, pronounced jaw, thick lips, and scraggly beard. It was Mahmoud Ahmadinejad, and Blake watched as he entered what appeared to be an inspection hatch on the near side of the gate. The Iranian president went in and he did not come out. He was followed five minutes later by a bearded, turbaned figure: Khameini—ayatollah, and Supreme Leader of Iran.

In ten minutes, only the drivers of the SUVs were left, and they departed in motorcade fashion again; the eastern sky was lightening and the fuel dump appeared to be nothing more than a fuel dump again.

The sky became gray and Blake used the rangefinder to measure the distance to the hatch the president of Iran and his entire security council had just disappeared through. The display showed him 421 meters.

Blake was almost positive the shock wave from a bunker-buster could do some pretty hefty damage at 421 meters.

He was just beginning to take down his camouflage netting when a pebble rolled down the hill.

Blake froze. Another pebble rolled down and he heard voices, laughter, and the distant squawk of a radio.

"So you boys think this hill is a good observation post as well," Blake whispered. "Ain't that inconvenient."

He listened some more. The Iranian soldiers sounded like they were on the very summit, fifty meters higher than him and a good two hundred meters distant. It looked as if he could still do his job.

Blake thought about the note he's sent to Alia: *If there's a way that's humanly possible, I'll come back to you.*

That's what he'd written. And there was a way that was possible. All he had to do was sit tight, let the window for the mission come and go, do nothing, and then walk out once the Iranian lookouts had left their hilltop post. That would get him home safe.

But that wasn't what soldiers do.

Blake thought the scenario through again. A regular general-purpose bomb, like the old Mk 84, had a blast radius of 365 meters. A GBU-28—a bunker buster—was better than twice as heavy.

Then again, part of its energy was going to be absorbed by the hardened installation it was hitting. But Blake wasn't about to kid himself; he knew he was going to get hurt in what was coming next.

Hurt, yes. But killed?

Blake thought of how he'd closed that note to Alia: *Pray for me, sweetheart.*
He hoped she was praying.

Blake uncased the laser designator, extending the back two of the tripod legs all the way, keeping the front one as short as it could go, and set it up on the side of the ravine. When he powered it up, it was noiseless, a black-on-green LCD power meter the only visible sign it was working.

Blake sighted on the hatch of the bogus fuel tank, pressed the designator button, and got a green light in the viewfinder: that and a confirmation that he was 421 meters away.

One of the distant Iranians began singing. He didn't have all that good a voice.

Twenty minutes later, there was a crack in Blake's headset.

"Evening star, morning star."

Blake checked the laminated card on his radio; the call signs were correct. "Morning star, this is evening star."

"Illuminate for function." The voice was very passable English, but the accent was odd. It was almost as if someone was trying to sound Israeli.

"Illuminating now." Blake pressed the switch on the laser designator.

"Good signal," the pilot radioed. Now his voice sounded middle-European; a Russian Jew, Blake supposed. "Evening star, interrogative: what is your position relative to target?"

"Morning star, I am on a reciprocal heading of 268 true from target."

There was a pause, then a response. "What is your distance?"

Blake hesitated, then responded, "Distance four-two-one meters."

This time the response was immediate. "Evening star, you are too close. Move back."

Blake put his hand over the boom mike, concerned the Iranians above would hear him. "Negative that. Enemy in area. Acknowledge drop is danger close. Proceed."

A longer pause. "Are you sure?"

Blake flicked the switch on the laser designator to steady-on and took his hands away, keeping his eyes near the viewfinder, trying to see if he could lay flat in the minimal cover of the ravine. The crosshairs in the viewfinder began to move up the tank.

"Oh, man . . ." One hand on the designator, holding it steady, he pressed the transmit button on the radio. "Morning star, now or never. Enemy right on top of me. Pull the trigger, bud; it's time."

There was a fifteen-second pause, then the pilot radioed one last time: "Weapon away."

For a full minute, nothing happened. Blake began to wonder if they'd dropped a dud. Then a garbage-can-size crater appeared just above the hatch on the tank, the tank bulged, and Blake could see a giant white bubble of super-compressed air rushing toward him. He released the designator and dropped, wishing gravity would work faster.

He never heard the explosion and never saw smoke or flame. There was pain throughout his upper body, as if the biggest, baddest dude in the whole world just hit him with a two-by-twelve, and after that, the universe went black.

Chapter Forty-Five

Rotor blades.

Blake groaned. Angels had wings. At least in his image of heaven, they had wings. So why would they need rotor blades to get around?

He even recognized the sound. It was a CH-53.

A Sea Stallion. The Navy used those. So did the Marines. And the Coast Guard.

"No way," Blake groaned. "If I got sent to squid heaven by mistake, I am going to be major-league hacked."

He tried to sit up and regretted it. He'd broken ribs before and this time it felt as if he might have broken all of them. His right shoulder roared with pain, dislocated. And Blake could tell he was bleeding from his nose, his ears, his lips.

Tinted brown by the rising sun, smoke washed across the blue sky above him. He saw it swirl in vortices and the rotor noise became thunder. The helicopter fuselage passed two hundred meters above him, flitting across the gap between the two sides of the ravine in a matter of a second.

"Here." The most Blake could manage was a moan. "I'm right here."

A small avalanche of pebbles washed down from above. Someone was coming.

Blake turned onto his good shoulder, tried to push up, and collapsed. He didn't have a firearm. He didn't have a knife. He couldn't even throw a decent right hook. He was an absolute Huggies commercial.

A tan suede boot appeared. Then a leg, BDUs, torso. The helmeted head came last as the man dropped into the ravine below Blake.

"Got him," the man called.

Blake blinked. That voice.

"Harry?" He tried to crane his neck up. "Harry Chee?"

The Navajo Indian, a member of Blake's old Special Forces team, smiled back at him.

"The last time," Chee told him, "was all about evening the score."

"And this time?" Blake tried to smile, but even smiling hurt.

"This time," Chee said, "you are going to owe me an Olympic swimming pool full of Budweiser. Now we'd better get you moving, Kersh. In about ten minute's time, stuff like radar and SAM sites are going to start working again here in dear old Persia and we want to be long gone when that happens."

IT TOOK JUST HALF of ten minutes to load Blake onto a stretcher. The helicopter, he noticed, bore the crest of the Kingdom of Jordan. He didn't even want to ask.

"The Iranians," he said, straining to be heard above the rotors. "Did they launch?"

"Sure did," Chee shouted back.

"And?"

"Looked like the drunks were running the fireworks at Disney World. Rockets overflew Israel and landed in the Med. One crashed and burned in Iraq. A couple fell short into the Gulf. All duds. No casualties anywhere, as far as I know. Might be some radioactive fish along the coast of Lebanon or Bahrain."

Blake motioned Chee closer with his good hand. "Did anybody strike back? Any missiles?"

"No." Chee laughed. "Ain't nobody starting World War Three around here except you, dude."

"How did you know I was here? Who sent you?" Blake was puzzled. He had told no American what he intended to do and it was just not like the American military to invade another country without orders from the very top.

Harry reached for his morphine syrette and paused briefly, looking directly into Blake's eyes, "Girlfriend saved your bacon, buddy. First thing she did was light up the phones to your DDO. He called the Mossad contact you'd sent that note to in Hebrew—and I'm not even going to ask when you learned Hebrew—and convinced him to talk to your girl. She got the dope on what was up, and the next thing I know, my cell phone is ringing, because besides about three people at CIA, I'm the only person she knows who realizes you're still alive, and she got my cell number last time, after that thing in Afghanistan. She asks me if I've got any Special Forces contacts in the Middle East, and I tell her that I'm stationed in Baghdad right now, a detailee with the Agency. So I talk to the chief of station in Baghdad, he talks to a friend in Mossad, they green-light the use of one of their helos, painted in Jordanian colors, and we put together a crew, mostly former Green Beanies. I'm the only active-duty in the bunch, so I guess that makes this an act of war, but only if the Iranians figure out what's going on, which they won't, as long as we move out soon. Which we're going to do right now, so don't move when I poke you with this needle."

Harry removed the cap and stuck Blake through his trousers in the leg.

In just moments Blake felt no pain and began to drift into a stupor.

It felt pretty good.

Chapter Forty-Six

It was late autumn, nearly winter, and the day was cool, too cold for bathing in the waters of the Black Sea. Seen from the cabana on the sand, the clouds building over the water to the west seemed to speak of winter and of times when holidays are better spent indoors, next to the fire.

But the old rabbi appeared deeply pleased with his surroundings. True, he wore a heavy woolen suit, appropriate to the season, but he reclined easily in the wicker chair, and smiled as he was handed a steaming tea glass by his good friend, the president of the Russian Federation.

"Thank you, Sergei Nikitavich," he told the younger man, his Russian voice still deep, still strong.

"And thank you for seeing me, Rabbi."

"Seeing you?" The old man chuckled. "You, the president of the country, have traveled all the way from Moscow to Anapa for this visit, and you thank me for the ten-minute journey from my humble shul to here?"

He made a dismissive gesture with his hand and cupped his hot tea.

The president cleared his throat and leaned toward the old cleric.

"I heard of your illness," he said.

"My cancer? It is nothing."

"Nothing?" The president sat up, eyebrows raised. "But, I was told that it is . . ."

"Terminal?" The rabbi nodded. "Oh, yes; that, it is. The doctors tell me I will most certainly be gone by Chanukah. And that, too, is nothing."

The president shook his head slightly and gazed at the old rabbi. "I don't . . ."

"Sergei Nikitavich," the rabbi laughed and patted him on the arm. "Have you forgotten your Scripture? Jews do not die. You learned that at your mother's knee, and I affirmed that as we studied together. The body dies, but this?"

270

The old man waved a hand dismissively at his shrunken, bent form.

"This, my old friend, is not worth keeping. I was given it to use and I used it well; it is all worn out. And besides, what will you be doing on the first day of the Festival of Lights? Watching it snow on the crowds in Red Square and eating brisket? I tell you, I have by far the better of the two situations."

The president looked unconvinced.

"I am old, Sergei Nikitavich," the rabbi told him. "I creak when I awaken in the morning. Some days, I must sit in the bath for an hour before I can fully straighten up. I tell you the truth: the pain of the cancer is very little, compared to the pain of the arthritis."

He pointed to his own face. "These eyes have seen eighty-seven winters, my friend. Eighty-seven! And believe me, they have no desire whatsoever to see their eighty-eighth, mild as the winters may be here. Jewish tradition ordains that I must go to be judged. And Jewish tradition also tells me that he who will judge is merciful. I am banking on the latter."

He smiled. "I can tell this talk is distressing you, my old friend. Let us speak of something else. Your son; he is well?"

"He is," the president told his old friend. "He was injured, ejecting from a multirole fighter, one of our Sukhoi stealth prototypes. But he has fully recovered."

The rabbi smiled, his eyes bright spots among the creases of his face. "He is back on duty, then?"

The president's face fell. "No, Rabbi. He resigned his commission."

"Ah. The stress of the accident. Of course. It is completely understandable."

The president looked down into his tea. "Actually, Rabbi, he resigned before the accident."

"Before? But then what was he . . . ?" The old rabbi set his tea glass on the table. "Sergei Nikitavich, I do not understand. Is your son in some sort of trouble?'

"No, my old friend." The president smiled thinly and shook his head. "It is nothing like that. In fact, last week, in a small ceremony in the Terem Palace, I personally conferred upon my boy the honor of Hero of the Russian Federation."

"Hero of the . . . ," the rabbi leaned forward. "I had not heard."

"Nor has anyone except the eight who were there," the president said. He began enumerating them on his fingers. "My wife, myself, the leaders of the air force and the secret service, and the Israeli, American, and British ambassadors."

He took a breath as if to say more. But he did not speak.

"Sergei Nikitavich," the rabbi said softly. "I have guarded all these years how you secretly reembraced your mother faith. I am also your friend and this worn-out old body will be cold and still as a stone within two months. If you wish a set of ears with which to share a confidence, then you could not choose more safely than mine."

The president set his tea next to the rabbi's.

"You remember when Iran launched their rockets," the president said. "When the whole world thought others would launch their own missiles in retaliation, but they did not?"

"I remember," the rabbi told him. "The response was limited to a single unmarked plane, and a single bomb. Not nuclear, but very effective. It eliminated practically everyone who had been holding Iran hostage; the talk is that a much more moderate government is forming there as we speak."

"My son," the president told him, "he was the pilot. No one could identify the plane because it was the Sukhoi, the stealth prototype. It will not go into production for another three years and, when it does, if someone makes the connection, we will claim the prototype was stolen, that we never announced it because of security concerns."

He picked up his tea, sipped it, and set it down again. "My Mikhail dropped the bomb. Then he flew the Sukhoi south, avoided radar thanks to the stealth technology, crossed the straits into the Arabian Sea, and ejected—that was where he sustained his injuries. A British Royal Boat Service team picked him up and returned to a Royal Navy submarine. He was taken to the British base at Diego Garcia for treatment, and returned here courtesy of the CIA."

The rabbi smiled broadly. "One man! Your Mikhail did all that, by himself!"

"No." The president shook his head. "Not by himself. The ordnance Mikhail dropped was provided by Israel. And it was laser-guided. There had to be someone on the ground, someone near enough to designate the target with a laser of the proper spectrum."

The rabbi leaned forward. "Who was it?"

The president leaned forward as well. "I do not know. Mikhail does not know. He spoke to him on the radio, but only a few words. All we know is that CIA and the Mossad told us he would be there, and he was."

The president picked up his tea again. "But I know one more thing, my dear friend."

The rabbi cocked his head. "What is that?"

"If ever I find out who it was . . ." The president sipped his tea. "I most decidedly assure you that I will confer the honor of Hero of the Russian Federation on one person more."

Epilogue
Outside Farmville, Virginia

Careful of her dress, Alia Kassab gazed out the window at the quiet lake. She had always imagined this day.

She never imagined it would be quite like this.

A lot was still up in the air. As far as the official record was concerned, Blake Kershaw still did not officially exist. His mother believed he was dead and had not been informed otherwise. The sum total of the people in the world who knew Blake was still alive was, as far as Alia could figure, eight.

Would there ever be wedding bells? A church? Pews crowded with family, with friends from around the world? She hoped so. She still dreamed about it. She had dreamt it just the evening before.

But for now she had this, and it was enough. Enough for her. Enough for Blake. And enough for God.

There was a knock at the door.

Alia looked in the mirror and checked the flowers crowning her long, dark hair. Raised in Islam, she would never again consent to wearing a veil, not even on a day such as this. She picked up her bouquet and opened the door.

Amos Phillips was standing there in a charcoal-gray, pinstriped suit.

"You ready?"

Her simple white dress rustled as she took his arm.

"Oh, yes," she told him. "I'm very much ready."

IT WAS A TINY group of people. Anatoly Warshowsky—he had officially changed his name back at the Russian embassy just as soon as he arrived in the States—was standing at Blake's side, ready to catch him if he needed it. Ten weeks after the bunker-buster bomb wiped away the entire top tier of the

Iranian government, Blake still ached and was less than 100 percent steady on his feet.

Zari was there as well, and the look she gave Anatoly made Blake wonder if perhaps General Sam shouldn't have pulled the strings to get two licenses. Olga looked on from one of two chairs on the lawn, smiling and weeping.

They stood at an arbor put up at the foot of General Sam's dock. There was no music; CIA retains a roster of musicians cleared to perform at state events, but not even they had the clearances required to perform at this event.

The door to the house opened and Amos and Alia stepped out.

Looking at her, Blake held his breath. Max, the German shepherd, freshly washed and wearing a black silk bandana, was sitting on his haunches near Olga, and Alia stopped for a moment to pet him, drawing a patter of laughter from the tiny group.

Then they were standing opposite Blake. Amos patted the back of Alia's hand, leaned forward, and kissed Alia on the cheek. Then Zari stepped forward to hold Alia's bouquet for her.

Blake tried to remember when he had ever witnessed such a perfect moment. He could not think of one. He could not think of one that even came close. The day was sunny, yet cool, with just the slightest hint of a breeze, that brought the distant cry of a bald eagle as it wheeled in a thermal, high on the far shore of the lake.

Blake thought of his father, dead so many years ago while he was deployed with the National Guard in Kuwait. He remembered the day he followed him in duty, enlisting in the Army, the day he first reported as a candidate for Special Forces. His missions came back to him one by one, including the mission that nearly ended his military career. He remembered his first day of college at Hampden-Sydney and the first day he met General Sam. Then he thought about all the events leading to this moment: his early graduation and commission, followed by the staging of his death, the weeks with Alia where he learned what he would need to know for his first mission, and when they—although they had not admitted it to one another at the time—first fell in love.

And then there were the months of action he could never talk about, that would stay there forever as gaps in his record. He remembered the times he nearly died and how the thought of Alia remained the spark that could keep him going. He looked at her and his eyes met hers.

"Okay, my friend," Anatoly whispered behind him. "Time to breathe again."

Blake smiled, took that breath, and offered Alia his arm. They stood beneath the arbor and faced General Sam.

"It is customary," General Sam said, "to begin this solemn occasion with the words, 'Dearly beloved.' But they seem, to my ears, inadequate. So let us begin, instead, in this way: Dear brothers, dear sisters, and dear friends. We are gathered together at the beginning of a journey, a journey that, like all perfect voyages, shall never end . . ."

And as General Sam spoke, the eagle soared and cried on the far side of the lake.

Glossary

CONUS—Continental United States

DIA—Defense Intelligence Agency

DDO—Deputy Director of Operations

DO—Director of Operations

FLIR—forward-looking infrared imaging technology

Green Beanies—Special Forces colloquialism for Green Berets (i.e., Special Forces soldiers)

GSW—gunshot wound

HAHO—high-altitude/high-opening, a type of parachute jump

HUMINT—human intelligence; i.e., intelligence obtained using people as a source

ICBM—intercontinental ballistic missile

IRGC—Army of the Guardians of the Islamic Republic, a.k.a. "Pasdaran" (Persian for "Guardians"); an Iranian police/military force primarily intended for internal or domestic use, and to prevent military insurrection.

LZ—landing zone, a place for landing aircraft, particularly rotorcraft

molon labe—Ancient Greek, "come and get them;" the response by King Leonidas the First of Sparta when the Persian army demanded that the Spartans lay down their weapons at Thermopolye

NCO—noncommissioned officer

NOC—(pronounced "knock") non-official cover, a term for operatives whose cover does not tie them to the government for which they work. Such operatives are more difficult to detect, but their activities are not conducted under the protection of diplomatic immunity.

Pasdaran—Persian, "Guardians;" an Iranian federal police/military force. See "IRGC."

POTUS—(pronounced "PO-tuss"), President of the United States

SIGINT—signals intelligence: intelligence gained through the interception of communications.